GOLDDIGGER

Hilary McCollum

Bella
BOOKS

2015

Bella Books, Inc.
P.O. Box 10543
Tallahassee, FL 32302

Printed in the United States of America on acid-free paper.

First Bella Books Edition 2015

Editor: JoSelle Vanderhooft
Cover Designer: Judith Fellows

ISBN: 978-1-59493-442-1

About the Author

Hilary McCollum is an Irish writer and storyteller. Her award-winning play, *Life and Love: Lesbian Style*, explores the highs and lows of lesbian existence. It received the Eva Gore-Booth Award for best female performance at the International Dublin Gay Theatre Festival in 2014 and was nominated for the Oscar Wilde Award for best new writing. After two decades in London, Hilary now lives in rural Ireland with her lover and furry family. *Golddigger* is her first novel. She is currently working on a second historical novel, set within the suffragette movement, with the support of Arts Council of Northern Ireland.

For more information, go to www.hilarymccollum.com or https://www.facebook.com/hsmccollum. Follow Hilary on twitter @hilarymcc7.

Dedication

To the lovely Darlene

Acknowledgments

The spark for *Golddigger* came from a collision of Kanye West's song titled "Gold Digger" with a memory that San Francisco's gay history dated back to the gold rush era. I am grateful to those who are reclaiming our lesbian and gay history, both imagined in fiction, and real. I believe these (hi)stories are important in giving us a sense of ourselves.

I would like to extend my heartfelt thanks to all those who have supported me during the writing of *Golddigger*. I started work on it in the novel writing class run by Irving Weinman at Birkbeck College. From that class, I became part of a wonderful novel writing group and would like to thank the members of that group (Marguerite Lazell, Maureen Austin, Monica Parle, Moshe Elias, Neil Heathcote and Sandra Lawrence) for their generous support and detailed criticism while I was writing the first draft. I would also like to thank Helen Morales, Amanda Gay Love, Claire Dooher, Morven McCallum and Helen Meadows for taking the time to read earlier drafts and for giving me thoughtful and encouraging feedback.

I have received ongoing help and support from a number of sources including Rachel Wingfield and the whole Wingfield clan, Joe Schwartz, Sinéad Smyth, Ann McKay, Simon Banner and Liam Campbell. I'd also like to thank Micheál Kerrigan, Alyson Campbell, Ruth McCarthy, Mel Bradley, Michelle Wiggins, Abby D'Oliveira, Pat Byrne, Ellen Factor, Kathryn Daily, Skye McCollum, Inishowen Rural Arts Network and Foyle Lesbian and Bi Women Writers' Group.

Special thanks to my mum, Marian McCollum, who gave me a love of stories as a young child that has stayed with me all my life.

This book is dedicated to Darlene Corry whose tireless support, enthusiasm, sympathy and encouragement have meant more to me than she will ever know.

I would like to thank Bella Books, particularly Karin Kallmaker and my editor, JoSelle Vanderhooft, for giving me the chance to tell this story. It is part of reclaiming our lesbian history.

"There is only one happiness in life, to love and be loved."
—George Sand

CHAPTER ONE

New York, August 1848

I woke this morning suddenly, as usual. Sleep is black and white for me. When I was growing up, I shared a bed with four sisters. They would moan and groan their way awake. Not me. Eyelids springing open, I'd leap out of bed ready for the new day.

Except for the nights I spent with Kitty. Then waking was a gentle stroll along a country lane, slowly becoming aware of her lying close to me, my breath on her skin, her foot on my calf, my eyes slowly opening to see hers looking at me. I couldn't help but smile. She'd kiss the edge of my upturned mouth. "Morning, Frankie," she'd say.

Now I spend my nights alone in a room in a boarding house in New York City. Sweat has pooled under my breasts as I have slept. New York is hot. I pour water from the jug on the dresser into the basin. My arms have tanned over the summer, up as far as the elbows, skin golden, splashed with brown freckles. But the upper half is pale, a creamy white. My arms are firm and strong. I like them.

I douse my face with water. It too is tanned, down to the collarbone. I catch my reflection in the mirror, eyes a bright blue, hair brown-black. I dip my flannel into the water, wring it out, then wipe my neck, beneath my breasts, under both arms, between my legs. Standing on one foot, I wash the other. I dry off with a rough towel. It is time to dress. I take a long piece of white cloth, tuck one end under my left armpit, and begin to wind it round and round my body, binding my breasts flat and tight.

I slip into my white shirt and the dark trousers that have hung overnight on a hook on my door. I bought them eighteen months ago in a pawnshop on the Lower East Side, the day after I'd arrived in New York on a coffin ship from Cobh. The trousers needed taking up and in, but I was good with a needle; my mother had taught me well. I borrowed shears from the landlady, then went back to my room and cut my hair short, peering into a spotted mirror. It was strange, not myself, but not entirely someone different—the son my mother never had.

I left the guesthouse and went in search of somewhere to live. It brought me here, to Mott Street. My room is tiny, space only for a narrow bed and the broken dresser I lugged up the stairs. I look again in the mirror above the dresser, adjusting my cap. It's time to set off.

I stop at the post office on my way to work, expecting a letter from home. My mother writes to me twice a year. At last it's arrived. My heart starts to beat faster—praying for good news. I read as I walk along.

Dear Frances
I hope this letter finds you in good health bad times are still with us and people are dying all bunched together Mary Quinn and her mother dead last week

The Quinns were neighbours, rather than friends. I stop, crossing myself, sending a prayer for their souls, thanking God it wasn't my family.

There is no sign of anything but hardship and poverty it has rained for months and your da is sure the potatoes will rot again thank God for our oats and the money you send Burnham has sent the wreckers in to destroy the cabins of them as cannot pay the rent but we have enough

That bastard Burnham. I turn and spit, as always when I think of him. Hounding people for the rent when he knows they have nothing to pay it with.

We found Dolly dead in the field some poor starving wretch had bled her she was such a good milker I hope it saved whoever done it

I am sorry I have no better news to tell you but pray God things will have
improved by the next time I write
  Everyone sends their kind love to you I remain until death
  your loving mother

Twenty minutes later I arrive at Harvey's grocery store. It sells all sorts—flour, sugar, tea and coffee, brushes and shovels, boots, tobacco and medicines. Gerry, my only friend in New York, works here. He's thin and wiry with jet-black hair, soft brown eyes and a lopsided smile. "Morning Frank," he says.

I nod.

"Don't you be wearing your tongue out," he says.

"What?" I say. "Oh, sorry. It's only…" I hesitate. Gerry is from Skibbereen. We've never talked about The Hunger.

"It's only what?" he says.

"I got a letter from home this morning."

It's his turn to nod. "Jaysus, I dread those letters. Me stomach clenches when I see one waiting for me."

We are silent for a moment.

I bang my fist down on the counter. "What am I supposed to do?" It takes me by surprise. Gerry too.

"Easy now there, Frank," he says. "I'm sure you're doing what you can."

"What? What am I doing?"

"You're making a new life for yourself here, you're sending money. Sure that's all you can do."

I don't answer. There is no answer. He's right, but it's not enough.

"Try and put the letter from your mind," he says.

I sigh, shaking my head.

"Listen," Gerry says, "why don't we go out later? We could have just the one drink. Sure, it'll lift your spirits."

I manage a smile. "I better get started if I'm to have money for a beer. I'll go and get my things."

I retrieve my chair and box from the back of the storeroom where Gerry lets me leave them overnight. Soon I'm on the sidewalk, placing the chair near the wall a few blocks down from Harvey's. There are shops here, a couple of restaurants, a theatre on the corner. It's a good spot. I get my brushes, cloths and polish out of the box, then turn it upside down in front of the chair. It's time to look for some trade.

I start off today with a pair of men's front-lacing shoes, made from the finest black leather. He's an older gentleman, with an eyeglass, gold pocket watch and bushy grey moustache. I set to with my black polish and brushes. I'm at the final cloth polish, bringing up a silky shine, when he leans forward.

"You've done a good job. I appreciate a young man who does a good job." He lowers his voice. "I bet you're good at all sorts of jobs, with hands like that. Perhaps I can interest you in a special job for me."

I pretend not to understand. "Have you some other shoes you want polishing?"

"Well, it is a polishing job," he says, coy, "a private polishing job, if you follow my meaning."

"Is it some boots, sir?"

He gives up. "No, no, not today at least."

Despite my refusal, he tips well then sets off down the street. I wonder about men like him. Is it just shoeshine boys? What about delivery boys? Messenger boys? Do they ever get a yes? I suppose they must.

I have four more customers in the next hour—men's black leather boots, ladies' soft grey leather side-fastening boots, ladies' ankle boots in red and burgundy and men's black shoes. A couple comes out of a shop twenty yards away, arm in arm. I'm hopeful—they look like a courting couple and men always tip more in front of their sweethearts than their wives. I watch them walk towardss me, ready to catch the woman's eye. But before she's got the length of me she trips and starts to fall. She's teetering, but he has her arm and manages to pull her back.

"Are you hurt?"

She shakes her head. "Thank goodness you caught me. Oh, but look at my shoes."

I step forward where they might see me but I don't say "Shoeshine." I'm not a hawker.

"My lady has scuffed her shoes," he says to me. "Can you restore them?"

I nod for her to take a seat. Her shoes are unusual, dark green leather, with a high heel and two pearly buttons on the outside of the ankle. Her trip has done no lasting damage and soon I have them polished to a high shine.

"Oh, they're as good as new. Why don't you get yours done too?" she urges him. He makes a show of reluctance, then sits down. He is wearing a well-made but dull pair of brogans. I give them my attention. He pays well, then departs with his beloved clamped tight to his side.

It is quiet now. Some days are like that. Usually I sit on my chair, waiting for trade to pick up again. But I'm restless today. I pace back and forth along the sidewalk, looking for a distraction. The newspaper stand down the street catches my eye. I fish two cents from my pocket for a copy of the *New York Herald*. Slowly I walk back to my chair, sitting down to read the first article, "Affairs in Our New Territory," the story of a New Yorker's journey to California. I settle down, taking my time, glad of the diversion. Until I get halfway down the second column. I sit up straight, sprinting through the words. Then I spring out of my chair and walk quickly down to Harvey's. I need to see Gerry right now.

But he's out on a delivery. I kick a stone in frustration as I walk back to my shoeshine stall. I try again later but he's still not there.

My hands are busy all afternoon with boots and shoes, but the *Herald* is flitting round my mind. "Gold mine discovered…abundant…a Peruvian harvest…as soon as a sufficiency of miners can be obtained." I am full of gold and what I might do with it.

At six o'clock I'm in the bar, waiting. "Over here," I say, beckoning to Gerry as he comes in. "I got you a drink."

"You're in a better mood."

"I am indeed. I found out something today that's going to change our lives. Gerry, they've struck gold in California. We are going to be rich."

"Will you talk sense. California. It's clean over the other side of the country. That's thousands of miles, as far as Ireland. How are we going to get there?"

"We'll find a way. I don't know how yet. But Gerry, we have to go. This is our big chance."

He is suddenly savage. "*We're going to get rich,*" he parrots. "*This is our big chance.* Would you ever listen to yourself? I've already had me big chance, Frank. It took me out of Skibbereen and got me to New York alive. It gave me a job when I got here. That's more of a chance than the rest of me family have had. Four brothers and me father all dead in Skibbereen. Me sister, Mary, dead in me arms on the boat to America. Me mother and last brother waiting for me to have the money to bring them over. And here you want me throwing it all away for some half-arsed plan."

I have never seen him like this. I have known him for almost a year and this is the first time he's been angry. He's usually funny stories, a smile dancing beneath his lips. Now they are tight, his face hard angles, eyes hot anger.

"Ah Gerry," I say. I go to touch him, but he flinches away. "Come on, don't take on so. I didn't mean to upset you. Listen, let's not talk about it now."

"And when would be a better time? When you've taken yourself off halfway round the world on a dream that will never come true?"

"Why shouldn't it come true? There's gold there for the taking, the paper says so. I'm as entitled to it as any man."

"As any *man*?" Gerry says.

"Yes, as any man," I say, but I can't look him in the eye. "Or lad, at least. As entitled as any lad."

His voice goes soft. "I know."

"Know what?" I say, wishing my face wouldn't redden. But it does. I can feel it burning up to my ears, hot round my throat.

"How old are you?"

"Twenty-two," I say, wondering where he is going. "Twenty-three next month."

"Yet still no sign of whiskers. Look at my face," he says, "after a day at work." Dark stubble shadows his cheeks and jaw. "And look at you, smooth as a baby's arse. Frank, I know."

I say nothing for several long minutes. I've been so careful, learning to stride like a man, sit with my legs apart, grunt answers to questions. "How?" I whisper at last.

He shrugs. "You'd me fooled for months. But one day…I just got a feeling."

I stare at my glass of beer, not knowing what to say.

"Anyhow, you will understand why I can't be letting you tear off across to California. You are but a girl. You may be man enough to shine shoes, but you've never the strength for gold digging."

"You're wrong. I'm as strong as many a man. I've been used to hard work since I was a child. I helped my father digging out the peat and preparing the fields."

"You were *helping* a man. A full-grown adult man. You were not doing it by yourself. Please, see sense. You will never manage on your own. And I can't be coming with you. I have steady money coming in. It's keeping me ma and brother alive. Promise me there'll be no more talk of California."

"I will promise no such thing." It is half shout, half sob. I'm on my feet now, bursting out of the bar, pushing away everyone and everything in my path, needing to get away from him.

You are but a girl! I can swing an axe all day, have a leg made for digging. I stride down the street, break into a run. I pound along, arms pumping, legs stretching. See how strong?

But in the back of my mind the fear nibbles, then gnaws. *You will never manage on your own.* I slow to a walk. Ahead I glimpse the East

River. At home there was an old rock on the cliff at Dunmore Head. I would sit there looking out across the sea to the Great Blasket, my mind drifting and turning till it found whatever answer I was searching. On that rock I decided that I needed to have me the loving of Kitty Gorman. There too that I first talked to her about leaving Ireland.

I sit down near the river. Boats are ferrying people across to Brooklyn, the tall ships delivering their cargoes at the South Street Seaport. This is where I arrived eighteen months ago. I had a little money, sewn into a secret pocket in my skirt, but no address to go to. I was washed along by the tide of people milling around the harbour. And then I felt a strong hand on my arm and I was propelled down a side alley, away from the crowd. He stank of sweat and dirt and something huge and animal. Forcing one filthy hand across my mouth, he pushed me hard against the wall.

"Shut up, whore," he said as I yelped in pain.

With his free hand he was fiddling with his trousers. But he couldn't get the buttons undone. Cursing he removed his hand from my mouth. It was my one chance. I clawed my fingers sharp down his left cheek.

"Bitch," he roared as he drew back his fist and swung for me. I dodged and he struck the wall. My knee came up hard and fast, catching him full in the groin. And then I ran and ran and ran. I couldn't tell if he was following, didn't dare look behind. Finally I stopped in a busy street, light and sound all around me. I leaned against a wall, my lungs burning. Slowly my breathing returned to normal. I looked up. There was a sign on the opposite side of the street. Guesthouse. I crossed over. They had a room free. I took it.

I lay awake most of the night. I'd heard stories of women molested, rumours whispered behind hands of girls disgraced and outcast. I knew these things happened, but they'd never happened to me, not until then. That's when I decided to become a boy.

Tears slip out. I have clawed a life out here—a room, a job, a friend. It is not enough.

You will never manage on your own. I came here on my own. I walked from Knockreagh to Cobh on my own. I sailed across the ocean on my own. The journey ahead is no farther than that behind. I am going to California.

CHAPTER TWO

Dunquin, March 1845

I have left my da finishing up in the fields and come home to prepare the evening meal. We have been planting potatoes all day, stopping only for boiled eggs and oatcake, washed down with water. It is hard on the back and on the knees—digging out the trough, laying in the seaweed, turning over the sods, planting the sprouters, covering them back up. Then on to the next trough. And the next.

Still, it is satisfying. Potatoes are great growers. And from the high field you can see right across the land, the patchwork of fields, the hedges of bright gorse, the road out to Slea Head, the sea.

We have a goodly sized farm, bigger than all our neighbours, fourteen acres rented from Lord Burnham. The house sits at the bottom of the farm, on a flattish bit of land, staring straight out to sea. My parents have worked hard for it—two rooms, three if you count the loft above the kitchen where my parents sleep.

The house is quiet. My mother is in Limerick helping my eldest sister, Marie, with the birth of her first child. Janet has been gone this year past, to Manchester after her marriage. And Peig and Lizzie are not yet back from market.

I start with the fire, breathing the embers back to life, adding sticks, letting them catch, then laying on sods of turf. I pull up my mother's rocking chair, sitting for a while by the fire, stretching out my legs, wriggling the twinges out of my back.

I am peaceful, but I can't sit here all day. This morning I boiled up a field of potatoes ready for making potato cakes tonight. It is hard to beat a potato cake hot from the pot. The praties are cold now and I skin them easily. I am mashing them in the big cream bowl when Peig dashes in.

"The dance master's back," she says, excited. "He's holding a cake dance on Sunday."

It's a while since I've been to a cake dance. I found myself with an unwanted suitor the last time. Mickey O'Connor was his name. Handsome enough but he thought too much of himself for my liking. He came calling the day after the dance. My ma made him welcome, setting a stool by the fire for him. He up and told her he was after marrying me.

My da laughed out loud. "Oh, you are now, are you?" he said. "Frances, what have you to say on this?"

I had been staring through the window at the donkey in the field, wishing I was out there with her. But I turned to my da. "I wish Mickey good fortune and happiness, but he'll not be finding it with me."

"Now don't be playing hard to get," Mickey said. "You are the woman I am after marrying, and you'll not find yourself a better offer than me. I have ten acres and four cows."

"I do not care if you have ten thousand acres and four herds of cows. You are not the man for me. And if you carry on talking such nonsense, you'll be doing it out of a broken mouth."

I haven't been to a cake dance since then.

"Oh, Frances," Peig says, "can we go? Please say yes."

I love all my sisters but Peig has always been special to me. After I was born, my mother had two children that died—Michael, who was stillborn, and Sally, who died at six weeks. Then along came Peig. You never saw a more beautiful child—dark curls, blue eyes, little button nose. And she never cried, just gurgled away to herself. She has always been easy and, being easy, perhaps a little indulged.

I smile at her. "We can go."

* * *

On Sunday morning we celebrate Mass at Saint Gobnait's Church. As I'm leaving the churchyard after the service, I hear Mary Garvey calling my name. I've known Mary since childhood, though she was a Begley then.

CHAPTER THREE

New York, September 1848

"So, you have Brendan's address now, don't you?" Gerry says for the third time as we approach the docks.

"I have it here." I take the piece of paper out of my pocket and unfold it, reading again the address printed in Gerry's most careful hand:

BRENDAN SCANLON
CALLAGHANS BAR
TWELFTH STREET
CHICAGO

"Don't forget to tell him I sent you," he says.

"I won't," I promise again. It's the part of the journey I'm looking forward to, meeting Gerry's cousin, Brendan, in Chicago—the only time in the first seven hundred miles I'll be on dry land. The North River, the Erie Canal, the Great Lakes, the Illinois Canal, the Illinois River, the Mississippi, the Missouri. So much water between me and the wagon trains heading to California. I can feel my heart pounding as we walk along the pier. In a few minutes I'll be boarding.

"That's the *Brilliant* there," Gerry says, pointing. "She's sturdy-looking, isn't she? See the..."

I try to listen as Gerry talks on, but I'm back on the *Margaret*, in the stinking hold, trapped with hundreds of others as the ship plunges and pitches, flung about like a doll. I hear again the retching, the moaning, see the face of the lad who landed on top of me as the ship heaved forward—his sunken eyes, his wasted face, his skin hanging in folds. Of all the people that died in that hold, it's always him who comes back to me. I never even knew his name.

"Frank?"

Gerry's voice pulls me back. His hand is on my arm. I take a deep breath, holding it in, then letting it out slowly. I feel the cobbles of the quay beneath my feet, hear the sounds of men unloading a cargo ship nearby.

"Sorry," I say. "I've not…since…"

"The one from Ireland? No, me neither. Listen, Frank, you don't have to do this, we can find another way."

"There isn't another way."

"You don't have to go at all," he says.

He hasn't raised this since the night in the bar, the night he told me he knew. This last month it's been as if we never had that conversation, never argued, as if I had never stormed off. When I saw him the next day, he was all "How can I help you with your plans for California?"

I turn to look at him. "You know I've my mind made up."

"Ah Jaysus, Frank, are you sure? That newspaper story might be a pack of lies. You've no idea what you might find out west."

"Perhaps not, but I'm going." Saying it out loud helps. I look at the *Brilliant*, taking it in this time—the gleaming black and red paint, the funnel, the propeller wheel. "You're right. It *is* sturdy."

We are both quiet for a minute. I adjust the pack on my back. "Well, I suppose I should get going," I say at last. I reach my hand out for a goodbye handshake, but instead he flings his arms around me, squeezing me tight.

"Good luck," he says. "And be careful."

* * *

"We'll moor here," Captain John shouts to me as dusk falls.

"Whoa!" I say, reluctantly bringing the mules to a halt. I'd rather keep walking. I don't want to be going below with him, don't want to be sharing a tiny cabin with him.

I was glad of the work when it was offered this morning. I'd been stacking crates on the quay at Albany, payment for my passage from New York, when the first mate of the *Brilliant* approached me.

"Gerry told me you'd be wanting work to take you on to Chicago," he said. "I know a man looking for a hoggee."

"A hoggee?"

He laughed. "It's the fella in charge of the mules that pull the boats up the canal."

It sounded just the thing—free meals, easy work, decent pay. I didn't pause to think about the risks.

I stand on the canal towpath wondering what will happen if he finds out I'm a woman. He might think I've made a fool of him. If it comes to a fight, I'll have no chance. He's a big man, strong from years of graft. In my mind I can see my face a bloody pulp, can hear the splash as he throws me overboard.

If only I hadn't been so foolish as to leave my pack in the cabin, I could take off now, carry on up the canal on my own. But everything I own in the world is in that bag. Not just my money, but my keepsakes, the things that matter to me. I can't leave without them.

I unharness the animals and settle them into the stabling area at the front of the boat, trying to calm my nerves. These past two years I've kept myself safe being a boy. People see what they think is there. Captain John will see Frank. And if he doesn't, I'll grab my pack and run.

As I make my way towards the cabin, I can hear him singing, a gruff voice that reminds me of my father.

The bowsman gave a bellow, and the cook she gave a squall,
And the waves run mountain high on that Raging Canaaal.

The captain stands in front of the range, stirring a pot of thick soup. Beyond him, my pack sits on the floor exactly where I left it.

"Can you lay the table," he says.

I look around the small room—bench, cooking range, cupboards, two stools, my pack. But there's no table that I can see.

He laughs and gestures to his right. "The table."

My eyes scan the surface of the wall, looking for some clue as to whether there really is a table or if it's a joke at my expense. Suddenly I see them—a pair of metal hinges, a couple of feet apart, halfway up the wall. Between them, almost on the floor, a metal catch. I bend down to release it, swinging out the tabletop concealed in the wall, unfolding the legs beneath it.

"A lad with half a brain for a change," he says.

A lad, he called me a lad. I feel like I've passed a test. Somehow it will keep me safe.

"Help yourself to bread," Captain John says, putting a loaf on the table before serving up. I blow on the soup, then take a spoonful. It is tasty, full of chunks of vegetables and fish.

"Have you worked on the canal for long?" I say to make conversation.

"More than twenty years on it," he says, "eight years before that building it. Clinton's Big Ditch they called it then. People said it couldn't be done but we showed them."

As I eat my soup he tells me stories about his life on the canal, the women he's rescued from drowning, the places he likes to go drinking, the friends he's made along the way. I can feel my fears slipping away.

At last he stands up and stretches. "I'm off to the tavern. The bunks are here," he says, releasing two narrow beds built into the walls. "You'll find blankets in the cupboard. I want an early start."

Darkness has fallen but the towpath is well lit. I watch till he's out of sight, then retrieve my pack from the corner and put it on my bunk. Everything's still there. I thought it would be but it's good to be sure. I take out Kitty's ribbon, holding it against my cheek for a moment. Gently I roll it up and place it back in the pack.

Tiredness is creeping up on me as I clear away the remnants of our meal and fold the table back into the wall. Exhausted I collapse onto my bunk, ready for sleep.

I am awoken sometime later by the sound of singing along the canal bank.

Now, if I live a thousand years…

Despite the slur I recognise the voice as Captain John's. I lie still, feigning sleep as he staggers through the door. But I am ready, one hand on my pack. There's many a man changed by the drink, Captain John wouldn't be the first. The other bunk creaks as he falls onto it.

For nothing in this whole wide world will ever raise my gall.

Thump. A boot lands on the floor.

Except the thoughts of my voyage…

Thump. The second boot.

…on that Raging Canaaal.

The bunk squeaks and complains as he swings his legs up and lies down.

"Uuuuurrrrrp." A loud belch rises from out of his guts and reverberates around the room, making me want to laugh, breaking the tension. I listen as he fidgets about, getting comfortable, still muttering the odd line from the song. Soon his breathing slows as he shifts into sleep. It's a long time before I drop off and I wake again every hour or so, always aware of the man sleeping a couple of feet away.

* * *

October 10th, 1848
Dear Gerry,

I am on the Queen of the West, a big paddle steamer heading towards Chicago. It is like a floating hotel with a ballroom, casino, two restaurants, three lounges and lots and lots of cabins. Mine is the smallest and the cheapest but it has everything I need—a bed, a nightstand, peace.

I slept for fifteen hours the first night on board, which was no wonder as I barely managed a minute the week before. Your friend Mick got me work on a canal boat owned by a man by the name of Captain John. He was a fair enough boss but the snores of him would have wakened the dead.

Still it was well worth it, the money I earned more than paid for my passage on the Queen of the West. I am well rested now and looking forward to catching up with Brendan in Chicago.

I will write again soon. Accept my best wishes.
Your friend,
Frank

* * *

I stride through the noise and clatter of the Chicago docks, my pack on my back, like a man who knows exactly where he's going. Around me gangs of men load and unload all manner of cargo, urchin boys offer to carry luggage to lodgings, carriages and wagons wait for passengers. I ignore them. A rank stench fills the air around the carcass of a rotting cow. I walk on, past the final grain store and emerge onto the street.

My eyes light almost immediately on the face of a pale young judy, her lips painted red, gaudy dress cut low to reveal a small bosom. She arches an eyebrow and starts to sidle over.

"Are you needing company?" she says.

I feel my face flushing and look away.

"I can show you a good time."

I continue walking, my cheeks scalding as "nancy boy" rings in my ears. There is none of the paving of New York here and I hardly know where to put my feet to avoid the filth and the dirt. The smell is worse even than the docks, a rancid mix of rotting vegetables, putrid meat and human shite.

I'm beginning to wish I'd never heard of Gerry's cousin when a woman emerges from a tenement doorway a few yards away. With her coarse dress, shawl and basket, she looks for all the world like she's on her way to the market in Dingle.

"*Dia dhuit*," I say, speaking in Irish without thinking.

"*Dia is Muire dhuit*," she replies.

I've kept away from the Irish in New York, Gerry aside, wanting to avoid anyone who might have known me as Frances, but there is a lump in my throat as she greets me in my own tongue. "Do you know Callaghan's Bar?"

She shakes her head.

"It's on Twelfth Street," I say.

She smiles, revealing broken teeth. "I'm going that way myself," she says. "You may as well come with me."

"Thank you. How long have you been in Chicago?" I ask as we walk along.

"Since June. I landed in Canada in May but it was America I was wanting. Are you only after arriving today?"

"This morning on the steamer. But I've been in New York since the beginning of forty-seven."

"I heard tell that was a mad place, stuffed full of people."

"It's busy, right enough, but it's a great city. You ought to go sometime."

"No, no. Chicago's too big for me, let alone New York. I amn't used to so many people."

"Where are you from?"

"Cúl Crann, County Mayo. And yourself?"

"D…" I go to say *Dunquin* but then panic. What if somehow she knows someone from home? "Castlemaine."

"De-castlemaine?" she says.

"I was born in Dingle but then we moved to Castlemaine."

"Castlemaine. Do you know Jimmy Conroy?"

"Jimmy…?"

"Jimmy Conroy. He lives in the next street. He's from Castlemaine." Holy fuck.

"Jimmy Conroy?" I say. "Are you sure he's from Castlemaine?"

"Definitely. He's never done talking about his Kingdom of Kerry."

"Oh, Kerry, Castlemaine, Kerry," I say as if I'm just beginning to understand. "I'm not from that one. I'm from the one in…Wexford," I say, grabbing for a county far from Mayo.

"Wexford? I didn't know there was a Castlemaine in Wexford."

"Ah well, it's only a couple of houses really," I lie.

"Wexf—" she starts, but I talk over the top of her.

"It's a terrible stink, Chicago," I say, wanting to change the subject.

"Oh, I know. I never met anything like it. It's shite upon shite. And there's all manner of animals running around half the time, if it's not cattle it's horses, if it's not dogs it's hogs. Shitting all over the place. And people swilling their pots out any which way. It's built for disease. They keep saying they're going to do something about it, but I amn't holding my breath." She laughs then. "Well, I am holding my breath, it's the only way you can make it down the street. Anyway, that's Twelfth Street there on your left. I hope you find who you're looking for."

I leave her at the grocer's shop on the corner and set off down Twelfth Street. A grubby group of children squat on the planked sidewalk, playing some kind of game with sticks. A brown-and-white terrier watches intently. Beyond them a wooden two-storey building proclaims itself Mac's Bar. I walk on down the road past a chandler's, a shop selling furniture and a dry goods store. At the end of the street I find another bar, but it's not Callaghan's either. Maybe I missed it? I walk back up to the junction with State Street, looking again at every storefront, every door. No Callaghan's. Either it's gone or it's been renamed. Mac's is nearer, so I try it first.

The street outside may be filthy but the bar is unexpectedly clean, fresh sawdust scattered on the wooden floor. It's mid-morning and there are only a few tables occupied. Behind the long wooden counter a big red-haired man is drying glasses, sleeves rolled up to reveal massive forearms. He doesn't look in the least bit like Gerry and to be honest I'm a bit nervous of the size of him. If the place was fuller, I might be inclined to slink out and try the other bar, but I've already been seen so I take a deep breath and walk up to the counter.

The barman looks up from his glass-polishing. "What can I be getting you?" he says, his voice deep but soft.

His slight smile encourages me. "I'm looking for a man called Brendan. Brendan Scanlon."

"Oh, you are, are you? And what would you be wanting with Brendan?"

"His cousin Gerry sent me."

The barman's face breaks into a wide grin. "Gerry? Is he here?"

"No, he's back in New York."

"I don't know why he stays in that town. There's plenty of work here in Chicago. I suppose that's why he sent you to me."

"So you're Brendan?"

"Who else would I be?" he says, putting the glass down and reaching his hand across the bar. His shake is firm but not bone-crushing. I try to return it in equal measure, though his great mitt must be twice the size of mine.

"So what are you after? There's the docks or building the railroad or—"

"I'm not looking for work," I say. "I'm heading west. Gerry asked me to stop by and say good day while I was passing through Chicago."

"Well, thank you for taking the trouble. Settle yourself there on a stool while I get you a drink. What would you be wanting?"

There are bottles aplenty arrayed behind the counter, but my eye is caught by one that takes me home. "I'll have a Guinness, please."

He pours it slowly, the ruby-black liquid foaming as it hits the tilted glass. I reach into my pocket for money but he waves it away. "Not at all, this one's on me. So how's the boy doing?"

"Gerry? He's grand." I start to tell him about Gerry's job at Harvey's, but I'm interrupted by a swarthy man looking for a round of drinks.

"And what about yourself?" Brendan asks when he's free again. "How is it you know Gerry?"

"I met him in Harvey's, when I was buying shoelaces."

"Shoelaces?"

"I was a shoeshine boy. That's what I did in New York."

"So where are you headed now?"

"California."

"Jesus, that's a hell of a long way. Whatever's taking you there?"

I feel strangely embarrassed as I say, "Gold. I heard they found gold there."

"Gold?" he says, laughing. "Are you sure? I've not heard anything about it." He calls across to a nearby table: "Denis, have you heard anything about gold in California?"

A dark-haired fella looks up from his bottle of stout. "Gold, you're saying?" He makes a face. "Not a bare word about it."

"Well, this young buck here's off to California looking for it."

They both laugh and I feel myself getting annoyed. "Do you not have a newspaper here?" I reach into my pack and pull out the front page of the *New York Herald*. "There it is in black and white."

"If you say so," he says. "But I think you're mad running across the other side of the country on the word of someone you've never even met."

"Mad or not, I'm going. I'm off down the Illinois Canal to St. Louis."

"Listen," Brendan says, "I'm serious now. The West's a dangerous place. I'm not saying you can't take care of yourself, but sure now we both know you're not the biggest of men. You've got to make other people worried about picking a fight with you. Make them choose someone else. Do you have a weapon?"

"A weapon? No."

"You need a knife, better still, a gun. There's people on those boats would cut your throat soon as look at you, turf you overboard without a second thought."

"I can't afford a gun. It'll have to be a knife."

"A knife it is. There's a hunting shop on Clark Street that should be able to sort you out. But take my advice—it needs to be big and it needs to be on show."

* * *

I stand on the dock at La Salle, waiting to board the ferry down to St. Louis, picking between my teeth with the point of my new twelve-inch Bowie knife. Occasionally I switch to cleaning the dirt from beneath my fingernails. Brendan had me practising this performance for an hour before he was satisfied that I could bring it off with any degree of menace. He wanted me muttering under my breath and staring suspiciously at people too—said people steer clear of lunatics. I practised that as well, just to humour him. But I've not tried it so far. There's no call for having people thinking I'm crazy, not unless I have to.

I remember a man in Dingle who was always talking to himself. Children used to dare one another to go up and taunt him until he'd had enough and would rush after them, his eyes wild, swearing and cursing. They'd scatter before him like birds. But the next day it would start all over again. I think he could have done with a few lessons from Brendan.

"Now, Ned," Brendan would have said to him, "that's not in the least bit threatening. Try slashing at one of them children with a knife. Or at least fire a few stones at them. Sure that would be a better job. As you are, you wouldn't frighten a kitten."

I didn't need any muttering on the canal boat down from Chicago; the performance with the knife was more than enough. None of the other passengers looked dangerous to me—mostly farmers, sitting or standing round the long, narrow cabin. A few of them had their womenfolk with them, some travelling with children. But they were all quiet enough and left me well alone.

The boat for St. Louis is a gleaming white three-deck paddle steamer called *The Victory*, topped with a pilothouse and two vast chimneys. The gangway's thick with people waiting to get on. The well-to-do are already on board, of course, gliding ahead, their poor Negroes following with bags and trunks. I imagine them now, sitting sipping tea in their suites, while we wait to squeeze into steerage. It's what that bastard Burnham would be doing, smirking to himself about the money he was making off the backs of his slaves, looking to where he could twist even more out of them, same as in Ireland.

Finally it's my turn to get on. The steerage cabin is already more than half-full with all manner of traders and hunters, farmers and labourers. There's even a party of Indians, adorned in feathers and beads and skins. These are the first Indians I've been anywhere near and I sneak a few glances in their direction, until one of them catches me and I look away.

I settle myself along the right-hand side, away from a card game that's already started in the far corner. I sit back in my seat, slowly cleaning my nails in as obvious a way as I can muster. Then I give the cabin my meanest glare. No one's looking back at me. I sheath the knife with some aplomb and settle down with a newspaper I picked up on the canal boat.

* * *

We arrive at St. Louis on Friday morning, the captain clanging the great bell as we approach the quay, water churning in a froth as the paddle wheels stop, then turn, slowing us to a halt. I lean against the white railings on the middle deck, watching as passengers surge ashore and dockers begin unloading the freight.

There are only a handful of people left when I finally make my way down the stairs. I walk along the dock, sitting for a while on a bollard looking out across the Mississippi. It must be more than a mile wide, bigger than any river I've seen before. I feel daunted by the task ahead, still thousands of miles to go.

What I need is a good night's sleep. I've not rested properly since Chicago, catching snatches of sleep sitting upright or curled up on the floor, my arm wrapped around my pack. If I'd the money I'd spend a night in St. Louis before pushing on to West Port and the wagon trains. Instead I decide to take a walk around the town before setting off along the Missouri.

They've done a much better job here than in Chicago. Instead of houses thrown up in all directions, beautiful white buildings stand elegantly back from the pavement. I drift along, taking in the sights.

Ahead a large crowd is gathering in front of a grand building, all pillars and copper domes. I wander over, wondering what's going on. And then I see them. Perhaps fifty or sixty slaves, both men and women, standing in chains along the left side of the courthouse.

When I first saw Negroes in New York, I couldn't stop myself from staring, thrilled by their dark skins, so different from my freckled paleness. But soon enough I hardly noticed them. I don't want to notice these slaves, but something in me makes me look. The one nearest to me is a big man, standing over six feet tall, his skin the colour of peat fresh from the bog. A white man stands in front of him. He pulls the Negro's mouth open, looking at his teeth like he's a horse at Dingle market, pinching his arms to check the muscle. The Negro submits without a murmur, standing straight with a quiet dignity that makes me want to cry. I wish I had a fortune. I would buy them all, set them free.

As the first Negro is led onto the wooden platform, I go to leave the auction. The crowds have squeezed closer for a better view, blocking my way. As I look for a way through, my attention is caught by a nearby slave couple, pleading with a white man.

"Please, sir," the woman says, "please sell us together. Please. We married. I's carrying his child."

The white man turns to her, contempt on his face. "I never let my niggers marry," he spits.

"Please, Mister Kingston," the husband says, "let me see my child."

Kingston turns his back on them, dismissing their pleas. The auctioneer's assistant walks over to the slave wife and unlocks her chains. I hear one last "please" to her owner before she's led onto the platform.

"Now here we have us a fine young housemaid. Well trained, obedient, skilled in all domestic services. Who will start the bidding? Do I hear three hundred and fifty?" He stares around the crowd. "Three hundred and forty, then? Who'll start me for this maid?"

A red-faced fat man on the far side of the platform opens the bidding at three hundred and twenty dollars. Soon three other men are making offers, bids swinging back and forth until there's only the fat man and a middle-aged man in a top hat left in it.

"Three hundred and ninety-five?" the auctioneer says.

The fat man nods.

"Four hundred?"

Top Hat indicates with his right hand.

"Four hundred and five?"

Fat Man nods.

"Four hundred and ten?"

Top Hat indicates.

"Four hundred and fifteen?" the auctioneer says, looking at Fat Man.

Fat Man gazes at the slave woman for a moment, then shakes his head.

"Four hundred and ten," the auctioneer says, looking round the crowd. "I have four hundred and ten. Is there any advance on four hundred and ten for this fine housemaid?" He looks around again. "Four hundred and ten once," he says. "Four hundred and ten twice." He pauses. "Four hundred and ten three times. Sold," he says, banging down a wooden hammer.

The slave woman goes straight to Top Hat, her face frantic as she talks to him, pointing to her husband as he's led up to the platform. He is dark, perhaps the blackest man I've ever seen, his skin gleaming, muscles showing clearly on his arms. "We've a strong young field hand here, experienced in planting and harvesting. Able to do some carpentry. Who'll start me?"

"Two hundred and eighty," calls a man wearing a green cravat.

"Thank you, sir," says the auctioneer. "Do I hear two hundred and ninety?" A short, grey man raises a paper he's holding in his left hand.

"Three hundred?" says the auctioneer.

I can see the woman, her hands held together as if in prayer, in front of her new owner. He hesitates for a moment, then raises his right hand.

"Do I hear three hundred and ten?" the auctioneer says.

He gets the nod from someone in the crowd, then three hundred and twenty from Green Cravat.

The woman's hands are cupped in front of her face, only her eyes visible, flicking from one bidder to the other, then back to her husband, as the price goes higher and higher. He stands silent on the platform, looking at the top-hatted owner of his wife, a silent plea across the crowd.

"Three hundred and fifty?"

At last Top Hat indicates.

"Three hundred and sixty, anyone?" the auctioneer calls, looking towards the other men who've been bidding. The grey man shakes his head.

I hold my breath.

Green Cravat raises a finger.

"Three hundred and seventy?" the auctioneer says, turning towards Top Hat.

Top Hat glances towards the wife, then back to the auctioneer. But he doesn't bid. I can't see the woman's face anymore, can't hear her voice. Top Hat doesn't signal, doesn't speak.

"Does three hundred and sixty-five help?" the auctioneer says.

Top Hat takes a deep breath, then nods.

"Three hundred and sixty-five. I have three hundred and sixty-five dollars." He turns to Green Cravat. "Do I have three hundred and seventy?"

I stare at Green Cravat, willing him to drop out. But his finger goes up. The auctioneer smiles.

"Three hundred and seventy it is. Do I hear three hundred and seventy-five?"

Top Hat gives a curt shake of his head, turning away.

"No," I hear the woman slave cry. "No! He's my husband. I's having his child. Please." But Top Hat starts pulling her away. She lunges back towards her husband. "Joseph! Joseph!"

Their eyes lock for a moment, but then his new owner steps in, dragging him one way as Top Hat pulls her the other.

I stumble a few steps, knocked by the crowd. I'm going to be sick. I put my hand to my mouth, swallowing back the bile. I have to get out of here. I start to push and shove my way through the throng. Breaking free at last, I start to run. I don't stop till I get to the docks. I buy a ticket for the first boat along the Missouri.

The *Valiant* is half-empty. I sit on my own, feeling numb, no energy for the knife performance. I am tired, but when I shut my eyes, the slave auction plays back through my head. When I open them, I see a couple of Negroes sitting nearby, travelling up the river for who knows what purpose. None that they have devised, their lives determined by the plans and whims of another. One of them's light-coloured, mulatto—part Negro, part white. Jesus, what kind of choice do Negro women have about laying with their white owners, about bearing their bastard children?

I thought I was past shocking after the things I had seen in Ireland. But slavery? At home I thought it was only the English who were such bastards. Maybe it's the rich. But I know that if I strike it lucky in California, I won't be using my gold to be owning other people.

* * *

The ship's bell clangs, ahead a rocky landing point at a bend in the river. I gather up my pack and make my way towards the lower deck. The trip from St. Louis has been frustrating—seven days pushing against the current, stuck for hours at a time on sandbars that litter the river.

My eyes are desperate for their first glimpse of a wagon as I walk from the landing point into town. The main street is lined with stores, the nearest signs proclaiming Middleton's Saddlery and Leather Store, Campbell's Blacksmiths, an apothecary, and Bob's Hardware. There's not many people about, just an old Indian sitting outside the Jumping Off Tavern and a bearded mountain man, dismounting from his horse outside Allbright's Gun Shop.

A man glances up from his study of a collection of saws as I walk into Bob's Hardware. I nod to him and carry on to the back of the store where a dark-haired man is leaning against the counter.

"Excuse me," I say. "I'm looking to go to California. Do you know of any wagon trains leaving soon?"

"California?" he says. "You best come back in the spring."

"I want to go now."

"Want or not, you've missed your chance. Should've been here months ago, boy. Don't you know nothing?"

I turn to the man at the saws. "Do you know of anyone heading to California? I'm desperate to get there, as soon as I can."

Before he can answer, the man at the counter cuts in. "Di'nt you hear me, boy? Ain't no wagon train heading there 'fore April. You can't get over the Rockies in the winter."

CHAPTER FOUR

Dunquin, March 1845

She is dancing a few steps ahead of me. I run, frantic, trying to catch up. Across field upon field, over hedges and ditches I run, but I never get close to her. Though I am desperate to touch her, to hold her. I slump to my knees. She'll never be mine.

She turns, dancing towards me, reaching out her hand. "Dance."

A wave of energy bursts through my body as my fingers touch hers, lifting me up, dancing me closer and closer to her. Her arms fold around me.

"All I want is someone to dance with," she says, her lips against my ear.

Her skin is soft on my cheek, soft and warm and dangerous. She tilts her head back, just far enough to look at me, and smiles. I smile back. I don't know who moves first, is it her or is it me, leaning towards each other, our lips—

I wake, startled. She was going to kiss me. Kitty Gorman was going to kiss me. My heart is thumping through my chest, my face flushed. She was going to kiss me. I sit up, looking anxiously at my sisters, but they sleep on.

Dressing quickly, I go through to the other room where my da sits at the table. "Have you been up long?"

"A while. I've the cows milked already."

"Thanks, Da. I'll go and gather in the eggs."

"Peig'll do it when she's up. You should have a day off."

"But there's work to be done."

"Nothing that won't keep. We've finished the planting—a day's rest will do you good."

I wander down the lane from the house, trying not to think of Kitty. I follow my feet with no clear idea where they are taking me as long as it is away from Ballyferriter. Drifting along the road as far as Dunmore, I decide to climb the headland. It's steep and my breath comes quick. The day is overcast, silver grey clouds patched together over the vast ocean. It will rain today, but it's dry for now. There used to be a fort here, but only a scatter of rocks and a few walls remain. Ahead lie the Blasket Islands, just offshore, then nothing till America. I wonder if Kitty has ever been here.

Why can't I stop thinking about her? It is bad enough that I dream of her night after night, now she is taking hold in the day. I remember watching her at the dance. I could hardly take my eyes off her. Then the tongue-tied moments after Peig introduced us. I can't remember her first words to me, only an awareness that she was speaking and me not able to answer. Till finally I forced out, "I'd love some."

I couldn't stop once I'd started. "It's very kind of you to offer. I love plum cake. And this one, all the way from Dingle on the top of a pike? Imagine. You'd think they would worry about dropping it. Shall we go and sit down somewhere? Look, over there, there's a space. Shall we go and sit there?"

Kitty and Peig followed me. We had no knife but Kitty broke the cake in half by hand. She took out a handkerchief and carefully wrapped one half in it.

"I'll take this home to have with my mother," she said.

She broke off a piece for each of us from the remaining half. It was a moist, dark brown cake with plenty of nuts and rum-soaked fruit. I hardly ever have cake and I savoured every mouthful. The slow chewing calmed me. I glanced at Kitty. Her cheeks were still pink from the dancing. She caught me looking at her and smiled.

"Do you want some more?" she asked.

"You've already been more than generous. But I did love it. You deserved to win, you were brilliant. Where did you learn?"

"At home."

"Me too. My da's a piper. He'd play and my ma would teach us the steps. She taught all of us, Peig and me, and my other sisters."

The music started up again in the background.

"It's the set dances," Peig said. "Are you coming?"

"Maybe later," Kitty said. "Unless you want to," she said to me.

I shook my head. We watched Peig go.

"I like this sister," Kitty said.

I laughed. "Everyone always likes Peig. It's been like that since she was a baby."

"So what about your other sisters? What are they like?"

I found myself telling her all about them, talking easily. "Have you any brothers or sisters?" I asked.

Her face darkened for a moment. "I had two brothers. But they drowned, out fishing."

"I'm sorry."

She looked away, then got to her feet. I thought she would go then, the magic spoiled. Instead she turned to me.

"Would you like to dance?"

I look out now at a currach fishing off the Great Blasket, tossed up and down by the sea. It looks so small from here, small and fragile. I think of Kitty's brothers. They would have fished from a boat like this. Now they're dead. I watch the boat for a while longer. Then I get up and walk back down the headland, past the old ogham stone to the road. To my right, the road twists down to Coumeenoole Strand. I love it there, where the waves beat in against the sand. Instead I turn left, towards Ballyferriter.

It is raining by the time I get there, a soft rain misting my hair, dampening my clothes. I do not know Kitty's house, but I get directions from a woman near the church. Their cabin is in a field beyond the village, off a track to the left. It is small, built of sods and stone. A couple of chickens peck around my feet as I walk towards it. I shoo them with my skirts.

My mouth is dry as I near the door, which stands slightly ajar. I do not know what I am going to say. I pause for a moment, thinking. I shout, "Good day. It's Frances Moriarty, come to see Kitty."

A voice croaks out from the midst of the cabin. "Come in."

I push the door open. There are no windows and it's dark inside, the only light from some low embers in the middle of the room. It takes a moment for my eyes to adjust, but slowly I make out a woman sitting in a chair in the corner.

"Good day," I say again. "I'm Frances Moriarty. I've come to see Kitty."

"Good day to you, Frances," she says. "You are very welcome."

"Is Kitty here?" I ask.

"Well now, do you see her?"

I peer round the tiny cabin. There is no sign of Kitty, but an area is screened off to the left behind an old blanket hanging from the ceiling. Perhaps she is there. My eyes flicker towards it in desperation.

The woman laughs, then dissolves into a fit of wheezing coughs. I go over to her. "Is there anything I can do to help?"

Slowly her breathing comes back to normal.

"Sorry," she says. "I've a bit of a cough."

"Shall I stoke the fire? My mother always says it's good to sweat it out."

She nods. "Thank you."

I fetch some sods from the stack outside and work the fire back to flame. She looks weak, now I see her in the light. The fire will help, but my mother swears by an onion soaked in milk for a bad chest.

"Do you have an onion, Missus Gorman? It is Missus Gorman, isn't it?" I say.

"It is," she says. "Kate Gorman. But no, I've no onion. Kitty's out finding me one. You're welcome to stay and wait, I'm sure she won't be long. Why don't you pull that stool up to the fire?"

I do as she says.

"So who are you?"

"My name is Frances," I say. "Frances Moriarty."

"Yes," she says. "I know that. You've told me that three times already. But who are you? And how do you know my Kitty?"

She starts to cough again.

"Perhaps I should go," I say. "Give you a chance to rest."

"I've been in my bed the last three days. I am sick to death of resting. Now take my mind off my woes and tell me about yourself."

"I'm from Dunquin. My father is Morris Moriarty, my mother Eliza Daly."

"Is that Morris Moriarty the piper?"

I nod. "It is."

"He's a fine piper, your father. Do you play yourself?"

"The pipes, only a little. It's the flute I play."

"Oh, I do love the flute. Would you play for me?"

"I don't have it with me," I say.

She nods towards a battered old box. "You'll find one in there."

I take up the wooden flute and test it out with a gentle scale. Then I start to play "Mo Ghile Mear." It is a tune that you hear in your heart more than your head. I have always loved it. I am lost in my playing, focusing only on the notes and the feeling, hearing them in my soul.

But as the last note falls away, I am suddenly aware that Kitty has slipped unnoticed through the door and is standing a few feet away, watching me. I stand up quickly, dropping the flute as I do so. It rolls towards her. I bend to recover the fallen flute but she beats me to it, holding it out to me.

"That was beautiful, Frances," she says.

Her hand grazes mine, touching for only the briefest moment, but igniting me like a torch. I see her hand stroking mine, holding it, kissing it, loving it. Flustered, I drop the flute again, fumbling round at her feet. I catch sight of her red petticoat and look away immediately, finally getting ahold of the flute and standing up again.

I can see a smile twitching at the corners of Kitty's mouth, hear her mother cackling behind me.

"You are surely a butterfingers and no mistake," she says. "But you have your father's gift for the playing."

"Will you play something else?" Kitty asks.

I hesitate, then nod. "What would you like?"

"How about 'She Moved Through the Fair'?"

I begin to play and after a few bars Kitty joins in. Her voice is strong and rich, full of sorrow as she reaches the last verse.

Last night she came to me, my dead love came in
So softly she came her feet made no din
And she laid her hand on me and this she did say
It will not be long now till our wedding day

I look at her as I finish the tune. She catches my gaze and smiles.

"You've a lovely voice," I say.

"Ah you're very kind, Frances, but you've not heard a voice till you've heard my mother's." She turns towards her mother. "But there'll be no singing till we can shift that chest. I have this onion sliced. I'm just going to put it in some milk to steep, then I'll heat it for you."

"You're a good girl," she says to Kitty. "Frances, would you mind playing me a few more tunes? Take my mind off that accursed onion milk I have in store."

I sit back down on the stool near Missus Gorman and begin to run through whatever comes to mind—"Bendemeer's Stream," "Eileen Aroon," "The Meeting of the Waters." Missus Gorman keeps time with her foot, humming gently under her breath.

When the onion milk is warmed through, Kitty pours it into a rough wooden bowl.

"Here you go now, Mother. This'll do you the power of good."

"Ah, Jaysus," Missus Gorman says. "Keep playing now, Frances, I need the distraction."

I start to play "She Is Far from the Land." As I finish, Missus Gorman says, "Poor Emmet, God rest his soul. It was terrible what the English did to him. Bastards." She starts to cough, wheezing and choking for more than a minute.

"Now Mother, don't go upsetting yourself." Kitty goes over to her and rubs her back. The coughing subsides, then stops.

"That onion milk has finished me off," Missus Gorman says. "I need to rest. Come again, Frances. I'll sing for you next time, if I'm rid of this chest."

"Thank you, Missus Gorman. I'd love to come again," I say, getting to my feet. "I hope you're feeling better soon."

"If you can wait till I get my mother settled, I'll walk a little way with you," Kitty says.

They disappear behind the old blanket, Kitty whispering and soothing to settle her mother. I watch the flames flickering in the middle of the room, thinking.

I start as I feel a hand on my shoulder. It is Kitty. "Sorry," she whispers. "I never meant to startle you."

"I was thinking about Emmet's fiancée. She wasn't much older than us when the English butchered him. And no grave to go to when they hid what was left of him. I don't know how she could bear it."

She shakes her head. "People find a way to bear the hardest things."

"I didn't mean to upset your mother, playing that song."

"She's always been dedicated to Emmet. Her uncle died in the rising. She's sleeping now. I'll walk you up the road a bit."

We are quiet as we walk along. She has hooked her arm through mine. It feels warm all down my side. We pause at the crossroads.

"Well, I must be going," I say, though I wish to stay where I am, her body next to mine.

"It was lovely to see you, Frances. Come again soon. You're always welcome."

"I will," I say.

"Promise?" She squeezes my hand.

"I promise."

CHAPTER FIVE

Kansas, November 1848

November 4th, 1848
Lassiter's Farm, West Port
Dear Gerry,
I arrived in West Port a week ago, ready to set off to California with whoever would have me. It turns out nobody would, not until spring. All that planning but we never thought of the winter coming.

I have stayed on here instead of going back to St. Louis. It is a terrible town, full of slaves and slave owners. I do not hold with slavery and neither does the man I am working for. Mister Lassiter is his name. He owns a farm about four miles out of town, breeding animals to sell to the overlanders and rearing cattle for market. I have three good meals a day and a place to sleep. He's given me a rifle and I've learned how to shoot turkeys and geese with it. He'll pay me the rest in supplies for my journey come the spring.

I am counting the time till I can get off to California. In the meantime you can write to me here. Accept my best wishes.
Your friend,
Frank

* * *

I am hard at work when Janey appears along the path from the house towards the barn. She's the Lassiters' only child, a fair-haired girl of seventeen. Her cheeks are flushed pink from the cold air.

"Hallo, Frank," she says, smiling, a wide grin full of white teeth. "I brought you something to eat."

"Thank you," I say as she hands me a plate of bread with cheese and pickle. I take a bite, savouring the tang of the cheese, the sharp of the pickle. "Mmmm, this is good."

"I made the bread myself," she says, flushing pinker still.

I take another bite.

"So what are you working on today?" she asks.

I struggle to swallow down what's in my mouth before answering. "Getting more wood laid in."

"Well you sure are doing a great job."

"Thank you."

"I guess I should let you get back to your work."

I nod, but still she lingers.

I set to, splitting timbers with my axe, aware of her watching, wishing she was gone.

"I'll see you tonight at supper," she says eventually, then sets off back towards the house.

* * *

I knock on the door. "Evening, it's Frank," I call. The door opens into the big main room of the house. Missus Lassiter emerges from the kitchen area to the left, wiping her hands on her apron. She's a tall, lean woman, not a spare ounce of flesh on her.

"Good evening, Frank. How are you?"

"Very well, Missus Lassiter. Can I do anything to help?"

"No, thank you. Janey and I have it in hand."

We sit down to a rich beef stew and plenty of freshly baked bread washed down with milk.

"I got the newspaper today, Frank," Mister Lassiter says. "Looks like you're right about all this gold in California."

These last months it has been like I'm the only person who has heard of the gold strike. If I hadn't kept the clipping from the *New York Herald*, I'd have begun to doubt it myself. Even the stores that kit the wagon trains out know nothing about it. Their minds are on what people will need for farming in Oregon, not prospecting in California.

"What did it say?"

"Got a report of President Polk's State of the Nation address. The president himself says there is a vast quantity of gold in California."

Mister Lassiter lets me have the paper. I sit up in the hayloft reading it. Nearly all the men in California are already at the mines searching for gold. Thousands more are expected to flood in from all across the country and beyond. I will be one of them. The wait for spring is maddening.

* * *

I make my way down to the bottom paddock, the sun shining on my back. The weather has changed over the past few days. The last week of March and spring is upon us.

Mister Lassiter's already at work in the field. "Afternoon, Frank. You know much about repairing fences?"

"It was all stone walls at home," I say, looking at the wooden fence in front of me. "But I'm sure I could have a go."

"Start by replacing this end post. Then renew any timbers that look weak or rotted."

"I can do that."

He nods. "You're a capable lad."

"Thank you, Mister Lassiter."

"You still intent on going? I could use you over the next few months, helping put together teams of oxen and mules for sale to the overlanders. We've a busy time coming."

They have been good to me, the Lassiters, but I can't stay here for them. I stand, awkward. "I'm sorry, sir. I'm still planning to go as soon as I can find a wagon train that will have me."

He sighs. "Well, I guess I expected you'd say that. And you may as well hear it from me. The first groups of overlanders have already started arriving. I saw them in town this morning."

"Really?" I say, excited. "I thought it wouldn't get started for a few weeks yet."

"Most years it don't. But this year there's people whose feet are itching to be on their way to California on account of the gold."

"I should get up to town soon," I say, wishing I could go right now. I don't want to be left behind.

"Listen to me, Frank. Anyone who leaves here in the next few weeks is a darned fool. I know those plains. The grass don't get growing till May. You take yourself off any earlier than the end of April, you're looking at big trouble. The animals'll starve for sure and then who's going to be hauling the wagons?"

I ponder Mister Lassiter's words as I set to repairing the fence. He's lived here long enough to know what he's talking about. Still, it won't do any harm to go up to town tomorrow, see if I can find someone leaving in a few weeks time.

I stand back from the fence admiring my handiwork, then push against it to test the repair. It'll hold. I'm packing up my tools when I hear someone calling my name. Looking up, I see a man walking towards me, wearing a cap and buried in a huge coat.

"Frank," he shouts again. "It's me."

I stare for a moment. Then I'm running, fast as I can, almost bowling him over as I skid to a halt.

"Gerry!" I throw my arms around him, unable to contain my delight at the sight of him. "What on earth are you doing here?"

"Heading to California to make my fortune."

"Really? You're coming?"

"Sure, Frank, didn't I always say you would need a proper man with you to make anything of gold digging?" He grins.

I grin back. "I still can't believe it's you. What changed your mind?"

The smile is gone. "They died," he says, his voice quiet. "My ma and my brother."

"Oh Gerry," I say.

"There's only me…"

"I'm so sorry," I say, not knowing what else to say.

He nods. "So anyway," he says, his voice businesslike though the pain's still there in his eyes, "have you a wagon train yet?"

"I'm going up to town in the morning to look for one. We can go together. All we need's space for our supplies, I'm sure we can find someone with a bit of room for rent in their wagon."

"How would you feel if I'd already found us a wagon?"

"A wagon? How much?"

"Nothing."

"Gerry, what are you talking about?"

"Well, it's like this," he says, "I was looking for directions to this farm when an educated gent came into the hardware store asking where he might hire help for getting to Sacramento. It seemed too good a deal to pass. He's after someone to buy supplies on his behalf, load and drive the wagon and look after the animals. In return we'll get our share of the food, room for our supplies and a tent to sleep in. What do you think?" he finishes. "I've not shaken on it yet, not till I talked to you."

I stare at him. In town for two minutes and already he has everything arranged. "Gerry, you're a godsend."

* * *

I let out a sigh of pleasure. "That was a wonderful meal. Thank you, Missus Lassiter."

"You're welcome," she says. "But it's Janey you should be thanking. She did most of the work, everything except the creamed corn."

I turn to where Janey sits next to me. "You've a real talent for cooking. I can't remember when I enjoyed anything so much."

She smiles but doesn't say anything in response.

"Hard to beat fried chicken," Mister Lassiter says.

"I'd never had it till I came here."

"I reckon my ladies took pity on you tonight. You ain't gonna have much in the way of good food in the next few months."

"You're right about that, sir. I think Gerry can cook stirabout, but that's about all."

"Stirabout?" Missus Lassiter says.

"Oatmeal. We call it stirabout in Ireland."

"Well that hardly counts as cooking," Missus Lassiter says. "Sounds like it'll be down to you, Frank. I suppose it's mostly flour and bacon you've got?"

"It is, ma'am. Hard tack and beans too. And rice, though I don't know the first thing about cooking it."

"I can give you a few easy recipes."

"Thank you, I'd appreciate that."

"Are you set for tomorrow?" Mister Lassiter says.

"I am, sir. Gerry and I finished loading the wagon today. It took some time. I never saw so many books as Doctor Dallas has, boxes and boxes of them."

"You wanna be careful, Frank. It's best not to overload the wagon. You don't wanna give the oxen any more work to do than they've got already."

"That's what the guide said. He made us get rid of loads of the books. Doctor Dallas was pretty upset, but it was the same with the other wagons. Anything that wasn't essential had to go—silver goblets, a rocking chair, a silk footstool—"

"A footstool?" Mister Lassiter says. "What in tarnation does anyone want with a footstool in the middle of the plains?"

"I didn't ask. We'd enough to do repacking our own wagon."

"It sounds like your guide knows his job. That's half the battle. Still I'd be happier if you were waiting a few days longer."

"Ten companies have gone already. We don't want to get left too far behind."

"Damn fools, those people that left last week. But I suppose it's almost May now and the grass is coming in. And them's good strong animals I've given you, the best oxen I've got. Not as fast as mules, but easier to handle. Start them easy, make sure they get enough forage and water and you shouldn't have any trouble with them."

We talk on into the evening about my forthcoming journey.

"It's time I was turning in," I say at last. "I've an early start."

"Good luck, Frank," Missus Lassiter says, hugging me. "Write and tell us all your adventures."

Mister Lassiter reaches out his hand. "Good luck, son," he says.

Janey has stayed seated. She's been quiet all evening.

"Goodbye, Janey," I say.

"Goodbye," she replies.

I walk across to the barn and climb the stairs for the last time. I am lying down on my old quilt, about to put out the lantern, when I hear the door to the barn creak open.

"Who's there?" I say.

"It's me, Janey. Can I come up?"

Before I can answer I hear her foot on the ladder. I sit up, waiting for her. She settles down on the hay next to me.

"So I guess you'll be on your way in the morning?" she says.

I nod.

"Are you sure about going? Pa says it's a long tough journey. You could stay here and work instead."

"I need to go. I have to try and make my fortune."

She's quiet for a moment, looking down at her lap. When she looks back at me, I can see tears glistening in her eyes.

"I'll miss you, Frank," she says. "You're the sweetest boy I've ever known."

"I'll miss you too. All of you. Your family has been very kind to me."

She throws her arms round my neck, her lips suddenly on mine, kissing me.

"I'll never forget you," she says, drawing back, as I sit there not knowing what to say or do. "Not till the day I die." She turns away quickly and is off down the ladder without another word between us.

too soon. Sunday is the soonest it would be seemly to call again. It is a whole three days away.

I think of things I might do to keep me busy and away from Kitty's door for three days. I could spin yarn for my ma or help her embroider some mats to sell at the market.

I stop. The market. Of course, the market. Kitty is sure to be at the market in Dingle tomorrow. I start to sing:

To market, to market,
To buy a fat pig
Home again, home again
Jiggety jig

I cannot shift this rhyme now that it has popped into my head.

To market, to market,
To buy a fat pig
Home again, home again
Jiggety jig

Though my marvellous Kitty is far as far can be from a fat pig. The thought makes me laugh. I jig along the path, laughing. Tomorrow, I will see her again tomorrow.

* * *

We are up before cockcrow this morning. While Peig and Lizzie eat breakfast, I load Bramble, our donkey, with our wares—butter, eggs, early carrots and peas and a few placemats my mother has crocheted.

"I'm glad you're coming to market," Peig says as we set off. "It's ages since you've been."

It's true. I prefer to stay at home, working in the fields with Da or roaming round the countryside alone. But nothing could keep me from the market today.

It takes three hours to walk to Dingle. Other stalls are already setting up—crates of live chickens, squawking and pecking; dead birds, hanging by their feet, waiting to be plucked; cows in groups of three and four; pens of sheep. We manoeuvre our way round all manner of animal droppings.

My eyes search for Kitty, but there is no sign of her. Still, it is early, there is plenty of time. Soon we have our first customer, an older woman with a harsh, lined face. She fingers the crocheted mats, sniffing.

"How much for these?"

"One shilling each, or six for five shillings," I say.

"I'll give you four shillings for six."

"You can see for yourself the fine craft in these mats," I say. "I can't take less than four and six."

She sniffs again but gets out her purse. The mats go into her basket. She moves off to the next stall.

"Oh, well done," Peig says. "Ma would have taken the four."

"I see the work that Ma puts into them. I won't have her sold short. And I could tell that the old baggage wanted them." I sniff pointedly. Peig and Lizzie laugh.

Our next customer is a young servant girl who takes a dozen of our eggs away with her. Customers come thick and fast after that and we are sold out by noon.

Busy as we've been, my eyes have searched the crowds all morning for Kitty, but to no avail. I haven't given up hope as I set off with Peig and Lizzie for a walk round the market, my eyes flicking in hope to every red-haired woman. She's not here.

"Let's go and find somewhere to sit a while," I say, wanting away from the crowded market, not yet ready to leave Dingle.

We walk towards the harbour. It's a cloudy day but dry, and the view is clear across to the other side of the bay. Peig and Lizzie chatter but I am quiet. I was so sure she would be here.

"I suppose we might as well go home," I say.

"Do you mind if we've a look round the town first?" Peig says.

"Look in O'Connell's Bakery, more like," Lizzie says.

"I don't know what you're talking about," Peig says, but she flushes.

"Oh yes she does," Lizzie says to me. "She's been making eyes at Liam O'Connell."

"So what if I have," Peig says. "It's no business of yours."

I look at Peig. I think of her as my little sister, but she is almost fifteen. There's many a girl married at sixteen.

"Is he nice, this Liam?" I ask Peig.

She nods.

"Well, why don't you go and see him? Lizzie and I can amuse ourselves for an hour."

"But, but…" Lizzie splutters.

"Ah now, Lizzie," I say. "Sure you won't mind keeping me company for a while. It'll be soon enough that you'll be making eyes at someone, and you'll be wanting the same chance I'm giving Peig here now."

I watch Peig's retreating back. "Come on," I say to Lizzie, "we may as well get Bramble."

We make our way to where she's tethered on the edge of the market. Her ears prick up, glad to see us.

"I kept her a carrot," Lizzie says, reaching into her pocket. Bramble munches her treat contentedly.

"What do you want to do now?" I say to Lizzie.

"Shall we take a walk up to Main Street, have a look in the shops?"

We carry on round the edge of the market, then turn left up The Mall.

"There's Esme and Maggie," Lizzie says, waving to two girls across the street.

"Why don't you go off with your friends for a while?" I say.

"Are you sure?"

"Go on ahead, have some fun."

I continue up the street with Bramble. As we near the junction with Main Street, I set her free to drink from the stream and graze on the bank. Music spills out of the pub opposite. I cannot help but tap my foot as I sit on the wall over the bridge, listening. I am drifting on the notes when I hear a voice saying, "Good day, Frances. I hoped I'd see you here."

It's Kitty. I get up in a hurry, stumble and almost fall back over the wall into the stream.

"Oh, Kitty," I say, blushing. "What are you doing here?"

"Well," she says, and there's a smile behind her lips, "I'm buying and selling things, like you do on a market day."

"But you didn't have a stall. I looked for you before."

"We sell our eggs straight to John Doherty."

I grin at her. "It's good to see you."

"And you," she says, touching me lightly on the shoulder. I have a sudden urge to kiss her. I look away quickly. Across the road a horse flicks its tail to the side and deposits moist brown droppings on the cobbles. I am able to look at her again.

"So are you on your own?"

"Peig and Lizzie are here too. They're off with friends while I'm looking after Bramble." I gesture towards our grazing grey donkey.

"I was going to ask you to come shopping with me, but it would be easier without a donkey in tow."

"I'm meeting my sisters shortly. I can leave Bramble with them."

We walk back down towards the harbour.

"So how's your mother?" I ask.

"She's definitely on the mend. I don't know whether it's my onion or your visit that's done the trick. You must come and play for her again soon."

"I'd be glad to. Anytime."

"How about today?" she says.

"Today?" If I go today, I can hardly go again on Sunday. I want to be with her now. But I need to see her again on Sunday. "Well…"

"If you're too busy, never mind," she says briskly. "I suppose you've got to get home with your sisters. Where the divil are they, anyway?"

Her tone stabs me.

"I'm sorry, Kitty. I do not mean to have offended you. You are the last person in the world I would wish to offend. It's not that I'm too busy, it's just that…" My voice trails away.

"It's just that?" she says, her tone still sharp.

I can see no way out but the truth. I put my hand on her arm.

"It's just that I thought I might come over to see you on Sunday. And if I come today, well, you might not want me to come again so soon. So…"

I look down. She puts her hand to my face, gently turns my head towards her. Looking straight into my eyes, she says softly, "Didn't I tell you just yesterday, Frankie, that you'll *always* be welcome in my house? Should you come every day, two or three times a day, you will always be welcome."

I stare back at her, but she holds my gaze for only a moment before looking away.

"There's your sisters at last," she says.

"You remember Kitty from the dance," I say, as they arrive. "I'm going to help her with her shopping. Can you two take Bramble home for me?"

"We don't mind waiting," Peig says.

"I wouldn't want to be putting you out," Kitty says. "I only want to borrow your sister for an hour or two."

"I'll see you back at home later," I say, ending the discussion.

Kitty and I head towards the market. "I want something to give my mother her strength back."

"How about a nice bit of fish?" I say.

"I was thinking of black pudding. It'll do her the power of good."

We stop at the butcher's, then drift through the market and up to Green Street.

"Can you imagine having a fine dress like this?" Kitty says, looking at a beautiful blue gown in the window of the draper's shop. She sighs.

I notice how shabby her dress is, how often patched and mended. I cannot afford the dress but I want to give her something.

"Can I buy you a ribbon?" I ask her.

"Ah Frances, I was only dreaming. You don't need to be spending your money on me."

"Please," I say. "I'd like to."

She ducks her head. "Thank you. I would love a ribbon."

"What would you like? Satin or velvet? Blue or green. Or red maybe?"

She laughs. "You have my head spinning," she says. "You choose. I'll wait here."

The ribbons are in a glass-covered counter on the left of the shop. I examine them carefully under the watchful eye of the owner's wife. I must have the right one. I am torn between a gold satin and a sea-green velvet. I wish I could buy both. The shopkeeper is getting impatient. I don't care about her but I don't want to keep Kitty waiting.

"I'll have this one, the velvet."

She cuts the length, wraps it in the smallest piece of paper she can spare and passes it over the counter to me.

"Sorry I took so long. It was hard to decide," I say to Kitty as I hand the paper parcel over, feeling excited and nervous.

She unwraps the paper and extracts my ribbon. "What a beautiful colour. Thank you."

I smile at her, proud and pleased.

"Shall I put it on?" she says.

She bends her head forward, white neck exposed, red hair cascading round her face. Her long fingers work quickly, gathering her hair together, twisting the ribbon round it, then tying it in a tight bow.

"What do you think?" she asks.

I think, *You are the most wonderful woman ever put on this earth.*

I think, *My heart is yours if you want it.*

I think, *I need to kiss your perfect lips.*

I say, "It looks lovely."

We walk together as far as Ventry where the road separates, one path leading northwest to Ballyferriter, the other west to Dunquin.

"So," she says, "am I to have the pleasure of your company for a few hours longer? Or will you make me wait till Sunday?"

I want to go with her. But ever since I watched her tying her hair with my ribbon, I have felt the desire to kiss her growing in me till I am fit to burst with it. I know now that she is fond of me, but how long will that last if she finds out the nature of my feelings?

She sees I am torn, though I pray she does not know the cause. "Well, if you are to make me wait, I would delay you but a little longer today," she says. "There is something I wish to show you a little way up the road. Can you spare me fifteen minutes more?"

I nod and follow her up the Ballyferriter road. A short way along she turns off onto a track on the right. In a few minutes we reach a copse that I haven't noticed from the road. She stops in the middle of it. I do too. She steps towards me. Her arms encircle me, pulling me closer. Her lips are on mine, she is kissing me. I pull my head back, looking at her, astonished. She holds my gaze. I pull her into my arms and kiss her.

CHAPTER SEVEN

The Great Plains, April 1849

"Pull your wagon in. We'll camp here," the guide says.

I shout at the oxen to whoa. Soon all nine wagons are parked up in a rough circle. They look so flimsy huddled together in the middle of nowhere. This morning I was swept away with the excitement of setting off, but I have felt a growing unease as we have journeyed into this wilderness. I've been living for months on the edge of the plains but it hasn't prepared me for being out here, adrift from the last signs of civilisation. No fields, no fences, no houses, no barns. Only the huge sky, swallowing me up.

"Shall I unhitch the oxen?" Gerry says.

"I can manage them. Why don't you go and find wood for a fire?"

He leaves me wiping the animals down. I start with Doctor Dallas's black mare, Thunder, running a cloth across her back and down her flanks. The oxen stand patiently, waiting their turn. I have named each pair—Bob and Billy, Jim and Georgie, Red and Rusty, Gold and Digger.

The spring grass is still thin and I put out a scattering of hay, then go to fetch fresh water. As I walk back from the nearby stream, I see Gerry talking to an older grey-haired man and two younger fair-haired ones. It was Gerry who kitted out the wagon while I sorted out the animals. He knows everyone in the wagon train.

"So, who was that you were talking to?" I ask Gerry when he joins me.

"The Fischers. The sons, Peter and Bertie, have been around in West Port the last few weeks but that's the first time I've met the father. He's been in America thirty years but he's still got a fearsome accent."

"Mister Lassiter was asking me last night how many people there were in the company. I hadn't a clue."

"Do you want me to introduce you to everyone?"

"Oh God no, not tonight anyway."

"Are you sure?"

"I'll have plenty of time over the next few months. Just tell me who's who for now."

"Well, let's see. You've met Jed Lawson already."

I nod, looking over to our bearded guide.

"We're lucky to have him," Gerry says. "He's taken two parties through to Oregon, knows all the best places to camp."

"Has he taken anyone to California?"

"Not so far, but we follow the Oregon Trail most of the way and we've the guidebooks for the last bit."

I give him a dubious look and he laughs. "There's plenty to worry about long before then."

"I'd be more worried if I were her," I say, indicating a woman on the other side of the wagon circle who's cradling a baby in her arms.

"That's Sarah Lewis. She's here with her husband, William. The littl'un's Martha."

"What can she be thinking, bringing a baby on a trek like this?"

"I know. But William was determined to come and Sarah didn't want them to be parted. So here the three of them are."

"You'd think she'd have been better off staying at home."

"Well, what can I say about stubborn women?" he says.

I shrug but don't answer.

"In the wagon next to them is Bernard Colville, who used to work for the *St. Louis Herald*. He has got the gold fever bad."

"St. Louis? He's not brought any slaves with him, has he?"

"He hasn't. He's with his in-laws, white people."

"I couldn't be trekking across America with a bunch of slave owners."

"There's no slaves here. And only Colville from St. Louis. All the rest are from round and about Boston. Except for the doctor."

"And us," I say.

"And us," he says. "But everyone's friendly enough, most of them anyway. The three Hain brothers are farmers. And the wagon next to them belongs to their cousins. Then there's a group of Scots—the MacGregor twins—"

I hold my hand up. "No more tonight, you'll have my head spinning. I'll never manage to remember them all."

"Of course you will. It's only thirty people."

"I suppose so," I say. "Anyway, it's time I was cooking."

Darkness is falling as we sit down to eat. There's little conversation beyond "Very tasty," and "Well done, Frank." We don't dwell after eating, Gerry and I checking to see that the animals are tied up before retiring for the night.

Doctor Dallas is sleeping in one tent, leaving Gerry and I the other. I have known Gerry for almost two years, but I feel awkward at the prospect of sleeping next to him.

He has made up a bed with blankets from the hardware store in West Port and my old quilt from the Lassiters. I take my boots off and lie down, facing the left wall. Behind me I can hear Gerry rustling around. Will he ever just lie down and go to sleep? It is worse, ten times worse, than being on the *Brilliant* with Captain John. At least then I had a bed of my own. Now I need a tent of my own. This space is so small, Gerry is so close. My body clenches, chest tightening.

"It feels strange, doesn't it?" Gerry says. "Out here in the open, miles from anywhere."

I don't answer. At last he lies down. I try to work out his position. His back, I think that's his back. I jiggle slightly, making sure. Yes, it's his back, he's facing the other wall. I don't know why, but I'm suddenly relieved.

"Good night, Frank."

"Good night."

* * *

I am awoken by a lantern shining in my face.

"Doctor Dallas?"

"No, it's Frank," I say, sitting up. I peer through the glare. It's one of the Fischer boys. "Is something wrong?"

"It's my father," he says. "He's ill. He needs the doctor."

"I'll take you to him," I say. We hurry to the next tent and rouse Doctor Dallas.

"What are his symptoms?" the doctor asks as we walk across to the Fischers' wagon.

"He's vomiting and has pains in his stomach."

"Any diarrhoea?"

Peter nods. "Yes, very bad. It's as if nothing will stay in his body."

Vomiting, stomach pains, diarrhoea. I stop walking. The Fischers' wagon is perhaps five yards away. I can hear a desperate moaning coming from it.

"I'll leave you here," I say.

"Who was that?" Gerry says as I clamber back into the tent.

"One of the Fischers. His father's ill. Jesus, Gerry, I think it's bad. Cholera or something like that."

He sits up. "Are you sure?"

"I'm telling you, it's some bad breed of sickness. Doctor Dallas better not take any chances. They need to be away from the rest of us till we're sure it's nothing that spreads."

I throw myself back down on my bed, full of rage. I will not think about Ireland, I will not. I work my nail into a scab on my arm, digging and picking till I have the scab off. It brings some respite. I drift in and out of sleep for the rest of the night.

The next morning, I am relieved to see the Fischers' wagon is gone. Gerry and I join the Lewises near the burned-out campfire.

"Hey, Gerry," says William Lewis. "Do you know what's happened to the Fischers?"

"The father's been taken ill. It could be cholera," Gerry says.

"Cholera?" Sarah says.

"Are you sure it's cholera?" William says. "I saw no sign of it in West Port."

"I'm not sure at all. But he's got the symptoms. And he only arrived from St. Louis the day before yesterday—he could have caught it there."

Sarah clasps her baby closer to her. "Oh my Lord. Has anyone else got it?"

"We don't know yet," Gerry says.

"But doesn't it spread? I heard if one person has it, everyone gets it. He was next to me yesterday near the campfire, breathing his bad air all around me and my baby." Her voice is edged with panic and Martha starts to cry.

"Hush now, Sarah," William says. "You're frightening the baby."

She's frightening me too. I decide to go and milk the cows, keeping myself busy with chores—feeding and watering the animals, checking the wheels of the wagon, mending a slight tear in my shirt. I harness my oxen, ready to yoke them to the wagon, but no one else is preparing to set off. People come and go from the campfire, standing together in clumps, then breaking up only to form again.

Gerry wanders over to me. "Are you going somewhere?"

"I want to get moving. Standing around doing nothing isn't going to make any difference to the cholera."

"Ah Frank, we can't be pretending there isn't a problem. We're waiting for Doctor Dallas to come back to decide what to do."

"Looks like your wait's over," I say, pointing at a lone figure on horseback approaching to the east of the camp.

Bernard Colville runs towards him shouting, "Doc, Doc, is it cholera?" But Doctor Dallas carries on riding. He stops in the centre of camp but doesn't dismount. Gerry and I join the crowd surrounding him, but it's impossible to hear a word over the voices shouting about cholera.

The crack of a rifle splits the air, bringing quiet in its wake.

"Thank you, Mister Lawson," Doctor Dallas says to our guide, whose gun still aims at the sky. Jed nods in return. "I am sorry to inform you that Mister Fischer is dead," the doctor says.

My hand's already at my left shoulder before I'm aware of making the sign of the cross.

"Was it cholera?" a voice shouts.

"Yes, yes it was."

"Cholera" ripples round the crowd as people start to take in the news. Doctor Dallas holds his hand up and we fall silent.

"I know this is a worrying time for all of us," he says, "but if we're careful, we can stop it spreading. First, has anyone else had any diarrhoea or vomiting overnight?" He looks around the group. I shake my head, others call out no.

"That's good news. So far only Mister Fischer has shown any symptoms. The Fischer boys will stay away from the wagon train for the next week as a precaution. And if any of you become unwell, you must tell me immediately."

"Will my baby be safe?" Sarah Lewis says, clutching Martha close to her.

"I believe we all will, if you do what I say. The most important thing is cleanliness. I want all food to be thoroughly washed and cooked right through. I want all drinking water boiled before use. I want all of you to wash your hands before eating and after relieving yourself. And I want the privy pit dug at least two hundred yards from the camp and all chamber pots emptied only into the privy pit. Is that all clear?"

Bernard Colville calls out, "I've seen outbreaks of cholera in St. Louis and I've never heard of all this water-boiling and hand-washing nonsense before. Are you sure you know what you're talking about?"

Doctor Dallas stares at him with some disdain. "And have many people died in these outbreaks in St. Louis?"

"Well, yes," Colville admits.

"Then I suggest you do as I say."

* * *

"It looks like it's going to rain again," I say, trying to make conversation. Doctor Dallas sits next to me on the wagon. He's been here for the last hour, since his horse went lame, and not a word has he said. Was he raised in silence? I wish he'd get off and walk instead of sitting here annoying me as he fiddles with his pipe.

"I said it looks like it's going to rain again, Doctor Dallas," I say, voice raised.

He turns to look at me, soft brown eyes full of apology. "Sorry, Frank, I've been rather rude this morning. Sometimes I get caught up in my own thoughts. My mind's been on cholera today."

Cholera. I'd rather have silence. But I don't want to be rude so I say, "Do you enjoy being a doctor?"

He thinks for a minute. "Yes," he says slowly, "when I can help people. But there's so much that medicine doesn't know. With Mr. Fischer I did what I could to try to keep him alive, but all I had was water against the diarrhoea and laudanum to ease the suffering. What I didn't have was a cure. Until we know what causes cholera, how can we hope to cure it?"

His face is animated, alive in a way I haven't seen before.

"With cholera," he continues, "people blame the air. 'Bad air,' they say. I'm not so sure. I think maybe it's the water."

"So is that why you have us boiling the water?"

He smiles. "Yes. I've learned that boiling the water and taking care with the food makes a difference. But I still don't understand why."

"I was surprised at a professional man like you heading for California."

"As soon as I read the reports in the newspaper I had to come."

"But weren't you making a pretty good living already?"

"California's about more than money, for me at least. My parents think I should be at home looking for the right girl to marry. But I wanted to take this chance for adventure. Maybe I'll make my fortune, maybe I won't. But at least I'll be able to say I was there, I saw the elephant."

He is quiet then for quite some time, chewing on the stem of his unlit pipe until he turns to me and says, "And what brings you here, Frank?"

"The chance to make my fortune."

"So is it only a question of money for you?"

"When you've never had any, only money is quite a reason," I say, trying to keep the anger out of my voice.

He nods. "Yes, I am sure that is so."

"But I suppose when it comes down to it," I continue, "it's not just money. It's what I can do with money. It's the chance to help my family, the chance to make something of myself."

"Well, I wish you luck, Frank. And please call me Charles."

* * *

"You sound happy enough, whistling away there to yourself," Gerry says as he returns from watering the animals.

"Having a bit of sun today has put me in a good mood," I say, looking up from where I'm cooking over the fire. "And I'm trying out a new recipe."

"Is that rice?" he says, staring into the pot.

"It is."

"Do you know what you're doing?"

"Of course. Missus Lassiter explained it to me. It's just like boiling potatoes."

"You've been doing a grand job with the meals." He fishes a flask out of his pocket. "Here," he says, handing it to me, "a little whiskey for the cook."

I raise the flask towards him. "May the hinges of our friendship never grow rusty." I take a slug, savouring the burn of the whiskey down my throat before handing it back.

"May misfortune follow you the rest of your life," Gerry says, raising the flask to his lips. "And never catch up." He wipes his hand across his mouth. "Jaysus, that's good stuff. We should have some music to go with it. There was always music on a Saturday night when I was growing up."

"Do you play?"

"No, not me. Our neighbour Ronan Collins was the musician," he says. "What about you? I saw you'd a flute in your pack."

It is the old wooden flute from Missus Gorman's box. She gave it to me before I left Ireland. "Think of the happy times when you play it," she said.

I will keep it always, but I will never play it again.

"I don't play either," I say, turning away and stirring the rice.

"Ah well," he says, "I guess we'll have to make do with my singing."

I carry on with the meal while Gerry sits nearby and sings the old songs of Ireland. He is halfway through "The Croppy Boy" when his voice is drowned out by an argument. I turn to see Angus MacGregor wagging his finger a few inches from Bernard Colville's face.

"What are you suggesting, man?" MacGregor says. "Tomorrow is God's day. We cannot be travelling on the Sabbath."

"No one said anything to me about not travelling on a Sunday when I signed up for this trip," Colville retorts. "And there's nothing in the Bible against Sunday travel."

MacGregor's voice is raised. "Just because we're living out on the plains, doesn't make us savages."

"Who are you calling a savage?"

"I've observed Sabbath since I was born. It's the Lor—"

"Every day not journeying is a day wasted. I'm not having your picky piety cost me in—"

"Picky piety," MacGregor roars, eyes bulging, spittle flying from his lips. "You're a heathen, man."

"Heathen. How d—"

"Heathen papist." MacGregor goes to grab Colville but Doctor Charles comes between them.

"Now now, gentlemen," he says. "Let's not have any unpleasantness."

"I will not have my faith mocked," MacGregor says.

"Your faith. What about my faith?" Colville says.

"You have no—" MacGregor starts, but Doctor Charles interrupts.

"Gentlemen, please, calm yourselves. I'm sure we can find a solution."

By now most of the company has stopped what they're doing and are following the exchange. "Maybe this is something for everyone to decide," William Lewis says.

"God has decided," MacGregor says.

"Your version of God," Colville retorts.

"Gentlemen, gentlemen. Mister Lewis is right. Everyone has a voice here. As I understand it, Mister Colville wishes to continue travelling tomorrow. Mister MacGregor believes we should not travel on a Sunday. Does anyone else have a view?"

"Animals could do with a rest," Walter Hain says.

"Hogwash. We barely travelled Wednesday with Fischer getting ill," Colville says.

"God tells us to rest on the Sabbath day," Duncan MacGregor says.

I stay out of it, standing on the sidelines as people talk round in circles—God says no; no He doesn't—back and forth, back and forth. It seems to me the no-He-doesn'ts have the upper hand when Doctor Charles steps forward again.

"I would like to propose a compromise. We observe the Sabbath in the morning, travel in the afternoon."

"It's the Lord's day all day," Angus MacGregor says, his face reddening.

"Whether we're travelling or not," Colville counters.

"Let's vote," Doctor Charles says. "Those in favour of travelling all day, please show."

The Colville party all indicate, as do Gerry and a few others.

"That's eight votes. Those in favour of no Sunday travel, please show."

The MacGregor brothers, their two Scottish friends and the Hain brothers raise their hands.

"That's seven votes," Doctor Charles says. "Those in favour of part observance, part travel?"

There's a lot of hands this time, including mine and the doctor's. "That's seventeen, by my counting. I'd be happier if we were all in agreement. How many of those who voted for all-day travel would compromise?"

All eight indicate their acceptance, though I see Colville muttering.

"And how many who voted for full observance would settle for morning observance only?"

Walter Hain nods and raises his hand. His brothers follow suit. The MacGregors' friend, Jamie, also starts to raise his hand before a glare from Angus MacGregor quells him.

Doctor Charles turns towards the MacGregor party. "I hope you can accept the compromise."

"Never," Angus MacGregor roars.

He is true to his word, on his knees praying loudly as the rest of the train prepares to depart the next day. Much of it seems to be his own invention, but as the final adjustments are made to the wagons, he starts reciting: "'Remember the Sabbath day, to keep it holy.'"

And not just the start of the commandment. He's quoting the whole thing, the six days; the manservant and maidservant, the creation of heaven and earth, and the resting on the seventh day. He has no sooner finished it than he starts again.

"'Remember the Sabbath day, to keep it holy. Six days shalt thou labour…'" Over and over again till it feels like he will never stop.

But he does. As the first wagon starts to roll, he's on his feet. "'The righteous shall rejoice when he seeth the vengeance,'" he shouts. "'He shall wash his feet in the blood of the wicked. Take heed of the word of the Lord.'"

As our own wagon starts to move, he carries on with, "'And I will execute great vengeance upon them with furious rebukes; and they shall know that I am the Lord, when I shall lay my vengeance upon them.'"

I wish I was up on the wagon driving instead of walking alongside with MacGregor raving in my ear.

"'Destruction cometh; and they shall seek peace, and there shall be none.'"

He carries on calling down all manner of God's vengeance upon our heads. Even as we leave the camp behind, I can still hear his voice booming out across the plains.

* * *

"Look who it is," Gerry says as we're harnessing the oxen a few days later.

I glance over to see the Fischer boys rejoining the back of the wagon train. Gerry waves at them but receives only the briefest of nods in response.

"Do you think they saw me? Maybe I should go and welcome them back," Gerry says.

"I'd leave them for now."

"Why?"

"I just would. Give them time."

"It's good to have them back at least," Gerry says. "Gets the numbers up."

"Surely you're not missing the Highlanders?"

"May the Lord in his vengeful glory smite thee down for suggesting such a thing."

"Do you think they've found another wagon train yet?"

"Probably. We must have seen at least a hundred wagons already and there's more joining the trail every day."

"God help whoever ends up with them."

* * *

We inch slowly west, each day much like the last—rising at dawn, milking the cows, hitching the wagons, trundling towards midday, stopping to eat, resting the animals, setting off mid-afternoon, travelling till evening, pitching camp. Some days we make eighteen miles, some days twenty-three, once twenty-six. With luck we'll be at Fort Kearney the day after tomorrow.

I hate the wet days, wheels sticking in the mud slowing us down, no dry wood for a fire, no cooked meals, bedding down cold and damp. Today is drier and I've been glad of the chance to cook again. I am waiting for the corn bread to be ready when I notice a group of riders away to the east, heading our way.

"Indians," the guide says.

A prickle of fear ripples through the company.

"Shouldn't we get moving again?" Sarah Lewis says.

"We'll never outrun them in the wagons," Jed says. "Most likely all they want to do is trade. But get all your weapons out and visible, just in case."

The Indians at the store in West Port always seemed to me to be minding their own business, but I know most of the wagon train is worried about an Indian attack. I get my rifle and knife from the wagon.

They are bearing down on us, perhaps thirty or forty horses, decked out in colours, riders wearing headdresses. I raise my rifle, finger pressed lightly against the trigger, sweat breaking out on my top lip. They look set to gallop straight through us but in the last few strides they pull up, coming to a halt perhaps ten yards away. We keep our guns high as they talk among themselves. After a minute, two of them dismount, one an older greying man wearing trousers and a jerkin of animal skins and a huge headdress of feathers. The younger one is bare-chested except for a necklace of some kind of animal tooth.

They approach our camp slowly, aware of the guns pointing straight at them.

"Peace," the older man says, hand held out before him. "Trade."

Jed nods. "Peace," he says. He gestures to us to lower our weapons. The chief turns to his tribe and raises his arm. They dismount and approach the camp. Soon it seems like everyone is involved in trading. Gerry gets a buffalo skin robe for a couple of blankets, Colville a beautiful piebald pony for a wooden trunk, Sarah a string of coloured beads for an old shawl. She gives them to the baby, who shrieks in delight.

"Are you not getting anything?" Gerry asks.

"I've nothing much to trade," I say.

"Sure you must have something. What about the old flute? You can't even—"

"No," I say, disgusted at the very thought, like he's suggested I trade myself.

"I didn't mean anything…"

I turn on my heel, leaving him where he stands.

CHAPTER EIGHT

Dunquin, May 1845

I am on my own up in the fields, clearing weeds from among the growing potato plants. It's been raining but the sun is breaking through. A rainbow arches from above my field down to the sea. And looking up who should I see, appearing as if by magic, but Kitty.

She is walking along the road, her step confident, head held high as usual. She has not seen me yet. It seems unfair to watch her when she doesn't know I'm here.

"Kitty," I call out, waving both arms. "Kitty, I'm up here."

She turns towards me. I run down to the road and vault the wall to land in front of her. Her hair is glistening from the rain, her shoulders damp, bare feet muddy.

"I can't believe you've come to see me," I say.

"Now what makes you think it's you I've come to see?" she says. "I could be on my way to many's a person in Dunquin."

"Oh," I say, crushed. "I thought…"

She leans forward and kisses me lightly on the cheek.

"Ah Frances, are you not used to my teasing yet? Of course it's you I've come to see. I woke up this morning and decided I couldn't be waiting till market day."

"I'm glad you didn't wait. I miss you every day."

"Me too. Our time together isn't enough, pleasant as it can be."

I blush, remembering the hour spent on Sunday kissing behind a hedge, halfway up the hill above Ballyferriter.

"I need to see you more," she says. "I don't want to be missing you, I want to be seeing you."

I nod. "I know. But we must be careful, Kitty."

"I don't want to be careful. I want to be kissing you now, here on this pathway."

I brush her cheek briefly with my lips. "Soon," I say. "But now I'm going to show you Dunquin."

I take her to the harbour, zigzagging down the path.

"It's different to Ballyferriter," she says. "Far steeper, more dramatic." She pauses for a moment. "I love it."

I smile, pleased, as if it's me she's praised. Manus and Jimmy O'Brien are setting off to fish. A dolphin appears near their boat, jumping alongside it as they pull out towards the open sea.

"Oh, isn't he wonderful?" Kitty says. "I wish I could leap and swim alongside him like a mermaid. Is he always here?"

"Only these last few days. He reminds me of you. Full of life."

We watch the dolphin and the boat for a while, then turn and walk back up the hill.

"So are you going to show me where you live?"

"Of course," I say, though I am nervous about bringing her home. My ma has been asking me what takes me to Ballyferriter every Sunday and not in a tone that encourages the trip. She is peeling potatoes when we arrive home.

"Good day, Ma," I say. "This is Kitty, my friend from Ballyferriter."

"You're very welcome," my ma says to Kitty. "Sit yourself down by the fire. We'll leave the potatoes to Frances while you tell me about yourself."

I have no choice but to take over the peeling. Like Missus Gorman, my ma starts with family. "Kitty Gorman, isn't it? Which Gorman is that?"

"We live in Ballyferriter, my mother and I."

My mother waits, expectantly, but nothing more is volunteered. "So your mother's a Ballyferriter woman?" my mother says, undeterred.

"She is," Kitty says, though I know from Missus Gorman's accent that this isn't true. I wish my mother would stop her prying.

"Now Ma," I interrupt, "what is it you're wanting doing with these potatoes?"

"What?" she says, turning away from Kitty, irritated by the distraction.

"The potatoes," I say. "I've them peeled. What is it you're wanting doing with them?"

"Anything at all, Frances. Sure you know as many things to do with potatoes as I do. Can't you see I'm busy now, getting to know your friend here?" She turns back to Kitty. "And your father, is he from Ballyferriter too?"

Kitty looks more awkward than ever.

"I think the fire'll want more turf for cooking the dinner," I say. "Kitty, maybe you could help me get some from the stack."

She starts to rise but my mother interrupts. "There's a whole basket of peat there in front of you, Frances, if you had but eyes to see it. Now away and give me peace."

I retreat from the fire with the cooking pot and begin to chop the potatoes into it, unable to help.

"Now, where were we?" my mother says. "Oh yes, you were telling me about your father."

There is no wriggling off the hook. "No, my father's not from Ballyferriter."

"So what brought him thereabouts?"

"He came there dancing and liked it."

"So you're *that* Gorman," my mother says, nodding, satisfied at last, "the dance master's daughter. Well, you're very welcome here, very welcome indeed. Isn't she, Frances?"

"That she is," I say, but Kitty doesn't return my smile.

My mother is soft as butter with Kitty for the rest of her time in our house. But I can see Kitty is on edge. After dinner I walk her back part of the way towards Ballyferriter.

"I'm sorry if my mother upset you. She likes to know exactly who's who and how they relate to everyone she knows."

She doesn't answer, just keeps on walking.

"You didn't tell me your father was a dance master," I say.

"Didn't I?"

"You know you didn't."

"Well maybe it's because it's none of your business." She is sharp, final. We walk on, silence stretching between us. Ten yards, fifty yards, a hundred yards. Till I can bear it no longer.

"Kitty," I say, pulling her round to face me. "Please. What is it?"

"Nothing."

"Then why are you so angry with me? What have I done?" I feel myself near to tears.

She must see it too. "I'm sorry," she says.

It makes the tears spill out.

"I'm sorry," she whispers, taking my hand.

"It doesn't matter."

"It does matter. I've made you cry."

She places little kisses under my eyes, licking away the tears. I laugh, weakly.

"Come and sit with me," she says.

I follow her off the path into the fields. We find a place to sit by the wall.

"I never talk about my father. But since your mother seems to know all about him, I see that I must talk to you."

I try to tell her that she needn't but she waves my protests away.

"My father, as you now know, was a dance master. But he thought it wasn't a great profession for a husband. So when he married he came to Ballyferriter with plans to be a farmer."

"Why Ballyferriter?"

"As I told your ma, he'd always loved the look of the place. But he never took to the land. He was miserable, so my ma encouraged him back on the road. He'd be gone for two or three months at a time but when he came home it was like magic." She smiles. "Then after three or four weeks he'd be off again."

"You must have missed him while he was away."

She shakes her head slowly. "It had always been that way, since ever I was born. I never expected it to change. Then, seven years ago, he went away as usual, but this time he didn't come back."

"Oh, K—" I start, but she talks on.

"He left in July, saying he'd be back in time for the harvest. At first we weren't worried. September became October and we gathered the potatoes without him. Still my mother was saying not to worry, he'd be back for Hallowe'en. But by December she was desperate, wondering was he dead or lying sick somewhere with no one to tend him. I remember her sitting up on Christmas Eve, pleading with the Virgin Mary to bring him home. But he didn't come. Not then, not ever again."

I want to put my arms around her, but she feels distant, beyond my reach. "Did you ever find out what happened to him?" I ask.

"Sort of. A friend of my mother's sent out word to all the places we knew of where my father danced. Months later we heard he'd got some girl pregnant down by Macroom. They eloped one night. We never found out where he went after that."

"That must have been hard for you."

She looks up. "'Twas terrible. The shame of it. For all of us, but especially for my mother. You know how people like to talk. You saw how your mother was."

"I'm sorry about my ma. And about your father. I could break his neck for abandoning you like he did."

"Don't say that, Frances," she says softly.

I look at her. She still loves him.

"Oh, Kitty," I say, drawing her into my arms. I stroke her silky hair. She is wearing my ribbon. I wish I could give her so much more, make up to her for the pain and disappointment of the past.

"I love you," I say, not knowing myself the words were on the way till they are out of my mouth.

She sits up, looking into my eyes. "I love you too," she says. Suddenly she is laughing. "It's the strangest thing," she says. "I'm sure I am not supposed to love a woman. But nothing has ever come so easily to me as loving you, Frances Moriarty."

I feel like dancing, like cartwheeling round this field. She loves me. Instead I kiss her, deep and long, pulling her down beside me, feeling her body against mine, soft and warm, hard and slim. I am awash with emotion as I finally force my lips away from hers. Her breathing is also fast, but a smile twitches beneath her lips.

"Is this your idea of careful?"

I go to silence her with my lips but she puts her hand on my arm. "You were right before," she says, sitting up. "We must be careful. If people found out, they'd stop me from seeing you. And I couldn't bear that." She gets to her feet. "Come on," she says, offering me her hand. "You can walk me to the next corner. Then you should get back home to work—I don't want your mother thinking I'm a bad influence."

* * *

Kitty's at the market on Friday but I have no time alone with her. "I'll see you on Sunday," she says as I set off home with Lizzie.

"See you Sunday," I reply, but as I walk back to Dunquin I decide to surprise her and visit tomorrow.

It's teaming down when I wake up on Saturday. I can make no excuse for a two-hour trek in this weather. I fret the morning away, starting tasks but not settling to them. By dinner it has rained itself out, a thin sun struggling through the clouds. I eat quickly, then make my excuses. I am in good spirits now that I'm on my way and I sing as I walk.

As I roved out on a May morning
On a May morning right early
I met my love upon the way
Oh, Lord but she was early
And she sang lilt-a-doodle, lilt-a-doodle, lilt-a-doodle-dee
And she hi-di-lan-di-dee, and she hi-di-lan-di-dee and she lan-day

The church clock shows half past two as I arrive in Ballyferriter. Kitty is cleaning out the chicken coop. I hear her muttering and cursing under her breath.

"That's fine language for a lady," I say, coming up behind her.

She whirls round. "Frances. What on earth are you doing here?"

"Visiting you."

She smiles. "Give me a few minutes and I'll have this finished."

"Do you want a hand?"

"You do enough work of your own."

"But I'd like to help. Let me." I pick up a shovel. "Where's your dung heap?"

"Are you sure?"

"I am."

"Thank you. It's round the back."

I scoop shovels of the fouled straw into a wooden wheelbarrow and ferry it to the pile behind the cabin, passing beds of turnips that line the left-hand side of their field. I enjoy helping her and the two of us make quick work of it. We are laying down fresh straw when the peace of the afternoon is disturbed by a terrible wailing sound, coming from a young woman walking towards us down the lane. Kitty runs to her.

"He's gone," the girl sobs.

"Come in to my mother," Kitty says, half carrying the young woman to the cabin. I follow them in.

"Siobhan's grandfather has passed," Kitty says.

Missus Gorman gets up from her chair and sweeps Siobhan from Kitty's arms into her own. "Ah, you poor child. You were that fond of your daddo, weren't you? But he's gone to a better place."

They stand there for some time, the girl sobbing into Missus Gorman's shoulder.

"Does your mammy want me to come?" Missus Gorman says at last.

"She does," Siobhan says.

"Do you want any help?" Kitty asks.

Missus Gorman nods. "There's always plenty to be done. You too, Frances."

"I don't want to be in the way."

"You won't be," Missus Gorman says. "Bring the flute with you. We'll want music later in the evening."

Missus Gorman gathers her shawl about her and sets off with Siobhan. Kitty and I follow behind.

"So who's the man that's passed?" I say quietly to Kitty as we walk along.

"His name was William O'Falvey. He's an old man who lives about a mile from here at Caherquin."

"Has your mother known him long?"

"Near enough since she's lived here. He used to run the shebeen that she went to with my father. But they'd have called her anyway— my mother does all the wakes round here."

The O'Falveys' house is closer to the sea than Kitty's. It is large, bigger than my parents' house, two proper floors, windows with lace curtains on both levels. The windows and door lie open. We follow Missus Gorman into the room on the right. It runs the length of the house, with a parlour area towards the front and a cooking area and table towards the back. Three women are in discussion in the parlour end. They break off as we enter.

"I'm sorry for your trouble, Bridie," Missus Gorman says, embracing one of the women.

"I know he was old but still…" the woman says, starting to cry.

"Oh, I know," Missus Gorman says, "'tis a terrible shock when it happens."

As the tears begin to lessen, Kitty goes forward. "I'm sorry about your father, Missus Sheehan. God bless him."

"I'm Frances," I say, "a friend of Kitty's. I'm very sorry for your loss."

Missus Sheehan nods. "Thank you," she says.

"So," Missus Gorman says, "where do you want us to start?"

"We've the mirror covered and the clock stopped," a small, wiry woman says.

"But we've not yet done anything with…" Missus Sheehan trails off. She takes a deep breath and resumes, "with my father. He's up above but I want to lay him out down here."

"I'm sure we could manage him down the stairs between us. Don't you think so, Mary? Maggie?" Missus Gorman says, turning to the other two women. "Kitty, will you and Frances give the table a good scrub and then bring it down to this end of the room?"

The table is big and old, made of planks. I sweep some breadcrumbs and other food remains off it into my hand and throw them into the fire. Kitty finds a scrubbing brush and sets to, vigorous strokes scouring the surface. I follow her, wiping and drying with an old cloth.

"I'll take this end," I say. Kitty and I heft the table a couple of inches off the floor.

"Jesus, it's heavy," Kitty says as she stumbles back towards the front of the room.

"Do you want to swap ends?" I say, wishing I'd thought to take the backwards end in the first place.

"No, I do not," she says.

We are just finishing putting the table in place when we hear the slow *bump-bump* down the stairs of the women with the body. I hold the parlour door open, catching my first sight of William. Eyes shut, face lined, mouth open, jaw slack, wet dribbling onto stubbly chin. Beneath his old stained nightshirt, his legs show pale and vulnerable, feet big, dry and scaly. Pure white hair flops over his face as they carry him past me into the parlour and ease him gently onto the table. The women are breathless, sweating. Kitty and I hover in the background, not sure what to do next. Missus Gorman solves our problem.

"I want you girls to set up the shebeen for the mourners while we get William here ready."

The room on the other side of the hallway smells of whiskey, porter and pipes. Like the parlour, it runs the length of the house. Two tables at the back are laden with assorted glasses and bottles of liquor.

"What do you think we should do?" I ask Kitty.

"I think a good clean first. Then we'll need to get a few more bottles in. They're out in the shed at the back."

We are busy for an hour perhaps, working quietly around each other. I am placing dishes of snuff on the windowsills and tables when the sound of a long single note takes my attention. A moment later it is echoed by a second voice. Then the first takes over, a beautiful, plaintive cry that brings a lump to my throat. Kitty takes my hand.

"That's my mother," she says. "The body must be ready. We should go and pay our respects."

Candles have been placed all round the room. The body is clean-shaven now, gleaming hair swept back from his forehead, mouth closed, dressed in a plain white habit, rosary entwined between his hands. He looks at peace.

I go over to the body, drop to my knees, and say, "The blessing of God upon the souls of the dead." As I get up, I cross myself. One of the women hands me a glass of whiskey and a tin of snuff. I take a pinch between my thumb and forefinger, place it on the back of my hand and inhale. The effect is almost instant, a feeling of goose pimples up my nose. I give my head a brief shake before downing the tot of whiskey.

I follow Kitty to the back of the parlour, where other women have been preparing food. We take dishes and plates through to the shebeen, moving some of the drink beneath one of the tables to make space for the food.

As the afternoon wears on, people begin to arrive. Some men start a card game, dealing William in and placing the cards in his hand.

"Ah, he was quite the card player," one of them says. "I've lost many a hand to the old trickster."

"He'd have his face as straight as a rule. You could never tell what he was up to."

"It wasn't just the cards though, was it?" a third man says. "At the Dingle races he'd be making the money hand over fist. He was always a great judge of horse flesh."

"Oh, that he was," the second man says. "Cards and horses, they were his strong suit."

The other men nod in agreement and lay down their first cards.

"Ah, you've a hand like a foot there, William," one of the men says. He discards the two of clubs and draws another card—the three of diamonds. "I think the luck died with you."

A bottle of whiskey passes between them.

"Here's to William."

The house is packed now and we spill out onto the patch of land in front of it. An older man starts up on the fiddle, a lament that I know well. I join in on the flute.

"He did love the music, my da," one of his daughters says, as we finish. "Would you play the 'Drinking Reel'? 'Twas his favourite. And Kitty, would you start the dancing? He always loved to watch the dancing."

It's a lively tune and the daughter starts to clap as it speeds along. Kitty takes to the floor, stepping up and back across the grass. Soon others are joining in. Another fiddle player takes up his bow and a man taps out the rhythms on spoons. We continue to play into the evening—reels, hornpipes, jigs and polkas.

As midnight approaches, we stop the music. The family goes in to be by the body, while everyone else crowds into the rest of the house or gathers near the windows or door. Kitty stands close to me outside the parlour. One of the men that was playing cards earlier begins the rosary.

"I believe in God, the Father Almighty, Creator of heaven and earth; and in Jesus Christ, his only Son, our Lord."

As the final Hail Mary is echoing around the crowd, Kitty turns to me. "I'll go and tell my mother we're away home."

"Shouldn't we wait for her?"

"No, she'll be here for the night, sitting up with Bridie. It's just you and me." She winks at me, an extravagant wink that sets me shivering and flushing at the same time. I'm going to be sleeping with Kitty. I have been wanting this chance, but now that it is upon me I am terrified. Will she just expect to go to sleep? It has been a long and tiring day, and she is surely exhausted. Or will she want something more? And what might that more be? I have seen the animals rutting in the fields. I know this happens between a husband and a wife to get a baby, though surely it must be a pleasanter process. But I have not the first idea about what I might be supposed to do with Kitty. I have no wish to be humping at her like a dog.

"You're a quiet one tonight," Kitty says as we walk back towards Ballyferriter.

"So are you."

"That I am," she says, hooking her arm into mine. "I've been thinking about old William."

"I was forgetting how long you must have known him."

She shakes her head. "It's not so much that I'm sad for him. Sure he lived till eighty-three and died with his family around him. It's my own life that has me thinking. I don't want to waste a minute of it." Her voice is urgent now. She pulls me to her and kisses me. She tastes a little of whiskey. I stand in her arms in the moonlight, moving my head back so I can look at her. Her face is serious, intent. "I don't want to waste a minute with you," she says, then kisses me again, a long kiss, minutes long. I can feel it everywhere. I am tingling and breathless. She breaks off. "Let's go home."

I am full of nerves again as we enter her cabin. She leaves me building the fire back up while she takes the lantern out to the privy. I can hardly look at her when she returns. She puts her hand on my shoulder. "Your turn," she says.

I hardly need the lantern to find my way, the moon is so bright. On the way back to the cabin I find water in the pail near the door. I splash my face and dry it on my sleeve, then swirl some water round my mouth. Finally I comb my hair with my fingers, wanting to look my best for her.

I open the door of the cabin. Kitty is already in bed. She holds the covers open. Below them she is naked. I look away, unsure what to do.

"Don't be scared."

I slip off my clothes, aware of her eyes on me, nervous and excited. At last I join her in bed. We lie side by side, looking at each other by the light of a couple of candles she has set into gaps in the stone above the bed. I have grown up in a room of sisters but I have never really looked at a naked woman before. Her skin is pale, arms lightly freckled, body soft curves, hair a dark red.

Slowly I stretch my hand towards her, touching her down her right side. A thrill jumps through me as I feel her warm flesh beneath my fingers.

I must kiss her. She answers me with one that is deep and strong, her arms coming about me, her breasts against me. I come away breathless, gazing into her eyes for a moment, then looking away.

"Don't be shy, darling Frankie," Kitty says, leaning in to kiss me on the cheek. "And don't forget to breathe."

I let my breath out in a rush. We both laugh.

"There's no hurry," she says.

I nod. "I could never have imagined feeling like this. It makes me tremble. Yet only a few months ago I didn't even know you."

I feel tears behind my eyes and bury my head in her shoulder.

She strokes my hair. "There now, darling." She lifts my hand towards her mouth and kisses it, gentle kisses landing on my fingers and palm. I look up at her. She kisses my forehead, below my eye where the tears have fallen, my cheek, to the left of my mouth, my lips. My mouth opens. I feel her tongue against mine.

I kiss her back, fierce and passionate. The whole of my body is alive and tingling. I seek her breast with my hand. I take my mouth away from hers so that I can look at it. Her breast is different than mine, fuller and paler, the nipple pinker. I circle the edge with my fingers, progressing slowly to the centre. It hardens and rises in response to my touch. I move so I can take it in my mouth. Her breath quickens.

"Is this right?" I whisper.

"Yes, oh yes," she answers.

We carry on like this long into the night, touching and stroking and kissing, till there is no part of her I do not know, till she has taken me to a place I had no idea existed, stripped not just to the skin but to the soul.

I fall asleep on my side, head in the crook of her arm, hand resting on her belly. It is early when first I wake, but there is enough light to see by. She lies on her back, both arms flung out above her head, the slightest smile on her face. I think I will lie here for a while, then get up and make my darling breakfast.

It is some time later when I wake again, slowly, gently coming to. I feel her breath on my shoulder, her foot on my calf. My eyes slowly open to see hers looking at me. I cannot help but smile. She kisses the edge of my upturned mouth. "Morning, Frankie," she says.

CHAPTER NINE

Oregon Trail, June 1849

24th June 1849
Sweetwater River, Oregon Trail

Dear Ma,

I am writing you a hasty line as we have run into a group of trappers who are taking mail back with them to the States. We have travelled a thousand miles since leaving West Port but we are still only halfway to the gold fields. You cannot imagine what a big country this is.

We are in the Rocky Mountains now. The guide is confident of our progress and we should be in California before the end of August. As soon as I have gold, be sure that I will be sending it to you. I have no news of how things are in Ireland but I hope and pray that you remain in good health and that there is a better harvest this year.

I think that you would like my friend Gerry, even if he is from Cork. We look out for each other on the trail. Doctor Charles is also a very fine person so you do not need to worry about me.

Please pass my love on to Da and the girls. I remain your faithful daughter, Frances

I stuff the letter into my pocket as Doctor Charles walks over, not wanting him to see my closing words.

"Are you a sweetheart or a mother?" he says.

"Pardon?"

"Sorry," he says, "it's my curiosity getting the better of me. Half the company's writing letters and they're nearly all to mothers or sweethearts."

"It's to my mother. And yourself?" I say, though I know it will be his mother. He's not a man I can easily imagine having a sweetheart. A betrothed perhaps, even a wife, but not a sweetheart.

"One to my mother, one to my brother, Nathaniel. He's a minister in Boston."

"A minister? Do you think he'd mind about your Sunday travel?"

"No, not at all. He's a Unitarian, not a Puritan. We all are in my family."

Unitarian? Puritan? Why they have to have so many breeds of Protestant, all disagreeing among themselves, I don't know.

"Any more letters?" the bushy-bearded trapper calls.

I fumble the letter out of my pocket and quickly seal it.

"Three more here," Doctor Charles calls, holding up his hand.

"That's fifty cents each."

"Fifty cents?" I say. "It was only twenty-five at Fort Laramie."

"Well maybe you should walk back there to send it," the trapper says.

"Here, this will cover both of us," Doctor Charles says, handing over the money and his letters. He turns for mine.

I feel my face redden. "No, I've got enough," I say, digging two quarters out of my pocket.

The trapper drops them in his fat moneybag. Our letters disappear into his sack, joining hundreds of others. He moves on towards the Hains.

"Hey," I call, "you owe the doctor fifty cents."

The trapper pauses. There's a flash of silver as he turns back towards us. "My mistake."

I stoop to pick up the half-dollar coin and hand it over to Doctor Charles. "Do you think there's any chance the letters will actually get there?"

"I hope so. But I wish I was receiving a letter today rather than sending one. I find it hard not knowing what's happening at home. It's foolish really. My worrying doesn't change anything."

Since I left home, I have had to learn to live with the worry, what news I get arriving months after it was sent, if it comes at all. "I think we all worry," I say.

"You have more reason to fear than I. I know these are hard times for your country."

I nod, not sure what to say. I have never spoken to him of the famine. "I'll go and get the oxen ready," I say, turning away.

* * *

We set off at six this morning after breakfasting on last night's corn bread. It is Gerry's turn to drive the wagon and I fall into step with Sarah Lewis. It's good to hear a woman's voice among so many men but it's the baby I enjoy the most, her delight in the slightest thing. We take it in turns to carry Martha, Indian style, wrapped in a blanket on our backs.

"Another cold one," Sarah says, pointing to the ice in the stream we're about to cross.

I sit down on a rock to take off my boots. They're a fine-looking brown leather pair, soft but strong with square toes, never worn till I found them two days ago in an abandoned trunk. The trail is strewn with all manner of debris—crowbars, clothes, furniture, books, shovels, even sacks of flour and bags of salt—thrown away to lighten the load.

"Half these streams aren't even here most summers," I complain. "They're not in Doctor Charles's guidebooks."

"Why this year?"

"It's the weather—bad winter then a wet spring. I heard Doctor Charles asking the trappers about it yesterday."

"William was talking to them too." She pauses. "They wanted Martha and I to go back to the States with them. They said we wouldn't make it to California, there's not enough grass for the animals ahead."

"No, I'm sure that can't be true. We've had fine grass these last few days."

"I suppose so. But it was poor for a couple of days before that."

"That was just a bad stretch. Even then, Jed found patches here and there. He knows what he's doing, he'll find forage for the animals."

"You sound like my husband."

"Well, we can't both be wrong."

"Let's hope not."

"Did you think about leaving with the trappers?"

"No," Sarah says, after a pause, "not really. I'd rather take my chances with the folk I know."

"You've done the right thing. A woman on her own has to be careful. You couldn't have been taking yourself off with a bunch of men you'd only just met. I wouldn't have…"

I stop. Maybe I should just introduce myself as Frances and be done with it.

"If I was in your position," I go on, trying to sound deep and gruff. "I mean, if I was a woman on her own. I wouldn't have gone with them."

She doesn't say anything. I no longer trust myself to speak. We walk on in silence.

* * *

Boooommmm.

I sit up in bed. Even Gerry's got his eyes open, and he's not a man easily roused.

"What the hell was that?" He yanks open the front of the tent and sticks his head out.

I clamber round him so that I can see outside too. The sun is not quite risen but there's enough light to see other members of our company emerging from their tents. William Lewis is nearest.

"William," Gerry shouts.

"Happy Fourth of July." He walks over to our tent.

"Oh, of course. Happy Ind—"

Boooommmm.

"Is that a cannon?" Gerry says.

"I reckon so. Imagine someone still carrying something that heavy with them. Shall we go and see it?"

Gerry looks at me.

"Why not?" I say.

Soon the three of us are strolling through the wagons encamped alongside the Bear River.

"It doesn't look like anyone's planning to move out anytime soon," I say. "There must be two hundred wagons here."

"I reckon most companies will stay put today to celebrate Independence Day," William says.

"It'll do the animals good to have a day of rest. That last hill yesterday was hard on them. Nearly too hard," Gerry says.

"That was nothing to what's ahead," William says. "I heard the Sierra Nevadas are so steep you can barely go ten yards without having to get out ropes and chains to haul the wagons up and down."

"It's a tough journey, right enough," Gerry says. "I've lost count of the number of carcasses I've seen, oxen especially. I sometimes wonder would we have been better off with mules."

"They're struggling too," I say. "Back at the Green River I saw a company whipping their mules across, rather than waiting for the ferry. One of the poor creatures stopped swimming, let its head go under and was swept away. I think it gave up."

"Some of these people don't know the first thing about looking after livestock," William says. "I take my hat off to our guide. Our animals look as well as any I've seen along the whole trail."

"Long may they stay that way," Gerry says.

We carry on among groups of men, sitting around campfires or standing talking, many of them already drinking. We can hardly walk five steps without hearing someone discharging a rifle or a pistol, and the notes of "The Star-Spangled Banner" and "Hail, Columbia" are all around us.

"Independence Day reminds me a bit of Saint Patrick's Day, but with a lot more shooting," I say to Gerry.

"I suppose so. But can you imagine Saint Patrick's Day if we had independence to celebrate? What a day that would be."

"I was in Boston a few years ago on Saint Patrick's Day," William says. "Lots of marching bands and people celebrating in the streets. I don't mind telling you I was impressed. I guess you had parades in Ireland?"

"Well, not so much parades, but it was quite a holiday," I say. "Church in the morning. Everyone would be there, the whole village. And after church the celebrations would start—eating and drinking, music and dancing till long into the night."

"Skibbereen was the same," Gerry says. "Not anymore, I don't suppose."

I hear the sadness in his voice but William doesn't seem to notice. "We should have a parade today," he says. "And then a party. I'll get Sarah to bake a cake. Soon as we've seen this gun."

* * *

"Ughhh," Gerry groans as I open the door of the tent, letting in the sunshine.

"Rise and shine," I say, unable to resist.

"Ughhh, leave me alone."

"It's time to get up."

"Not yet."

"It's already past nine."

"Nine? Shite," he says, throwing off the covers. A moan escapes his lips as he fumbles around for his boots.

"They're still on your feet," I say.

"What?" He looks down. "Oh." A wan smile hovers briefly but is dismissed by another moan. "I feel terrible."

"I'm not surprised. You had a skinful last night."

"Is everyone waiting? You should have woke me."

"We're not setting off for another half an hour. Turns out you're not the only one fishy about the gills this morning. I suppose you carried on drinking after I left?"

"Unfortunately. My head's thumping. Even my hair hurts."

"It was some night all the same. But I'm glad I went to bed after the dancing."

"I blame the Hain brothers. Turns out their great-grandfather fought for the Yankees against the English. If we toasted him once, it must have been twenty times."

"What you need is a hearty breakfast. I've the cow milked, the horse saddled and the oxen harnessed. All that's left is for you to get something down you and we'll be ready to roll."

* * *

I slap my hand hard against my cheek, hoping to crush the life out of a mosquito that's wriggled its way under my scarf. They call this place Fort Hall Valley but to me it's Mosquito Valley. The air is thick with them, intent on my blood. I am near eaten alive. And the poor animals are demented, their coats covered in a layer of biting torment.

Not to mention the heat. It would roast the arse off you today, worse than anything I knew in New York. Sweltering by day, freezing by night. And the road's dreadful, just dust and sand, sand and dust. You can't see the lead pair when you're driving the wagon.

Poor beasts, sunk to their knees, grit in their eyes, a plague on their backs and barely a shred of grass to share between them. They've not had so much as a mouthful to eat today and little more the two days before that. I hope to God we find some forage tomorrow.

* * *

I've got to go, got to go now. I look around, desperate for some semblance of shelter in this barren valley. I dash behind a rock, undoing my buttons as I run. I've barely got my trousers down before it's bursting out of me. I crouch down, my hands holding tightly to my trousers to protect my privacy.

It seems to have stopped. I wait a minute longer before carefully pulling my trousers back up and walking back to the wagon.

"What's the matter with you?" Gerry says.

"Nothing," I say, as I fall into step beside him.

We've taken to walking alongside the oxen, cajoling and encouraging them as they struggle through the heat and the dust. They're exhausted. We all are. The Humboldt has to be the worst river in the world, all twists and turns, never going in the right direction for more than a hundred yards, valleys full of sage and willow when what we need is good grass. It's sucking the life out of our animals. In a couple of days we'll be at the sink where the river disappears for good. After that it's the desert.

"So you're galloping off the trail in this heat for nothing?"

"My stomach's not quite right."

"How not right?"

"Just a touch of diarrhoea," I say, embarrassed.

"You should talk to the doctor."

"Not yet."

"This could be something serious, Frank."

"But if he examines me—"

"And if he doesn't?"

We walk on in silence. Until I have to make another dash for the rocks.

"You have to talk to Doctor Charles," Gerry says, when I return. "If you don't—"

"I know. Where is he?"

"Up at the front."

I walk along the side of the wagon train, hoping there'll be no need for any examining. If he asks me to take my trousers off, I'm going to refuse. He can't make me.

Ahead, Doctor Charles plods through the sand, leading his horse.

"Frank," he says as I catch up with him.

"Gerry thought I should come and talk to you. I've a bit of an upset stomach."

"What kind of upset?"

"Diarrhoea."

"How often?"

"Only the twice."

"Good. And how loose?"

"Loose?"

"Was it very watery? More water than solid."

"No, the other way round," I say, feeling my face hot. I do not want to be talking about this.

"Any blood?"

"No."

"Any vomiting?"

"No."

"Stomach cramps?"

"No."

"Any irritability?"

I pause. "A little…"

He smiles. "Any more than usual?"

"No."

"Any other symptoms at all?"

"No."

"That's good. Well, you're not the only one in the company. But I don't think it's anything too serious."

"I told Gerry—"

"No, you were right to come. And come straight back to me if it gets worse. As I said, it's nothing serious, probably just the state of the water."

"If you can call it water. It's more like drinking mud."

"It's all we've got. And you need to keep yourself hydrated."

"Hy—"

"You need to keep drinking. Even if it is mud."

* * *

"Whoa," Jed says. "We'll noon here."

We still call it nooning even though we often stop as early as nine or ten in the morning to avoid the worst of the heat. Gerry joins me unhitching the animals. We let them loose among the willows near the river.

"Would you look at that?" Gerry says as the animals set about the young, tender trees with relish. "Doesn't that do your heart good?"

"Thank God to have something for them."

"Maybe we should stay here overnight, give the animals the chance to recruit before the desert."

"There's not enough eating for that. They'll be through those leaves and shoots in no time."

Gerry glares at me like it's my fault there's not enough. "Jesus, I hate this journey," he says, his good mood vanishing in an instant. He kicks a stone towards the water but it buries itself in the dust a few yards away. I can think of nothing to say that might help and plenty that might make it worse.

"Can you watch the animals? I'm going hunting before it's too hot."

I don't wait for his answer, leaving him glowering under the willows as I make my way back to the wagon for the shotgun. For all the lack of vegetation, I've had some luck hunting along the Humboldt—an antelope, plenty of sage hens, a few jackass rabbits. I've never had so much meat in my life. Maybe it'll raise Gerry's spirits if we've got something tasty to roast over the fire tonight.

As I head out of camp, I notice a man with a pack mule heading in my direction. "You're going the wrong way," I say. "The sink's in the opposite direction."

"Sink's where I came from. Left there yesterday. I never saw suffering like it."

"What do you mean?"

"Animals are dying in their hundreds. Ain't no grass."

"Are you sure?"

"I saw it with my own eyes. There's seven hundred dead already, maybe more. People dying too, so I heard. I'm going home. And if you've any sense, you'll do the same."

CHAPTER TEN

Dunquin, June 1845

The Garvey twins are being christened tomorrow so I'm stealing another Saturday away from my chores to see Kitty. As I gather my boots from where they've been drying on the hearth, my mother says, "Where are you taking yourself off to?"

"Clogher Strand," I mutter.

"What on earth is taking you there in the rain and with jobs still needing doing?"

I don't say anything, just carry on padding out the hole in my right boot with an old piece of leather. I push my foot into it without looking but I can feel her staring at the top of my head as I tie my laces.

"I'll catch up with my chores tomorrow," I say, avoiding her eyes. "Bye Ma."

I set off at a quick pace before she can call me back. I don't like to annoy my mother. But I have arranged to meet Kitty near Clogher Strand and I don't want to be late.

The rain has barely halted this last two weeks and the mountain stream gushes along beside me, hidden from view by a bank of green ferns, fronds glistening with raindrops. At least it's not heavy today, more a settling drizzle that seems to freshen the colours of the fields around me as I climb away from Dunquin. The gorse has faded now, replaced by hedges blazing with scarlet fuchsia.

I try to leave my mother behind, but she won't let me go. Jobs still needing doing. There's always jobs needing doing on a farm. I do my share of the work, more than my share. Why's she making such a fuss? It's only two Saturdays in ten years of working on the farm.

I want these worries gone before I see Kitty. I don't want to be turning up with a sour face and a funeral air. Especially not at Clogher Strand. I have looked down on it whenever I have walked to Ballyferriter. I love the way the sea rushes in to the beach, have noticed it every time, imagined strolling along the sand with her, arm in arm, looking out at the crashing waves.

I turn down towards the beach but immediately break into a run, shouting as I do, "Jaysus, Kitty, will you get out of there? It's dangerous."

In answer she laughs, head thrown back, standing out in the sea, hair wet and wild from the rain.

"Ah you old woman, how can I be in danger in six inches of water? Sure it doesn't even reach my knees," she says, hitching her skirts higher as a larger wave approaches, and flashing her thighs as she does so.

I am caught for a moment by the sight of those beautiful, firm, white thighs and my visit between them two weeks past. But then another wave breaks against her, and I scream, "Get out of that sea now, Kitty Gorman. Do you want to get yourself drowned?"

She starts to make her way towards me, face closed. "I'm the last person you need to be reminding about the dangers of the sea," she says, and I remember too late about her brothers.

"I'm sorry, Kitty. I was frightened."

She doesn't say anything and I can see she is still put out.

"Please forgive me. I can't bear it when you're cross with me."

"I'm careful, you know," she says, still brittle.

I put my hand out towards her, not sure if she'll shrug it off. But she lets it stay on her arm.

"It's good to see you," I say.

"You too," she says, thawing at last. She strokes my arm softly and I let out a sigh I didn't know I'd been holding in. She hooks her arm into mine as we walk along the shore.

"I love the feel of the sand on my feet, even more so when I'm in the sea with the water washing it away," she says.

"Isn't it cold?"

She laughs. "Only at first, then you don't notice." She leans towards me, head gently tipping. My eyes close and I kiss her. I pull back first.

"You taste of salt."

"That's what happens when you've come from the sea."

"There was a moment, when I first caught sight of you. You looked so wild and like…" I hesitate. "Like you belonged there. Like you belonged to the sea. But then I thought the sea might not give you back."

"The sea couldn't keep me from you. Nothing could." She looks into my face, fierce, intense. "Come on," she says, setting off up the beach, "I've got something to show you."

"Where are we going?"

"You'll have to wait and see."

We head west towards Sybil Head, the rain still drizzling down, misting the air.

"Did you tell your mother where you were going?" I say as we begin the climb.

"I told her I was meeting you."

"Do you think she's suspicious?"

"About us? Nooo. No. Sure she thinks you're wonderful. 'Oh isn't she a lovely girl, that Frances Moriarty?' she's always saying. 'I'm glad you've got yourself such a good friend.'"

She stops, pulling me towards her. "And sure you are a good friend," she says, kissing me. "The very best of friends."

"Kitty," I say, pulling away, "we must be careful. Someone might see us."

She laughs. "Oh, you're such a worrier, my poor Frankie. But soon you'll be able to stop worrying."

She dances away from me, then breaks into a run, hair streaming out behind her. I follow her off the path onto a barely visible track that disappears into the heather. She skids to a halt just over the brow.

"You see," she says, panting.

Tucked away into the side of the hill is a small wooden plank door, half hanging off its hinges.

She looks triumphant but I'm not sure why. "It's a scalp," I say.

"Is that all you have to say?" she says. "You may look and see a scalp; I see a hideaway where I can kiss and love you for hours and hours without having to worry about who's watching."

I turn towards her, uncertain. They're always small, scalps, bad-luck places, full of shame.

"Now Frankie. I hope you aren't going to give me any nonsense. You haven't even looked at it yet. This wasn't built for some girl in trouble—it belonged to a family."

"A family?"

She nods. "Mairead and Brian Costello they were called. They fell on hard times, got evicted, ended up coming and living here with their little girl."

"What happened to them?"

"She had a brother in Liverpool who sent them the money to take them over there. But they lived here for a few months and it was well enough built. It's bigger than your usual scalp, more of a scalpeen. Have a look."

I follow her through the low door, ducking my head as I step inside. My first impression is of darkness and the smell of earth. But as my eyes adjust, the room takes shape around me. It's about six feet wide, burrowing eight feet into the hillside, roofed with sticks and planks, laid under the turf, walls reinforced with large stones.

I squeeze Kitty's hand. "You've found us a home."

* * *

We have only gotten as far as the door of the church when Malachy starts to cry. He is squirming in his father's awkward arms, face red and contorted, eyes squeezed shut, mouth stretched wide, bawling out his protest. I hope he doesn't set his brother off—it is my first time as a godparent and I'm nervous enough without having a crying baby to contend with. I've been rehearsing the Latin all week, wanting to be sure of getting my responses right.

Father Michael raises his voice loud above the crying child. "*Quid petis ab Ecclesia Dei?*"

I answer "*Fidem*" in time with the twins' parents, Mary and Peter Garvey. The other godparent, Seán Malone, echoes "*Fidem*" half a beat later. Clearly I'm not the only anxious one.

"*Fides, quid tibi præstat?*" the priest says.

"*Vitam æternam,*" we manage, almost in unison.

The grizzled old priest takes over, exorcising any unclean spirits from Dominic and claiming him for Christ. I watch as the priest wets his fingers with his own spit and traces a cross on the baby's forehead. Mary and Peter repeat the sign, then Seán and I do the same.

The priest turns to Malachy. Ignoring his screams, the priest repeats the process and the second boy is claimed for Christ. At least Malachy's got a strong pair of lungs on him, I think, as he roars his displeasure.

The preliminaries completed, we proceed into the church. It is fuller than usual, packed with Begleys and Garveys from across the peninsula, many of them turning for a look at the babies. I nod to Mary's younger sister, Angela, and her sharp-featured husband, John. It feels like every eye is upon us. I've always loved babies, their delight in the slightest thing. And these boys, my first godchildren, I love even more. But standing up in front of the whole church is a daunting matter. Proud as I am, I will be glad when it's over.

Beside me, Mary takes Malachy into her arms and begins to soothe him. Soon he is quiet, dozing through the prayers. Mary gives me an encouraging smile as she hands Malachy over to me. His eyelids flicker briefly but he sleeps on. I hope he stays that way.

Father Michael calls us forward to the font for the promises. Next to me Seán Malone carries Dominic, looking as terrified as if he was going to be renouncing Satan to his face.

"*Abrenúntias satanæ?*" the priest says.

"*Abrenúntio,*" we answer.

We get through the "credos" without a stumble, Seán and I managing to keep in step.

Father Michael turns to me. It'll be the water in a minute. Please don't let it waken the baby.

"*Vis baptizari?*" the priest says, already filling the small pitcher.

For a moment my mind is blank, as if the sight of the water has washed the answer out of my head. I want to say "*Credo,*" but I know it's not right.

Father Michael stands expectantly.

Vis baptizari? I repeat in my head. "*Volo,*" I say with relief.

I hold the sleeping baby over the font as Father Michael begins the baptism. Malachy doesn't seem to notice the first splashing of water on his head or the second. It is only on the third dousing that his eyes blink open. He looks up startled into the priest's face but, to my relief, he doesn't cry. I step back from the font, making room for Seán to bring Dominic to be baptised.

After the service, people gather in the churchyard, and the area beyond it, congratulating Mary and Peter, the women taking it in turns for a hold of one of the twins. Father Michael doesn't seem to notice the flask that passes between some of the men. I stop to talk to Angela, who's cradling Dominic in her arms. I haven't seen her for more than six months, since she married and moved to Annascaul.

"So how's married life treating you?" I ask.

"Oh, grand," she says. "John finished building our house a few weeks ago and it's as cozy and comfy as you could imagine. But it's good to get back to Dunquin for a visit. Any sign of wedding bells for you, Frances?"

"Not yet," I say. Not ever. Kitty and I will never have that, never have a day of everyone's blessings on our love, never have their wishes for a long life together.

"—with us today. Come on and I'll introduce you." I stare blankly at Angela, wondering what she's been saying. She continues talking as I follow her to the gates of the churchyard. "He's a fine-looking man, you know. Not as handsome as John, of course, but fine-looking all the same. And he's wanting a wife. Here, take Dominic. Men love to see a woman with a babe in arms." She dumps the baby on me like a sack of potatoes. It's too late to escape as Angela comes to a halt beside John and a tall, thin man I do not know.

"Good day, Frances," John says.

"Good day."

"So what do you think of our nephews?"

"They're great lads, the both of them."

"The lungs—"

"Matthew," Angela says, "this is Frances Moriarty, an old friend of the family. Frances, this is Matthew, John's brother."

I shift the baby onto my left side to get a closer look at him. His face is narrow, but not as pointy as John's. Angela can think what she likes, this is the better-looking brother. He takes my free hand in his, looking into my face with his soft grey eyes.

"It is my great pleasure to meet you, Miss Moriarty," he says. I am torn between a desire to hit him and to laugh.

"She's a great dancer, is Frances," Angela says. "And you never heard anyone like her on the flute."

She will be showing him my teeth next, like a prize mare. But it seems it's Matthew's turn for the big buildup. "And Matthew here, he's a proper tradesman, a carpenter, you know. He's made a double crib for the twins. You want to see the work in it."

Matthew flushes, as embarrassed now by Angela's matchmaking as I am. I take pity on him. I must introduce him to some nice available young women during the christening party. Deirdre Kavanagh, who is standing by the well, will do for a start.

"My friend Deirdre has always had a great interest in carpentry," I lie. "Come on and I'll introduce you."

I leave Deirdre and Matthew talking by the well, my conscience clear, and fight my way over to the proud parents.

"My little rascal," Mary says, reaching out for her son. I hand him over.

"The more I see that child, the more I see your father looking at me. Sure isn't he a dead ringer for him?" I say.

She nods and hugs the baby to her bosom. "He is that. I think Malachy takes more for Peter's family."

"He's certainly got a quaire set of lungs from somewhere."

"Oh, he can be murder at night. I'm surprised you don't hear him, the roars he makes."

"My mammy says I was just the same," Peter says.

"Well I wish you every blessing with the pair of them. I'm so glad you asked me to be godmother."

I look at Mary, Dominic nestled in her arms, and it suddenly dawns on me that if she stays with me, Kitty will never have her own baby. I can never give her a child. A cold fist clamps around my heart. I follow the crowd up the hill, trying to blank my mind.

The last thing I want is to be with other people. I wish I could get away to Dunmore Head to think, but the Garveys are great ones for a party, and as godparent, I must go. I watch Peter's mother stirring a big pot of soup over a fire outside their house, wondering how long I will have to stay.

"I see you passed Matthew on to Deirdre Kavanagh," Angela says, settling herself next to me.

"I thought they might like each other."

"Well, it looks like you're right," she says, looking over to where Matthew and Deirdre stand talking. "I was hoping for you as a sister-in-law, but maybe it's Deirdre I'll get."

"You could do worse," I say.

She arches her eyebrow. "Like who?"

I search my brain for someone I know Angela doesn't like.

"Mary Quinn."

"Oh, I always thought there was something sly about her. Who's she courting now?"

"Nobody, as far as I know," I say, wondering how I might escape without offending Angela, who's getting herself up for a long gossip. "Shall I go and get us some soup?" I say.

"Sure, I'll come with you," she says. "Give us the chance to catch up."

I am trapped in the queue with Angela, who is going through potential candidates for Matthew's hand, all of whom are found wanting. Soon there are only two or three people ahead of us.

"Well it seems like Deirdre's your best bet," I say.

"You know, you're right, Frances. Deirdre would suit me down to the ground. I'll need to work on Matthew these next few weeks. I've been stoking him up for you, to be honest."

"Today's your chance," I say, seeing my opportunity to get away. "Get them dancing. A good dance is always great for getting a romance going. I'll go and see if my father will play with me."

I take long strides up towards our house, leaving Angela, my da, everyone behind. Tears swim across my vision as I reach the door, my mind full of Kitty. I love her. I haven't had a single second's qualm about loving her. Until today. I don't know what I've been thinking. Maybe I haven't been thinking at all. A love that has to be secret, that no one can ever know about? A love that can't give her marriage, can't give her children? How can this furtive love ever be enough for Kitty?

I sit on the floor, not sure how I even got here. My da will be expecting me back at the party. I splash my face with water from the bucket, tie my hair back, get out the instruments and make my way back to the Garveys.

"You've had me like a hen on a griddle, waiting here," Angela says as I return. I don't answer but carry on over to my father. He is talking to Seán, an empty cup of soup in his hand.

"Angela's raring for a bit of dancing," I say. "Will you play with me?"

He looks deep into my eyes for a long moment. I don't know if he can tell I've been crying. "I will," he says. "Away and fetch me a stool."

It is good to be playing. I don't have to think, don't have to talk, don't have to listen except to the music. It has always helped me, never more than today. We weave from one tune to the next, picking up requests from the crowd and carrying them away in new directions. He is a great player, my father, and I have grown up playing with him. I could follow him anywhere.

I am safe for a little over an hour, but then my father's ready to stop. He stretches up, rubbing the bottom of his back.

"I doubt there's two better players anywhere in the Kingdom of Kerry, maybe even the whole of Ireland," my mother says, coming over to us.

Peter offers a cup to my father. "There's a drop to slake your thirst."

My father takes a sip of the *poitín*, turning his head to the side as he swallows. "Jaysus, that's powerful stuff, Peter. Where are you after getting it?"

Peter laughs. "That's one I brewed up with Frances here. 'Tis strong, I know."

"If it wasn't already illegal, I'd be wanting that banned," my father says.

"I hear you and Angela have been matchmaking," Mary says to me. I follow her gaze to where Matthew is leaning against the wall, still talking to Deirdre Kavanagh. "She was hoping to get you as a neighbour in Annascaul. But I think she'll be happy enough with Deirdre. Have you seen the crib Matthew made for the twins?"

I follow her to the front of the house where an ornately carved wooden double crib sits on the grass. The twins lie inside it, fast asleep. The sight of them brings the tears back to the surface.

"Is there something wrong?"

"I'm grand, only a bit tired."

"Your turn will come," she says, misreading my sadness. "Matthew wasn't the right man for you."

"You won't mind if I take myself off home."

She shakes her head. "Of course not, Frances. But come and see us soon." She hugs me tightly, then lets me take my leave.

Now I'm free to go, I want to get it over with. I am striding up the hill, wondering how I'm going to get onto the Ballyferriter road without Mary seeing me when I hear a voice calling my name. It's my mother. "Frances, where are you off to in such a hurry?"

"Oh, I was…I was…" I say, grasping for an easy lie that doesn't come.

"Surely you're not off to Ballyferriter again."

"*It'll be the last time*" is on the tip of my tongue, but I swallow it back. I need my mother less interested in what I'm doing, not more. "I was just going for a walk," I say instead.

"In the middle of a party?" she says.

"It's not the middle," I say. "Look, there's other people leaving." I point back down the hill towards the track from the Garveys.

"But they're not the godparents."

"Mary doesn't mind."

"*I* mind. I don't know what's going on, but you're not yourself. You've always been so responsible. Now you're missing your Saturday chores, leaving parties early. You're not in some kind of trouble, are you?"

"Trouble?" I say, forcing out a laugh.

"There's something you're hiding. A mother always knows. You're seeing someone, aren't you? Someone unsuitable. A man at Ballyferriter. Who is he, Frances? Is he married? Is there going to be…" She swallows before continuing. "Is there going to be a baby?" She whispers the final word.

I stare at her.

"Please, Frances, tell me."

I shake my head. "No Mother, there's no man at Ballyferriter. There's no baby," I say, but my voice breaks.

"Oh God," she says, starting to cry.

My mother never cries. I don't know what to do. I put my arm round her, feeling awkward. She shrugs me away.

"Is he free to marry you?"

"What?" I say.

"Is he free to marry you? The father?"

"Mother, there is no father, there is no baby. Please believe me."

She looks at me. "Do you promise me?"

"I swear on my life."

"Oh, thanks be to God. I've been so worried."

"I'm sorry. I didn't mean to upset you."

"I couldn't...You know how it is for girls that fall. Jaysus, I don't think I've ever been so relieved. I could do with a drink. Maybe even some of that poitín." She offers me her arm. "Come on, let's go back down to the party."

I have no choice but to take it. We make our way back down the hill.

CHAPTER ELEVEN

California Trail, August 1849

It's cold when we rise before daybreak. We hitch the wagons quickly and roll towards the Humboldt Sink. I thought the company would argue for hours yesterday when we got the news about the grass. We didn't. There's too many of us, too many animals to think about turning back.

After half a mile we pass an abandoned wagon. Next to it lie the carcasses of four oxen, their eyes pecked out by birds, their bodies bloated and stinking from the sun. I turn away, sickened by the stench, and pull my handkerchief over my mouth. In the next mile we pass another nine or ten wagons, at least fifty carcasses and a wooden cross, names and dates scratched into it. With each wagon, my sense of foreboding grows. We trudge on in silence.

An hour brings us to the slough that marks the end of the Humboldt. Not that it's much of a marker, just a little ravine with several small springs, a few tiny patches of parched grass, trampled and crushed by those before us. Broken bits of wagon and jettisoned luggage lie scattered round the sink.

I'd expected there to be lots of people here, preparing for the crossing of the desert. There are but a few. A big fella's sitting out behind the nearest wagon, dipping corn bread in mashed beans like he hasn't a care in the world, a steaming cup of coffee at his feet.

"Howdy," he says, smiling.

"Morning," Jed says. "Are you planning on setting off across the desert today?"

"No sir, I am not. I'm off to the meadow, soon as I've my breakfast down me."

"Meadow?"

He laughs. "I guess you ain't heard. A scout found a vast quantity of grass yesterday. It's only six miles from here."

"Vast?" Jed says, suspicious. "How vast?"

"I mean vast," the big fella says, throwing his arms wide open. "Thousands of acres vast. 'Enough for feeding up your stock' vast. 'Enough for harvesting to take with you' vast. Vast." He grins at us, delighted at being the bearer of such good tidings.

Everyone's cheering and crying, slapping one another on the back. I throw my hat in the air, letting out a whoop of joy. We're saved.

* * *

"So, you and Gerry are off tomorrow?" Doctor Charles says.

"First thing, as long as you're sure you can manage without us," I say, looking up from my packing.

"Sacramento's not far now. And the Lewises are coming too. I'm looking forward to being in a town again."

"I don't think it's as much of a town as you're used to."

"At least I'll be able to stock up on medicines."

"So you're going to carry on doctoring now you're here?"

"I can't imagine a time when I'll ever stop. But I'll dig for gold too. I'm still hoping to make my fortune, same as you."

"You're a good doctor. Without you, we'd have lost more than Mister Fischer. I've heard of wagon trains with as many as nine or ten deaths in their company. Drownings and shootings and all manner of illnesses. You kept us alive."

"Thank you, Frank, though I don't know if I could have helped a lot of the people that have died. Except maybe for those with the cholera. You should keep up your precautions against it."

"I will."

"Good, good."

He lapses into silence. This is his way; I have learned it these past months travelling alongside him. He has a burst of speaking, then disappears back into his own world. Sometimes another burst might follow, sometimes not.

"It's been a pleasure," I say at last, "knowing you."

"You too, Frank. I wanted you to have this." He hands me a wooden box he's been holding. "Look after yourself. I hope we meet again as rich men." He places his hand briefly on my shoulder, then strides away.

I watch his retreating back. I've learned so much from this man. He has talked to me about his theories of hygiene, God and raw vegetables, taught me the basics of dressing wounds and setting bones. But I don't begin to understand him.

I turn the box over in my open hands, find and release the catch. Inside, on a bed of green velvet, sits a silver-grey pistol with a wooden handle. I lift it out, weighing it in my hand. It is beautiful, engraved with a coach and horses around the cylinder.

"Thank you," I say, though the doctor's too far away to hear. "Thank you."

* * *

"Look, Frank, we must be nearly there."

I follow Gerry's finger, glimpsing a patch of canvas ahead through the trees. My heart is pounding. It has taken me a year to trek from one side of America to the other, but now I'm within touching distance of my gold. I break into a run, but it lasts only a few yards. The path is narrow, full of tree roots to trip on, and my pack is heavy on my back. I settle into a brisk walk, Gerry close behind.

We have been walking for about an hour, following a track from the main trail towards Sutter's Mill. Gerry and I soon reach the tent, one of three scattered in a small clearing. I follow the sound of axe on wood to find a group of men building a log cabin nearby. They are the only people we see as we snake our way through the trees towards the river but as we get closer, there is no doubt that we are close to a welter of humanity. The air is full of the sounds of people at work, the ring of metal on rock, grunts of effort, shouts of frustration. But even the noise can't prepare me for the frenzy of activity that greets me as we emerge from the trees. Along the banks men with picks and shovels are forcing their way down through gravel and rock. But the busiest area is the river, which teems with men, knee- and thigh-deep, shoveling sediment into all manner of contraptions or simply swirling it round in big metal pans. They seem oblivious to the water that spills around them and the grime that cakes their clothes.

"Ah, Jaysus," Gerry says. "Will you look at the number that's here already? Will there be anything left for us?"

"The newspapers say the rivers and hills are thick with gold," I say, sounding more certain than I feel as I look at the hordes of miners swarming in front of me.

"Where in the name of God have all these people come from?" Gerry says. "How can so many have got here ahead of us? We were one of the first trains out of West Port. I know we had wagons overtake us on the road, but not this many."

"I suppose they've come by the sea routes. Or from round and about California."

"We should get started," Gerry says, "before these bastards rob it out from under us."

"Look, if you want to start, we can," I say. "But neither of us knows a lot about mining yet. Why don't we try to pick up a few tips from those as have been here for a while?"

He lets out a sigh. "You're right, you're right," he says.

We walk down to the river still carrying our packs. Men are panning in ones and twos every ten yards, scooping up silt and water, swirling it round and peering at what's left. One, who sees us watching him, turns his pan towards me. Three or four nuggets glisten on the last dregs of wet sand. A little farther on, three Indians squat over woven baskets they have dredged through the riverbed. I watch them picking out bits of gold.

"You see, Gerry," I say in excitement, "we're not too late."

But the next fifty yards has men cursing and complaining as they chuck the contents of their pans into the river and start again. We pause near a gang of four men working with a strange wooden box. Two of them are shoveling great mounds of riverbed in the top while the other two are pouring on water and shaking it back and forth. There is little visible of their faces, covered as they are with great bushes of beard.

"Right, let's see what we got," one of them says, an ugly bastard with a fresh cut above his left eye. I step forward, wanting to see whether their contraption has worked.

"And what in hell's name do you think you're looking at, boy?" he says to me. I take a step back.

"Ah now, we didn't mean any harm," Gerry says. "We've just arrived today and yere box caught our eye."

"Christ," the man explodes. "If it weren't bad enough with the savages and the spicks, now we've got the thieving Irish. This is the *American* River. The gold in it's *American* gold. You stay away from me, you know what's good for you." He spits on the ground, an inch from my boot.

Gerry pulls me stumbling away upriver.

"Jaysus, do you think they're all that crazy?" Gerry says. "I thought he was going to take you apart."

"We shouldn't have let him do that. Shouldn't have let him push us around."

"Sure he would have murdered you if we hadn't cleared out."

"We need to look tougher, Gerry. We can't be easy pickings."

"Well how are we supposed to do that? You look like you're scarce past twelve with your pretty-boy looks and bald cheeks. And I'm like a streak of piss." He sits down suddenly on a rock. "Ah Jaysus, Frank. We should never have come here. What were we thinking?"

"I was thinking about making my fortune," I say, bristling. "I still am. I never asked you to come."

"Yes you did. You told me the gold was there for the taking. Said you'd as much right to it as any man."

I can't believe he's throwing this in my face. We have slept next to each other for four months, helped each other over the mountains, through the nightmare of the Humboldt.

"Fuck you, Gerry," I say and storm off up the hill.

"Frank," I hear him calling. "Frank, come back."

"Fuck off," I shout back over my shoulder, taking my eyes off the bank I'm scrambling up and tripping over a rock. I crash to the ground, scraping my hands, burning my knees, the pack thumping me hard in the back of my head. I struggle back to my feet, but my fall's given Gerry the chance to catch me up. He grabs my arm. I spin round. "Leave me alone," I scream, but he clings on.

"Not until you let me say sorry. I'm sorry, Frank." He drops his grip.

"I never made you come here," I say, still angry.

"I know," he says. "I'm sorry."

"I may have suggested it when I first made up my mind to come, but I left you in New York. I never made you come."

"I know."

"You're not here on my account."

"I know. I was panicking, but I shouldn't have taken it out on you. I'm sorry."

"No, you shouldn't," I say, ready at last to accept his apology, "but I forgive you."

I take my pack off and sit down. Gerry settles himself next to me.

"So, we've got two problems as far as you see it. The first is getting the gold, the second keeping it," I say.

He nods.

"Well, on the first, we're going to start digging and panning, same as the rest of them, and hope for the best. For the second, I would refer you to the advice of your own cousin, Brendan."

"Brendan? I've never had any advice from Brendan. I was always terrified of him."

"Well, I can still remember his exact words to me. 'You've got to make other people worried about picking a fight with you. Make them choose someone else.' He knew what he was talking about."

Gerry stares at me.

"Look, for people like you and me, not perhaps the biggest of men, or," I say, lowering my voice, "not even men at all, we need to find some other way to make the roughnecks choose someone else. I was good at this on my own, Brendan was a good teacher. We've got to look crazier than them."

"So Brendan explained this all to you?"

"He did."

"Well he may have helped you, but he certainly didn't tell me." Gerry is tetchy, resentful.

"Ah, Gerry, we've no time for any nonsense. We're both a hairsbreadth away from having our throats cut and our entrails fed to the birds. What does it matter how I learned it, as long as I can still do it and you can too?"

"I suppose," he says.

"Right," I say. "What would make you frightening to people?"

"Well, nothing," he says, "sure isn't that the problem?"

"Gerry, I'm not talking about the real you. I'm talking about who you could become that would scare the arse off that bastard back there. Now how I did it on the boat was mostly through picking my teeth and cutting my nails with my knife. Nothing like a great big knife on show to encourage people to give you a wide berth. Except of course a gun. Nothing beats a gun."

I get the pistol Doctor Charles has given me out of my pack. "Here's what we're going to do. I'm going to learn how to use this pistol and you are going to learn how to look dangerous with your knife."

We find a quiet spot away from the river. I show Gerry all the moves Brendan taught me and a few I picked up myself. Gerry's not great, keeps dropping the knife, but I say a few encouraging words and leave him to it.

I look for a tree with a branch at the right height to practise on. I've never used a pistol but from the moment the doctor gave it to me, I've thought of it as a new friend. I open up the box.

"You need a name." As I say it, *Sarah* comes into my head. "Right then, Sarah, it's time for us to get to know each other." I feel a thrill as I lift her out of her box. She's solid but not too heavy, the wooden handle nestling into my palm. I take aim at the branch, slowly squeezing the trigger, loving the kickback as the bullet flies towards it.

It misses, rupturing a branch about six inches below the one I'm aiming at. But I know it won't be long. With my third bullet I hit my target. I kiss the barrel of the gun. "Well done, Sarah."

I tuck the gun in my belt, then try drawing it quickly. It's a bit of a fumble and even after a few attempts I'm not fast enough. I need a holster but it will have to wait till we've found some gold. In the meantime, I will wear Sarah in my belt, on show.

I return to Gerry. His cheek is bleeding.

"The feckin' knife slipped," he says.

"Well, at least a scar will make you look meaner," I say. "I was going to talk to you about your face in any case."

"What about my face? There's nothing wrong with it."

"Maybe not in the grocery store or on the wagon train, but here it looks far too friendly. You've got to stop smiling so much. You need to look like a killer, not a man that coddles babies."

"Look, the Lewises weren't well. I was only helping out," he says, scowling at me.

"That's more like it. That's the face I want when we meet anyone new. No smiling till you get the nod from me."

"Now listen here, Frank. I amn't your toy to be pushed and pulled as suits you. I am my own man. And don't you forget it was my smiles that got us the job with Doctor Charles that's brought us this far. You're not the only one as knows how to get things done."

"I never said I was."

"Well it sounds like it. 'Use the knife like this, Gerry. Don't smile like that, Gerry. Can't you look a bit meaner, Gerry.' If you're wishing I'd stayed in New York, then why don't you come out and say it."

"Oh Gerry, of course I don't wish you'd stayed in New York. I don't know how I would have managed without you. There's lots of things you can do far better than I can."

"You were ready to set out on your own earlier today. I want to know if that's still your mind."

"Have you been listening to a word I'm saying? I'm not looking to go it alone," I say, then realise what he's angling for. "Unless you are. If you want to split up, that's fine by me. I'm not keeping you."

We stand in silence, glaring at each other.

I pick up my pack. "So, shall I set off on my own?"

"That's not what I'm saying. Put your pack down, Frank."

"So what are you saying?"

"Oh Jaysus, I hardly know myself. I just didn't like you telling me what to do."

"I'm sorry. I was just trying to find a way to keep us both alive. I didn't mean to offend you."

"A man," he says, "has his pride."

So he's back on this. Is this how it will be from now on?

"Why is it suddenly such a problem that I'm a woman?" I say, my voice low, though there is no one in sight. "You've known for ages, since before you left New York. You've known the whole time we've been crossing America. But it's only today you've been like this. Why today?"

He looks down. "Till today I've been a help. Not anymore. I don't know how to protect you. Men are supposed to protect women. It's you who's working out how to look after me."

"Gerry," I say, putting down my pack at last, "I don't need you to protect me. I just need you to be my friend."

"It's only a matter of time before you start looking for a man who can be more to you than a friend. Where will that leave me?"

"I can promise you, Gerry, that's never going to happen."

"How can you say that? You'll want to settle down, find yourself a husband."

A husband?

"I'm not going to get married. I will never marry."

"How can you be sure of that? You'll fall in love, sooner or later."

"I've already been in love. There'll never be anyone else for me."

"What happened?"

"I never talk about her."

"Her?" he says, and the shock in his voice chases away the thought of Kitty. I sit down, hiding my face in my hands. He is still for a moment, then he sits down beside me.

"Her, you say. You were in love with a woman?" Gerry says softly.

"I was."

"And was she in love with you?"

His voice sounds almost hopeful.

I take my hands away from my face and look at him. "Yes," I say, "yes, she was."

CHAPTER TWELVE

Dunquin, June 1845

Ma keeps me busy all week—churning butter, dyeing wool, darning socks. There's no chance to get away to Ballyferriter. But as I go about my jobs, I'm thinking, thinking all the time about Kitty. The way she turns her head, the quickness of her thought, the softness of her touch, the smell of her. Loving Kitty has changed me, brought me to life. Everything is sharper, clearer, brighter since her. I have known her for only three months, but she is woven into my very fabric.

It's not that I didn't have love before, the love of my family and my friends. But with Kitty it's different—she has chosen me; we have chosen each other. How am I to do without her? It's like taking a branding iron to my own flesh. Worse, because flesh heals, new skin grows.

But how am I to stay with her? We'll be outcasts if anyone finds out. A mortal sin. That's what Father Michael would call our love, a crime against God and nature. It has never felt like that to me. It still doesn't.

I keep thinking of the christening party, of Mary with Dominic in her arms. Children are the greatest blessing in life. You come of age, marry, settle down, have children. Then you watch them grow, marry, settle down, have children. I always thought it would be this way for me too. Until I met Kitty. Now I think maybe I could live without children if I could but have her. But how can I ask her to pay this price?

I get up at dawn on Friday, dressing quickly before waking Peig. It's drizzling when I go out to milk the cows. By the time we're on the road to Dingle, it's pouring.

"I hate this feckin' rain," Peig says as we trudge along beside Bramble. The sky is leaden, sea slatey, as we come into the harbour and set up our stall. We've not much to sell—butter, a few carrots, some runner beans. We haven't brought the mats because of the rain. No one browses on a day like this. Even so, customers are in short supply and it takes a while to shift what little we have.

"Well, I suppose we should pack up," I say to Peig. "Is there anything you're needing to do before heading home?"

"No, I've had enough."

"Not seeing Liam?"

She shakes her head. "I wouldn't want him seeing me looking like a drowned rat."

"Well I think I'll have a look round first. You can take Bramble, she'll get you home quicker than walking." This is not strictly true but at least she'll have company and I need to go and find Kitty. As I turn into the bottom of Main Street, I hear a familiar voice emerging from Paddy Shea's public house. I'm sure it's Missus Gorman. I duck my head under the low door and go in. The bar is packed with damp farmers and shoppers, drinking, smoking pipes, exchanging gossip and listening to the music. Kitty is sitting at a table to the side of where her mother is singing. I make my way over, smile painted onto my face. There's not a seat to be had so I stand next to her, feeling awkward, wondering how to get started on what I have to say.

"Good day," I say, looking past her to the table of drinks.

"Good to see you," she says, shifting over on her stool and patting the other half of her seat with her hand. I perch on the edge, trying not to touch her but catching the smell of her above the damp of her clothes.

"Jaysus, Frances, I'll not bite," she says. "Will you get your arse onto the seat properly."

I shuffle up, feeling the warmth of her down my left side.

"Could you be any wetter?" she says. I pull away but she puts her hand on my leg. "Don't be so twitchy, I don't mind." Her hand remains, distracting me. "Do you want a drink?" she says, offering me her glass of porter.

I shake my head.

"Is there—" she says, but the rest is drowned out as Missus Gorman finishes singing and the crowd starts to clap and cheer. She picks her way over to us.

A big farming man to the right of me leaps to his feet. "Can I offer you a seat now, Kate?" he says.

"That's very kind of you, Bernie."

"Shall I get you a drink? You must be thirsty after your singing."

"Well, I wouldn't mind a glass of porter. Tell the barman it's for me—I get them on the house."

"A glass of porter it is. A glass of porter for the voice of an angel."

"And I'm sure the girls will have a thirst on them," Missus Gorman continues, nodding towards Kitty and me.

"Ah, right," he says, reluctant, "ah, what can I get you?"

"I'll have another glass of porter, please," Kitty says.

He looks at me.

I cannot talk to Kitty here. And I cannot carry on sitting next to her, her hand still on my leg, body pressed down my side, and not be telling her what's on my mind.

"Nothing for me," I say. "I'm not stopping."

"Not stopping?" Kitty says, taking her hand away and turning to stare at me as Bernie blunders off towards the bar. I look away.

"So how are you, Frances? I see it's still raining," Missus Gorman says.

"Heavens hardest," I answer.

"I have never known a wetter June," she says. "If I hadn't promised Paddy that I'd sing today, I'd have stopped home in Ballyferriter."

"Wet or not, I've a bit of shopping to do," I say. "I best be on my way." The table rocks as I get to my feet. Kitty stands up too. I feel her eyes on me.

"I may as well do our shopping now too," she says.

"Will we be seeing you tomorrow, Frances?" Missus Gorman says.

"I don't know yet."

I push my way through the crowd to the door, Kitty hard on my heels. It's still raining and I pull my shawl over my head at the door.

"What on earth's wrong with you, Frances Moriarty? You've barely looked at me, hardly spoken, and you'd have taken yourself off shopping on your own if I hadn't followed you out."

She's angry already. I turn towards her, shaking my head. "I'm sorry," I say, but before I get any further, a farmer bursts out of Paddy Shea's, singing "The Minstrel Boy."

"Tho' all the world betrays thee, / One sword, at least, thy rights shall guard," he slurs as he staggers off up Main Street.

"Can we go somewhere else? I can't talk to you here," I say.

"You're not having me tramping round in the rain with you till I know what's—"

We are interrupted again, this time by an older man on his way into the bar. "Is that you, Kitty Gorman?" he says. "'Tis a terrible day to be outside."

"Oh that it is, Mister Daly," Kitty says, forcing a smile. He disappears into Shea's.

"You see. How can I talk to you here?" I say.

"If you've something to say, you can spit it out here and now. And you can look me in the eye while you do it," she says, reaching out and lifting my chin up. There is a look of fury in her face. She's only been angry with me once before, the day I told her I loved her.

I gather up my courage. I'm doing this for her. "I think...I've been thinking maybe we need to stop."

"Stop?" she says. "Stop what?"

"Stop...seeing each other." I feel my tears brimming and blink them back. She stares at me as I struggle for words.

"You should be free...to marry and have—"

"What are you talking about? I don't understand what you're talking about."

"I'm talking about you. I'm trying to do what's best for you."

"What's best for me?"

"So that you can be happy. I want you to be happy."

The pub door opens again. It's Missus Gorman.

"Ned told me you were standing out here in the rain. Come on back inside. You can shop later."

Kitty turns to her mother. "I'll be in in a minute, Ma. I'm just sorting something out with Frances here."

"Don't be long," Missus Gorman says. "You'll catch your deaths, the pair of you." She closes the door behind her as she returns to the pub.

"If you've met someone else, I'd rather you said so, instead of dressing it up as being about me. I suppose it was at the christening. Handsome was he?" Kitty says.

"What?" I say.

Her hand's in her hair, pulling off my ribbon. She hurls it at my feet. "If you want to be free, consider it done."

She pushes past me back into Paddy Shea's.

I'm in a daze, not entirely sure what just happened. I shake my head, trying to clear it. *"If you want to be free, consider it done."* I hadn't expected it to go like this. In my head it had gone quite differently.

"Kitty, I think I need to stop seeing you."

"But why, Frankie?"

"You deserve the happiness you can get from marriage and children. It would be selfish of me to stand in your way."

"But I'm happy now."

"It can't last. You need to be fulfilled as a woman, as a mother. I can never give you that."

Eventually she would nod. "I will always love you, Frankie, somewhere in my heart."

Or maybe she wouldn't. In my dreams she'd say, *"You're enough, Frankie. I don't want to be free. I don't want to marry. I don't want to have children. All I want is you."*

Instead she thinks I'm a liar and a cheat. *"Met someone else."* How can she not know there will never be anyone else?

I bend down to recover my ribbon, sodden and dirty from the puddle at my feet. I squeeze the brown water from it, then smooth it out. A couple of strands of red hair still cling to it. It can't finish like this. I roll the ribbon up carefully, slip it into my pocket, then turn and walk back into the pub.

"I'm glad to see you back inside," Missus Gorman says. "It's pouring out there."

I nod.

"I hope you girls weren't arguing over some man."

"It's nothing like that," I say. "But I could do with a word with Kitty."

Kitty sits beside her mother, sipping her drink. She doesn't look up.

"Kitty, can I have a moment?" I say.

She continues to ignore me.

"Kitty," Missus Gorman says, "Frances is talking to you."

She looks up at last, glaring at me with a hatred that hits me like a physical blow.

"I'm listening," she says.

So is Missus Gorman. And Bernie.

"It's something outside. I need to show you."

"It's raining," Kitty says.

"She's a stubborn one, my Kitty," Missus Gorman says, laughing. "Always has been. Why don't you sit yourself down, Frances? Have a drink with us. I can tell you now she's not going to budge."

She is wrong. At the prospect of me sitting down, Kitty gets to her feet.

"I'll be back shortly, Ma," she says.

I follow her out of the pub. The rain is, if anything, heavier than before.

"Say what you've got to say."

"Kitty, please. You don't understand."

"No, I don't," she says. "I don't understand how I could ever have given my heart to you."

"I gave mine to you. It will always be yours, always. I will love you forever. That's what I wanted to say. There is no one else. There will never be anyone else."

"Is that it?" she says. "I'm getting wet."

"Please, Kitty. Please believe me. I haven't met anyone else."

"I trusted you."

"There isn't anyone else. I'm doing this for you. At the christening, I suddenly realised I could never give you a child. I don't want to be selfish."

"What do you call deciding what's best for me, if not selfish?" she says. "What do you call ripping your love away so you can feel noble?"

"I didn't mean it like that," I say, desperate. "You've got to believe me. I didn't want to stand in your way." My voice trails off.

Hers is strong and hard. "You're in my way now," she says. "I'm going back in to my ma, and I don't want you following me."

Dunquin is the longest of long walks home. It pours all the way but I don't bother with my shawl. I want to be drenched.

"Look at the state of you, Frances," my da says when I arrive home. "Away out of those damp clothes. You'll catch yourself a chill."

I cannot move. I have walked home by just keeping on putting one foot in front of the other, one foot in front of the other. "It's over," on the left foot. "You've lost her," on the right. Through puddles and squelching mud, one foot in front of the other, it's over, you've lost her, over, lost her, over, lost, over, lost.

Now I stand dripping in the kitchen. I don't know how to move anymore. My da puts his arm round my shoulders. "Come on, Frances," he says. I let him guide me to the chair by the fire. I start to shiver, my teeth chattering, hands shaking.

"I'm putting on the kettle. You need a warm drink."

While the kettle boils he fetches a blanket and an old sheet. He drapes the blanket round my shoulders and begins to gently rub my hair with the sheet. It is soothing.

"I'm going to make you a hot whiskey." He slops the whiskey into an old blue cup. "Your ma's been worrying about you," he says, pouring in the hot water. "It's as well she wasn't here when you got home. She thinks you're in some kind of trouble." His voice is full of concern. "We wouldn't turn you out, Frances, no matter what."

I am touched by his kindness. "Thank you, Da. You don't need to worry. There's no married man. I'm not pregnant."

"So what is wrong?" he says, bringing over the cup.

I sip it slowly, letting it burn its way down my throat, wondering what to say. Suddenly I'm too hot, my skin prickling, face flushing. I throw off the blanket, retching, vomit hot at the back of my throat.

My da puts his hand to my head. "You're burning up, child. I think you should get yourself to bed."

He helps me into the bedroom, then unlaces my boots. He leaves me on the bed, undoing my dress. Even sitting down I feel dizzy. I pull my nightgown over my head, then slip into bed. My stomach is churning, the room shifting around me. I feel sick. I welcome it. I have thrown away the best thing in my life, thrown it away with both hands.

CHAPTER THIRTEEN

American River, August 1849

"So, are you ready to seek your fortune?" I say to Gerry.

"I am, but I don't think we should start here."

I nod. "I was thinking the same thing. If we go back down there, we'll have to fight that bastard for sure."

We hoist up our packs and begin to walk, keeping the river in sight but staying away from the banks.

"Do you think this is far enough?" I say to Gerry after about an hour.

"A bit farther. I don't feel this is quite the right place."

Thirty minutes later we stop on a wide shallow stretch curving gently round a broad left-hand bend. About twenty yards along the bank, half a dozen men are hard at work, with another three or four panning on the opposite side.

"I think this is it," Gerry says.

"Shall we pitch camp first?" I say, not yet ready for our first confrontation with the getting of gold. We erect our tent about twenty yards from the river, near a wooden sign stuck into the ground, scarlet letters spelling out Ruby's Bar, Hotel and Restaurant, Hangtown, 1 mile. There is nothing now to prevent our starting. I wrap Sarah in a piece of oilskin and hang her round my neck, take off my boots, roll up my trousers, grab my shovel in one hand and my pan in the other.

"Well here goes," I say to Gerry. I leave my shovel on the edge of the bank and step into the river. The water feels pleasant on my hot, dirty feet but the river is gritty and not entirely comfortable to walk on. I take a few steps away from the bank, water splashing up my trouser legs.

Gerry's chosen a spot a couple of yards away. "Do you know how we're supposed to do this, Frank?"

"The men at Sutter's seemed to be scooping the riverbed up with the pan and swirling."

I sink my pan under the surface and dig it into the riverbed, forcing it through the silt and gravel. The water splashes up my arms and down the front of my shirt. I heft the pan out again, three-quarters full of riverbed, topped with water. I try to swirl but the material doesn't want to move. Soon the water's splashed out, leaving behind the same mound of dirt. Carefully I edge the tip of the pan back under the surface and allow more water in. Then I try to swirl it again, but it's still not moving. I groan in frustration.

"How are you getting on?" asks Gerry.

"I don't think I can be doing it right."

"I think you've got too much material in there. Ditch half of it and try again."

"But what if I throw away gold?"

"Dump it on the bank. You can go through it later."

I scoop two-thirds of the dirt out and replace it with water. The material moves more easily now, water and dirt washing over the sides until the pan's almost empty. I search for a glint of gold, but all that's left is a layer of dark sand.

"Any luck, Gerry?" I say.

"Not so far," he says, "but we couldn't expect it first time."

I load the pan and start again, praying for gold as I swirl out the water. But there's still no glimmer.

"Third time lucky," I say to Gerry, loading the last scoop of dirt off the bank with the shovel. No gold.

I take a couple of steps farther out into the river, yelping as a sharp stone jags my foot. Now thigh-deep in water, I try a fourth time, fifth time, sixth time. No gold.

Now soaked to the skin, I go to the edge of the bank, scooping the riverbed up at the shallowest point. Nothing. I can't help but feel disheartened.

I stretch my back before bending to my task again, swirling the pan left to right then back and forth. As the dark sand settles, I see a glint of colour. I peer into the pan, my heart beating fast.

"Gerry, Gerry, come here. It's gold. I've found gold!"

He splashes over towards me, staring for a moment at the tiny nugget before whooping in delight. He starts singing, "Gold, gold, gold, we've got gold," while kicking up plumes of spray.

"Careful, careful," I say.

"Here, put it in the pouch," Gerry says, taking out a small leather bag.

"No, I'm going to hold onto this one," I say, picking the nugget out of my pan and wrapping it carefully in my handkerchief. It is barely more than the size of a freckle, but I don't care. My lucky first nugget.

Gerry comes to work on the bank next to me. Soon we are depositing more and more tiny specks of gold into the leather pouch.

As evening draws in we stop for the day. Gerry sets about making a fire while I rummage through our limited supply of food—a bag of weevil-infested flour, a couple of handfuls of oatmeal, a few beans and a little dried meat. I pick out as many weevils as I can, then make flat pancakes. They cook quickly. I wrap one around some dried meat and hand it to Gerry.

"It's not much of a meal to celebrate our first gold," I say.

"Sure it'll do. We're sat under the stars with gold in our pockets. With luck we'll find enough to stock up at Hangtown in a couple of days. We'll need flour, oatmeal, beans and bacon. Oh and I hope I'll be able to get coffee. I've been missing my cup of coffee."

"I'd love a bar of soap. I worked in the fields all the time in Ireland, but my clothes were never dirty like they are now."

Gerry laughs. "Ah you're a girl after all." Then serious, he says, "Did you dress like a boy in Ireland?"

"No, of course not," I say. "But I wasn't safe as a girl on my own in New York."

"So will you be going back to looking like a girl when we've made our fortune?"

"I don't know. I've got used to being Frank. But it's hard too, worrying about being caught out. Do you think if I was rich enough I could be a girl that wears trousers?"

"If you're rich enough, you can do just about anything. I'm going to build me a big white house with a huge great wooden bed with fresh white sheets and big fat pillows. And I'll have a tall clock that chimes. There was a house I used to deliver to in Union Square that had a lovely big clock in the hallway, the face inlaid with gold, and it played a tune when it struck the hour."

"The only rich person's house I've ever been in was Lord Burnham's," I say, turning my head away to spit. "And I never got beyond the room where they cleaned the shoes."

"I've not been beyond the kitchen in many of them myself. Delivery boys didn't get the grand tour. But sure even the kitchens were great—huge sinks and cast-iron ovens instead of a pot over the fire. Store cupboards filled with every kind of food you could imagine. And I went to a few that had whole rooms full of bottles and bottles of wine. Wine," he says, drawing the word out. "It's made out of a fruit called a grape. Have you ever tasted a grape?"

I shake my head. "I don't think I've even seen one. What are they like?"

"I've only seen a picture myself. But when I'm rich I'm going to be eating grapes and drinking wine." His voice is fierce and I see tears glistening in his eyes. He is quiet for a moment, then asks, "What about you, Frank? What do you want once we're wealthy?"

My first thought is my family. My gold can keep them safe. But Gerry has no one left, so instead I say, "A house sounds like a grand idea. A big strong house that'll last forever. And some land, plenty of land for growing food and for…"

"For what?" he says. "Go on, I told you about my grapes."

"For keeping horses. When I'm rich I want a stable of racehorses."

"Racehorses?"

I nod. "Have you ever seen horses racing, Gerry?"

"No, I can't say that I have."

"There's a big horse race in Dingle every August. You should see them flying across the field, over the fences, everyone cheering. I always loved going to the Dingle races." And now it is me close to tears, glimpsing August in Dingle with Kitty.

Gerry pretends not to notice. "So how much do you think we'll need for my grapes and your racehorses? How much will make us properly rich?"

I have never had more than a few dollars. I have no idea how much we'll need. "Thousands," I say. "Thousands and thousands."

"Well we best get off to bed, then, if we're to be fit to find it."

* * *

I wake at dawn and make my way down to the river. I have always liked to be up at daybreak, the freshness of the new day, the only noise the greetings of birds. Early-morning rabbits scurry about the banks, their white tails catching my eye. I wonder if I might manage to get one with the rifle. I slip back to the tent to retrieve it.

The shot is obscenely loud, scattering the rabbits, birds flapping up from the trees. Gerry bursts out of the tent in his long johns, black hair wild about his head, knife in hand, looking as mean as ever I've seen him.

"What is it?"

"I'm just shooting us dinner," I say, going to retrieve the rabbit.

"Jaysus, you nearly gave me heart failure," Gerry says as I return to the tent.

"It's time your lazy Cork arse was up anyway," I say, laughing. "So do you fancy a spot of rabbit stew tonight, or would you rather the dried meat?"

"I can't wait to get stuck into some decent food," he says, putting on his trousers.

The shot has roused some of the other miners. I keep my rifle in my hands as I watch a few of them emerge from the nearest tent, about forty yards away. They're looking in our direction. "Keep your knife about you," I say to Gerry as one of them starts to walk towards us. As he approaches I see that he is young, perhaps eighteen or nineteen, with soft, brown, curly hair and only the scratchiest of beards. He holds his hands up, smiling nervously, as he gets closer.

"Trade," he says.

I hold up my hand, indicating that he should halt. He does.

"*Lapin?*" he says. "I give gold?"

I stare at him.

He points at my rabbit. "Gold?"

"He wants to buy your rabbit," Gerry says. He points to the rabbit, then turns to the young man. "Rabbit," he says.

"Ah," the boy says. "*Lapin*, rabbit. I buy rabbit?"

"No," I say.

He looks disappointed. Then he points at me. "You kill rabbit for me? For gold?"

I glare at him. "What's he after?" I ask Gerry. "Why can't he shoot one himself?"

"Maybe he's not a very good shot," Gerry says, grinning, even though I've given him no sign that it's time for smiling.

"How much gold?" he says to the boy.

"'alf a ounce."

"You"—Gerry points—"cook for us too," he says, miming eating and pointing at himself and me.

The boy seems to understand. "Two rabbits, half ounce, we cook for you."

"Now listen here, Gerry," I start to say, but he ignores me. Instead he spits lightly on his hand and offers it to the boy, who looks alarmed but takes it. Gerry smiles, then points to himself. "Gerry," he says, then points to me, "and Frank."

The boy points to himself. "Jacques." He offers his hand to Gerry and then to me, but I ignore it.

"Come on now, Frank," Gerry says. "Be a bit friendly, shake the boy's hand."

I take it, scowling. "Can I just have a word, Gerry?" We turn away from the boy. "What kind of a deal are you making here? He might not even be able to cook. And what if I can't get us another rabbit?"

"Ah Frank, trust me. You've said yourself that there's things you're good at and things I'm good at. And I can see a good deal when it's offered. This boy's French, or at least I think he is. They know how to cook, the French. And even if he's not that good, it'll still save us skinning the rabbits and cooking them ourselves. Now away and shoot us another rabbit."

I can see his point but I still feel a little knot of irritation. I mustn't let it distract me. The rabbits have reemerged from their burrows. They won't be out all morning. I raise the rifle to my shoulder, focus on a plump buck and fire. Jacques cheers as the animal falls. I leave him to go and fetch it while I get my pan and make my way back down to the river.

Gerry and I work our bank all day, stopping only for a handful of oatmeal around noon. It's hard on the back and the arms and the legs, but we're slowly accumulating fragments of gold. Judging from what Jacques gave us for the rabbit, we got perhaps three ounces yesterday, maybe six today. I have no way to tell yet whether this is a little or a lot. But we'll find out soon. We've almost no food left and will have to go to Hangtown in the next couple of days.

As evening approaches I see smoke from the Frenchmen's camp. We continue to work for another half an hour. "I suppose we should get ourselves off," I say, as the sun sinks, streaking the sky and water red.

Gerry lets out a deep moan as he stretches out his back. "It's good to be stopping," he says, getting out of the river.

I wash my face and hands in the cool water, then make my way back to the tent. My trousers are still damp and my feet feel stiff as I stuff them into my boots. I tuck my pistol into my belt.

"What are you bringing that for?" Gerry says.

"As far as I'm concerned, we still don't know that we can trust them. I'm taking no chances. And I wouldn't leave Sarah here anyway in case she got stolen."

"Sarah? You've named your gun Sarah?"

I feel myself redden. "What of it?"

"Nothing, nothing. I was just curious. Was that the name of your girl in Ireland?"

"It's after Sarah Curran, Emmet's fiancée. Anyway, it's time we were going. Bring your knife. And the rifle."

I am tense as we make our way along the bank. But as we get closer I hear laughter. Two men are sitting by the fire while Jacques is on his feet, stirring the pot. The smell is rich and succulent. The two men stand as Jacques introduces them, holding out their hands and smiling behind their wild beards. Their names are Alain and François, and they look older than Jacques, perhaps mid to late twenties. François laughs as he hears my name. I catch what sounds like "noo zav" followed by a few more words I don't understand. I shake my head. What's he saying? He points to himself. "François." Then me. "Frank. François, Frank, François, Frank," he repeats, and I nod, realising at last that we share a name and smiling back.

The first stars are pricking the purple sky as we sit down by the fire. Jacques starts to serve up the food immediately. It tastes even better than it smells—our first decent meal in weeks. The stew has all sorts in it, mushrooms and root vegetables as well as the rabbit, which is spicy yet tender. It's served up with proper bread and a dish of green leaves. Gerry was right—the French know how to cook.

"Delicious," I say, smacking my lips and pointing to my mouth and nodding.

Jacques smiles. "Thank you," he says.

Alain offers us some kind of drink, rough but powerful, while François fetches a fiddle from their tent. The tune is jaunty and we join in clapping while Jacques sings along. After a few tunes François offers the fiddle to Gerry and I. Gerry shakes his head but I reach across him to take it. I played the fiddle for a few years before settling on the flute, and I'm sure I can get a tune out of it as a thank-you to our hosts.

"Can you dance?" I say to Gerry.

"Not all that well."

"Well do your best," I say and start into a simple jig.

The Frenchmen seem delighted, laughing and cheering, whether at my playing or Gerry's jigging I cannot say. At the end I hand the fiddle back to François.

"Thank you," I say.

He smiles. "Thank you."

We take our leave, wanting a good day's panning tomorrow.

"That was a good night," I say to Gerry as we walk the few yards back to our tent. "And all from shooting a rabbit. I think I'm going to like California."

CHAPTER FOURTEEN

Ballyferriter, June 1845

I pause at the church at Ballyferriter to catch my breath. Two wood pigeons are perched on a tree in the churchyard. I take it as a good omen and carry on walking. In a few hundred yards I'll be at Kitty's. I can't decide whether it is better if Missus Gorman is home or not. If she is, Kitty will have to be civil to me, and maybe it will soften her for when I speak to her on her own. If she's not, I can get straight to the point.

My ma was far from happy about me coming. I had to swear on the Bible that I was only visiting Kitty and her ma. At least it wasn't a lie.

I have prepared myself as best as I can, rehearsing what to say as I walked from Dunquin. Not that my previous rehearsals did me any good. But I'm hoping "I've been a fool; have me back" will do better. I've written her a letter in case she won't listen to me.

My dearest Kitty,

Please read this. I know you are angry. You have every right to be. What can I say in my defence? Nothing. Or perhaps just three things.

Firstly, sometimes I can be very, very stupid. But I learn quickly and won't make the same mistake again.

Secondly, I will always love you. And I'd like you to feel the benefit of it.

And finally, I throw myself on your mercy. If you give me another chance, you'll never regret it.

I wish I had better words to plead my case. I put my trust in your kind and loving heart.

Forever, your Frankie

I hope she can read.

I woke in a burst of optimism this morning and decided to come today. It wasn't raining—well, only barely raining, not the torrents of recent weeks. I took it as a good sign. And by the time church was over, the sun had broken through. That's when I told my ma that I was off to Ballyferriter.

"You've been sick in bed for the last day and a half," she said. "You can't be off gallivanting all over the country."

"I won't be gallivanting," I said. "I'm just off to see Kitty and her mother. I told them on Friday I'd be coming."

That's when she dragged me back to the church and had me swearing on the Bible I wasn't going calling on anyone else.

I can see the turnoff to Kitty's field just ahead.

I'm walking towards the door.

I'm knocking.

"Good day. It's Frances," I call out.

"Come on in," Missus Gorman replies. She has the fire lit and is shelling peas into a bucket. There is no sign of Kitty. I am undeterred. It hasn't rained today—well, only barely.

"How are you, Missus Gorman?" I ask.

"Will you ever be calling me Kate?" she says.

I let out a half laugh. "I have tried Kate," I say, "but my tongue seems to find Missus Gorman easier."

"It being so much shorter," she says.

"Is Kitty here?" I say, though clearly she's not.

"Do you see her?" she asks.

I shake my head. "Where is she?"

"I don't know myself. She said she had something to do after church. You know Kitty, there's no point pressing her when she doesn't want to be pressed. She's as stubborn as stone when her mind is set."

"Would you mind if I wait for a while?"

"Not at all. Sure you're always welcome in this house."

"Shall I give you a hand with the peas?"

There is a pleasing rhythm to the shelling of peas. Split, *ping, ping, ping, ping, ping*. Split, *ping, ping, ping, ping*.

"'Tis a shame that Kitty's not home. You might have shaken her out of her mood."

"Her mood?" I say.

"Oh she's been in the most powerful mood the last couple of days. You couldn't look at her. Eat your head off at the slightest thing. I thought you might know what's wrong."

I shrug, but my heart is soaring. There's still a chance.

"I was wondering was there a man on the horizon?" Missus Gorman says.

"Not that I know of."

"So that's not what you were talking about on Friday?"

"It wasn't."

"You're both at that age now. I thought maybe she had her eye on someone, maybe even that you both had your eye on the same man."

"Honestly, she's not mentioned any man to me."

"Well, I'm sure she'd tell you first. Mothers are always the last to know."

She is silent for a moment, then starts to sing "She Moved Through the Fair." I join in on the chorus, though my voice is far from the greatest. We finish shelling the peas, but there is still no sign of Kitty. I wonder how long I can wait.

"Can I get you a cup of rosehip, Frances?" Missus Gorman says.

"I'll do it," I say, getting up and filling the kettle from the bucket. "Shall I go and draw you more water? There's not much left in your bucket."

"That would be very kind of you. Do you know where the well is?"

"I do. I pass it on the way here."

I walk back along the road to the well. There's no one else fetching water and soon I'm hauling the bucket back up, handle squeaking as I do so. If she hasn't come in another hour, I'll have to go home. I can't be cluttering up Missus Gorman's house all afternoon. If only I knew where she'd gone, I could wait for her on the route. I check that the letter is still in my pocket. Can I risk leaving it?

"What are you doing here?"

I slop water down the side of my dress as Kitty's voice brings me up sharp. She is standing near the gate into her field, perhaps ten yards away. I walk towards her. "I've come to see you," I say, trying to keep my voice steady. I put the bucket down, standing close enough to touch her. But I daren't.

"See me? But weren't you just saying two days ago that you didn't want to see me anymore?" Her voice is sharp but I see the tears behind her eyes.

"It was never that I didn't want to see you. Never." I try to get across all my sorrow, all my regret, as I look into her face.

"Well it's what you said."

"Kitty, I'm so sorry. Please, please believe me. I wish I could take it all back. I never meant to hurt you."

"What else would I be but hurt? It's too late for sorrys." She turns away from me, head down.

"No, Kitty, no, it's not too late. I made a mistake."

I bend so I can see her face. She is crying.

"Oh God, Kitty." I put my arms around her. She doesn't resist, just leans against me, body limp. "I didn't mean to hurt you. I just thought you'd be better off without me."

She straightens up, pulling away, wiping her eyes. "Maybe I would."

"No, you wouldn't. Nobody will ever love you more than I do. Even if you turn me away I will go on loving you. Till the day I die."

She looks at me for a moment, then picks up the bucket.

"Where are you going?" I say, panicking.

"I'm taking this bucket in to my mother."

"Let me take it in."

"No," she says, "I don't want you to come in."

I start to sob. "Please, Kitty."

"Shush now, Frances," she says, touching my arm. "If you come in there'll be no chance for us to talk. If we're to have any hope, I need to understand. Leave me to put my mother at ease. I'll meet you up the hill in ten minutes."

I make my way slowly away from her house, following the rough track leading away from Ballyferriter. How am I to help her understand? There is only sorry. It is not enough.

I should have given her the letter. The letter had more of a chance. She could have read it on the way, arriving with one of her wonderful smiles. *"I don't know what I'm going to do with you, Frances Moriarty. But I do forgive you."* She would have sat down beside me, kissing away my tears, holding me close, back where I need to be.

I try to calm myself as I see Kitty climbing up the hill. She's making her way across the ferns and heather to where I sit, close enough now that I can see her face. And I know I'm not going to be able to explain. I will say everything wrong. My tears return.

"Come on now, Frances," she says, her voice soft, "don't take on so." She reaches her hand out and strokes my hair.

"I can't bear to lose you."

"You don't have to lose me," she says, still gentle. "But I have to understand. I never imagined a love like this could come into my life. I thought it was like that for you. And then you broke it off."

"I'm sorry."

"I can see that. But what if you do it again?"

"I won't," I wail. "I swear I won't."

"That's not enough," she says, still gentle but also firm. "Come on, dry your eyes. It's time for you to explain."

If I am to talk, I need to blow my nose. My mother has always been keen on handkerchiefs. But all I have is my sleeve.

"Don't look for a minute," I say.

"What?"

"Please, look away." She turns her head and I wipe away the worst of the snot and tears. "Right, you can look."

She turns back towards me.

"I bet I look terrible," I say.

"You'll do."

"I don't know where to start."

"Try the beginning."

I take a deep breath, letting it out slowly. "I suppose it was the churchyard after the christening. I'd finally managed to escape from Angela and her matchmaking—"

"Angela?"

"She's Mary's sister. Angela Begley, she was. She married a fella from Annascaul. I hadn't seen her since she married."

"And the matchmaking?"

"She's looking for a sister-in-law, to brighten up her days in Annascaul."

"So you were tempted?" she says, an edge to her voice.

"Kitty, no, no, I wasn't tempted. I'm not interested in anyone but you."

She stares at me. I return her gaze. She nods. "Sorry, this is hard."

I take her hand and squeeze it. "I know."

"Go on," she says.

"Before that, Angela, she was saying, you know, any sign of wedding bells? We'll never have that. Always, always, this will have to be a secret."

"I know," she says softly.

"And then I looked at Mary, holding her baby in her arms, and suddenly it hit me—I can never give you a child."

"I can't give you one either."

"I don't mind," I say. "I'd rather have you."

She looks me in the eye. "So why did you decide I'd rather have the child?"

I shrug and sigh. "I just felt so…selfish."

"It's not your decision. Do you understand that? I need you to know it's not your decision. It's up to me what I do with my life. I can't have you deciding for me."

I squirm under her gaze. "It's not what I meant."

"It's what you were doing."

"I'm sorry. I don't know how to explain it. Being there, it made me feel so…wrong. Like I could never make up for all that you'd miss out on. Like I could never be enough."

"And do you still feel wrong?"

"Nothing's ever felt so right as being with you."

She leans over and kisses me, not a soft, gentle kiss on the cheek but a powerful, passionate one. We cling together.

CHAPTER FIFTEEN

Hangtown, August 1849

"Are you not finished with that letter yet?" Gerry says. "I want to be there and back this side of Christmas."

He is tetchy. The riverbank paid almost nothing yesterday and little more this morning. We don't know if we've made enough yet for the supplies we need from Hangtown.

"I'm nearly done," I call to Gerry, adding *Your ever loving daughter, Frances* to the bottom of my letter. With luck my family will get it by January.

"Have you got everything?" Gerry says as I stand up stretching. He means the gold. I've sewn the leather pouch into my trousers. I pat them to check it's still there, then nod to Gerry.

"I'll get my weapons, then we can be off."

The sun splinters the trees as we make our way upriver, air fragrant with pine and sweet-smelling flowers, a rush of white water below us. "I don't like this," Gerry says. "I bet these woods are full of robbers."

"We've got our guns," I say, taking my pistol out of my belt, but I'm nervous too, seeing ambush round every corner. We are out of food and can't afford to lose our gold. "Let's get closer to the river. There'll be more people there."

Two shots crack out. Gerry throws himself to the ground. "Get down," he hisses.

I hunch behind a tree, trying to hone in on the exact direction of attack. In the distance I think I distinguish a faint cheer.

"Did you hear that, Gerry?"

"Of course I feckin' heard it."

"Not the shots. Afterwards. Did you hear someone whooping?"

"What? Start firing back, I don't want to die here."

"I don't think they were shooting at us. Someone was celebrating, I think they got what they were after."

"Are you sure?"

"No, let's wait here a while."

Gerry crawls over as I lean back against my tree, trying to slow my breathing, my hand going again to the little pouch.

"Ah Jaysus, Frank. Maybe we should just go back to the camp. Try again tomorrow, maybe bring the Frenchmen with us."

"We can't be running to someone else to be looking after us. Anyway, the store mightn't be open on—"

"What's that?" Gerry says. But the sound of someone crashing towards us has me on my feet already, edging round the tree, pistol raised. Perhaps fifty yards away a man is swaying between the trees, the front of his shirt stained with blood. Over his shoulders he's carrying a young deer, its smashed head lolling onto his chest, blood and brains dripping from its wounds.

I move out from behind the tree where he can see me, cocked pistol pointing straight at him. He stops in his tracks.

"Whoa," he says, "easy does it."

"Jaysus, Frank, what the hell are you doing?" Gerry says, coming alongside me. I ignore him, not sure myself. The sight of this big blood-splattered man has unnerved me.

"I mean no harm," the man says. "I been out hunting."

"Frank, will you stop," Gerry says, but I can't lower my gun. "What's your name?" he calls to the blood man.

"William Burns, but they call me Bear Man."

I nod slowly. William. His name is William. William Bear Man. Letting out a long sigh, I lower the pistol.

"Thank God," Gerry says. He walks forward, reaching out his hand. "I'm Gerry, that's Frank."

Bear Man wipes his bloody hand on his trousers and shakes Gerry's hand. "Pleased to meet you." He smiles. "Even if your friend here did give me a bit of a fright."

"Ah, don't mind Frank," Gerry says. "He's friendly enough when you get to know him. Aren't you?"

I am not feeling particularly friendly, but I slip my gun back inside my belt and offer Bear Man my hand. He takes it, swallowing mine up. He's even bigger close to, perhaps six foot six, with broad shoulders and massive forearms. "Nice to meet you, Frank," he says. "You new here?"

"What makes you ask that?" I say.

Bear Man laughs a deep belly laugh. "Met many miners yet?"

"A few."

"When they arrive, men are William or Thomas or Matthew or Frank. Within a few weeks they're Stumpy, they got a limp; or Tucker, they come from Kentucky; or Bear Man, they fool enough to wrestle with a bear. You'd be Pistol Boy."

I'm not sure if he's mocking me, but Gerry is taken with the game. "Or Sure Shot, maybe. Or Quick-Finger Frank."

"And you'd be Jaysus Gerry," I say.

Bear Man smiles. "Sorry I spooked you. I s'pose you've heard of the robbers round these parts. On your way to Hangtown?"

"We are indeed. How much farther is it?" Gerry says.

"A bit less than a mile, I s'pose," he says, putting down the deer, wiping the gore off his neck and flicking it onto the ground. "First visit, I'm guessing,"

"'Tis," Gerry says. "We saw a sign for Ruby's. Have you been there?"

Bear Man laughs again. "Sure is one helluva place. It'll be bursting tonight. She always puts on a bit of a show on a Saturday. You can't miss it, on Main Street opposite the hanging tree."

"The hanging tree?" Gerry says.

"Ain't you heard how Hangtown got its name? I was there when they strung them up, three robbers, from the old oak on Main Street. It must have been maybe January or February. They ain't been the last."

"I hadn't really given the name any thought," Gerry says.

"'Fore it was Hangtown it was Dry Diggings, on account of you had to dig your dirt up above, then take it down to the creek to wash it. Worth it, though; I made me quite some gold down there. Lost it too, mind, playing Monte. That is the most accursed game in all these hills. You take my advice and steer well clear of the Monte tables. 'S why I don't go in bars much nowadays. I'm saving, buying me a ranch. Seen enough men ruined by this place."

He is quiet for a moment. "Make your gold, boys, but leave 'fore it kills you, that's my advice, 'f you wanna take it."

We shake hands again as we leave the Bear Man to his deer.

"What a nice fella," Gerry says as we carry on towards Hangtown. "Especially after you were pulling a gun on him."

I don't answer.

"Didn't hold it against us at all," he continues. "There's many a man wouldn't have been so forgiving, would have taken it personally."

I carry on walking, saying nothing. What can I say? I nearly shot a man dead because I was panicked by the sight of blood?

"Pistol Boy, eh?" Gerry says. "I wish I'd asked what my name would be."

"What would you want it to be?" I say.

"I don't know. What do you reckon?"

"I already said, Jaysus Gerry."

"No, Feckin' Frank," he says. "Not that."

I laugh at his scowling face. "Lucky Gerry would sound good."

"Or Gold Man. That's what we're here for."

Twenty minutes hard walking brings us to Hangtown.

"Did you ever see so many tents?" Gerry says as we gaze down on the camp. "It's worse than Sutter's Mill. There must be thousands here."

Tents have been thrown up along half a dozen streets, spreading into the steep hills that hem the camp in. Sturdy square tents, Indian-style round tents, plank hovels, draped with canvas, that don't look like they'd keep out the first spot of rain. There are log cabins too, with proper windows and chimneys.

"They're even digging up the road for gold," Gerry says, as we steer our way round several miners hard at work on the street into town.

All of the men sport beards of varying lengths and condition. Even Gerry's stopped shaving. My hand goes to my smooth chin, hoping the dirt will be enough to keep me safe.

A sign proclaiming *The Gold Bar* hangs from one of the wooden buildings we pass. I peer in at the open double doors, glimpsing a group of miners playing cards before the stench of tobacco, beer, stale sweat and vomit turns me away.

"Jaysus, did you ever see a filthier place?" Gerry says. "What would make you want to spend your hard-earned money in that hole?"

"Do you think that was Monte they were playing?"

"Probably, from what Bear Man was saying."

"Have you ever gambled?"

He laughs. "Well, that depends what you call gambling. Cards and horses? No. But running my arse across America looking for gold?"

"Well you found some, didn't you?"

"And now it's time to see what we can get for it," Gerry says, approaching Sam's Stores, a big square tent on the left side of Main Street. But before he makes it through the canvas opening, he is knocked aside by a large Indian squaw, dragging a younger girl by the arm. She turns round in the doorway to shake her fist and shout, "Bad man," then marches off down the street. A cackling laugh follows them from inside the store.

"Don't you forget my offer," a high-pitched American voice calls from inside the tent, followed by a fresh cackle. Gerry and I exchange a glance, then enter the store.

The rear end is a wooden cabin to which the tent is tethered. Flies buzz around bits of dried meat hanging on metal hooks above my head. A couple of roughly hewn tables down the left side of the tent area hold a box of shriveled carrots, a few heads of brown-leaved cabbages, potatoes, a straw-lined tray of eggs, four loaves of bread, glass jars of pickles and preserves. Down the right are bins of flour, oatmeal, dried beans and coffee.

The cackling man stands behind the counter in the cabin end of the store, which is lined with cases of guns and knives and shelves of brandy. He is small and wizened with shoulder-length sprays of yellow-grey hair sprouting out around the edges of his bald head. Several teeth are missing, the others dark and stained. He has the palest eyes I've ever seen, the merest hint of washed-out blue. I draw in my breath as I take in the prices scrawled on a blackboard to his right—flour fifty cents a pound, eggs two dollars a piece, coffee five dollars a pound and he wants a whole dollar for bread that I could buy for four cents in New York. I hope to God we've made enough.

"What do you want?" he says, not in a tone offering help.

"We've come for supplies," Gerry says. "We have gold."

"Gold? Imagine that," he says, rolling his eyes.

"You do take gold, don't you?" I say.

"Of course I take gold," he snaps. "How much you got?"

I turn away to hack the pouch loose from my trousers, then hand it over to him.

"You got no scales?" he says. "I'll just weigh it for you."

The scales are on his side of the counter. He shakes our gold onto the left pan, then adds weights on the right, muttering and sucking his teeth.

"You got eight ounces, one hundred and twelve dollars worth."

One hundred and twelve dollars. In New York I might make ten dollars in a good week.

"I don't think your scales can be working quite right," Gerry says.

"You calling me a liar?"

"I'm just saying there's more than eight ounces there. Perhaps you've made a mistake." Gerry's voice sounds calm but I can see fury in his face. Maybe Wizened can too as he makes a show of redoing the weighing.

"Well, I'll be damned. There's twelve ounces. That'll be—"

"One hundred and ninety-two dollars. I know the rate—sixteen dollars an ounce."

Ten minutes later we're back on Main Street, packs full of flour, oatmeal, sugar, dried pork and beans. We've a bottle of brandy and Gerry has two pounds of coffee. Best of all, my pistol is now nestled against the outside of my right leg in a tan leather holster.

"It suits you," Gerry says as he sees me glancing down at it. "You look the part, Pistol Boy."

"Forget Jaysus Gerry," I say, "you should be Genius Gerry. How did you know he was after cheating us?"

"I was working in Harvey's for more than a year, weighing things every day. A pound of coffee, eight ounces of sugar, two pounds of flour. I knew for sure we had more than eight ounces."

"Well, thank God you did. Do you think the old bastard tries it on everyone?"

"I'm sure he does. And it's hardly like he needs to, the prices he's charging. Jaysus, Mister Harvey's eyes would have dropped out on the counter at the sight of two dollars for an egg. The man's making it hand over fist."

"And we are too. One hundred and ninety-two dollars in three and a half days. Whoever could have imagined it?"

"I couldn't have imagined spending more than a hundred dollars on a few provisions and a holster."

"I'm sorry it cost so much. We can take it back."

"No, I wanted you to have it. But with prices as they are, we can't afford too many days where we don't find any gold."

"We'll be fine. This time last week we had nothing but our shovels and a handful of grain. Now we've enough supplies for at least three weeks, four if I can shoot a few rabbits. There's money on the way to my family. And we still have more than sixty dollars."

Gerry smiles. "Not for long. Come on, let's go and spend a little bit more on a drink to good fortune."

Twenty yards away scarlet letters on a gold background proclaim Ruby's on a sign hanging from the first floor of a three-storey wooden-framed building. The building is painted a dark berry red, except for the lintel and the windowsills, which are the same gold as the sign. Gerry pulls open the heavy wooden door and we make our way inside.

"This is more like it," Gerry says.

Ruby's is as bright and clean as The Gold Bar was grim and filthy. The polished wooden floor reflects the light of three chandeliers suspended from a white ceiling decorated with golden flowers. Dark red curtains, fringed with gold, hang over a low wooden stage, which runs the length of the left side. On the opposite wall stands the bar, a counter of dark wood, fronting shelves and shelves of bottles. Perhaps thirty round tables, covered with red cloths, are scattered in between. Although it's still mining hours, a few are already occupied.

A pretty young woman approaches us, her blond hair set off by her red dress. "Can I 'elp you, gentlemen?" she asks in a soft voice tinged with a French accent.

"We were wanting a drink," Gerry says.

"Of course," she says, leading us to a table near the bar. "What would you like? We 'ave everything—wine, champagne, beer, whiskey, brandy, port, liqueurs. Whatever you want."

"Everything?" Gerry says, a mischievous smile playing around the corners of his mouth. "How about Guinness?"

"Guinness? I do not know of this Guinness. It is alcohol?"

"Indeed it is. From Ireland."

"Is there something else I can get you?"

"I would like wine," I say.

"Red or white?"

Red or white? How would I know? I've never tried wine before. I didn't know it came in colours. "Red," I say.

"I'll have the same," Gerry says.

She is back quickly with two short-stemmed glasses.

"*Sláinte*. May good luck pursue us." I clink my glass against Gerry's before taking a cautious sip. It has a strong taste, penetrating round my mouth and warming my throat as I swallow. "Mmm, I like this," I say, taking a swig.

Gerry laughs as I splutter and cough. "Easy does it now, Frank," he says, patting me on the back. I look around to see if anyone else is laughing at me, but no one seems to have noticed. At one table a red-dressed woman is dealing cards to a group of miners; a red-shirted man is doing the same at another. The group nearest to us is tucking into great platefuls of some kind of food that I don't recognise.

"What would we have, if we had the money to be eating here?" I ask Gerry, opening up one of the menus on the table. The left side is labeled Oriental, the right Mexican. Both are full of dishes I've never heard of—tacos, foo yung, enchiladas, chow mein.

"Did you ever try Chinese in New York?" Gerry says. "There was one not far from Harvey's. Gave us money off in return for cheap supplies from the store. Mister Harvey loved to try different kinds of food. Italian, French, Chinese. He had deals with all the restaurants. They weren't as good as the French, but the Chinese surely did know how to cook. Chow mein, I've had that."

I look at the description—*noodles fried with vegetables and chicken.* "What are noodles?" I say.

"See that man's plate, there, on the right. That's chow mein. The noodles are those long, flat things. They don't have much of a taste themselves, but they fill you up. And they take on the flavour of everything else, the vegetables and the chicken and the sauce. It's really good."

"So is that what you'd have?"

"No, I'd probably try something Mexican. I've never had that before. Maybe enchiladas—'corn pancakes with ground beef, spicy sauce and cheese.' They sound good."

"Excuse me. Do you inquire about a drink we do not have?" a woman's voice says. She speaks with an accent but not one I am familiar with. I look up. She is small and slim, wearing a sumptuous red velvet dress edged with gold brocade.

"We did," Gerry says. "Guinness. But we're enjoying the wine."

"The wine is free if you tell me about Guinness. I like to stock everything my customers want."

"Oh, there's no need," I say. "My friend was joking."

"Oh," she says, sounding disappointed, "is there no Guinness?"

Gerry laughs. "There is, surely. Have a seat and I'll tell you all about it."

"Thank you," she says, offering her hand to Gerry, then me. "I'm Ruby Alvarez. Nice to meet you."

"Frank Moriarty," I say. "So is this your place?"

"Yes," she says, sitting down next to Gerry. Her face is lit by the lamp on the table. Golden-brown skin and the darkest eyes I have ever seen, topped with thick, strong eyebrows.

"It's a great bar," I say. "I loved it from the moment I saw it."

She smiles, a broad smile with plenty of teeth, a gap between the front two. "Thank you."

"What's it like running a bar here? Especially with you…" I trail off, worried I might offend her.

"Especially?" she says, eyebrow raised again.

"With you being a woman," I say, laughing nervously. "You know, with it being such tough country round these parts."

"Maybe I'm a tough woman," she says, smiling.

I ignore Gerry's smirk. "Well you're doing a great job," I say.

"I want Ruby's to be the best bar in California. That is why I like to have all the different drinks, like your Guinness."

"Oh yes, the Guinness. Now what can I be telling you about it?" I say. "It's a dark drink, almost black. A reddish black."

"And it tastes slightly bitter, but smooth too," Gerry says.

"It's a porter, a kind of beer I suppose," I say.

"And Guinness isn't the only brewer. Beamish & Crawford do a lovely porter."

"We never had that in Dingle. It was always the Guinness."

"Well as a Cork man, I would have to say I prefer the Beamish, but it stays close to home. I don't know if they sell it outside Cork. When I came to America I was very glad of the Guinness."

"You've been able to buy in America?" Ruby says.

"In New York. You could get it in the Irish bars in New York," Gerry says.

"And in Chicago," I say. "They had it in Brendan's bar. He stood me a pint."

"Could you help me find a supplier? Perhaps this Brendan's Bar?"

"I'm not sure if Brendan—"

"Of course we could help," Gerry says. "You leave it to me."

"Thank you," Ruby says, smiling again. "What else do people drink in Ireland?"

"There's a lot of poitín, though them as are in charge don't like it. And whiskey too," Gerry says.

"I have whiskey. But I have not heard of this *pot-cheen*. Is better than whiskey?"

"Oh, it's powerful stuff altogether," Gerry says. "It would blow the head off you."

"But when it's made right, there's nothing better for loosening your cares," I say. "At least while you're drinking it."

"Are they selling *pot-cheen* in New York and Chicago?"

"I've not come across any in America," Gerry says. "Even in Ireland, it's not strictly legal. You'd have to get someone to make it for you. I don't suppose you know how, Frank?"

I am back in the outhouse with Peter Garvey a few weeks before the christening. "Get that fire going, Frances," he says. "If we don't get this distilled, I'll have nothing to give people to toast my boys."

"Don't be worrying. We'll have plenty for the christening."

"I want everything to be perfect for my boys."

"It will be."

"I feel so blessed, having them. So blessed." He wipes his face on the back of his sleeve, then laughs. "Away and scatter that by the bush for the fairies," he says as the first draw comes through. "They like a woman's touch." He always says this when we're making poitín and he always laughs. I don't know why.

How can he be dead? How can they all be dead?

I shake my head, trying to clear it. "I know how to make it," I say slowly.

Ruby frowns, her eyebrows converging. "Are you certain?"

"Of course. I've made it before, hundreds of times. But I'll need a still and supplies. For the best poitín, you germinate—"

"'Scusez, Madam Alvarez," our waitress says. "There is a customer at the bar wanting the most expensive meal we can possibly make. 'E does not wish for anything that is on the menu."

Ruby stands. "I must go. Tell Clarice what you need." She gives us a last smile, and then she is gone.

CHAPTER SIXTEEN

Dingle, August 1845

Peig and I pause, waiting for Lizzie and her friend Ellen who are straggling behind, talking and giggling.

"Come on you two, keep up," I say.

If we don't get a move on I'll be late. I'm going to the Dingle races with Kitty. I love the races—the roaring crowds, the wild gallop of the horses. I can't wait to be there with her.

"You two walk ahead," I say to Lizzie and Ellen, wanting to be able to keep an eye on them. "I don't think I've ever seen two girls walk as slowly," I say to Peig.

"Oh, I know. She drives me mad, Lizzie, when she's in her dithering mood. Honest to God, some days if I'd a whip I'd take it to her. She can walk that slow, sometimes you think she must be going backwards."

I laugh. "Well at least we're behind them now. We can drive them on like two reluctant sheep."

Peig whistles as if she was directing a dog.

"You best not let Ma hear you whistling."

"Oh she caught me only yesterday when I was feeding the chickens. 'A whistling maid and a crowing hen are neither fit for God nor men.' She says I'll never find me a husband if he hears me whistling. But I love to whistle." She blows out a verse of the "Queen of May" reel.

"Whistle away," I say, "it's not like you're short of suitors. I suppose you'll be meeting Liam today."

"Maybe," she says, coy, then laughs. "Oh, I do like him, Frances. He looks so fine. And he's so funny."

"Is it love?"

"I don't know. Yes. No. Perhaps. I know I like to be with him. I look forward to seeing him. I wish you could meet someone too, Frances. I know Ma's worried you'll never be settled. Maybe today. I've heard the races are a great place to find a suitor."

I *have* met someone. Oh I wish I could tell her, tell her about Kitty. How I hate this secrecy. Instead I say, "Shall we sing? It might get the girls moving a bit quicker."

We run through all the old favourites, singing our way into Dingle, joining the crowds down Goat Street. I have to stop my feet skipping over to Kitty when I see her over by the junction with Green Street. She is tapping her heel against the wall to the sound of the fiddle player across the road.

"Ah, there you are," Kitty says. "I was wondering if you'd find me among these hordes. So are we set for some fun, girls?"

Our progress is slow down Main Street, full as it is of people milling round stalls selling sweets and cakes. The pubs have come outside to serve ale and stout at makeshift booths, and there are plenty of tinkers on the street selling pots and pans, belts and buckles.

"There's Liam," Peig says, pointing to a little knot of lads towards the bottom of the hill. She rushes on ahead.

"Which one's her sweetheart?" Kitty says.

"I think it's that small, dark one. Liam O'Connell's his name, from the bakery on Green Street," I say. "What is he up to?" At the sight of Peig, Liam is encouraging his dog onto its back legs. Peig laughs as it wobbles around barking. "He surely does know how to entertain the girls."

"You know a bit about that yourself," she says, softly. I feel myself blush.

"Frances," Peig calls, looking over towards us, "come and watch Liam's dog dancing."

Close up Liam's not a bad-looking chap, with sparkling blue eyes and high cheekbones, though he'd do better without the reluctant moustache on his upper lip.

"Did you hear Liam's dog singing?" Peig says. "Wasn't it great?"

"Did you teach him yourself?" Kitty says.

"I did surely," Liam says, puffing himself up. "That dog would do anything I ask him, wouldn't you, Curly?"

"Are you heading out to the course?" I say.

"Oh, not for a while yet. There's plenty of time," Liam says. "Me and my friends were hoping we could escort the young ladies for some refreshment. With your permission of course, Miss."

He is beginning to irritate me but Peig says, "Please, Frances, say yes," her face shining.

"You have my permission," I say, turning back to Liam. "But you'll have Miss Gorman and I for company."

His face falls for only a second before he smiles and says, "We'd be delighted, wouldn't we, lads?" He hasn't introduced his companions yet, a spotty, fair-haired lad and a thicker-set, surly-looking young man, whose eyes seem fixed to the ground.

"You don't mind, do you?" I whisper to Kitty as we proceed up the street. "I promised my mother I would keep an eye on the girls and I haven't got the measure of these lads yet."

A few steps away there's a booth serving drink but it's heaving with people.

"We'll try up John Street, shall we?" Liam says. "I've a friend running a bar there."

He stops outside Hoolihan's. They've fashioned some benches outside the bar with planks balancing on empty barrels. We squeeze on at the end.

"What can I get you, l-ladies?" the fair-haired lad says.

Kitty and I order porter and the girls follow suit.

"Jim," he hollers, all confidence now.

The drinks are just arriving when a big, red-faced man staggers over, bulbous nose betraying years of drinking.

"That you, Liam?" he says, bracing himself against our table.

"It is, Uncle Tommy."

"Ah, blood knows blood. Blood knows..." he slurs.

"Here, have a seat, Uncle," Liam says, getting up to make way for the older man.

"Good lad...Always my favourite."

I get a good grip of my drink as he stumbles onto the opposite bench.

"Favourite nephew. Would you ever be...ever do me another kindness?"

"Anything Uncle Tommy."

"Robbed. I was robbed. Would you be getting me a drink?"

I see Liam suck in his breath a little—his uncle's already had a skinful.

"Ah well, Uncle Tommy, we're not really stopping."

"Not stopping," Tommy roars, banging his fist on the table and spilling Peig's drink. "Never thought a nephew of mine…Begrudging his own uncle."

"Ah Uncle Tommy, it's not like that. I was only meaning you'd enjoy a drink better at the racecourse. Why don't you come on with us? You've always loved it out at the races."

"Some days out. Ballintaggart. D'you remember that year… Chieftain? I won on Chieftain," he repeats quietly, disappearing into his thoughts.

"So are we nearly ready to go?" I say, trying to help Liam out. "We don't want to leave it too late or we'll not get a good spot on the course."

"Come on, Uncle Tommy," Liam says.

Tommy lurches from his seat and staggers from the booth, Liam close behind.

"Do you think the fresh air'll sober him?" Peig says.

"He's absolutely bladdered," Kitty says. "He needs more than air, the man needs his bed."

"He'll never get there on his own. Liam'll have to take him," Peig says.

"Let's give him the chance to walk it off first," I say, not able to face her disappointment yet. "Sometimes that works."

But as we reach the corner with The Mall, Tommy breaks into a run and clatters into a table.

"Ye feckin' hypocrites," he roars. "Can't ye let an honest man enjoy his day out without yere no-drinking nonsense?"

"See here," the man behind the table calls out, pointing at Tommy. "See here the curse of drink upon our nation. Join us today in signing the pledge."

"Stick your bloody pledge," Tommy says as Liam tries to pull him away. A woman scurries round their feet, collecting the pamphlets that Tommy has sent flying.

"Come on, Uncle Tommy," Liam says. "Come on away now." His fair-haired friend takes Tommy's other arm and they succeed in getting him moving down the street, Kitty and I following with the girls.

"Shower of shite," I hear Tommy grumbling. "Won't let the people alone. And he's a Protestant, that one. I'm listening to no preachin' from a bloody Protestant." He turns round and shouts, "Leave us alone, you bloody turncoat."

"Do you think he's one of that lot from down at Colony Gate?" I say.

"What lot?" Lizzie asks.

"That Protestant lot. They were sent here to convert us all."

"Not all of them were sent," Kitty says. "I heard they were led by a Dingle man by the name of the Reverend Francis Moriarty."

"He's got your name," Lizzie says to me. "We're not related, are we?"

"Of course not. He's nothing to do with us," I say, looking pointedly at Kitty.

She smiles back. "At least you hope not."

Ahead of us Tommy has come to a halt. He leans against a wall, breathing heavily.

"Come on, Uncle Tommy. Come and get a drink of water. That'll do you good."

"Lea' me alone," Tommy says. He slumps down the wall, his shirt dragging up out of his trousers as he does so.

"Come on now. You can't be staying here," Liam says.

"Leave me be," Tommy says, shutting his eyes and letting his head drop forward.

"Up you get, Uncle Tommy. Come on," Liam says but there is no response. He turns to Peig. "I can't leave him here like this. I'll have to take him home."

"Can I help?" she says.

"No, no. Brian and Mickey'll help me carry him. You go on out to the races. I'll come along later."

"You'll never be able to find us," Peig says.

"Don't worry," I say. "We'll get a place near to the finish. Look for us there," I say to Liam.

We carry on down The Mall, leaving Liam and his friends struggling to get Tommy to his feet. Half of Kerry seems to be on its way to the races and it's slow going as we make our way up the hill out of town. There's stalls galore on either side of the road, selling cakes, apples and drinks.

We stop to watch a man performing a trick. "See here," he says. "I have three cups." He holds each one up in turn, then places them back down on the wooden box in front of him.

"Now what good are three cups on their own? I'm sure I'm missing something. I think maybe you might have what I'm looking for," he says to Ellen, who looks back startled, shaking her head.

"Do you mind if I check?"

Ellen gasps as he reaches over and produces a small red ball from behind her ear, then holds it up to the crowd.

"This is what I was looking for. Now I have three cups," he says, holding each of them up to the crowd again, "and one ball. But this isn't any ordinary ball. This is a magic ball." He pauses, holding the ball up, showing it to the crowd. "So do you want to see some magic?"

"Yes," a few people say.

"I didn't quite hear you," he says. "Do you want to see some magic?"

"Yes," we cheer.

"That's more like it. Now the magic red ball goes under the middle cup. So under the left cup, we have nothing, under the right cup, we have nothing, and under the middle cup, we have our magic ball." He lifts each cup as he speaks. "Now keep your eyes on the middle cup."

He starts to shuffle the cups back and forth and round and about till my eyes are nearly crossed trying to keep track of the middle cup.

"So which cup do you think the magic ball is under?" he calls.

Some people including Kitty call out "left," others "right," but most, like me, say "middle."

"Well, let's see." He lifts the right cup but it's empty. "Perhaps it's under the left." Kitty groans as it comes up empty too. I feel smug as he says, "So it must be here."

But as he takes the middle cup away, there's nothing there either.

"Not here, not there, not anywhere. I told you it was a magic ball. And a magic ball needs magic." He replaces the three cups, then taps each one with a little black stick.

"Let's see if that's done the trick." The crowd cheers as the red ball is revealed under the left cup. "So that means these two must be empty. But what have we here?" he says, lifting the middle and the right cups to reveal two more red balls. He juggles with them briefly.

"Well, I hope you've enjoyed my little entertainment. And you're welcome to show your appreciation," he says, passing round his hat.

Two girls come running over as we turn away from the magician to carry on our journey. "Ellen, Ellen," they call.

"Did you see me?" Ellen says. "The magician used me in his act."

"Oh, I wish he'd chosen me," the taller one says.

"Did you feel anything when the magic came over you?" her pudgy friend asks.

"Not really."

"Oh," the pudgy friend says, disappointed.

"Shall we stay and watch him again? Maybe he'll choose me next time," the tall girl says.

"Can Ellen and I stay?" Lizzie asks me.

"If you want to, but you'll miss the start of the races."

"We don't mind."

"Look for us near the finish. And be careful."

Ten minutes walking brings Peig, Kitty and I to the course. There are plenty of people here already but it's not so busy that we can't slip between the crowds to a spot near the finishing post.

"This is perfect," Kitty says. "All we need now is for the rain to stay off."

From here I can see back down to Dingle Harbour and the crowds snaking along the road out to the racecourse. The fair's already getting going, tinny music, laughter and shrieks reaching me from the field below. I breathe in deeply, then let out a sigh of pleasure. "Oh, I love race day."

"Do you fancy a drink?" Kitty says.

She reaches into a deep pocket in her skirt and brings out an earthenware flask, unscrews the top and passes it over. The whiskey has a warm, spicy caramel taste.

"That's good stuff," I say. "Where are you after getting it?"

"Ah, now that would be telling," she says, laughing.

Bookmakers are milling about on the course, calling out odds on the first race. Two to one for Laughing Lord; four to one, Silver Rod; sixes on Hedgecutter, Irish Warrior, Mad Marauder and Frisky Boy; eight to one, Henry the Hunt and Dingle Diamond; ten to one bar.

"Are you putting a bet on?" Kitty says.

"Not yet. But if I was betting, I'd be on Hedgecutter," I say. "What about you?"

"I've no money for the betting but I'd go on Silver Rod. I love grey horses."

"I think I'll go for Frisky Boy," Peig says.

"I wonder why that is?" I say.

She blushes, then laughs. "Oh I do hope he comes."

"He seems a nice lad," Kitty says. "Have you known him long?"

"About six months. He works in his father's bakery on Green Street."

"Is that where you met him?"

She nods. "I helped him out one day when an old lady collapsed in the shop. He offered me a cake for my trouble."

"There's a lot to be said for a man that can offer you cake," Kitty says.

The horses are gathering on the far side of the course.

"I wish I knew which one was Frisky Boy," Peig says.

"There's only the one grey. That'll be Silver Rod."

Suddenly they're off in a wild dash, a cheer rising up from the crowd. Even from here you can hear the pound of the hooves. Nobody's sitting anymore. I'm shouting for Hedgecutter, excitement fizzing through me though I still don't know which horse he is. Kitty's jumping up and down as Silver Rod battles for the lead with a big black beast. They round the bend into the finishing straight, Silver Rod half a body ahead of the tiring black horse.

"Come on, Silver Rod! Come on, Silver Rod!" Kitty shouts.

A brown horse flies round the bend, bounding down the stretch towards the finish line. He's catching Silver Rod with every stride.

"Come on, Silver Rod," I call out.

They cross the line neck and neck.

"Did he win?" Kitty says. "Did he win?"

"I don't know, I couldn't tell."

"Who won?" Kitty says to a man next to us.

"Hard to say. I think it was Laughing Lord. But on the other hand it could have been Silver Rod. One or the other of those two. No use to me. I was on Irish Warrior. Irish Waster more like."

A huddle of men are conferring near the finishing post, the crowd waiting expectantly around them. A fellow with a top hat emerges from the huddle. "Silver Rod wins, by a short head."

There are boos from the crowd but Kitty's shrieking in delight. "He won, he won!"

"What would you be like if you'd had money on him?" I say, laughing.

"Don't you be giving me that, Frances Moriarty. I heard you shouting for him."

"That's only because—" I'm interrupted as the crowd pushes back from the finishing post. Fists and feet are flying in a brawl between three or four men.

"Break it up, break it up." A few men intervene to pull the warring parties apart. There's blood gushing from the nose of one of them, the man who announced the result, now minus his top hat. Opposite him a red-faced jobber's being held back by a couple of men.

"You bloody cheating bastard," he shouts. "It was Laughing Lord that won. You bloody robber." His friends drag him away.

"Well, after all that excitement, I think it's time for another drink," Kitty says, passing round her flask.

"Oh, it was an exciting race, wasn't it?" Peig says. "But I wish I'd known which one was Frisky Boy."

"Here he is now," I say.

"What?" Peig says.

"Guess who," Liam says, putting his hand over Peig's eyes.

"Liam," she says, spinning round into his embrace.

"I told you I'd find you," he says, grinning.

"Oh, I'm so glad," she says. "Did you get your uncle sorted out?"

"I've left him sleeping up in my bed. He's a good man really, you know. Just every now and then he gets himself a bit carried away. 'Tis a shame it happened today; he always did love coming to the races."

"Where are Brian and Mickey?" Peig says.

"They're down below at the fair. I thought we might go later, if your sister will allow it."

"Of course," I say. I'm beginning to like him. Out of the corner of my eye, I see Kitty smiling.

"Have you ladies eaten?" he says.

"Not yet, though I was about to offer round my boiled eggs and cheese," Peig says, digging into her pocket.

"Perfect, I brought a loaf of bread," he says, unwrapping it from a piece of cloth. With a flourish he places the cloth on the grass and beckons Peig to sit down. "And a couple bottles of ale," he says, relieving his pockets.

A bookmaker is calling out his odds as we sit down to eat.

"Who do you fancy?" Liam says to Peig. "I'm backing whoever you choose."

She listens carefully as the bookmaker gives the odds. "Jack of Spades. I like the sound of him," she says.

"I'll go thruppence on Jack of Spades to win," Liam says to the bookmaker.

"I'm on Celtic Sunset," Kitty says. "Who are you backing?"

"Kerry Lad," I say.

"How much are you laying?" the bookmaker says.

"Oh, sorry, I'm not betting this time," I say.

He turns away in disgust.

"Bet with me," Kitty says quietly.

"What's the bet?" I say, voice low.

She leans in to whisper. "My horse wins, you owe me ten kisses. He loses, I owe you ten."

"Deal," I whisper back, then pretend-spit on my hand and offer it to her. As she takes it I begin to lift her hand towards my lips, then realise what I'm doing and let it go quickly. I glance around to see if anyone's noticed but Peig and Liam are deep in conversation and the crowd around is going about its business. But I must be careful. I smile at Kitty, who winks back.

A roar goes up from the crowd.

"Oh, they must be off," I say, getting to my feet. "Come on, Kerry Lad."

The race is won by miles by a brown horse with a big white face. We crowd down round the bookie with Liam.

"Was that Jack of Spades that won?"

"No."

"Where did he come?"

"Not placed."

"Where did Kerry Lad come?" I say.

"Not placed."

"What about Celtic Sunset?" Kitty says.

"Not placed. Now stop wasting my time and let me deal with my punters."

"I'm sorry, Liam," Peig says. "I've wasted your money."

"Ah, never mind. Shall we go down to the fair and have a bit of fun losing some more of it?"

Peig looks at me.

"Go ahead. Enjoy yourself. Maybe we'll see you later."

I watch her go, arm in arm with Liam. "Come on," I say to Kitty. "I can't stand another race where I don't know what horse I'm backing."

We make our way over to the parade ring. The horses are being led round, ridden by young men in all manner of jockey outfits. Among them is a beautiful chestnut mare, head tossing back and forth.

"What a horse," I say. "Imagine owning a horse like that."

"I'd say she'd be a handful," Kitty says.

I approach the nearest bookmaker, a fat-bellied man with heavy jowls and droopy eyes.

"What's the odds on the red horse, number three?"

"The Red Queen? I'll give you eight to one."

"Tuppence each way." I take my slip.

"Come on, let's get back to the finishing post," I say to Kitty, taking a last glance at my horse.

We dodge between people, hurrying back to our place. I can see the Red Queen rearing up as she waits for the off, turning away from the other horses to face the wrong direction.

"Oh no," I say. "What are you doing, Queen?" She's on her back legs again, seeming to pause in midair as the other horses gallop off. She's already a couple of lengths down as the jockey wheels her round. At last she's into her stride.

"Go on, Red Queen," Kitty shouts. "Go on."

She's moving now, tearing up the ground, overtaking the last and the next to last.

"Go on, Red," I shout as she moves up to fourth. I grab Kitty's arm as they round the final bend, my Queen trailing the leader by about a length. She's closing in, three-quarters of a length, half a length. She's going to do it. The Red Queen takes the lead, but not till she's past the finishing line.

"Oh," Kitty says. "Oh, that was so unlucky. If only she'd started right. Didn't I say she was a handful?"

"But what a horse," I say. "And I went each way. We're still in the money with second."

"Ahh, you clever darling."

"It's only a shilling, but we might get us something nice on the way home. I was wondering if we might go soon."

"But you love the horse racing," she says.

"I know, but there's only a couple more races and what could top the Red Queen? Now, all I want is to be on my own with you."

"Me too," she says. "I keep wanting to kiss you."

I stare into her eyes for a moment but look away before I kiss her there and then.

We set off to our little scalp at Sybil Head, back through the crowds, past the stalls, the tricksters, the jugglers and the tinkers. There's a dance going on in one of the fields.

"Do you want to stop?" I ask.

"No," she says. "Let's have our own dance. We can dance our way there."

Off she goes with a forward, forward, forward step, none to the side, none back. She grabs my hand as I catch up, throwing her head back and neighing.

"Giddyup there, Frances, be a racehorse, not a carthorse."

The weather keeps off till we're perhaps four hundred yards from the scalp. But suddenly the skies open, large drops splashing down on our heads.

"Come on, let's run," I say, grabbing her hand. We arrive laughing and just a little wet.

* * *

I wake snuggled in against Kitty's back. It's dark in the scalp, though I can see it's past daybreak from the chinks of light slipping through the gaps in the door. We have fashioned a bed from armfuls of heather stuffed into old sacks. It rustles as I lean forward to kiss Kitty's shoulder. She murmurs, then turns and puts her arms around me, gently pressing her warm nakedness along the length of my body.

"Morning, Frankie," she says.

I pull her closer. "I love waking up with you, being able to hold you here next to me. Our bodies fit together so perfectly."

"Mmm, don't they," she says, nudging her leg between my thighs.

"I wish I could stay here with you all day."

"What time are you expected back?"

"In time for Mass. I mustn't linger or my ma'll think I'm involved with some married man again."

"Well, I suppose I should make the most of the time I've got," she says, running her hand down my flank.

We have to rush when we finally get up, untangling our clothes from where we cast them off the night before.

"I'll have to clip along to Dunquin," I say.

"Are you sorry I kept you?"

"I'm never sorry for an extra second with you." I hold her tight. "I love you, Kitty. I wish I could be with you all the time. But for now I must go."

I set off, running down the hill and out onto the road to Dunquin.

CHAPTER SEVENTEEN

Hangtown, September 1849

Gerry groans. "Oh, my throat's killing me." He rubs his neck tenderly with his hand. "And under my arms."

I am at his side in an instant. "At least you're not hot," I say, checking for fever with the back of my hand. "It's probably a chill, but you best spend the day in bed."

"We need me working," he says, struggling to sit up.

"Not today," I say, pushing him back down. "I'll manage on my own for a day or two. But first you could do with a hot drink."

I stoke the fire back up and get our battered old kettle going. Coffee's not the thing today. When I was young my mother used to give me hot water with sage, but I have no herbs. Hot brandy will have to do.

If only we still lived near the Frenchmen, they'd be sure to have something. We moved away from our river camp three weeks ago. "Hangtown's the place," Gerry said. "Sure didn't Bear Man tell us how much gold there was to be had at Hangtown? And there'll be less risk of ambush if we're closer to town."

We tried the road into Hangtown first but found only the merest sprinkling of dust. The past week we've been pitched up in Cedar Ravine, a gully overlooking the sprawl of the town. Soon the frenzy of digging will start again but for now it's quiet. I fetch Gerry's cup and splash a generous measure of brandy into it, then pour in the boiling water.

"Drink it as hot as you can bear, that's what my mother always said with her sage water."

"Sage water?" Gerry says.

"It was my mother's remedy, she swore by it. God, it was disgusting, would have turned the heart out of you. And she'd have the throat seared off you, she had it that hot. At least you're drinking brandy."

"It'll be the last bottle we'll ever have if our luck doesn't change."

"Try and stop worrying. You need your strength for getting better."

"How can I help but worry? We've found no more than six ounces this last three weeks. All the easy gold's gone."

"We're just in a lean patch. Our luck could change any day. And we've enough to buy food for another couple of weeks." I say. "Come on now, all this talking is keeping you from that hot brandy. Get it down you. You can have a griddle cake once you've finished."

I can't keep this cheeriness up. I leave Gerry to his bed and his brandy and take myself, my pick and my shovel off up the mountain.

"Come on, mother lode. Please give me something today."

I start by shoveling dirt into my sack. When it's nearly full I slip my arms through the straps I've added to it and stagger down to the creek to wash it. The first load delivers nothing, the second two tiny nuggets, then nothing, and nothing. This is not a lucky place for us.

I check on Gerry on the way back up to the dig but he's sleeping. He looks worn out. I hope it is only a chill. There is sickness everywhere in the camps around the diggings, all manner of fevers. Between the cholera, the fighting and the lynching, there are plenty of ways to lose your life here.

I walk back up to the diggings and start to fill my sack. Maybe this time.

* * *

Gerry is sitting up in bed when I get back at sunset. His nose is red, eyes watery.

"How are you feeling?" I ask.

"My throat's not so raw, but my head's all stuffed up and everything aches."

I feel for the heat on him but there's still no sign of fever. I don't think it's anything serious.

"How did the digging go?" he says.

"Better this afternoon than this morning," I say, passing him my little leather pouch.

"Maybe an ou-ou—" He beckons for me to take it back as a large sneeze explodes out of him.

"Bless you."

He wipes his nose on his sleeve. "About an ounce I think."

An ounce. It's barely enough to keep body and soul together here, let alone make us rich. But tonight's worry is helping Gerry get better so I say, "What you need now is a decent meal inside you."

"I built up the fire but I couldn't manage the cooking," he says.

"I'll put on beans and bacon. And I've picked some of those greens that the Frenchmen showed me. I thought they might help. Doctor Dallas was always talking about fresh fruit and vegetables."

"Ah Jaysus, I hate greens."

"Oh stop fussing," I say. "They'll do you good."

"I can see the kind of wife and mother you'd make. It always comes out when someone's ill. God help your poor husband."

"I've told you before, there'll be no husband."

"What about a wife?" he says as I get the beans and bacon cooking.

"What?"

"A wife. Seeing as you're dressing like a man, you could go courting as one." He laughs.

"What?" I say. "What's so funny?"

"I was just imagining your wife's face on her wedding night." He laughs again.

"If you've time enough to be making jokes, you can be getting on with washing and chopping the greens."

"Oh don't go all tetchy, Frank. I didn't mean to annoy you."

"Well, what do you expect? Mocking me."

"I wasn't mocking you," he says. "Really, I wasn't. It was just the wedding night amused me. But you know, you might have more chance of finding someone as a man. Wouldn't it be harder to meet a woman, dressed like a woman?"

"I don't want to meet a woman. I've told you before, I'm done with all that."

I go out to stir the pot. Oh, he can be aggravating. A wife. As if there could be anyone—"Ouch!" I burn my hand on the stupid fucking pot. I stomp back into the tent for a cloth to lift it with.

I cannot look at Gerry. As if I'd be after conning some woman into thinking she was getting a man.

"Frank," he says, "I'm sorry."

I turn towards him. "You don't know what you're talking about."

"I've said sorry," he says, before another sneeze interrupts. "I didn't know you'd take on so. I was only…" He hesitates.

"Only what?"

"It doesn't matter."

"Only what?"

"Only thinking about the future. To take my mind off the present. Just thinking about how each of us might go about finding someone to love."

"I don't want someone to love."

I see him flinch, sitting on his bed, big feet sticking out of the blankets, a drip on the end of his red nose, cowering as I shout at him.

I shake my head. "I shouldn't be shouting at you."

He shrugs. "And I should know by now you don't like to talk about that part of your life. It's only…" He stops again.

"It's only?" I say softly.

"I don't know. I don't know how to say it."

"Just get on with it."

"You did it. You were a girl and you found a girl to love you. How did you know she was the kind of girl that would love you? How did you know she was the kind of girl who wouldn't spit in your face? Who wouldn't batter you for it? How did you know?"

I shake my head. "I don't think I did know. But she did. Kitty knew."

We are quiet over dinner, though I catch Gerry looking at me a couple of times like he's about to say something. I escape afterwards back out to the fire, this time with my still. Tonight's as good a time as any for finishing the poitín. The *braichlis* has been fermenting for three weeks. Three times through the still and it'll be ready.

"Can I help?" Gerry asks.

"Are you up to it?"

"I've been living with that poitín for the last three weeks. I can't miss out on this last stage."

"Well only at the start and the finish, in between you're to rest."

It is late by the time I've finished distilling. I wake Gerry to witness the last bottle being filled.

"Oh, it's great to see all these bottles. Imagine—*we* made this, out of little more than barley and water," Gerry says. "Can I try a drop?"

I pour him a measure and a glass for myself. "*Sláinte*," I say, sitting down next to him.

He puts the glass to his lips, then takes a swallow. "Hoooo," he says, shaking his head once sharply. "Jaysus, Frank, that's some drink."

"Do you like it?"

"Like it? I love it. Great flavour. If I'd known how good it would be, I'd have held out for twice what Ruby's giving us."

"Really?"

"Definitely. We could sell this, Frank. Not just to Ruby but all up and down these gullies. Undercut that cheating bastard at Sam's Stores."

"But would people buy it? Most of them won't have heard of poitín."

"Of course they will, once they've had a sample. Especially when the alternative is that swindler. I still can't believe the prices he's getting away with charging."

"There's not much choice. I'd never darken his door again, if there was anywhere else…" The words echo in my head. "That's it, Gerry. That's it," I say, excited.

"What's it?"

"*If there was anywhere else*. Maybe there should be. You've seen for yourself—"

"A shop?" he asks. "Are you suggesting we open a shop?"

"Why not? Look at the money there is to be made. There's more people arriving every day. It would be far easier than digging for gold ourselves. You've worked in a store be—"

"Have you any idea how much it costs to set up a shop?"

"No, how much? To get going, how much?"

"I don't know…A hell of a lot more than we've got, I can tell you that for nothing." He looks at me. "You're a one for the big ideas, aren't you? For months it was all 'let's go and dig for gold,' but ten minutes after getting here, you want to be opening a shop."

"I thought you'd love your own store," I say, disappointed.

"How can you expect me to be excited when we've barely enough money for a couple of weeks' food? We'd need thousands of dollars for supplies, for premises. Not to mention finding suppliers—"

"Maybe we don't need it all at once," I say, not ready to let my idea go. "We could start out with selling poitín, make it at night, carry on digging in the day, then expand—"

I'm interrupted by the loudest sneeze I've ever heard. He looks terrible. "We should get to bed," I say. "It's late. We can talk about this another time."

* * *

"I don't think I'll be very long. It's not far into town from here," I say to Gerry the following afternoon.

"Are you going like that?"

"What's wrong with me?"

"Your hands are filthy, your shirt's grey with dirt. And as to the state of your boots, Jaysus, you wouldn't think you used to make your living cleaning shoes."

I look down at my clothes. I would never have gone out like this in New York. But then I catch sight of him.

"You're one to be talking with that wild-man beard and grubby vest. Everyone's like it here."

"Not Ruby. Nor any of her staff. You're off to make good on our first deal with her. You can't go looking like some savage."

I scowl at him but I know he's right. "Fine," I say grumpily, rooting around among my things for my old brush. I start battering the worst of the dirt off my boots, then apply some polish. I scrub my neck, face and hands clean with a cloth dipped in water, then run my hands through my hair a few times, removing as much grit as I can. Finally I slip into my cleaner shirt.

"That's better," Gerry says, before being taken over by a coughing fit.

"I'll bring you back an onion."

"Ah no," he groans. "Not onion milk. I hate onion milk."

"We need to stop that getting a grip on your chest. Don't be such a baby."

He mutters to himself.

"What?" I say, catching the word *baby*.

"Nothing."

"No, what? Baby what?"

"Look Frank, I amn't after a fight."

"You may as well tell me. You've got me annoyed already."

"I was just wishing there was something we could do with your baby face, those smooth cheeks."

"I can't sprout whiskers. And you made me clean all the dirt off, if you remember."

"I know, I know, but you need something." He stares at me for a moment. "The shoe polish. Rub some of that onto your chin. It'll look like five-o'clock shadow."

"I'm not putting fecking shoe polish on my face."

"Just a little bit. Go on. It'll work."

"No."

"You're fierce stubborn," he says. "But I'll wish you luck anyway."

I grunt, then heave the heavy sack onto my shoulder, the bottles clinking as I do so.

"See you later."

The straps of the sack bite into my shoulder and one of the bottles keeps banging into the bottom of my back as I make my way into town. It's not a long trek and within fifteen minutes I spot the scarlet letters proclaiming Ruby's up ahead of me. But now I'm here I'm reluctant to go in. I set the sack down, rubbing my shoulder. What if Ruby doesn't like it? I don't fancy lugging this lot back up the hill. Or worse still, what if she's forgotten all about me and my poitín, looking through me before dismissing me out of hand? I imagine the stares as I clink, clink, clink back out of the bar.

Don't be ridiculous. She's paid for the still and the ingredients. She won't have forgotten.

I take a deep breath, lift the sack back over my shoulder, then pull open the heavy wooden door.

The chandeliers give off plenty of light. I look around for Ruby but she is nowhere in sight. Clarice approaches. "Can I 'elp you?" she asks.

"I'm here to see Ruby. I've the poitín she wanted."

"Ah, yes, I remember. Please, take a seat. I will just go and fetch her."

It is still early and the bar is quiet with only one Monte table occupied. A few miners prop up the bar. I pick a table near the door, as far as possible from the customers, settling my sack at my feet. Should I get a bottle out, ready to show her? I reach into my sack, then change my mind and sit up again, catching one of the miners at the bar staring at me. I sneer back, then get my knife out and start cleaning my nails.

"Excuse me."

My knife clatters onto the table as Ruby's voice pulls me from my performance. Getting quickly to my feet, I knock over my chair, which crashes to the floor. "Pardon me," I mutter as I bend over to pick it up, then fumble my knife back into my belt. I redden as Ruby suppresses a smile.

"Mister Moriarty?" she says, stretching her hand towards me.

Moriarty. How did she remember that? What on earth's her other name? Oh Jesus, I wish Gerry was here.

"Frank. Call me Frank," I say.

"Nice to see you again." She sits down. I follow suit.

"Sorry about the knife business," I say. "It's a habit I picked up, travelling on my own."

"I understand." She smiles, hitching her dress up slightly to reveal a small gun in a holster above her ankle. My cheeks burn as I notice deep red stockings under her gold dress.

"Clarice tells me you have the pot-cheen."

"I have. Would you like to try it?"

"Of course," she says. She walks quickly to the bar, returning with a small shot glass. While she's gone I grope in the bag for one of the bottles and place it on the table.

"Shall I pour?" I ask.

"Please."

She brings the glass first to her nose, inhaling gently.

Please let her like it.

"Interesting," she says, arching her eyebrow at me. She takes a small sip, holding it in her mouth before swallowing. "Very interesting." She nods. "I like. Of course, I don't know how is supposed to taste, but I like." She takes another sip. "If my customers like too, I will want much more."

I cannot stop the smile that breaks out across my face. "Oh, thank you."

"No, thank you, Frank. I love to find new things for my bar, to give people much choice. My favourite is champagne. Have you tried?"

I haven't even heard of champagne, let alone tried it. I'm guessing it's a drink, but it could be food or perhaps even a card game. Before I have time to answer she calls, "Clarice."

"Yes, madam."

"Bring us a bottle of the Renaud-Bollinger. Thank you."

Clarice is back soon with an elegant green bottle and two stemmed glasses topped with wide, shallow bowls. The dull hiss as she eases the cork out of the bottle is no preparation for the fizzing froth that pours into the glasses.

"God, it's lively," I say.

Ruby laughs, picking up the nearest glass. "*Salud*. To pot-cheen in Hangtown."

"*Sláinte*," I say, taking my first mouthful of champagne. It tingles up my nose and buzzes inside my mouth before I swallow. "Oh, I like this." I take another sip. "This might be the best drink ever."

"I think so." She smiles. I notice again the gap between her teeth. She in turn is looking at me. Her eyes linger on my chin. I look away.

"Is *slan-cha* Irish?"

"It is," I say. "It means 'good health.' Though there's all sorts of drinking toasts in Ireland. My favourite is 'May you be in heaven half an hour before the devil knows you're dead.'"

She laughs again, a warm, rich sound. "I like this toast. More interesting than *salud.*"

"What language is that?" I ask.

"Spanish."

"So are you Spanish?"

"Mexican," she says.

"Have you been in America long?"

"Since California become America. And you?"

"A couple of years."

"What brought you here?"

Death, I think. Death brought me here.

"A ship," I say. "As far as New York. Then when I heard about the gold I decided to come to California and seek my fortune."

"To good fortune," she says, clinking my glass.

"To good fortune."

CHAPTER EIGHTEEN

Dunquin, September 1845

"I surely am sick to death of oats," my da says to me as we sit at the table eating stirabout. "Thank the Lord we start the harvest today, I woke up dreaming of a decent feed of potatoes."

Since last year's potatoes ran out eight weeks ago, we've been managing on oatmeal, buttermilk, eggs and whatever else can be fashioned into a meal. I love September and the return of the potato. It's the time I was born. Maybe that's why autumn's always been my favourite season. If I'd sprung out in March, would I feel differently about the leaves changing colour, the crisp sharp mornings? Mister O'Connor, who taught me as a child, told us about countries where there are no seasons. I wouldn't like that, same weather, day in, day out, same sunrise, sunset.

"Shall I get the girls up?" I say.

"Leave them sleeping. Your ma'll send them up in an hour or so."

I am glad we'll be starting without them. I like working up in the fields with my da. "It's probably just as well," I say. "You know how bad tempered Lizzie can be if you rise her too early."

"She takes after your mother. Come on, let's be off."

It's a clear enough day as we make our way up the hill, following the path to the high field. It's our smallest field but the furthest from the house. We always start up here. I begin this morning with digging a storage pit in the bottom left-hand corner of the field while my da does the same in the top right. I don't make it too deep, just enough to keep the light and frost out, not so deep as to break your back finding them again.

"How are you getting on?" my da calls from his end of the field.

"Nearly finished," I say, leaving my shovel standing in the earth next to the pit.

The furrows have stayed neat, our lines of potato carefully weeded over the spring and summer. The white flowers are long gone, leaving a foot of yellowing leaves above the surface. These are our lumpers, large knobbly potatoes with pale yellow skins. We grow two acres of them for ourselves, four more of Queens for sale. My da precedes me down the first furrow, digging in with his spade along the side of the ridge to avoid damaging the potatoes. I follow him, half crouching, half crawling, extracting the potatoes where they lie exposed amid the broken earth. Dark soil clings to them, especially around the bumps and knobs and deep eyes. I rub it off, then place each potato on the ground to dry out. In a few hours, once the sun has hardened their skins, they will be ready to store.

Gathering potatoes is hard, slow work and my da has more than half the field opened up before I have finished even the first row. Tomorrow my thighs will burn, my back ache, from the crawling, crouching, reaching, gathering. But for now I'm fine. My mind drifts as I find my rhythm. It lands at Kitty's doorstep. We went to a dance yesterday outside the shebeen where the old man died in May. I smile, shutting my eyes for a moment, remembering that first night with her. How shy I was, how nervous. I have learned a lot since then about the giving and getting of pleasure, though I only spend the night with her every few weeks. We mustn't raise suspicions. She tells her mother she'll be staying over with me, I tell mine I'll be staying over with her. Instead we meet at our scalp. Not that we spend all our time there out of clothes. We sing, we dance, tell each other stories, talk of our future, sometimes just sit.

"Morning."

I look up to see Lizzie and Peig coming through the gate towards me. "Good afternoon," I say, smiling.

"Ah Frances, we've not done badly. Ma says you only set off an hour ago," Peig says.

The girls mutter and grumble to each other as they start on the next two furrows, but soon they too are in a rhythm. My da has finished uncovering the furrows. I join him at the far end of the field, working our way back towards the middle. When there's only one row left, my da stands up and stretches.

"Would you go and fetch the sand, Frances?" he says. "Then you can catch us up in the west field."

It is good to be upright after more than four hours on my knees. I shake out my arms and legs as I walk back down the hill to the outhouse, breathing in deeply, looking out to sea, glad to be alive.

Bramble walks over to the wall, snorting a welcome as she sees me approach. "Good girl," I say, scratching the back of her ears. She's a lovely donkey, soft grey with a strong dark line across her shoulders and down her back, patient and hardworking. She smiles when she sees you and never kicks or bites. Not like Samson, the first donkey we had. He liked nobody but my da. Anyone else went near him, he would kick and bang and create a commotion. You never met a noisier donkey, braying and hee-hawing at all times of the day and night. Before we had the house we used to share the old cabin with the animals. I don't know how we ever got any sleep. The least thing would set him off and my da would have to sing to him to put him back over.

Bramble waits patiently as I hitch the cart behind her and start loading it with sacks of sand brought up from the beach. The sand protects the potatoes in the pits. There's not enough room for all the potatoes in the cabin, half full as it is already with oats. It's the oats that pay the rent. My ma hoards any profit. "I'll take that for a rainy day," she says, ferreting the coins away in every nook and cranny round about the house. Even my da doesn't know how much she's saved and where half of it's hidden.

The top field is empty when I return, just rows and rows of harvested potatoes, the odd bird looking for worms among the dirt. I shake a layer of sand from my sack into each pit, then make my way down to the west field, where my da has started uncovering the furrows.

"Ah, there you are," he says. "Would you line the pits, then take Peig with you and start in the east field."

Peig sits on the little cart as we bump along the track to the east field perhaps sixty yards away.

"My back's aching already," she says.

"You'll forget about it tonight when you've got a decent meal in your belly," I say. "I'll make—"

The putrid stench of rotting flesh hits me, forcing my mouth shut. I turn my head away, my face screwed up, gripping the side of the cart to stop from retching.

"What's that smell?" Peig says.

I put my hand to my nose and speak round it as best as I can. "Some animal must have died somewhere near. We'll have to move the body."

Peig slips off the cart. "There's no sign of a body here. It must be in the field," she says, opening the gate. "Eucchhh. It's even worse in here."

The air is rank with the bodies of a herd of rotting cows. I look around but there isn't a single corpse.

"What is it?" Peig says. "Where's it coming from?"

I scan the field, looking for a body. And suddenly I see what's out of place. There are no green stalks here. The plants are grey black slime.

"It's the potatoes," I say, leaning down to get a closer look. My stomach rises in my throat as the smell takes me over. I turn away, vomiting onto the ground.

It catches the edge of Peig's dress. She doesn't notice. "Look at the potatoes," she says. "What's happened to the potatoes?"

"I don't know," I say, fighting down the panic. I put my hand over my face, trying to shut out the stink. "Maybe it's just above ground. Perhaps the potatoes themselves will be fine."

The spade is still lying on the back of the cart. I fetch it. It goes in easily along the side of the furrow. I squeeze my eyes shut. "May the potatoes be safe. May the Lord bless us with a good crop."

My left hand slips down the shaft. There's a sucking sound as I open up the ground. I stagger back from the sight and smell. There are no solid potatoes, just an oozing sludge of stinking grey rot.

"Oh Jesus," Peig says. "Oh Jesus." She turns away, running from the field.

"Da!" she screams. "Da! Da!"

CHAPTER NINETEEN

Hangtown, September 1849

"I've heard a lot of men have had luck here," Gerry says as we walk up Log Cabin Ravine, the other side of Hangtown from Cedar Ravine.

I grunt.

"We can put the tent up over there, by the big tree."

I grunt again.

He throws his pack down. "Will you stop with the grunting? It was you that wanted to move."

"Not here. This isn't the r—"

"Will you give my head peace about the river? It had stopped paying."

"There's many a man taking great lumps of gold out of that river."

"And they're digging it out up here too."

"I've a feeling about the river."

"Well maybe I've a feeling about here."

We glare at each other. I've been trying to persuade him to move back to the river for the past week after day upon day of fruitless digging in Cedar Ravine. We need gold and soon. I'm sure the river is the place to get it—we were lucky there before. But Gerry point-blank refuses to consider it. The other side of Hangtown was as far as I could budge him. We put the tent up in silence.

"Listen, Frank," he says as we finish, "let's not quarrel."

I sigh. Life is tough enough without falling out with Gerry. Now that we're here I should give this place a chance. "So where do you want to start digging?" I say.

"Well, I thought we'd have a look around, find a promising spot."

"When I was at Ruby's the other day, she told me something about the course of rivers."

"Oh Frank, not the river again. We haven't even—"

"Will you stop? I'm trying to help. Ruby said that the Mexican miners know where to dig. They go for the inside of the river bends."

"There's no river in this ravine."

"I know. But there used to be. The gold's still there on the inside of the bends. We just need to work out where the bends are, where the river used to be."

"Did Ruby tell you how to find the inside bends?" he says, excited.

"Well, no. She didn't really know the details. That's why I've not mentioned it till now. But surely it's not beyond us to work it out. If you were a river, where would you go?"

"Am I supposed to be thinking like a river?"

"It's worth a try."

He sighs, putting his hand to his forehead the way he sometimes does when he's thinking. "The sea, I suppose. Rivers are always looking to go to the sea. Or a lake. If they can't get to the sea, they'll make do with a lake."

"Great. So. The sea. Where would the sea be from here?"

"West," he says. "The nearest sea will be the Pacific."

"But west's that way," I say, pointing to my right. "Up over the hills. Rivers don't flow upwards. It would have to go down first, down and then round to the west."

He nods. "It would have joined up with the American. The creek down below in Hangtown probably flows into it too."

"So maybe our missing river flowed into the creek? You can just about see part of the creek from here, down through that gap," I say, pointing. "Maybe that's where it joined. We should work back from there."

I scan the hillside, following the lines and shelves. A dense clump of bushes halfway down the hill catches my eye.

"Look there," I say. "Do you see those bushes? They look extra thick. Maybe they're being watered from below. Maybe that's where the river went."

so sure the deer would bring us luck. But then I've been sure about a lot of things. Better a rabbit in the stew than a deer in the bush. I wish I knew how to make that stew the Frenchm—

"Aahhhh."

I crash to the ground, rifle clattering from my hand.

Ow. Owww.

Sharp pain radiates out from my ankle. Jesus, fuck. It's broken, I know it's broken. I try to move, but my foot's stuck down a hole among the tree roots. I start to cry. Minutes pass and still I cry, great huge sobs.

I remember Thomas, a fella from Dunquin who mangled his leg out on the bog one day. He never walked right again, limping and hurpling round the village.

That's going to be me.

We're never going to find any gold.

We should never have come here.

CHAPTER TWENTY

Dunquin, October 1845

"Frances! Frances!"

I go to the door, wondering who it is. Mary Garvey stumbles towards me, half running up the track towards our house.

"What's the matter?" I say.

"Our potatoes," she says, starting to cry. "They're rotten."

"What? But…" She must be wrong. Their crop was safe, not a potato lost to the blight.

"They're rotten, rotten," she says, her voice rising.

"Were they…You hadn't left them in the pits, had you?" I say. Burnham's agent was very clear in his instructions about storing the potatoes out of the ground this year. A third of the crop was lost in the harvest but he said the rest would be safe. He can't be wrong.

"Peter built a shed. We've done everything Campbell told us to do. Everything."

I feel dizzy, like a breath would knock me over. He said they would be safe. He said they would be safe.

"What are we going to do?" Mary says, her face twisting as she tries to stop the tears falling.

I put my hand on her arm. "People will help, we won't let you starve."

"It's not just the food. We've nothing for the rent."

"Burnham'll have to wait for it. You can pay him after the next harvest."

"What if he puts us out?"

"He won't do that. With what's happened to the crop, he'd have to put out half the parish."

"Do you think so?"

"My mother always says, 'God will provide.' The saints will protect you, you and the little ones. Try not to worry." I stroke her arm, trying to send out a calmness I don't feel. Things are going to be bad.

I watch her retreating back, dread building inside me. I have to check our potatoes. We were lucky, only the east field lost to the blight. Pray God the rest are safe. A nasty smell reaches me on the air as I make my way round the house towards the old cabin, a vomity kind of reek.

I put my handkerchief to my mouth to ward off the stench and open the cabin door. It's dark, even with the door ajar, but I can see the sacks of potatoes piled into every inch of the cabin. I put my hand cautiously into the nearest sack, ready to draw back at a trace of slime. But the potatoes feel whole. I take a couple out and put them to my nose, inhaling deeply. They smell slightly earthy. I try the next sack and the next. All whole, no trace of rot, nothing bad. I sniff the air. The cabin is safe, there is nothing rotting here. I let my breath out slowly. Thank you Lord.

I go outside, mouth open, sucking in the air. There is no taint. Maybe I imagined it. Slowly, I retrace my steps, sniffing as I go. A few yards from the cabin I detect again a note of vomit. I scan the ground around me. To my left, I spot a slimy mess of feathers, the discarded meal of some local tom. I shake my head, then walk back to the house.

* * *

The sea is roaring today, waves battering the beach. The tide's on its way out, leaving behind fierce, black rocks. And clinging to the rocks are the mussels that have brought us down to Coumeenoole Strand.

"Are you sure we can eat these?" Mary says, looking warily at the blue-black shells, still gleaming from the sea.

"They're really tasty," I say, "if you know how to cook them. Mussels in beer or with butter and onions, or mussel chowder."

"We never ate anything like this. It was always potatoes."

"My ma never fully trusted the potatoes. There were problems before, thirty years ago."

"I'll never trust them again either." Her voice is bitter.

"No, I don't think any of us will."

"I suppose we should make a start," Mary says.

"It's easy enough. First, you choose your mussel. Not too small—they're still growing. And not the ones that are half open, they're already dead and gone bad." I point to a shell about an inch and a half long. "This one's perfect," I say, taking hold of the shell a little more than halfway down its length. "You get a firm grip of it, then twist sharply and—pull." I tug hard and the shell comes away from the rock.

"Your turn," I say, dropping it into my bucket.

Mary approaches the rock cautiously, pausing to peer at the shells. I realise I'm staring and get on with finding my next shell. I'm on to my third one when I see Mary staggering backwards.

"Oh, I think I pulled a bit hard," she says, laughing as she recovers her balance. Soon she is picking her way across the rocks. It is not difficult work but it's hard on the hands, the bitter wind biting through the flesh to the bone.

"That's probably enough," I say, once she has half a bucketful. "They don't keep long so there's no point getting too many. Come on, let's go back up to the house and I'll show you how to cook them."

The shells click-clack together as we walk up the steep hill from the beach towards Mary's cabin. Her mother is sitting in the kitchen, Dominic sleeping in the wooden crib, Malachy shuffling around the floor on his bottom. He holds his arms up to Mary, who scoops him into a hug.

"How's my baba?" she says. He squeals as she blows a raspberry into his neck.

"Good afternoon, Missus Begley," I say.

"Afternoon Frances."

"Frances has been showing me how to gather mussels," Mary says.

"It's a terrible day to be reduced to eating the likes of them," Missus Begley answers.

"Ah, Mammy, it's not so bad. Frances is going to teach me how to cook them up nice and tasty."

Missus Begley shakes her head, then gets up from her seat without another word and goes out the door of the house. I exchange a glance with Mary.

"She thinks it's paupers' food," Mary says quietly.

"Would it be better if I took them with me?"

"No, no, Frances. We need to learn to manage on things besides potatoes."

"I didn't mean to be upsetting your mother. There's other things than mussels you can try. You can gather mushrooms in the forest for a stew and nettles for making soup. And we'll give you what potatoes we can."

"How will we ever repay you?" she says, tears welling up in her eyes.

"There's no need." I look away as Mary wipes her face with the back of her sleeve.

"Anyway, you were going to show me what to do with my bucket of mussels," she says, putting Malachy down.

I sit on the floor with Mary and the bucket, showing her how to remove the beard from the mussels. We place the debearded ones in a bowl of fresh water.

"What next?" she says.

"Well, it depends how you're cooking them. Shall we make soup this time?"

"Soup sounds great."

"The mussels need to soak for about twenty or thirty minutes, but we could be getting on with chopping vegetables for the pot."

"I have turnips and carrots."

"Great, we'll scoop the turnips out for the soup and make jack-o'-lanterns with what's left behind."

Jack-o'-lanterns have always been one of my favourite things on earth. I can't have been more than five or six when my da first told me the legend of Stingy Jack.

"Oh, he was a terrible man," he said, sitting me on his lap opposite one of the lanterns, its flickering light casting shadows round the old cabin. "A terrible, greedy drunk of a man. Always trying to cheat people. He even thought he could cheat the Devil."

"Oh, not the Devil," I said, shivering as I peered around the cabin, checking for a horned beast with seven heads.

"The Devil himself," he said. "It was a dark Hallowe'en night, a night like tonight, and Jack was out drinking in a shebeen. And who should he run into but the Devil himself. Says he to the Devil, 'Will you be buying me a last drink?' Quick as a flash the Devil replies, 'Of course. But on one condition. I want your soul.'

"Stingy Jack thought about it for a moment. His soul or a drink, his soul or a drink. And he decided he wouldn't be needing his soul for a while, but he needed a drink right now. Jack nodded his head.

Immediately the Devil turned himself into a sixpence to pay the bartender. But Jack was a quick thinker. He snatched the coin and put it into his pocket, where he carried a silver cross. Well try as he might, the Devil couldn't change himself back while he was next to the cross.

"Each day the Devil would call out to Jack asking to be set free. And in the end they made a deal. The Devil could go free so long as he promised not to claim Jack's soul for ten years. Ten years seemed a long time to Jack, who was still a young man, and so he set the Devil free. But the ten years came and went very fast and soon the Devil came calling while Jack was out walking on a country road.

"'You owe me a soul,' the Devil said.

"But again Jack was quick in his thinking. 'You can have my soul,' he said, 'but first would you get me an apple from that tree?'

"So the Devil jumped up into the tree and as soon as he did, Jack placed crosses all around the trunk, trapping the Devil once again. This time, Jack made the Devil promise that he would not take his soul when he finally died. Well the Devil was furious at being caught out again but he could see no option but to agree.

"Years went by, and finally Stingy Jack passed away. He went to the Gates of Heaven and Saint Peter came down to see him.

"'Can I come in?' Jack said.

"'No,' Saint Peter answered. 'It's too late. You've spent your life lying and drinking and cheating. You can't come in.'

"So, then Jack went down to Hell. The Devil was waiting at the entrance. 'Well, Jack, we meet again,' he said.

"'Can I come in?' Jack said.

"'Don't you remember our deal?' the Devil said. 'We agreed I wouldn't get your soul and if I can't have your soul, you can't come in.'

"'But where am I to go?' asked Jack.

"The Devil laughed his evil laugh. 'From now on you are doomed to roam the earth without a resting place.'

"'But it's windy and dark and I'm all on my own,' Jack said.

"The Devil doesn't have much pity but he tossed Jack an ember straight from the fires of Hell. And till this day Jack wanders the earth, his only light the ember from Hell in a hollowed-out turnip."

My mother was furious with my da for telling me this story; I had nightmares for days afterwards. But since then I've always loved the flicker of a turnip lantern.

"Pass me one of the turnips," I say to Mary. "I'll carve it for you." I carefully slice the top off to make a lid for the lantern, then set to extracting as much of the orange flesh as can be usefully cooked. "Have you any plans for celebrating tomorrow?"

"The boys are too young for—"

"You're never too young for All Hallows Eve," I say. "Why don't you come over tomorrow night?"

* * *

"Ah, Kitty, it's lovely to see you. Come on in and sit yourself down," my mother trills. Since that first day when she came to visit, my mother has nothing but her best words for Kitty. "This is our neighbour Mary Garvey and her sister Ellen."

It is three days since I last saw Kitty and I'm itching to touch her. I keep my hands busy, chopping cabbage for the colcannon.

"I've no call to be sitting when others are hard at work," Kitty says. "Give me a job to do."

"I wouldn't dream of it," my mother says. "Sure aren't you a guest in this house? Put your feet up after your long walk."

"Well, before I do that, have you anywhere I could be hanging this?" she says, taking an apple threaded onto a piece of string out of her pocket.

"Oh I love snap-apple," Lizzie cries.

"There's a nail on the beam above your head," I say to Kitty, smiling at her. "You could put it there."

She's beyond handsome today, her cheeks slightly pink from the walk, red hair wild from the wind, turquoise eyes shining with life. Oh, she surely is the finest-looking woman in the world. I watch as she stands on the little stool that normally sits by the fire, ready to catch her if she overbalances. Her nimble fingers have the string tied in seconds and she leaps off the stool as light and easy as a mountain goat.

"Are you the Kitty that won the cake dance?" Mary asks.

"She is indeed," my ma answers. "I'm hoping you'll take a turn later at the party, Kitty. My husband's quite the player."

"I suppose that's where Frances gets it," she says. "Was she always musical?"

"Well, I suppose so. She used to tap along with her little fat hand when she was a toddler."

"Fat hands? She had fat hands?" Kitty says, amused.

"Not just hands. Fat everything. The fattest of all my babies. The fattest baby in Ireland."

I feel myself redden.

"Well, I'd always rather a fat baby than a scrawny one," Kitty says, turning towards me and giving me the most outrageous flirty wink. I redden further.

"We should sort out the games before the men are back from lighting the bonfire. What shall we play?" I say.

"Apple bobbing," Peig says.

"And that apple-peeling one that tells you who you're going to marry," Mary says. "I'm sure that one of you girls will be wed before next Halloween."

"Do you know the apple-and-mirror one for telling your fortune?" Kitty says.

"I've tried it," my ma says. "But I prefer puicini."

"Puicini?" Kitty says.

"Oh, it's a great game, isn't it Ma?" Peig says. "Why don't we let Kitty have a try of it now?"

"I'll take her into the other room out of the way while you get it set up," I say, seizing my chance for a moment alone.

"You look so beautiful, today," I say to her, shutting the door behind us.

"You too," she says, slipping her arms around me.

Her lips are soft and welcoming as I lean forward and kiss her. I intend just a brief kiss but her warmth so close is impossible to resist.

We burst apart as the door opens.

"I can't see anything," I say to Kitty. Then, turning to Peig, I say, "Kitty could feel some grit or something in her eye."

Peig stares at me. Did she see anything? I don't know.

She turns to Kitty. "I need to put this blindfold on you."

CHAPTER TWENTY-ONE

Hangtown, September 1849

"Gerry," I shout. "Gerry."

He doesn't come.

"Gerry!"

He still doesn't come.

"*Gerry!*"

There's men camped all over this hillside. Why can no one hear me?

Shutting my eyes against the pain, I try to pull my foot out of the rabbit hole. But it's stuck fast. I mustn't start crying again. I keep taking deep breaths, trying to think.

Looking around I see the rifle. I stretch out my right arm towards it. But it's just out of reach. Twisting as far as I can, I inch my fingers across the dirt. Nearly there. Pain jags down my neck as I make a grab for the strap.

Got it. I pull the rifle towards me, then fire it.

"Gerry," I shout as the noise of the gun fades away.

I reload and fire again.

"Gerry!"

At last I hear the sound of feet pounding.

"Frank, where are you? Frank."

"Over here, I'm over here."

It is so good to see him. Tears start again.

"What happened?" Gerry says.

"I fell. My foot's trapped."

He crouches down. "Stay still," he says, easing his hand down the hole.

"Careful," I say, wincing.

"It's the lace. It's tangled round one of the roots."

"Can you get it free?"

"I'm trying. Christ, it's tricky."

"Cut it. Just cut it."

He pulls his hand out of the hole and takes the knife from me. "Keep still. I don't want to cut you."

I feel him sawing back and forth against the lace.

"I'm through," he says at last, easing his hand back out. "Can you move it?"

Sweat breaks out on my forehead as I inch my foot gently out of the rabbit hole. *Please don't let it be broken.*

"Can you help me off with my boot?" I say.

But he's not listening. He leans forward, reaching into the hole. "Jaysus," he says, turning back towards me. In his hand lies a large nugget. It's the shape of a pear but bigger, nearly the size of Gerry's hand. A big fat golden pear. We both stare at it for a long moment.

"Jesus," I say at last. "Jesus, God." I can hardly breathe. "How… how much?"

"I don't know." He moves it from one hand to the other and back again. "A lot. Maybe one hundred and twenty ounces. Phew," he says, blowing his cheeks out, "that's two thousand dollars sitting right there. Fuck, Frank."

"Two thousand dollars. Jesus. Is there," I say, hardly daring to ask, "is there any more?"

He hands me the pear as he leans down to look into the hole around the root. It's knobbly and pockmarked, dirt lining the grooves. And heavy, almost too heavy for one hand. I clasp both hands around it, my heart beating faster as I feel its solid weight.

"It's too dark to see," Gerry says. He rolls his sleeve up and sticks his hand into the hole, feeling around. He withdraws it with a grin, grains of earth spilling onto the scrub around the tree roots. In his hand are two chunky nuggets, each the size of a large blackberry.

"This is it, Frank," he says, his face lit up by a smile. "This is it. There's more in there, I'm sure of it, but we'll need the pick and the shovels to get it out."

"We can't take the chance of someone else finding it before we've got it staked. Can you get the equipment while I stay guard here? I don't think I can walk anyway."

"I'd forgotten about your ankle."

"Me too," I say, suddenly noticing the pain again. I wince as I try to rotate it. "It hurts, but I don't think it's broken. Doctor Charles taught me that much. I might be able to walk if I can strap it. The old sheet will do. And can you bring the pan—I can't dig, but if I've a pan I can sift what you dig."

"You'll be calling me 'donkey' by the time you've finished loading me up," he says, but he's smiling.

I take my boot off while I'm waiting for him to return. A grey-purple bruise extends from the heel across the top of my foot and my ankle's already starting to swell. But it was worth it.

Suddenly I'm back at the quay in Cobh, crowded in by people, desperate people, jostling and pushing, crying and pleading, begging to get on a boat. In front of me there's a couple with their mother, waiting for the next ship. The mother has a terrible stink about her, like the flesh is rotting on her bones. She doesn't last. There's nowhere to bury her, nothing to bury her with. They cover her in their only blanket and leave her there on the quay. The man has to drag his wife onto the ship. She's sobbing and wailing, he's saying it's their only chance. It doesn't save them. Within a week they're both dead.

Tears well up in my eyes as I sit now below the tree, holding our big lump of gold. Gerry drops what he's carrying with a clang. "Is your ankle bad?" he says, coming over to me.

I can't speak for a minute. I wipe my face with my sleeve and whisper, "Why me?"

"What do you mean?"

I shake my head. "Why did I live when so many people died? They were dying in Dunquin, dying on the way to the ships, dying on the ships. They're still dying. Why should I be alive when all those people are dead? Why should I have this gold when there's people at home with nothing? People dying in droves because they've got nothing?"

He sits down heavily beside me. "You mustn't give in to this, Frank."

"The day I left…" I start to cry.

"Don't think about that."

"I can't help it. This old woman—"

"Don't tell me," he says, standing up. "I know what Cobh was like. But we can't help anyone if we give in." He picks up the shovel and begins to dig.

* * *

"I think we should bring the tent up here," Gerry says as dusk approaches. "I won't be able to sleep tonight unless I'm close to the gold."

"Can you bring everything on your own?" I say, still not able to walk far.

"It'll take a few trips but I'm sure I can manage."

"I'll get a fire going while you're gone. If you bring the food on the first trip, I'll do the cooking."

He mock spits on his hand, then offers it to me. "Deal," he says.

Fifteen minutes later he is back with the cauldron, filled with our food supplies. By the time he returns with the tent I've got a stew cooking. We've driven four stakes in a square round the tree to mark our claim. We pitch our tent alongside, only a few feet from the bonanza.

"This night deserves a celebration," Gerry says, fetching a bottle of poitín from the tent. He passes me a cup. "Health and long life to you."

"And to you," I say, taking a swig.

"I can't believe how much gold we've gathered in one day," Gerry says, looking at the pan of gold, which I've placed near the fire. As well as the pear, we've found five blackberry-sized ones and countless little kernels.

"When I first decided to come to California, this is how I dreamt it would be," I say. "After the hard times we've had, it doesn't seem real."

"To the end of hard times," he says, knocking his cup against mine.

"The end of hard times," I echo. I look again at the gold, the dull yellow glinting in the firelight. "There must be thousands of dollars worth," I say, dropping my voice to a whisper.

"I'd be guessing about three thousand dollars. Jaysus, three thousand dollars in a day."

"The most I ever made in a day in New York was three dollars."

"That's better than I was doing at Mister Harvey's."

"Ah, it was only the one day. Most days it was a dollar, maybe a dollar and a half." I shake my head. "Now we're rich," I say, as if hearing the words out loud will help me to believe them.

"Well, I'm not sure we're rich yet," he says.

"Not rich? We've three thousand dollars."

"Don't get me wrong," he says, "it's a good start. But how long will it last in California?"

"Years," I say.

"Months, you mean. The cost of food alone. And we'll need a cabin for the winter. We've made enough today for eight months in California, nine if we're lucky. We'd need ten times as much to be rich."

I feel like all the breath's been sucked out of me. A minute ago three thousand dollars was a fortune. Now it's not enough. "I thought this was a night for celebrating," I say, feeling a surge of bitterness towards Gerry.

"It is," he says, "of course it is. But it's a night for planning too. And there's no point pretending what we've found today will be enough if we stay here."

"If you're saying we should leave California, you're on your own. I'm not making that journey again," I say.

"No, I'm not saying that."

"What are you saying?"

"I've been thinking about what you said a few weeks ago. About a store."

* * *

"Feck off, y'bastard," Gerry says. I can't help but laugh as he jumps away from the mule. He scowls. "It's no wonder those men were glad to be shot of you. You surely are the most ungrateful half-breed I've ever come across. Trying to bite my arse."

He bought the mule yesterday from a couple of miners further down the ravine. Guinness, we've named him, on account of his black coat.

"You're going to have to load him. He likes you better than me. Maybe it's your *woman's* touch," Gerry says with an edge of sarcasm that I decide to ignore.

We are both tired after five days of hard digging around our tree. All the big nuggets came in the first day but we carried on picking out the little grain-sized pieces. Gerry reckons there's about four thousand dollars worth of gold, enough to build and stock a store and send money to my family. And we've kept a bit for a rainy day. I will be glad when we've got it to Hangtown and the safe at Ruby's.

The nuggets are hidden among our bedding and dirty clothes to fool any would-be robbers. It takes close to an hour to get ready for departure as I move things between the mule and our own packs, adjusting the loads to keep them balanced and secure. I take a last look around the campsite, the half-exposed roots of our tree, the remains of the fire, the flattened ground where we pitched the tent. Down the gully I can see knots of men, busy looking for a lucky strike. But it's quiet up here.

"Come on, Frank," Gerry says, "let's get going. Hanging around here's making me nervous."

Reluctantly I turn away. It is time to weapon up.

"Right, is your rifle loaded?" I say.

"Yes, I've already checked."

"And have you—"

"Yes, there's more ammo in my pack. And I have my knife here in my belt."

I check my own knife and rifle, adjust my pistol in its holster, put my meanest face on. No one's taking this gold off me without a fight. With one hand on my pistol, the other on Guinness's reins, I set off at a slow limp down the mountainside. Gerry follows behind, just out of range of the mule's hind legs.

The ground is rough through the trees towards the main path down the ravine. I have made perhaps one hundred and fifty yards when I hear twigs cracking nearby. I signal to Gerry to halt. We both hold our breath. Guinness doesn't. He starts with a kind of whinny ending in a bellowing *hee-haw, hee-haw*. A big reddish-gold dog bursts out of the undergrowth, barking exuberantly at Guinness who whinny-haws in reply, kicking out with his back legs. The dog circles Guinness a couple of times, then comes and sits in front of me, pink tongue lolling out of its black muzzle. I holster my pistol and reach down to stroke its solid head.

"Jaysus," Gerry says, "that dog nearly scared the arse off me."

As we set off again, the dog decides to come too, sniffing along five yards ahead, looking back every now and again.

"I wonder if it's with someone," I say, hoping not.

"It looks well enough fed," Gerry says. "The owner's probably off digging somewhere."

In ten minutes we are free of the trees and out onto the path down to the creek. We should be safe here, among the miners hauling pay dirt back and forth to the water to wash it. Goldie, as I have named her, bounds up to a couple of miners, barks and then runs back to me.

"That damned dog again," one of them says, a young, dark-haired man with the customary wild beard.

"Is she yours?" I ask, wondering if he might sell her.

He shakes his head. "Belonged to some critter got hisself shot dead in Hangtown last week. Now she's just hanging around gitting on my nerves."

I fondle Goldie's silky ear, smiling. No one else is going to claim her. There's a piece of dried meat in my pack. I fish it out and hold it on my palm for Goldie. She takes it gently, then chomps it down. "Good girl," I say.

"I take it the dog's coming too," Gerry says.

"If she wants to," I say. "What do you think, Goldie?" She nuzzles my hand with her dark nose. I stroke her again, feeling her short, fine coat. She is well-muscled, strong and powerful, and her tail whips back and forth as I pet her. "Come on then," I say. She barks then bounces off ahead of us down the path, pausing to sniff at what looks like mule droppings, then running back to me for another stroke. She is mine.

We pass plenty of miners hard at work, but they barely grunt at us.

"Not like Ireland, is it?" I say. "You wouldn't be passing all these people without a word."

"I'm in no mood for talking. I just want to be safe at Ruby's."

But Goldie makes me feel safe; she's such a big, bold dog. And then I see something that makes me certain we are going to be fine.

"Bear Man" I shout, as he joins the path twenty yards ahead of us. "Bear Man." I break into a limping run, pulling Guinness behind me. Goldie sees me running and comes alongside, barking excitedly. It sets Guinness off on his whinny-hawing. The commotion is enough to catch Bear Man's attention.

"Frank," he says, "good to see you." He reaches his huge hand to me. "And you, Gerry. How are you doing? You found much gold?"

"A bit," I say, cautious. Gerry and I have agreed we should play down our strike. "We're on our way into Hangtown."

"Me too," he says. "I find it easier to resist the lure of the Monte if I go in the morning. I've bought me a piece of land. And I've ordered some vines. Once they arrive I'm done with gold mining."

"Vines?" Gerry says.

"Yeah, I've been reading all about them. The weather here's perfect. I'm going to be growing me some grapes and then making me some wine."

"I've only had wine once," Gerry says.

"I'm hoping to supply Ruby's," Bear Man says.

"We've been selling her poitín," Gerry says.

"Pot-cheen? I ain't heard of that. Though last time I was in she sold me a lethal brew she was calling Ruby's Reward. It nearly took my head off."

"I'll bet that's our poitín," I say. "Was it a bit like whiskey, but clear?"

"Yeah, that's the one. You made that?"

"We did. Do you want a bottle?" I say, stopping Guinness and extracting a bottle from his saddlebags.

"Well, thank you," Bear Man says. "I really appreciate this. I'll save you one of my first bottles of wine."

It's only half past nine as we reach Hangtown. We stop outside Ruby's, Goldie panting at my feet. "I need to go get me some supplies," Bear Man says. "It was good to meet you boys again."

"Have you time for a drink? To celebrate your vineyard?" I say.

"It's a bit early for me. But I'll be back in on Friday evening. Maybe I can catch up with you then."

CHAPTER TWENTY-TWO

Dingle, December 1845

It's cold and damp when I get to the scalp. Kitty arrives as I'm squatting over a little pile of sticks, trying to coax them to flame. Nine months into our love, her beauty still takes my breath away. I gaze up at her face, get lost in her. Then realising I'm staring, I look away.

Kitty laughs. "Come here," she says, pulling me away from my crouch by the fire into a warm embrace. Her lips find mine, her mouth open, welcoming. I press against her, my right leg firm between hers.

She laughs up at me. "Have you missed me then?"

"I have," I say. "You know I have."

She strokes my hair, smiling. "Me too," she says softly. She pulls me down onto the floor, kissing me again. And again.

I pull a cover over us, keeping Kitty warm as my fingers rediscover her body. She says my name as I touch her, stroke her, "Frankie, oh Frankie," till she is beyond words.

Afterwards I lay with my head on her chest, listening to her breath returning.

"You're looking pretty comfortable there," she says eventually. "Shouldn't we be getting off to Dingle?"

"Just a little longer," I say as she plays with my hair. "There's plenty of time."

"Plenty of time?" she says, kissing my cheek, once, twice. I turn my face towards her. She kisses me, gently biting my bottom lip, her hands finding their way inside my dress. I stop her long enough to take it off.

* * *

"We should get ready," I say.

"I knew my charms couldn't keep you from Dingle for long," she says.

"Your charms could keep me here forever," I say, softly kissing her cheek, her lips. "I love being with you."

"I love it too. Kissing you, touching you, stroking you, tasting you. I love it all."

I can feel my body starting to throb again. She lets out a long breath. "I mustn't let myself become distracted again or we'll never get there."

I grin at her. "So is that what I am, a distraction?" I throw off the covers and get out of bed.

"You are at the minute. What else would I be but distracted with you standing there naked before me?" She pulls the covers back over her. "You get ready first, we'll only end up getting in each other's way if we're both trying to dress."

I step into an old pair of black trousers that belonged to my da.

"Shame," she says, "the lovely legs have gone."

I slip a dark gansey over my head. "It's your turn to get ready," I say to Kitty.

"In a minute. Put on your mask first. I want to see the whole costume."

I have been working on the mask for weeks, ever since Kitty and I came up with the notion of disguising ourselves for today's Wren Day celebrations. The wren has been hunted and paraded on St. Stephen's Day for as far back as anyone can remember. It's strictly for the boys, dressed up in their costumes, accompanied by their bands. Girls stand on the sidelines watching, clapping, cheering, maybe dancing if some fella grabs them. But today Kitty and I will be in the thick of it.

My mask sits in the far corner of the scalp, stems of willow woven together, covered with old pieces of sack, painted black. Carefully I fit my head inside it, peering at Kitty out of the eyeholes.

"Even I wouldn't know it was you." Kitty laughs delightedly, sitting up in bed. "I'm telling you, if you were on four legs you'd pass for a real donkey."

"But will I pass for a Wren Boy?"

"The best Wren Boy I've ever seen."

"Are you sure? I don't want to get caught. Can you imagine the scandal? My ma would never let me out of the house again."

"We won't get caught. Oh, now I want to be ready too," she says, getting out of bed.

It's dark in the scalp with my mask on and I want to be able to watch her dressing. I take it off and sit down on the bed, looking at her pale, slim body, the dark red hair between her legs, the smudge of blood on the top of her thigh.

"What are you staring at, Frances Moriarty?"

"You," I say.

"Well stop. You're distracting me again. Now where did my rags end up?" She roots around under the covers for them, then presses them between her thighs to stem the flow. Slowly she starts to dress. First a pale camisole, then a fisherman's sweater, followed by a frayed grey shirt, left open.

"Where did you get those?" I say as she puts on a pair of dark grey breeches.

"Ah now, Frances, I can't be telling you all my secrets," she says, tucking in the shirt.

"Oh, tell me," I say. "They look great."

"They do, don't they? But believe me, you're better not knowing where they came from," she says. "Now for my mask." She slips a white-painted sack over her head, aligning the holes with her eyes and mouth. "Will you tie this on for me?" she says, handing me the gull's beak. I made it myself, whittling a branch, painting it yellow, hollowing out the end to fit onto Kitty's nose, then attaching strings to either side. I position it gently against her nose, then tie the strings behind her head.

She laughs as it slides down off her face. "A bit tighter, darling. Don't worry, I'll tell you if it's hurting."

This time I'm firmer and the beak stays in place. "It suits you."

"What, having my face covered by a sack?"

"No," I say, looking into her eyes, "being a seabird. You're not supposed to be hemmed in."

She touches my hand. "Thank you," she says. "And for thinking of doing this. I was always jealous of my brothers, God rest them, gallivanting all over the country in their masks and straw suits. Today it's our turn."

There is no one to see our departure, a donkey and a kittiwake walking at a fast clip down the slope from our scalp to the road to Ballyferriter.

"We'd best go round the village," Kitty says. "It's close to home where there's most chance of us being found out."

"Especially with your eyes, I've never seen anyone with eyes like yours. People from round here would be bound to know it was you."

"I'm sure most of Ballyferriter hasn't a clue what colour my eyes are. It's just you with all your gazing into them that knows."

I feel myself blush and am thankful for my mask. It is true, I am forever wanting to be staring into her eyes. Since the start I have never been able to get enough of looking at her, trying to make her stick. When we're apart I wonder sometimes did I dream her up, is she real at all? I get a fear in my heart, feel her slipping through my fingers, leaving me empty. Then I conjure her in my mind—those eyes, that smile that undid me. And I know I couldn't have imagined feeling like this. I tell myself she's real, she's real and she loves you.

"You have the most beautiful eyes I have ever seen and I don't believe for a second that I'm the only person who has noticed them," I say.

She stops and turns me to her, perhaps thinking of a kiss. But she can't get near me with the great donkey head in the way. We burst out laughing, which carries me away into a bit of donkey braying, which sets her off swooping round me, crying like a gull.

"Ah, Kitty Gorman, I love you."

"You couldn't just be shouting my name a bit louder now, could you?" she says.

"Oh, I forgot," I say, looking around, but there's no one in sight. "I'll have to be careful. You'll have to give me another name to be calling you for the rest of the day."

"What kind of a name?"

"A boy's name, you eejit, like a Wren Boy might be having."

"I don't know that I'm wanting a boy's name. But maybe a nickname. Yes, a nickname." She pauses. "Chancer."

"Chancer? Ah Jesus, Kitty, I can hardly be calling you that."

"Sure isn't it my choice? Chancer's what came in my head, and Chancer I will be."

I sigh. I know her in this mood and there will be no turning her from it. "So what about me? What shall my Wren Boy name be?"

"Well Frankie, of course," she says.

* * *

"We should put our masks back on," I say as we approach the last stretch into Dingle.

I have been barefaced for most of the journey from Ballyferriter, feeling too hot and closed in to be keeping the mask on for the walk. "Sure I'll be wearing it all the time once we're in Dingle," I said to Kitty when we got beyond Ballyferriter, and she nodded and followed suit. Though it delayed our progress, bare faces making it harder to resist the urge to be stopping every now and again for a kiss. And I had no will to resist, no wish to when there's nothing in the world I would rather be doing than kissing Kitty out in the open in the midst of God's creation.

I look up and down the road. There's not a sinner in sight. I pull Kitty towards me for a final kiss, letting my tongue linger, wanting her all over again. I hold her in my arms, looking again into her sparkling eyes, smiling.

We leap apart at the crunch of a twig. I stagger slightly at the edge of the ditch, looking around. But it's only a cow in the field, staring lazily at us before bending to tear at the grass.

"You should see your face," Kitty says, laughing. I put my mask back on to hide my embarrassment.

We pause at the crossroads on the edge of town.

"Which route shall we take—the top road or along by the water?" I say.

"Well, do you have a preference as to which Wren we join? The top road we're likely to catch up with the Goat Street Wren or maybe John Street. By the sea, it'll be the Quay Wren or the Green and Gold."

"Oh, let's try for the Green and Gold. They've always the best costumes."

"And the best party."

We have scarcely turned onto the lower road when there's a great roaring and cheering from somewhere behind us.

"Come on," Kitty says, "it'll be one of the Wrens on the way back from Lord Burnham's." She sets off at a run back towards the crossroads and onto the road towards Ventry. I follow, one hand holding on to my mask to stop it bumping up and down. As we get closer I can hear music beating out. And suddenly, in a burst of noise and colour, round the corner appears one of the Wrens.

"It's John Street," Kitty says, pointing at the red flag bearing the legend *Sráid Eoin* in blue. The flag is held aloft by a man wearing women's clothes, down to a red-and-blue-striped petticoat, his face smeared in black shoe polish, which is still not enough to obscure a great thicket of moustache on his upper lip. Alongside him capers a white hobbyhorse, worn on the shoulders of a tall, skinny man, its wooden jaws snapping open and shut in time to the music. A masked group of young lads follows close behind bearing a huge holly bush on a pole, lit up with bits of coloured cloth. I wonder if I might sneak a couple of ribbons off it later to give to Kitty. From where I stand at the side of the road I can see at least two dead wrens tied to the bush, their heads lying limp on their breast bones. Weaving round and about the holly bush and the hobbyhorse are two men in full straw suits, each of them carrying a bladder on a stick.

Beyond this front group is a rabble of men, numbering twenty or thirty, shouting, laughing and banging on drums. Among them is a core of players, mainly flute with the odd fiddle. They start a new tune and the voices of the Wren fill the air:

The wren, the wren, the king of all birds,
St. Stephen's day was caught in the furze,
Although he was little his honour was great
Jump up, me lads, and give him a treat.

Kitty and I join in on the chorus:

Up with the kettle and down with the pan
And give us a penny to bury the wren.

One of the straw men swoops towards us, whirling his bladder in our faces.

"Friend or foe?" he chants. "Friend or foe?"

I am transported for a second back to my childhood, a man like this diving into the crowd, dark eyes glittering behind his mask, bearing down on me. Clinging onto my father's leg, wailing, not wanting to be stolen away, people around me laughing.

"Friend," Kitty says, in a gruff voice. "Up John Street."

"Up John Street," he shouts, waving the bladder in the air and leaping off to jig round the hobbyhorse.

"Come on," Kitty says, falling into step with the John Street Wren. "This one's as good as any."

We carry on back to the crossroads and along the lower road past the wood, singing and shouting with the rest of the Wren. The day has brightened enough to see Beara on the other side of the bay. I hope the rain stays off.

As we get closer to town there are more people on the road. The lads with the wren-bush go up to them, accompanied by the straw men.

"A penny for the wren."

Those that give, receive a blessing and a feather plucked from one of the wrens for their trouble. Those that don't get a smack from a straw man's bladder.

"If I had a penny to my name, wouldn't I be spending it on food?" one woman says, her face flushed.

Prices are certainly higher at the market than they were last year. But most people are managing, bedded down for a lean year till the next crop. There's talk of public works in the spring for the worst off, maybe building roads. It won't come to that for us, though there's men like Peter Garvey might be glad of the work.

The musicians start up another Wren song:

Droleen, droleen, where is your nest?
'Tis in the tree that I love best
'Tis in the holly and ivy tree
Where all the birds come singing to me

As we reach the crowds on Strand Street, people on either side of the road clap along in time to the music. We pause outside Dan's Pub on The Mall, the haunt of the Green and Gold, battering out a racket on the drums. A few lighthearted insults are exchanged as some of their Wren come out to jeer at us, before we carry on to the end of the road, then right up John Street to Malone's Bar where we settle for a round of drinks.

The others are taking their masks off, making an easy path for the glass to their mouth. I lean towards Kitty, resting my donkey head on her shoulder, wanting my words close to her ear. "I could really be fancying a drink," I say quietly. "Do you think I could chance tilting the mask or would I be getting found out?"

"Say that again," she says. "I can't hear you with all this noise."

"Is there a way for me to risk having a drink?" I say.

"There's an answer to every dilemma."

She pushes through the crowd and into the pub, leaving me standing on my own.

Not for long. "Is that you, Muiris, under the mask?" It's one of the straw men, now unmasked, a red-haired man spattered with freckles even now in the middle of winter. "I might have known you'd be late."

Shite. Should I be Muiris or not? It'd help us be accepted if I play along, but if he starts asking me things only Muiris would know the answer to, I might be found out.

"Quite a turnout," I say, sidestepping the issue.

"'Tis," the straw man says. "Though we'll not be collecting our usual haul. Still, I'm sure we'll be getting enough for a good party tonight, isn't that right, Muiris?"

"My name's Frankie," I say.

"Frankie? Which Frankie is that?"

I am saved by Kitty's return with a pint of Guinness.

"This is Chancer," I say.

"Chancer who?" he says, his face suspicious.

"Chancer Doherty," she says, without so much as a moment's hesitation. "John Doherty's my great-uncle. I'm over staying with him, thought I'd see how you do the Wren in Dingle." Oh Jesus, why John Doherty? Everyone knows him.

"Ah, he's a great man, your uncle," Straw Man says, reaching out his hand.

"And you are?" Kitty says.

"Terry Kennedy."

"Good to meet you," Kitty says, shaking his hand. "I'll remember you to my great-uncle. You don't mind if I borrow Frankie here."

Whether he minds or not we're off into the pub. It's heaving inside, so packed you wouldn't hit the ground if you fell. She leads me over to the far corner.

"Ah Jesus, Kitty," I say. "I don't think this is too safe. He was on to me before you came back."

"Stop fussing, Frankie."

"How can I?"

"Why don't you have yourself a drink of Guinness?"

"You drink it," I say. "Then we should go."

"I bought it for us to share," she says, an edge to her voice. "And I've a pie ordered. Calm yourself."

I look around, seeing danger everywhere. "How am I to calm myself? The game's up if that straw man finds out you're nothing to do with John Doherty."

"Will you keep your voice down? I don't know what's got into you, but you'd better get it out again and quick. And just so as you're clear,

I have known John Doherty since I was a child. He'll swear anything I ask him, on a stack of ten Bibles if he has to."

She glares at me, eyes hardening behind her mask. I glare back. "Well how was I supposed to know that?"

"You could try trusting me," she says, her tone if anything harder and sharper.

I bite my lip. "I'm sorry."

She grunts, shaking her head. "And that makes it right, does it?"

I reach out and touch her arm. "I'm sorry," I say again. "I shouldn't have got so exercised."

She sighs. "Would you look at you, standing there with that big long donkey face? I suppose I'll have to forgive you," she says, softer now. "Here, have a drink of the pint."

I look round. The bar is so busy with men chatting and joking, I think they'd hardly notice if I stripped to my bare skin. I slip the mask up carefully, adjusting the angle to expose my mouth while keeping the rest of my face covered. I take a deep pull on the Guinness.

"Ah, that's good, Kitty," I say, savouring the strong bitter taste before handing it back.

"It's Chancer."

"Chancer," I say. "Sorry, I keep forgetting."

"You're not much of a one for the disguises, are you Frankie?"

I can see the sparkle in her eyes, gently mocking me. I shake my head. "No, I don't think I am."

"I'm glad," she says. "I wouldn't want you to be too good at playing games." She stares at me with a real warmth in her eyes now and I find myself smiling and blushing.

I watch as she takes a sup of the stout through a hole she's made in her mask, leaving behind a creamy moustache on her top lip. Her tongue slips out to lick it away and my body clenches as I am taken back to this morning, remembering it inside me.

"You'd think they were only out slaughtering the cow now, the time it's taking that pie to be ready," she says, glancing over to the bar.

"Shall I go and ask about it?"

"No, I'll go."

I watch her weave her way through the crowd towards the bar. She is back in five minutes.

"The cheating bastards," she says. "They said I never ordered a pie, that they serve them up at the time. And they weren't going to give me back my money until that straw man overheard and made them. But now I'm bloody starving."

"Drink up," I say, handing her the pint. "I'm sure we'll find something."

As we reach the door to the street, we are sucked back into the John Street Wren, gathering for another turn around the town. The crowd is thick as we make our way up Main Street, and it brings out a raucous singing from the Wren. The straw men are everywhere and the coins fairly rattle into the boys' caps as they chase down the money. It's as well that they caught more than one bird, for the first one's just a poor naked body now, every feather plucked and handed out. Other Wren Boys dash into the crowd to grab a girl and whirl her in a dance along the street, sometimes demanding a kiss to let go. As we climb the hill I see Peig up ahead and without pausing to think I pull her into a polka down the top of Green Street.

"Liam," she says. "Liam, that's not you, is it?"

I am chastened by her uncertainty, the confusion in her voice. "No, not Liam," I say, "but no one to fear."

She pulls me up short. "Frances, that's you, isn't it?" Her hand reaches for my mask but I dodge back into the Wren and weave my way quickly over to Kitty.

"Come on, let's get nearer the front," I say, wanting to put some distance between my sister and me. We nudge our way into the third row of marchers. "Oh, Jesus. Whatever possessed me?"

"Just as well for you it was only your sister you took for a dance," she says, laughing, "or you'd be feeling a peck of my beak."

"It upset her. I should have known it would. And then she realised it was me and I ran for it."

"You can trust Peig, she'll not tell on us."

"Is she following? You look."

Kitty peers into the crowds on either side. "There's no sign of her," she says.

"At least that's something. Oh, but I feel ashamed at carrying on like that. I've always hated how girls are thrown about the place on Wren Day."

"You were only having a bit of fun," Kitty says.

"I'm sure that's what the Wren Boys tell themselves."

We are interrupted by a wild neighing from the hobbyhorse, who breaks into a run down the hill, followed by the lads at the front. From the right, along Strand Street, another hobbyhorse appears.

"It's the Green and Gold," one of the straw men shouts. "Step on, we're marching Holy Ground first." He charges down Green Street, urging the rest of the Wren to hurry, and we are swept along by a surge from behind.

In front of us, the younger lads are shouting and clapping as the hobbyhorses battle, wooden jaws snapping as they push and shove for advantage.

"Make way for the Green and Gold," a tall man wearing a woman's wig roars, "the best Wren in the land."

"We will not make way," our hobbyhorse shouts back. "We were here first."

Another man, his face blacked up, steps out from the Green and Gold, a pitchfork in his hands. "You will make way," he says, swinging the fork at our hobby. With a sudden splintering of wood, our hobby's head is knocked sideways, wobbling for a moment before clattering to the ground. A great cheer goes up from our rivals.

"You cheating bastard," one of the straw men shouts, running forward and swinging his bladder on a stick at the pitchfork man. It glances against the man's cheek, but a bladder doesn't deliver much of a blow and he follows in with his fist.

The man puts his hand to his lip, pulls it away, registers blood. The pitchfork swings through the air, handle hitting the straw man hard on the left side of his head. The blow knocks off his mask, leaves a bloody wound on his temple. I watch him fall backwards, his skull hitting the kerb with a low *thud*, blood blossoming onto the road.

My heart is pounding with fear as the hobbyhorse bends down over Terry Kennedy's still form. He crouches there for a minute, blood beginning to stain his white outfit. Suddenly he lunges for the pitchfork man, grabbing him round the throat.

"You murderer," he screams, pushing him back against O'Connell's bakery. It is the last thing I see clearly as I'm knocked to the ground by a surge of our Wren behind me. My mask caves in, the wooden frame digging into my face as I fall forwards landing hard on my right knee. Above me, I feel feet kicking, fists thumping as the Wrens join in battle. A boot crushes down against my hand. Women are screaming, voices shouting.

A hand closes on my arm. Kitty bends over me, hauling me to my feet. "Come on." She drags me out of the thick of the fray, pulling me behind her around the edge of the warring factions, down Green Street. I stumble, barely able to see through my damaged mask, but not daring to take it off.

"Hurry," she says.

CHAPTER TWENTY-THREE

Hangtown, October 1849

I don't know how she can tell, but the minute I'm awake Goldie is on her feet and over to the bed, slobbering at my face.

"Get off," I say, laughing and putting my hand between her tongue and my cheek. She carries on licking, then clambers her front paws onto my bed. "No," I say, pushing her back down. "You can't be messing up Mammy's bed. You'll get us thrown out."

Gerry and I have taken rooms at Ruby's for a few days while we make our plans for the store. The bed is the most glamorous one I've ever seen—dark carved wood, white sheets, feather pillows and a deep red cover.

"Shall we get up then?" I say to Goldie, fondling her ear. She looks up at me, dark wrinkles where her brow furrows slightly. I cross to the window, twitching aside the curtains so that I can peer out. My room is at the back of the building, looking out onto the trees stretching up the hillside.

There's a knock at the door. "Mister Frank?"

I clamp my hands over my loose breasts in a panic, hoping I'll be left alone if I don't answer. But Goldie gives me away, rushing to the door, barking.

The knock comes again, but louder.

"Mister Frank? You ready for bath?"

The bath. Shite, I'd forgotten about that.

I dash back to the bed and throw myself in, pulling the blankets up to my chin.

"Goldie, settle," I say in my stern voice. She looks at me reproachfully, then retreats to her blanket. "Come in," I call.

The door is opened by a young Chinese woman. "Good morning, sir," she says, picking up two steaming pails of water and coming into my room. "My name Ai-Li. You sleep well?" She walks over to the bathtub in the far corner of the room and tips first one, then the second pail of hot water into it. The tub is the size of a short, deep horse trough, covered in black enamel embroidered with red roses linked by chains of gold leaves. I wonder if all tubs are so pretty.

"You want salts?" she says.

Salts?

"Erm, yes."

She takes a glass bottle filled with pale crystals from a deep pocket in her apron and shakes them into the water, filling the room with the smell of lavender. "I be back in minute," she says.

"I bet you've never had a bath, have you?" I say to Goldie. "No? Well me neither."

It seemed such a daring thing to do when Ruby's hotel manager asked if either of us wanted a bath.

"I'm definitely going to try one," Gerry said.

"And you're sure it's safe?" I said to him. "I heard tell they were after banning it some places."

He snorted. "Nonsense. A wealthy family I delivered to in New York had them all the time. Every day, I heard. And they were fit as fiddles."

And since I'm on the way to being a wealthy person and I didn't want Gerry thinking I was a-feared, I said I'd try one too.

It smells nice but it looks very hot. Surely that can't be good for the skin, or any other parts. Ai-Li returns with her two buckets, accompanied by another girl with two more.

"You want get in now?" she says. "We top up round you?"

Top up around me? Jesus, they can't be seeing me naked.

"Ah no, no, you're fine," I say. "I'll wait for you to finish."

"It get cold, Mister Frank," she says. "Better to get in."

"No," I say sharply, then recovering with a half laugh, "it'll be fine. I don't like it too hot," as if I were having baths all the time.

"I leave you soap," Ai-Li says, pointing to a small wooden table, set next to my bath. "Towel on top shelf of dresser. You want something else?"

"No, thank you. Thank you very much."

"Very well." She bows her head slightly and then leaves me to my lavender steam.

I slip out of bed and quickly go and lock the door. Then I heave the armchair over to block it. I should be safe now.

"Wish me luck," I say to Goldie, stripping off and walking over to the bath.

I dip my finger into the bath. It is hot, but not boiling. I take a deep breath and stick my right foot in the water.

"Ahhh." I hop away from the bath. My finger was lying. The water would roast you, melt the skin off your bones.

"Jesus," I say to Goldie. "Are they after killing me? This is the last bath I'll ever have. Wealthy people are full of shite. It'll be a jug, a bowl and a cloth from now on." Goldie pads over, her nails clicking on the wooden floor, and licks my bare leg.

"No, don't be doing that."

If I wasn't so dirty, I would give up on the bath. But it's five months now since I had a decent wash. Dirt has wormed into every wrinkle and crevice of skin, caked all round my toes, inside my elbows, underneath my breasts.

There is nothing for it. I put my foot back into the bath. It's not so hot now. Warm, very warm, but not hot. I step in with the other foot, spreading my toes, feeling the water between them, the slight grit of the salt beneath. I take a deep breath and sit down. The water laps up above my belly. I shuffle my arse forward, lowering my upper body into the warmth.

Oh it feels good, soft and gentle, caressing my skin, loving away my aches and pains. For some minutes I lie there, letting my mind float free, thinking nothing in particular.

Goldie brings me back to the present with a little yelpie pay-me-attention bark. I reach my hand out to stroke her. She snuffles it with her nose, then settles down next to the bath.

As the water begins to cool I duck my head under the surface, running my fingers through my hair, feeling the grit beneath the tips. I sit up, groping for the soap on the table. This is nothing like the coarse soap I used to make with my mother on the farm. It smells of lavender and something else, perhaps roses. I lather up and start to wash.

The water is scurfy, grimy and brown when I step out of the bath, but I feel fresh and clean. I rub my hair vigorously with the towel, then wrap it round my body. It is so much thicker and softer than anything I've ever known before, a soft golden colour with an elaborate red *R* embroidered in the corner.

"I think I'm converted," I say to Goldie. "These baths are a great thing. I'm going to have one when we build our house."

My new clothes are in the dark wooden dresser. I have lived my life in the hand-me-downs of my sisters and neighbours and in the discarded clothes of strangers. Today, for the first time, I'm putting on clothes that didn't belong to someone else before me. I bought them yesterday at a little shop Ruby told me about, Woolf's, off Main Street heading out to Cedar Ravine. Though the tailor's not so much a wolf as a rather fussy little dog. A bell clanged as we entered the shop and he emerged from a door behind the counter, a small, neat man with a balding pate, round, wire-framed glasses and pale, fluttering hands.

"How can I help you, gentlemen?" he said, in a clipped, sharp accent.

"We're after buying us some new clothes," Gerry said.

"Indeed," he said, with a brief look of distaste as he took in our shabby appearance—my cracked, mud-caked boots, snagged and grubby trousers, stained, fraying shirt, filthy nails. I stuck my hands in my pockets out of sight.

"Vich of you vill go first?" he said.

"He will," I said, pointing at Gerry.

I watched the pale hands flashing around Gerry, measuring his neck, his waist, his inside leg. His inside leg? Ah, no. Would he notice anything out of place? Or, more to the point, not in place? The thrift shops I've been to before haven't been caring about your inside leg. You bought as seen and sorted it out yourself. Jesus, being wealthy could be complicated. I was just thinking I should leave when Mister Woolf turned to me.

"Ah, no," I said, "there's no call to be measuring me. Sure I'm only a bit smaller than my friend there."

He gave a slight snort. "That vill be no good," and before I could say a word he was upon me. "I knew it," he said as he wrote down the measurements. "Your shape and size are completely different. You vill need quite different clothes."

He disappeared into the back of the shop and emerged with an armful of trousers, a pile of shirts and, to my relief, no dresses.

I open up the doors on Ruby's dresser. On the shelves inside I have laid out my clothes. Three white shirts, two of linen-cotton with buttons and fold-down collars, and one of pure cotton, with a keyhole neck. I cannot help but bury my face in the bright white smell of my shirt as I take it from the shelf and lay it out on the bed.

On the next shelf, a deep red silk cravat, charcoal waistcoat and three sets of undergarments. I slip into a new pair of white cotton drawers, pulling them up so the waistband settles softly against my belly.

Which trousers? The charcoal wool mix or the pale cotton drill? I hesitate for only a moment before picking up the drill. They've got a fly-front design, different to the flat-front I'm used to. I step into them, first my left foot, then my right. I leave them unbuttoned as I sit on the bed to put on my socks. My ankle is still bruised, but it has faded from purple-blue to a greenish brown-yellow. And the pain has mostly gone.

I take a fresh strip of cotton and bind my breasts, then slide an undershirt over my head. I unbutton my shirt, feeling the stiffness of the new buttons, then put it on and button it up again. I tuck it into my trousers, then button up my flies. Finally I pull on my new boots and run my hand through my damp hair.

"We're ready," I say to Goldie. "Let's go."

Goldie waddles down the stairs in front of me. She turns at the bottom to bark.

"Shush," I say.

"Would you like breakfast?" Clarice says, as I follow Goldie into the reception.

"Yes, please, but I need to take my dog out first."

Clarice stoops to fondle Goldie's head. "She is beautiful."

"Thank you," I say smiling, proud.

"Do you want to order now? I will 'ave it ready for when you get back."

"Oh, great. What do you have?"

"Anything you want. Eggs, bacon, bread, pancakes—"

"Pancakes, I'll have pancakes, please."

Goldie and I stroll up Main Street. To my delight she squats outside Sam's Stores. "Good girl," I say quietly. When she's finished we turn back towards Ruby's.

"Frank."

Looking up I see François, one of the Frenchmen from the river, walking towards me. My face breaks into a broad smile. "*Bonjour*," I say, dragging up one of the words I learned during our time on the riverbank. He kisses me on either cheek while I stand, wooden.

"Nice shirt. You look like you are being lucky."

I nod. "A bit. Enough for now. How about you—are you still at the riverbank?"

"*Oui*, but closer to 'angtown."

"So what are you doing in town today?"

"My 'andle broke," he says, showing me his shovel. The wood has split down the middle of the shaft. "I get a new one at Sam's Stores."

"You need to watch him. He's a trickster, that Sam."

"Trickster?"

"Ermm," I say, thinking for a word he'll know. "A liar, a cheat."

He shrugs. "I know."

I am tempted to blurt out our plans but Gerry and I agreed we'd try to keep them quiet. We don't want to alert Sam too soon.

"It's good to see you again, François. How about a drink on Friday? Gerry and I are staying at Ruby's."

"I would like that. Jacques and Alain also."

"Friday it is."

I carry on back to Ruby's, Goldie at my heels. We make our way through the kitchen garden at the rear of the hotel. It's full of all sorts of plants, most of which I don't recognise. There's a coop in the far corner but to my relief Goldie shows no interest in the eight or nine chickens scratching around in the dirt. She trots up the steps behind me and flops down on the back porch. I leave Goldie where she is and make my way into the residents' dining room. Gerry is sitting by the window overlooking the garden. His new blue shirt looks well on him; in these months of dirt and exhaustion I'd forgotten how handsome he is. His face is animated as he talks to Ruby, who's sitting opposite him. I falter, not sure whether I should interrupt them, but Gerry looks up and calls me over.

"You'll never guess what, Frank. Ruby is getting supplies all the time from San Francisco. Marco's going next week. I can travel with him and he'll introduce me to all the contacts."

He looks as pleased with himself as if he'd just invented storekeeping. I stare at him, still standing. *Don't tell anyone anything*, he said. *We must keep our plans to ourselves.* Now here he is cooking up deals with Ruby.

"Sit yourself down, Frank," Gerry says.

Ruby gets up. "Perhaps I should leave you to talk."

CHAPTER TWENTY-FOUR

Dingle, December 1845

I pelt along Strand Street, the roar of the riot at my back, ahead the grey blur of Kitty's shirt. There are people all around, women and children wanting away. I stumble, falling over a girl that's tripped ahead of me. Stooping, I drag her free of the feet pounding out of Dingle.

I pause at the side of the road, scanning the crowd ahead for Kitty. I crane my neck, looking and looking. I wish I could take off the mask; I can't see properly and my face is hot, so hot. Where is she?

I plunge back into the throng, pushing past people, searching for Kitty. I'm out beyond the harbour, the wood on my right, sea on my left. The crowd's thinner here but still I don't see her. A stitch is forming in my side. I start to slow down. Barely running now. Stopping.

I stand in the middle of the road, my hand pressing on the pain in my side, sucking in great breaths of air, wondering what to do. I'm safer out of Dingle but I don't want to leave without Kitty.

Or Peig. Jesus, I can't believe I forgot about her. I've got to go back.

A whistling maid and a crowing hen. My mother says they're always bad luck. We should never have done it, passing ourselves off as Wren Boys. Then we'd have been nowhere near the fight. And we'd have been with Peig; all three of us would be safe.

I hurry towards Dingle, trying to dodge the people coming in the opposite direction.

"Frankie! Frankie!"

Peering through my broken mask, I see Kitty running towards me. She throws her arms around me, clattering against my mask and battering it further out of shape.

"Oh, thank God," she says. "I was so—"

"Have you seen Peig?"

"I haven't. The—"

"I have to go back. I have to find Peig."

"It's too dangerous."

"My little sister's back there," I say, my voice rising. "I can't leave her."

"Please, Frankie, think. Peig was at the top end of Green Street. She'll have got away by the top road. You'll never get to her up Green Street."

"I've got to try."

"Listen to me," she says, grabbing my arm, holding me back. "Our best chance is out to the crossroads. You won't get through if you go back, and you might get us killed trying."

I take one last look along the road back into Dingle. "Come on, then," I say, turning and setting off towards the crossroads.

There's a thin drizzle falling. I wish I could have the wetness on my bare face; my head feels like it's been baked in the fire. A sickness rises in me. I remember Peig going missing as a child, hardly past toddling, everyone out searching, my mother hysterical. I found her playing with a kitten in one of the top fields. Completely content, singing away to the little creature, in a world of her own. My mother wept with joy when I brought her home. I don't know how she'd ever survive the loss of Peig, how she'd ever forgive me for not looking after her.

It's not long to the crossroads. People are flooding along the top road, away from Dingle. I try to search among them for Peig but the mask is in my way. I scramble up the grassy bank above the road and take it off, hoping that people will be in too much of a hurry to notice me. At least I can see properly now. But I don't see Peig. Kitty joins me scanning the crowds. There's no sign of my little sister.

"I don't know how I could have left her," I say. "What kind of a sister am I?"

"Oh Frankie, what else could you do? We'd never have got back up the hill to her. And you could have been killed trying. I'm sure Peig is safe."

"So why isn't she here?"

"She's probably gone on home. We should go too," she says.

"But Peig might come any minute."

"I think she'll have gone already. We can't stay here. If that fella's dead, someone'll have to pay for it. The police will be looking for people in costumes. Please Frankie. There's nothing more you can do."

We wait a while longer before I finally turn away from Dingle. The light's beginning to fade and the rain's coming on hard now. Wren Day's supposed to brighten up these dark December days. Now there's a man dead, who knows how many injured. And my sister's missing.

We walk towards Ventry in silence. The light's gone by the time we reach the turnoff for the road back to Ballyferriter and the scalp. I speak at last. "I have to go home. I have to know she's safe."

"I know," Kitty says. "But look out for yourself too. You can blame me for the dressing up if it helps."

"I'll do no such thing. We were in this together, Kitty Gorman."

"I don't want you to be in trouble."

I shake my head, past caring about it. "Are you safe on your own?" I say, suddenly imagining her journey on the road over the mountain in the darkness.

"Many's the night I've walked this road alone before I met you."

"Why don't you come with me?" I say, needing to know she's not in danger. "There's room enough for you to stay."

"I don't know, Frances," she says. "Your mother and father will be angry enough without me landing up on your doorstep."

"They won't care about that," I say. "Please come. I don't want to be parted."

She stands there thinking for a long time. "I don't know," she says, at last. "Surely it will make things worse?"

"Please."

At last, with a brief nod of her head, she agrees to my request.

"Thank you," I say, squeezing her hand.

"Well, what's keeping you then?" she says, turning away and starting out along the road to Dunquin.

It's a grim journey, dark and wet, full of fear about Peig and half-formed thoughts about how I'm to explain why Kitty and I ended up in the middle of a Wren Boy riot. There's a silence between Kitty and me that I'm not used to and don't know how to break.

My boots have long since seen their best days and are leaking badly as we finally pass the first of the cottages on the edge of the village. I've my mask back on but there's hardly a sinner about—only Mick Malone staggering along Main Street. He stops and stares as we make our way past him. Music drifts up from the shebeen on the road towards the harbour. It seems out of place for people to be enjoying themselves after all that's happened today.

I take my mask off as we turn away from the village and onto the track up towards the house. It feels like forever since I set off this morning.

"Not long now," I say.

"No," Kitty says.

"I hope she's there."

"She will be."

My left boot has started to make a squelching sound with each step.

"What are you going to say about us?" Kitty says.

"I don't know. Maybe they'll just be glad to see us, especially if Peig's told them about the riot. And if they're angry, I'll say…I'll say I thought girls could be Wren Boys too."

"Well there's a clue there in the name," she says. On another day we'd both have laughed but her tone is sharp.

"What are you worrying about? My mother's always thought you're halfway to sainthood. It's me will be in trouble."

"Oh, Frances, do you understand nothing? Do you really think they'll be leaving you free to be going wherever you please after this? It'll be the end of nights away at the scalp. Maybe they'll stop you seeing me altogether."

I stop, taking hold of her arm. "Nothing could keep me from you now."

"I'm scared. I might lose you if we stroll in there without a plan."

Kitty's right. I shouldn't have brought her home with me. It would have been easier to make up a lie if I were on my own. "It's my ma we need to worry about," I say. "My da will think it's funny, but she won't. She can't abide being lied to. And the idea that we planned it will be one big lie to her."

"Well then let's not tell her it was planned. Let's say it was just spur of the moment. A dare that got out of hand."

"But how will we explain the costumes?"

"We'll say we found them and thought it would be a fine laugh to dress up in them."

"Oh, I don't know, Kitty. She'll want to know where we were finding two Wren Boy costumes. And she'll think it was stealing that we took them."

She's quiet for a moment. "My brothers," she says. "They were in the Wren. We'll say these are their old costumes. We found them in my house and couldn't resist trying them on."

"Jesus," I say, half laughing. "That might just about work."

We hug each other briefly, trusting the darkness to keep us safe, then carry on up the hill towards the house. There's a light at the window of the kitchen, warming the dark evening. I'll be glad to get in and get this over with.

"Ready?" I say to Kitty.

She nods.

I open the door and let myself into the kitchen. It's warm, a fire glowing in the grate. But there's no one there to enjoy it. The quiet unnerves me.

"Ma? Da?" I shout. But there's no answer. "Where is everyone?" I say to Kitty. "Why aren't they here?"

"I don't know," she says.

"Peig must have been hurt. Why else would my parents be gone? What if she's…" I start to cry.

Kitty puts her arm round me. "Come and sit down," she says, guiding me over to the settle. "Maybe it's not as bad as you think. Maybe they've all gone out. She mightn't be hurt at all."

I shake my head. "I knew it. Right from the moment I realised I'd left her behind. I knew then something terrible had happened to her. We should never have dressed up. Everyone says it's bad luck for a woman to take on a man's ways."

"Oh, Frankie, you can't be thinking that. The fighting was nothing to do with us."

"But if we hadn't been dressed up, we'd have been with Peig and she would've been safe."

I stare into the fire, imagining Peig, her head covered in blood, wondering what to do. I can't just sit here. "I think we should get changed and go out searching," I say, standing up.

"My dress is back at the scalp."

"There's an old one Marie left behind when she got married. You can wear that."

We take the lamp through to the bedroom. I root in the chest at the bottom of the bed for Marie's dress.

"Maybe we should hide the costumes," Kitty says, after we've changed.

"We can put them in the old cabin on the way out."

Kitty comes over to stand next to me as I sit by the kitchen fire, tying my soggy boots back on. I feel her fingers in my hair and pause, nuzzling in against her leg. She crouches down in front of me, looking into my face, leaning forward to kiss me. She pulls away suddenly, overbalancing and falling onto her back on the floor in front of the fire. Behind me, I hear the door close. Kitty struggles to get up as I turn, dreading my mother's face. But it's not Ma, it's Peig, dripping water all over the floor. I jump to my feet, rushing over to her.

"Oh Peig, thank God, thank God. Are you hurt?"

She shakes her head but starts to cry.

"You're safe now," I say, putting my arms round her.

She pulls away. "It's Liam," she sobs. "He's been arrested for murder."

CHAPTER TWENTY-FIVE

Hangtown, October 1849

The first thing I'm aware of as I wake is a rough dryness in my mouth, the second a warm wetness between my legs. Squeezing my thighs tight together, I ease my way out of the bed, praying there's no damage.

"Ah Jesus," I say, looking at the blood on the bottom sheet. I sway slightly, feeling the effects of last night. "Not today."

I didn't mind my monthly bleeds when I was a girl. But since becoming Frank they've been a torture to me, forever checking for a show of blood. Usually I'm so careful, packing plenty of wadding into my undergarments when I know it's due. I count back through the dates in my head to the last one. Three weeks ago. It has no business coming again already.

"Not now," I say sharply to Goldie as she sniffs along my thigh. She slinks back to her blanket, furrowing her brow in a look of reproach. I fumble for a rag to wipe away the blood trickling down my thigh, then press it tight against me.

I look again at the sheets and groan. Sinking to the floor, I curl up on my side, rag still in place. I'm so tired of pretending all the time, so tired of being something I'm not, never wanted to be. My womb aches, my back aches, my head's pounding, my stomach's churning.

Goldie pads over, nuzzling my neck, then lies down next to me. I reach my hand out to stroke her silky ear.

"Poor mammie," I say.

The floor is hard but Goldie is soft and warm. I feel better lying here next to her. The room is steady, unlike last night. I half remember staggering across to the bed. Then nothing. My clothes are folded neatly across the chair though I don't remember taking them off. I had on my light-coloured flat-fronted trousers. Just as well my bleed didn't start last night.

I sit up suddenly. It didn't, did it? I struggle across the room to the chair. Lifting up my trousers, I check the area between the legs. No stains, thank God. My secret's safe. But I have to sort out the sheet. What I need is water and something to scrub with. A glass stands next to a small water jug on the nightstand. It's never enough to sort out my sheets. Jesus, why couldn't it have been a little show, instead of this huge great bleed? You'd think someone had cut me open. I pour myself a glass of water, sipping it as I think about what to do.

Maybe I could disguise it as something else. I could cut my arm with my knife and say that's what caused the blood. But why would I have had a knife in bed with me? Perhaps I could make myself sick over it, I feel ill enough that I'm sure it wouldn't be hard. But how would I ever face Ruby again?

A knock disturbs my pondering.

"Frank, it's Gerry. Can I come in?"

"Hold on a minute," I say, pulling on an old pair of drawers and slipping my white shirt over my head. I unlock the door and ease it open.

"Jaysus, you look shocking," Gerry says.

"Thanks," I say, looking at his washed-out face. "You've looked better yourself."

He gives a rueful smile. "I think I maybe had a glass too many."

"A glass? More like a bottle."

"Still it was a great night," he says. "They're good company, those Frenchmen."

"Bear Man too."

"Did you see the way he threw that gobdaw out the door? Jaysus, just lifted him clear off his feet and slung him like a sack of spuds."

I had forgotten all about the fight. It happened after the show finished and the waitresses were busy among the crowds, serving drinks and taking orders. Through the noise I heard a man's voice. "You ready to suck my cock again, whore."

I turned to look at the speaker, a thin, dark-haired man, sitting at the neighbouring table. His hand was on Clarice's neck, pushing her head downwards. I was starting to my feet but Bear Man beat me to it, pushing the man's hand away from Clarice. He pulled the creep to his feet, huge hand closing round his throat.

"You apologise to the lady, mister," Bear Man said.

The man clawed ineffectually at the great mitt clamped round his throat.

"Apologise," Bear Man said as the man's face began to purple.

I stood beside Bear Man, wanting to help, but misunderstanding me he growled, "Stay out of this, Frank."

"I'm on your side," I said, "but you need to loosen your grip if he's going to be able to say sorry."

"What?" he said. "Oh, right." He shifted his hand from the man's throat to the top of his shirt, drawing his other back in a great fist ready to strike.

The man was gasping for air, face full of shock, fear and a note of anger, dark red finger marks already showing on his throat.

"Apologise to the lady," Bear Man said.

"It does not matter," Clarice muttered, her head down.

"This lowlife insulted you, of course it matters," Bear Man said.

"Ain't no insult if it's true," Lowlife said, forgetting too soon the hand round his throat. "She's a whore. Fucked her myself over at Sutter's Fort."

A roar emitted from Bear Man as he smashed his fist hard into Lowlife's face.

"Apologise!"

Blood from his cut, swelling lip was seeping onto Lowlife's teeth as he finally said to Clarice, "I'm sorry, ma'am," though a sneer lingered in his voice on the final word. Clarice nodded, not looking at any of us, face flushed, then hurried away.

"Hell, that wasn't so hard now, was it?" Bear Man said. "You take my advice and get your sad, pathetic self outta this town." With that Bear Man dragged him to the door and threw him into the street.

Gerry dumps my clothes on the floor and sits down on my chair. "I tell you, Frank, I'll be careful what I say round Bear Man in future. Especially about women. That maggot didn't know what hit him."

"He deserved it."

"So you don't think it was true, what he was saying about Clarice?"

On the contrary, I do think it was true. I saw her face when he mentioned Sutter's Fort, I could feel the shame coming off her. Poor woman. I wonder if Ruby knows.

"I don't know," I say to Gerry, not wanting to discuss it. "Anyway I've no time now to be contemplating it. We've plenty to do before you get off to San Francisco. And since you're already dressed, you can do me a favour. Go and get me a jug of water and plenty of salt."

"What for?"

"Never you mind."

While he's gone I strip the bloody sheet from the bed and make the rest up neat as could possibly be. With any luck the maid won't bother doing it again herself. Which will give me the chance to soak the sheet. My mother swore by cold, salty water for shifting bloodstains. I hide the bloody sheet in the cupboard for now, then sit down on the chair and sip at the last of the water. I still feel shocking. It'll be a day or two before I drink again.

Gerry is back soon. "Here's your water and your salt," he says.

"Thanks. I won't be long. Why don't you go and order us the biggest breakfast you can think of and I'll be along shortly."

I have a quick wash, focusing on the important places, but making sure to leave plenty of water in the jug. I add a good dose of salt, then put it on the middle shelf of the cupboard. I bunch up the bloody bit of the sheet and dip it into the salty water, swirling it around, then leaving it to soak. With any luck, a few hours will lift the stain.

"So what have you ordered?" I ask Gerry when I join him in the dining room.

"I pushed the boat out," he says. "Bread rolls, toast, butter, jam, cheese, and a Hangtown Fry."

"Hangtown Fry? I've never heard of it."

"Do you remember that first time we were here there was a miner wanting the most expensive meal possible? The chef invented the Hangtown Fry—oysters and bacon fried up with eggs."

"Ah Jesus, Gerry, are you sure that was a good idea? We're both a bit fragile this morning."

He laughs as he leans forward to pour me a coffee. "Here, this will help with the hangover."

The coffee is strong and bitter but welcome.

"What time are you setting off?" I ask.

"About eleven. There's plenty of time. I thought we might go and have another look at our plot."

We decided on it yesterday, a great site at the start of Main Street on the way into town, flat, with plenty of space to expand.

I smile. "I'd like that. Have you had any thoughts about a name?"

"Nothing beyond Frank & Gerry's. How about you?"

Unbidden, Kitty comes to my mind, burning my throat, prickling my eyes. This might have been our store.

"What is it?" Gerry says.

I shake my head.

"You were thinking about her, weren't you?"

I don't answer.

"I'll leave the name to you," he says. He pours himself another cup of coffee. "I'm glad we've found a site. I'll be able to imagine you here, getting on with building our store ready for the goods I'll be sending on from San Francisco. We're a good team."

I nod. We have spent nearly every minute of the last seven months together. He is my brother. We niggle and fight, but I love him. "Be careful, Gerry. Don't forget everything I taught you with the guns and the knife."

"I won't," he says.

"Keep them on display at all times, especially your new pistol."

"I will."

"And make sure you keep the guns clean, you never know—"

"Enough, now. Stop your fussing. You're like a mother hen."

"I'm just worried about you. It's rough country between here and San Francisco."

"I'll be fine," he says. "Sure won't I be with Marco?"

Marco works for Ruby, keeping the restaurant and hotel well supplied. He couldn't look more different to Gerry, a big boulder of a man with missing teeth, a scar stretching from his cheekbone into his lip, great big meaty fists. He's done the journey to San Francisco a hundred times.

"Well make sure you do what he tells you," I say.

"Enough." He looks up. "Here's the food."

"God, Gerry, there's enough here to feed half of Hangtown," I say as Ai-Li brings plate after plate to our table.

He laughs. "Sure did you not tell me to order the biggest breakfast I could think of?"

"I don't know where to start."

"Start with the special, the Hangtown Fry," a woman's voice says. I look up to see Ruby, her deep red blouse revealing a triangle of golden skin. "Do you mind if I join you?"

"Not at all," Gerry says as I drop my knife. Leaning over to retrieve it I bang my head on the corner of the table. Jesus, it hurts.

"I think you might still be drunk," Gerry says.

"I'm fine," I say, resisting the urge to rub my poor sore head. I shovel some egg, bacon and a couple of oysters onto my fork and transfer it to my mouth. "Oh, I like this. If it doesn't make me feel better, I don't know what will."

"I hear you were celebrating last night."

"Oh, indeed we were," Gerry says. "We met up with our French friends from the river. And with Bear Man. I think you know him?"

She nods. "Yes, of course."

"Did you hear about the trouble? Bear Man threw some fella clear into the street for insulting Clarice," Gerry says.

"How is she?" I say.

She hesitates for a moment. "Clarice is used to the insults of miners. I hope this does not spoil your night."

"Ah, no," Gerry says, "we had a great night, a real celebration. We've found a plot for the store—near where The Gold Bar is."

"Congratulations. You should do well there. I tell Marco to help you as much as he can in San Francisco."

"Thank you so much," I say. "You've been very kind to us."

"Is nothing," she says, smiling. She looks at me for a long moment, her eyes on my hairless face. She knows. I'm sure she knows.

CHAPTER TWENTY-SIX

Dunquin, February 1846

"At least it's not raining," I say as we walk to market.

"Mmm," Peig grunts.

"And mild for February."

She doesn't even grunt this time. She's changed these weeks since the Wren Day riot. Liam's still locked away, him and eight other Wren Boys, all charged with murder. The police don't even have the real culprit. Cormac Walsh his name is, so the talk in the market says, and he's long gone from Dingle, away on his toes the day of the riot.

"I'm sure they'll find Cormac Walsh soon," I say.

"The trial's only a month away. A month, Frances. And they'll hardly be finding him when they're not even looking."

"The truth'll come out in the end. And then Liam's sure to be released."

"The truth's been out there for weeks. It's made no difference. The police don't care whose neck gets stretched."

She lapses back into silence. We've been over this before. And always we end up in the same place, no nearer helping Liam. Maybe we should stop talking about it.

"I told Kitty we'd meet her later," I say.

"You go."

"Ah Peig, you can't be hiding yourself away from everyone."

"I don't want to see anyone but Liam. And the next time I do, he could have a rope around his neck." She starts to sob. "I love him, Frances," she says through her tears. "We were going to get married. He was planning to ask Da, once he'd a bit of money saved."

I knew she was keen on Liam, but this is the first time she's mentioned marriage. She really has grown up. It'll be Lizzie next. And then there'll only be me left at home. The spinster daughter. Nothing unusual in that. But the spinster daughter and her very close spinster friend? How long will it take my mother to work out where my heart lies when the others aren't there to distract her?

* * *

There's already a crowd gathered in the churchyard as we make our way down for Saint Gobnait's Pattern Day. I walk at the back with Peig, my mother in front, arm in arm with Lizzie, my da striding out ahead, greeting our neighbours.

"Do you have your votive with you?" I ask Peig.

It was my idea to make an offering for Liam on Saint Gobnait's Day. In weeks of thinking, this is the best I've come up with—prayer. At least it's given Peig something to do. She took a while last night deciding on the wording. But once she had it settled, she wrote her prayer out on a card of Saint Patrick.

Blessed Saint Gobnait, healer of the sick, friend to the needy, I pray for you to watch over the life of Liam O'Connell and bring him safely through his trial.

"It's in my pocket," Peig says.

I give her arm a squeeze. "I need to have a word with Peter Garvey," I say. "Will you manage without me for a minute or two?"

I weave my way through the crowd, nodding and smiling to friends and neighbours as I pass them. There's always a good turnout but it seems busier than ever this year. There's hardly a soul in the parish not here. Peter's standing near the church door, Malachy in his arms. The lad's face is wan and thin, none of the plump little cheeks he used to have.

"No Mary today?" I say.

"She's up above with Dominic. He's a bit of a cough."

"How was Killarney?"

"It's too busy a place for me. But I think Ellen will settle well enough in service."

"She must have been glad of you taking her."

"I'd never have heard the end of it from Mary and her mother if I hadn't."

"I know you, Peter. You wouldn't have rested yourself."

"I was glad to go, right enough. It's good to see her safe. I'm telling you, Frances, I saw people on the route that were barely hanging on by the skin of their teeth. Far worse off than we are."

We're silent for a minute as I try to find the words for what I wanted to say to him.

"I've been meaning to call in," I say at last. "I was wondering if you might be needing any seed potatoes."

He flushes and drops his eyes. I feel for him, standing there, covered in shame, like it's his own fault his potatoes rotted.

"We've enough," I say to him in a rush. "We didn't lose that many to the blight."

His eyes are still on the ground, his toe working round a big stone, trying to loosen it. He doesn't speak, not for a while. "I never wanted it to come to this. Not able to support my own family, relying on the charity of my neighbours."

I thought it would be easier coming from me rather than my da, but still his pride sits between him and help.

"It's not charity, Peter," I say. "It's friends helping each other out."

"And what can I do to help you out in return?"

I can almost taste his bitterness in my own mouth. "I know that you'd help me and mine if we ever needed you."

His body droops a little as a great sigh slips from between his lips. He shifts the child to his other shoulder. Finally he nods. "If I have to have help from someone, I'd sooner it was you."

I can't help the smile that breaks out across my face. I've been worried about the Garveys, living on air for weeks now.

He has his old energy back suddenly. "I'll get them planted and then I'm planning to go to England for work. I can send money back for my family. You'll keep an eye on Mary while I'm away? And my boys?"

"Of course. You know I love Mary, and sure who wouldn't love these fine boys of yours? And I'm their godmother besides. Of course I'll look out for them."

"I appreciate your help. You and your da's."

Behind us the church door opens.

"Looks like we're near ready to go," Peter says.

"Ah, I better dash. I promised Peig," I say. "Tell Mary I'll be over tomorrow."

I jink my way back through the crowd, whispering "sorry" and "excuse me" till I reach my family. I turn to face the priest, who's standing on the steps of the church. He holds a jar of honey, symbol of Saint Gobnait, keeper of bees, healer of the sick. To one side, two men hold a wooden figurine of Gobnait. She's hundreds of years old, carved from a single piece of yew, a luscious brown, polished up with beeswax till she gleams. Her face wears a calm, gentle expression, serene I suppose, even though there's a snake curled around her feet. Mind you, everyone knows that Saint Patrick banished the last snake from Ireland before she was even born. She's standing on a beehive, arms held out in front of her, offering help to all who need her. I have always loved this statue.

"We are gathered here today," the priest begins, "to mark the Pattern Day of Saint Gobnait, our very own saint. Gobnait performed countless miracles of healing here in Dunquin, using honey like we have in this jar and water drawn from her holy well down below us.

"I call upon Saint Gobnait to aid us in these days of hunger and injustice. Heal our blighted potatoes and give us a good harvest. Look after our faithful children in Dunquin.

"In the name of the Father, and of the Son, and of the Holy Ghost. Amen."

"Amen," we chorus.

He turns his back on the crowd, positioning himself on the far side of the statue, then stepping forward to begin the rounds. Slowly we move off along the path through the churchyard to a wrought-iron archway, following the priest, the statue and the jar of honey, echoing his prayers for healing and help. Through the archway and down to the well, the whole congregation following and praying, watching the statue swaying back and forth on the shoulders of the two men.

The congregation stands back as the priest and the elders make their way round the well, clockwise, always clockwise, no need for bad luck here, no wish for blasphemy.

Round the well once.

Twice.

Three times.

A wooden cup sits beside the well. The priest dips it into the water, then scatters the contents on the ground in front of him.

"I offer this sacred water to the earth, which our Father in heaven created for us."

He dips the cup back into the well and takes a sup from it. "This is holy water," he says, "healing water. Let any of you who wish to be healed come forward."

Slowly people make their way to the front, circling the well three times, then crossing themselves before sipping from the wooden cup. Peig is one of the first to go forward. I watch her slip off to the tree behind the well and tie a rag to one of its branches. I look away, out to sea, over towards the Blaskets. Some of the islanders have come over for the ceremony, filling bottles with well water to keep their boats safe for the year.

At last I make my way round the well myself, taking my sup of water, praying that Liam be set free and our crops be safe this year. The tree behind the well is fluttering now with countless ribbons and rags, the ground below strewn with saints' cards, rosaries and all manner of offerings to the Saint to help her needy flock.

There are only a few people left wanting to take the water. I watch as Peter does his rounds with little Malachy. He nods at me before leaving. But I am not ready to go yet. I stand for a while, looking out to sea, taking in its steely green, the dashes of white, feeling the edge of wind beginning to bite my skin. A rag comes loose and whips past my face, blowing away in the air, out to sea. Finally I turn away, walking back up the hill, climbing towards home.

* * *

"I'm going over to the Garveys," I say after breakfast on Thursday morning. I'd meant to go over yesterday but the rain was too hard and heavy. It's a better day today. Still no sign of the sun, but the sky's a lighter grey, not the dark that closed in over us on Tuesday evening. It rained like it would never stop, drumming on the roof as I lay in bed, battering away all day yesterday. It kept us all at home—my ma spinning, Da whittling, Peig fretting and Lizzie moping. I sat by the hearth, knitting a blanket to sell at the market. I like to knit, the *click-clack* of the needles, the fabric growing beneath your hands, spreading onto your lap.

And it gives you time to think, to dream. I imagined the blanket was for Kitty and me to snuggle under in our own cabin, a proper place with our own kitchen, our own hearth, a big comfy bed, a shed for our animals out the back, a few acres for our crops. I would see her every day, go to sleep with her every night, wake up with her every morning.

How lucky men are that they can live out their life with their sweetheart. That they can marry her, settle down with her, farm their patch, raise their children. And that everyone is happy for them when they do. It'll never be like that for me, I'll never get to live with Kitty.

But at least I have the days when we escape to the scalp. Tomorrow night. We will be together then, after the market. And maybe I could go and see her today, if the weather doesn't turn again. Yes, I'll go today, after I've been to see Mary.

The stream's gushing as I make my way along the track towards the Garveys'. The ground's wet and my boots are leaking already. I shouldn't complain, at least I have boots. We're better off than most— more land, bigger house. And we were luckier with our potatoes, lost fewer in the field, none in the store, plenty of seed for planting next month. I'm glad Peter will take some from us. I wonder if he *will* go away once they're sown.

The chickens are pecking in the yard as I open the gate and make my way up to the Garvey's cabin. I knock on the door and turn the handle. It won't open. Something's blocking it on the other side. I push harder but it still won't open.

"It's Frances," I call out.

"Go away," a voice calls back.

"Mary, is that you?"

"Go away," she calls again. "You're not safe. We've…" Her voice breaks.

I stand in the pause, waiting for her to go on, dreading her words.

"We've got the fever."

I want to run, get away while I can. But these are my friends. I force my feet to hold the ground.

"Are you sure?" I say.

"The twins, Peter, they're burning. My ma's got the cough."

"What about you?" I say.

"I'm fine, so far. But if they've got it…" She starts to cry. "My boys. What am I going to do for my boys?"

"Oh, Mary."

"You should go. I don't want you getting sick."

"I'm away to fetch my ma, she'll know what to do."

The chickens scatter as I dash through the yard and out the gate, clattering it behind me, running for home. This fever's come on quick. I only saw Peter two days ago and there was no sign of it. I burst through the door into our kitchen.

"Jesus, Frances," my ma says. "What kind of a way is that to come in a door?"

"The Garveys have got the fever," I say, panting from the pace I've come across the track.

"Who told you this?" Ma says, standing up from her spinning wheel.

"Mary. I was just up with her. She says they've got the fever. Peter, the twins, her ma."

"Did you touch her? Did you touch any of them?" Her voice is urgent. It has me terrified. My mind is whizzing from the exchange at Mary's door to Tuesday at Saint Gobnait's.

"I put my hand on Peter's arm," I say. "At the Pattern Day." I feel my skin prickle with fear. "But he was fine then."

"How are you feeling? Have you been coughing?"

She puts her hand to my head. "You're hot. But most likely it's from the running."

I can feel the tears gathering. I touched him.

"I'll make you a tonic with some of Gobnait's water," my mother says. "And you should rest for a day or two. Peig can go to the market on her own tomorrow." She's not a toucher, my ma, not of me anyway. But her voice is soft, reassuring.

"I said I'd go back up. I told Mary you'd know what to do."

She sighs. "You can't be going. I'll do what I can for them. It'll depend what breed of fever they have. And whether God wants them now or not. Have they a rash?"

"I don't know. I didn't ask."

"Is there diarrhoea or just the burning?"

I shake my head, feeling stupid, useless.

"I don't suppose you know whether they've any food in the house?" she asks.

"I didn't check. But they've barely had a thing for weeks."

"Well, we'd best make a stirabout. For Mary at least. Then I'll away up to their cabin."

I mix a few handfuls of oats with some water and put it over the fire to cook while my mother bustles about, packing her bag with willow bark, eggs, dried nettles and who knows what else.

"I'll finish that," she says as the stirabout starts to thicken. "Away you and get the long-handled spade."

I stare at her.

"I can't be touching them, Frances. I'll need the spade to hand things through the window."

I hear my da singing in the field above as I make my way up to the shed. I can't make out the song. His gift isn't in his voice, even though he loves to sing while he's working. I wonder should I go and tell him about the Garveys. But my ma looked nearly ready to go and she's not a woman to keep waiting. She's sat on the stool by the front door when I return with the spade.

"Would you look at the muck on that?" she says. "How am I to be using it to hand anything in?"

"Sorry," I mumble, wiping the spade on the damp ground as best as I can.

She stands up, checking my forehead again with the back of her hand. "You feel cooler now. Hopefully it was only the running around."

I nod, relieved. "I don't want you going up to the Garveys on your own. I'm well enough to come."

"No," she says, sharp. "No, you're to stay here and rest. I can manage fine without you." Her tone is final. She hooks the pot of stirabout onto the end of the spade, picks her basket up with her other hand and sets off across the track.

I sit down on the stool but I can't settle. What if I do have the fever? I don't want everyone else getting sick because of me. Maybe I should go away for a while. I could go to the scalp, stay there till I'm sure I'm not a danger. But then I'd have to tell everyone about the scalp and I don't want to do that.

Maybe the shed would be far enough, I could sleep in with the animals. It did us fine when I was a child.

I don't know what to do for the best. I put my head in my hands and let the tears flow. I'm still sitting there when my mother returns.

"There's only prayer will help them now," she says. "They've got the typhus."

CHAPTER TWENTY-SEVEN

Hangtown, October 1849

It is almost dark as I finish work for the day. Everything aches—my back, my legs, my arms. I have worked as hard the last week as ever in my life. "Find good builders," Gerry said. Jesus, finding any would be a start. Whatever they did before, men in Hangtown have one occupation now—digging for gold.

I'm living in a large tent pitched at the front of our plot. It will be the display area and entrance for the store once it's built. I have swapped the hotel's wonderful bed for a narrow cot, the bath for a bowl, the wardrobe for hooks hanging around the tent. But at least it's free.

God knows how long I'm going to be here. My plan is for a wooden building twenty-five feet wide by thirty long, the bulk of the space given over to the store with a loft above for sleeping, a room at the back for eating and cooking. But it feels like it will never be built. I've been working on my own, digging down into the dirt to create a flat base on which to build. There's gold even here—just a couple of small nuggets, though I'm sure I'd find flakes if I washed out the dirt. But I've no time for that, just loading it into sacks and dumping it on the edge of town. In my first week I've cleared maybe seven feet. At this rate I'll be lucky to manage the foundations by December. Gerry'll be back with our merchandise long before then and no building to sell it from.

"Come on, Guinness," I say. "Let's get you home."

I've got him stabled further up Main Street, not willing to share my tent after the years of Samson in our old cabin. I whistle for Goldie, who's always rooting around somewhere near the plot. There's a crowd gathered outside Ruby's, raised voices carrying towards me. I tether Guinness and walk cautiously towards them, hand on my pistol, ready to draw. Jacques, one of the French miners, hurries over to me.

"*Mon Dieu*, François. I am so sorry," he says.

"What's wrong?" I say.

"Your friend is being found murdered."

He reaches an arm out to steady me as I stagger backwards.

"Gerry?" I say, not wanting to believe it.

"Ah, *non*," Jacques says. "He is not Gerry. The other friend. The big man, we go drinking with."

My brain has slowed and I can hardly think who he means. All I can feel is relief that it's not Gerry. And then suddenly it hits me.

"Bear Man? Do you mean Bear Man?"

"Bear Man, yes, that is his name."

Bear Man dead? How can he be? He is the size of a mountain. If anyone can take care of himself, it's him.

"But how?" I say.

"Shot, so they are saying."

I need to see for myself. I push my way to the door to Ruby's bar but find it locked. Maybe the rear entrance will be open. It is strangely quiet at the back of the hotel as I slip through the garden, onto the back porch and into the rear lobby. The silence unnerves me and I draw my pistol as I make my way into the bar. It's almost empty—just Bear Man, laid out across two tables near the bar, and Clarice, sitting silently next to him. I look around the bar again, making sure there's no immediate danger.

"Clarice," I say, going to her. "I heard…"

I look down at Bear Man. A bullet hole marks his right temple. Neat, tidy. A little blood, nothing dramatic. I retch as I begin to register the left of his skull—a great oozing mass of brain, bone and skin, black clots of blood. And his shirt is covered in blood and gore. I look away.

"What happened?" I say to Clarice, but she doesn't respond. Her face is pale, eyes glassy. "Where's Ruby? Everyone?" She doesn't answer, sitting by the body, still and silent.

I don't know what to do about Clarice. What I do know is that I can't leave Bear Man like this. He needs to be cleaned up and prepared by someone who cared about him in life.

I make my way behind the bar and into the kitchen in search of a bucket of water, soap, cloths. Ruby's standing with her back to me in front of a linen cupboard, a bucket of water at her feet.

"It's me," I say, not wanting to startle her. She turns around but for a moment it's as if she's looking straight through me.

"We are closed tonight," she says, her voice stiff.

"I came to get some things to…to…" I try taking a deep breath. But I can feel my eyes brimming, throat tightening. For a moment I see a field in Knockreagh.

I shut my eyes, forcing it away. Think of Bear Man. Think of his grave to be. Bear Man, shot dead, 15 October, 1849. Except we can't write Bear Man. That was his nickname. The marker should have his real name. What was his name? He told me once. And suddenly I'm desperate to know.

"What was his name?" I ask Ruby.

She stares at me.

"His name, his real name. What was it? He told me once. Before he was Bear Man, who was he?"

Why doesn't she answer? Surely she must know. She knew him before I did. She's here in this kitchen, eyes red-rimmed, finding water and cloths to clean him up. She must know. I start to sob, slumping to the floor.

She comes over to me, crouches down, puts her hand on my arm. Her eyes glisten with tears ready to fall.

"William. His name is William Burns."

"William Burns." I remember now. He told me in the woods, the first time we met. "William Burns," I repeat. "And I am Frances Moriarty. Not Frank. Frances. Third daughter of Eliza and Morris Moriarty of Dunquin, Ireland."

Ruby looks at me for a moment, then, nodding slightly, she offers me her hand. "Please to meet you, Frances."

I start to laugh, gulpy laughs mixed with sobs. It is good to hear my name again. I start to wipe my face with the back of my sleeve but Ruby takes a cloth from the cupboard. "For your face," she says, handing it to me. "I must go and prepare William."

"I'd like to help."

She nods, helping me up from the floor. "Of course."

In the bar, Clarice is still sitting by the body. Ruby puts her arms around her. "Ah, Chickadee," she says, kissing her gently on the forehead. I look away.

"I cannot believe it," Clarice says.

"No," Ruby says. "I cannot believe either." It is quiet for several minutes. I sneak a glance, wanting to know what's happening. Ruby still stands, Clarice's head buried in her bosom, their arms around each other. I clear my throat, feeling I should remind them that I'm here.

Ruby looks up briefly. She strokes Clarice's hair. "We are going to prepare him now. Come, sit over here." She eases Clarice out of the chair and leads her to one of the nearby tables. Then she turns to me, suddenly businesslike. "My staff is getting a coffin, clothes, oils to dress the body. We should begin."

I wonder at the trouble she's gone to, used as I am to men barely thrown into the ground.

"How did you know Bear—William?" I ask.

"He played Monte here when I begin Ruby's." She looks at the body. "Where to start? I think the clothes."

"I'd like to clean up his head first," I say. It feels wrong to be doing anything else while his head looks such a mess.

She squeezes my arm. "You are right."

I steel myself for my first touch of my friend's dead body. His skin has not yet chilled. Carefully I wipe the area round the head wounds with a damp cloth. The cloth is soon stained red, covered in blood and brain. I rinse it out and continue with my task.

"Do you have something I could bandage his head with?" I say, at last. "Maybe an old sheet." She disappears behind the bar and into the kitchen. While she is gone I clean the blood out of his hair.

"Do you know anything about what happened?" I ask Ruby when she returns.

"I hear gunshots but…" She shrugs—gunshots are nothing unusual in Hangtown. "Then Old Joey come to tell me Bear Man is shot dead."

"Did he see it happen?"

"No. He is at the stables when he hears the first shot. I think is the one in the back, then the second shot, in the head, to be sure."

"Who did it?"

She shakes her head. "Joey does not know."

"Do you think they were after money?"

"Perhaps. But why shoot him in the head this way?"

"So why—"

We are interrupted by the return of Ai-Li with Mister Woolf, the tailor. He shakes his head, looking down at Bear Man's blood-soaked clothes.

"He needs a suit and shirt. Can you get them in an hour?"

"I vill do my best, Madam Alvarez," he says.

While he is measuring up, two of the barmen return. "The coffin?" Ruby says to them.

"George is making it now," the taller one says. "He'll bring it over when it's ready. What do you want us to do now, boss?"

"We reopen in an hour for Bear Man's friends. Let people know."

The barmen depart with the tailor who promises to be back soon with the clothes, leaving Ruby and I free to get on with preparing the body. His skin feels cooler now as we cut off his clothes and clean him up. The body is beginning to stiffen.

"We need him sitting to clean his back and bandage the wounds," I say.

It's an effort to get him upright. As with his head, the entry wound is small but his chest is an oozing mess where it came out again.

"We're going to need to pack it," I say.

Ruby tears off strips of sheet for me to wad and press into the hole. I hold the body still while Ruby ties a bandage round and round his torso till there's no red showing through. We are just finishing as the tailor returns.

"I vill help put on his shirt," he says.

We struggle with the arms, he is getting stiffer all the time. My face is hot, sweat prickling under my skin as we edge the shirt onto his body. Clarice comes over with a cravat, peacock blue. She ties it carefully round Bear Man's neck.

"My lovely man," she says quietly. She kisses his cheek, his lips, tears dripping down her face. "My silly great bear."

I swallow hard to keep from crying. Mister Woolf clears his throat. He stands to the side of the body, holding a dark blue jacket in his hands. Clarice kisses Bear Man one last time, then steps back into Ruby's arms. They hold each other as I work with Mister Woolf to finish the dressing.

We are easing the trousers up his big, hairy legs when the air is shattered by gunfire. Shot after shot, pistols and rifles. I drop to the ground. But Mister Woolf hurries over to the door.

"They have got him," he shouts.

"Got who?" I say, cautiously getting to my feet.

I am almost knocked back down by Clarice as she breaks out of Ruby's arms and runs into the street. Ruby dashes after her.

The gunshots have died away to be replaced by a loud chanting.

"*Ing im um. Ing im um.*"

I strain my ears, trying to understand what they're saying, half chanting myself as I make my way to the door. "*Ing im um, ing im um.*" The street is full of miners and suddenly it becomes clear.

"String him up. String him up."

Below the big tree is an open wagon, lit by torches, miners jostling around it. And on the wagon are three men. One of them's a mass of blood, battered face seeping red onto his spattered shirt. His hands are tied and bound in front of him. A second man has a pistol rammed up against the bloodied man's temple. The third man, in a blue shirt, is holding his hands up trying to get silence. To no avail. With every second, more men are spilling out of the bars and eating places, joining in the chant. "String him up. String him up."

Blue Shirt takes his pistol out and fires into the air. He's answered by air shots from dozens of miners. But as the gunfire dies out, the chanting subsides. Blue Shirt seizes his moment. "Sideburns Sennen stands before us accused of the murder of Bear Man," he shouts.

"String him up," ripples round the crowd but doesn't take ahold.

"We may well string him up, but first he's entitled to a trial. We ain't savages. Can any witnesses please come forward?"

The crowd churns as several people push through it, making their way over to the wagon. I wriggle closer to the front. Blue Shirt leans down, talking briefly to the clump of witnesses.

"I call the first witness—Old Joey," he says, standing up.

Old Joey lived in the mountains, trapping for pelts until a fall did for his leg. Now he runs the stables where Guinness beds down. He struggles to get onto the wagon till a couple of miners give him a hefty shove from below. He sways for a moment, then turns to face the crowd.

"Can you tell us what you know about Bear Man's murder?" Blue Shirt says.

"Well, I was down in the stables starting to feed and water the horses when I heard a shot. It was right close by and it set off one of the horses kicking and banging. As I tried to calm him there was another shot. I went out to see who was creating such a fuss outside my stables and that's when I found him."

"Do you mean Bear Man?"

"Well of course. Who else would I be meaning?" he says, drawing a few laughs from the crowd. But Old Joey carries on. "Face down, he was, face down in the dirt. Knew it was Bear Man, of course, I ain't never met another man that size. Woulda helped him if I coulda. But he was already dead. Bullet straight through his brain, saw the hole myself. All black it was round it. Weren't nothing I could do for him but shut his eyes."

"Do you know who shot him?" Blue Shirt says.

"Reckon it was this lick-spittle here."

"I never done it," Lick-spittle says, but a chorus of "String him up" drowns him out.

Blue Shirt holds his hands up and the crowd slowly returns to quiet. "You saw him do it?" he says to Old Joey.

"Not exactly. But everyone knows he's been itching for vengeance since Bear Man threw his sorry ass out of Ruby's last week."

Threw his ass out of Ruby's? I look again at the bloodied man on the wagon, trying to recall the face of the lowlife that insulted Clarice. Dark-hair, big sideburns, just like this man. I notice for the first time a noose hanging from the tree above the cart.

"Were you at Ruby's when it happened?"

"Well, no, but—"

"I was there," a voice from the crowd shouts.

"We'll hear from you next," Blue Shirt says, before turning back to Old Joey. "Have you anything else you wanted to say?"

"Just that you can tell a lot about a man by his horse and his is a mean, evil-eyed creature if ever I saw one."

Joey limps to the edge of the wagon and is helped down into the crowd. He is replaced by a tall, young man. As he takes his place on the wagon, I see that it is François.

"Can you start by telling us your name?" Blue Shirt says.

"I am François Duflot."

"And what can you tell us about what happened at Ruby's?"

"Last Friday I go out drinking with Bear Man. 'E was with my friends, Frank and Gerry. This man," he says, gesturing at the bloodied man, "insult one of the waitress. Bear Man, 'e goes mad. 'E throw this man into the street."

"And how did Sennen respond to that?"

"'E threaten Bear Man. 'E say, 'You will be sorry.' Bear Man laugh. But now 'e is dead and this man should pay."

"String him up. String him up. String him up," thunders through the crowd.

Blue Shirt tries to pull them back to the trial but his words are lost in the chants echoing through the throng. He fires his gun into the air again and again but it's some time before it's quiet enough for the next witness, a man in his thirties who gives his name as Stuart Gordon.

"Can you tell us what you know about Bear Man's murder?" Blue Shirt says.

"He did it, that man there," Gordon says, pointing at Sennen.

"You saw him?" Blue Shirt shouts as "String him up" begins again.

"I didn't need to see him. I caught him on the road out of town. His face was pure guilt."

"I didn't do it," Sennen shouts, fear clear in his voice. "It wasn't me."

"It was, you stinking coward," Gordon says. "You paid him back for what happened at Ruby's. Now it's your turn to pay." He jumps on Sennen, punching and kicking him. Two more men jump on the wagon, pushing aside Blue Shirt and the guard. Another man joins in, and another, kicking and punching Sennen as they drag him over to the rope.

"*String him up. String him up.*"

Sennen's still struggling, smashing the nose of one of his attackers with his head and kicking out at another. But there's too many of them. Two of them hold his head back while Gordon places the noose round his neck. There's a sudden silence in the crowd as they push Sennen off the cart. I can't stop watching as he twitches and sways above us, gasping for air, chest heaving, legs jerking out of control.

It feels like forever before his body goes slack. A sickness rises up from my guts as I stare at Sennen, his face dark and discoloured now, a damp patch at the front of his trousers. I stumble through the crowd, back towards Ruby's as the air erupts around me, men discharging rifles and pistols, whooping and hollering.

I slump onto the steps at the back of the hotel. God, even if he did kill Bear Man. To die like that? I take deep breaths. In. Out. In. Out. Pushing the sickness away.

At last I get up and make my way into the bar. It's still empty, just me and Bear Man. "You've been avenged," I say as I neaten his trousers. "They strung him up. Sennen. The man that insulted Clarice. The man they say killed you."

I brush back his hair, away from the bandage. "He said he didn't do it." I shake my head. "I don't know. He was caught running away. And he wanted to get back at you."

I twitch the cravat into place. "He's no loss. He was a creep and a coward. Not like you. You were a good man. You didn't deserve this."

"No."

I start at the voice behind me. It's Ruby. "I didn't hear you come in."

"I am sorry to surprise you," she says.

The door to the bar opens and four of Ruby's staff come in.

"We open in five minutes," Ruby says to them, "for Bear Man's friends only." She turns to me. "Will you light candles around the body?"

I nod. "I will. And I'll lead the music at the wake."

"The wake?" Ruby says.

"You know, the time now to mark Bear Man's life, to send him on his way, before we bury him."

"I understand."

"Do you have any instruments? A flute or a fiddle?"

"Only the piano," Ruby says. "Now I must go."

The piano? I have never even touched one. I grew up playing music. The fiddle, the pipes, especially the flute. There is a flute in my tent. It's the wooden one Missus Gorman gave me before I left Ireland. A few months later she was dead. I think of what her last days must have been like. Weak with the hunger, terrible pains in her stomach, her skin rough and dry, hanging in folds, her eyes sunk into the back of her head, her face and neck wasted, her bleeding gums. I imagine her hobbling out from her cabin, dragging herself step by slow step from Ballyferriter, up over the mountain road to Dingle. I wonder where she fell, how long she lay by the side of the road. Did she cry out to the Virgin for help? Did she pray for death to come at last or did she hope that someone would come and save her?

I wipe away my tears. Bear Man was a friend. I am sorry he is dead. But I cannot play my flute for him.

CHAPTER TWENTY-EIGHT

Dingle, March 1846

You know you've been working when you've been planting potatoes. I stand up, feeling the numbness in my knees, the ache in my back. The Garveys' cabin catches my eye as I stretch. I look away, turning so it's no longer in my line of view. But I can't make it go away. It's empty now, empty and silent. Silent as the grave, people say. But that cabin was more like a coffin, holding them in, waiting for them to die.

Malachy was first. Sunday, 15 February. I was walking back from church with Peig when I heard a terrible wailing coming from the Garveys' up above. My ma had kept me from there since we'd had word of the fever. But I had to go then. I found Mary wailing at the window of the cabin, the dead baby in her arms.

My father made the coffin, a wee wooden box, not much needed for a boy of ten months. We had the wake as best we could, the Garveys inside the cabin, the rest of the village gathered outside. You could hear the shouts of Peter, deep in the fever, not even knowing his son was dead, her mother hacking and coughing, the keening of Mary.

The young and the old, they're always the ones most likely to die when there's fever. Dominic followed his brother into the ground. Mary's ma was bound to be next. I never expected Peter to die. Even though both twins were taken, even though I knew he was sick, I was sure he'd pull through. It was the finish of Mary. By the time her mother died, two days later, there was barely a whimper from her. Two weeks shut in with the fever, she never caught it. Maybe it would have been better if she had. She's gone. Nobody knows where, disappearing in the night after her mother died.

Campbell's been offering their patch for rent. No one round here could afford the extra cost, even if they wanted to. Except maybe my da. But he wouldn't take it. I'm glad. I couldn't have brought myself to farm that land.

So I'm here in the same fields we planted last year, and the year before, trying to keep my eyes from the Garveys' cabin, my mind from what happened there. Though I hear Mary's cries in my mind every day, have no peace from them. "*No, no, not my baby, no, no. Please God. No.*" Over and over. "*No, no, not my baby, no, no. Please God. No.*"

My family was lucky last year. We only lost the one field of potatoes, had enough left to feed us. And we've the other crops, the oats and the turnips, our sheep and cows. We can pay the rent in May. All Peter had was his acre. All he had was the potatoes. It's all a lot of people have.

Kitty and her ma don't have even an acre. Their patch is scarcely more than half of that. They've no oats, only a couple of chickens. Please God may they have a good harvest. I take her ribbon out of my pocket. It's the one she threw back at me last year after I'd been so foolish about us being together. I've kept it ever since as a reminder of what it means to have her in my life, of how near I came to losing her. I kiss it for luck, then put it back in my pocket. I crouch back down and plant the next potato.

* * *

It's raining again when I wake on Saturday morning. I sit up sighing. There's been hardly a dry day this last month, grey skies closing in over us, as if times weren't hard enough already. Peig stirs next to me but doesn't wake. I'm relieved. The only time she's not been crying this last week is when she's sleeping. Liam and the others were found guilty and sentenced to be transported to Van Diemen's Land. I don't know what to say to her anymore.

I dress quickly, wanting to get off to see Kitty.

"Surely you're not going out in this weather?" my mother says as I tie my boots.

"It's easing off," I say.

"It never is. That's on for the day."

"I'll be fine."

"Soaked through, that's what you'll be. I suppose it's Kitty Gorman's you're off to again?"

I don't answer.

"I said I suppose you're off to Kitty Gorman's."

"I am."

"Well what's so urgent about seeing her today? In weather like this? And when your sister needs you?"

She is going to keep me here. She is going to keep me and I can't bear it. The only thing that's been keeping me going all week is the thought of Kitty.

"I wouldn't go, but I promised to help Kitty practise her dancing. I think there's some fella she has her eye on." I can feel myself blush at the lie but push on. "She's expecting me. I don't want to let her down."

My ma sighs but doesn't say anything. Gathering up my basket, shawl and flute, I head for the door, going while the going is good.

The rain is teeming down, as if the sky is siding with my mother. I pull my shawl close around my head and stride out across the track, wanting to put distance between me and my ma. *Off to see Kitty Gorman again.* There was a tone in her voice that I didn't like. Oh and it's so unfair when I've barely even seen Kitty this last month, what with the Garveys and the trial. Not to mention the potatoes and the rain.

Sometimes I wish we could run away, run away where no one knows us, run away and be on our own. Away from the questions and the lies and excuses to be together. But where could two women go away from prying eyes?

The rain eases off as I reach the last stretch to the scalp. There's smoke coming out of the chimney—Kitty must be home. I run the last stretch, arrive panting at the door. I haul it open, struggling with the stiffness.

"All this rain," Kitty says, "it's warping the wood." She kisses me briefly, then helps me off with my damp shawl. "You're soaked through. Come and get warm."

I stand close to the fire, rubbing my back.

"Potato planting. It's a killer, isn't it?" Kitty says.

"Especially in this weather. It was heavy work, getting the ground dug."

"Don't I know it? But at least they're in. I passed a couple of people still planting on the way from Ballyferriter, trying to turn the earth in the pouring rain. I know I should have felt sorry for them but all I could think was thank God it wasn't me."

"I can't remember a wetter winter," I say, sitting down on the edge of our mattress. "Now a wet spring. I suppose we're due for a good summer."

"It couldn't beat the one I had with you last year," she says, raising an eyebrow. "Remember the afternoons behind the hedge up above my ma's place?" She shakes her head. "Jesus, we've taken some risks." She laughs.

"It's a wonder we were never caught. Thank God we found this place."

"Thank God we found each other. It's a year, you know."

"I know, I've been thinking of it too. At last year's planting I hadn't even heard your name. Kitty Gorman. I do love the sound of it. Kitty Gorman."

"I love hearing you say it. Even now, I love hearing you say my name."

We are quiet for a moment, looking at each other, smiling.

"I've got something for you," I say at last, "something to mark it. You know, a year passing." I hand over the old pillowcase from my basket, suddenly nervous.

She takes it, a slight frown on her face. "A pillowcase. Tha—"

"It's inside," I interrupt. "The pillowcase was to protect it."

Kitty laughs, blushing and biting her lip. She opens up the pillowcase, groping inside for my gift. Slowly she draws it out, spreading my sampler out on her lap. She sits quiet, staring at it.

"It's beautiful," she says, turning to me with tears in her eyes. "It must have taken…It's beautiful."

"Do you really think so?" I say, grinning.

"I love it. The colours, such lovely colours."

"I dyed them myself. Beetroot, onion skins, lichen, berries. I've been working on it for ages."

"And the little pictures. They're all about us, aren't they?"

I nod.

"The flute here, that's you. And the dancing shoes is me. And this is our scalp, isn't it?" she says, pointing to a little brown track leading to a wooden door in a green hillside.

"And this is the first day you came to see me in Dunquin," I say, pointing at the grey dolphin's head above a turquoise sea.

"What about the fire?"

I start with the easy answer. "It's the times we've sat together here, warming ourselves."

"Like now," she says.

"Like now," I say, struggling for my next words, not wanting to sell her short. "It's about the love I have for you. How strong it is. How it feels like it'll never go out. And it's also about…" I stop, looking away from her into the flames, suddenly shy.

"About?" she says.

"You know."

"I want you to tell me."

"It's about how it feels between us. You know, when we're touching. About the…passion." I feel my face burning. "You know."

"Show me," she says, pulling me down beside her.

Afterwards, Kitty lies in my arms, drifting to sleep. There's no sound but the soft in and out of her breath, the odd crack from the twigs in the fire. Her hair fans out across the pillow and down onto my breast. I remember again that first time seeing her, her hair bouncing on her shoulders as she danced, my first stuttering words to her. I wasn't aware of anything missing before I met her, was content enough up in the fields with my da, planting potatoes. Now I can't imagine my life without her.

She mutters as I gently stroke her hair, then goes back to sleep. I let my breathing fall into time with hers, at peace for the first time in weeks.

CHAPTER TWENTY-NINE

Hangtown, October 1849

"Jesus."

I wake with a start, eyeball to eyeball with Guinness. He lets out a loud bray, then tries to bite my shoulder.

"Go on," I shout, sitting up. "Away with you."

Goldie looks up from her blanket.

"Don't be blaming me," I say to her, rubbing my shoulder. "It was that bloody mule."

It's the last time Guinness spends the night anywhere near me. I tied him to a post outside the tent last night after seeing Old Joey slumped across a table, an empty bottle next to him. In the future, I'll open up the stables myself if I have to.

I should take him down there now, stop him sniffing and snorting his way round my tent. But my head's pounding. He ambles over to my pots of barley, fermenting for the next batch of poitín. I've got twice as many on the go now so I can start selling myself as well as supplying Ruby.

"Stay away from that," I say.

Guinness ignores me, dipping his nostrils over the edge of one of the pots. He lets out a deep snort. I jump out of bed and pull him away.

"You're going outside," I say, tugging on his reins.

The street is quiet. The sun's coming up and I can just make out the big tree, Sennen's body still hanging from it. Someone should cut him down. I turn away and go back into the tent. I rub my hand across my face, trying to clear the thickness in my head. Goldie pads over to me, her wet nose nuzzling my bare leg.

I sit on the bed, leaning over to take in her sleepy-dog smell.

"Mammy's girl," I say to her.

She licks me, tail wagging, making me smile. I am glad to have her with me, especially now that Gerry's gone. I wonder how he's getting on. He'll be in San Francisco by now. It's a wild town, so I've heard, I hope he's keeping out of trouble. I should write to him, tell him about Bear Man.

"Mammy's worn out," I say to Goldie, lying back down on the bed. She rests her head close to my hand, making it easy to stroke her silky ears. I should get up and get on with clearing the site but I'm exhausted, working all the time. I shouldn't have stayed so late at the wake. And I shouldn't have drunk so much. Mind you, I wasn't the only one, toast after toast to the memory of Bear Man. There'll be plenty of sore heads today.

"I wish you could dig the plot for me," I say, sighing and pushing myself slowly up onto my elbow. I swing my legs out of bed. I want to be able to tell Gerry I'm making great progress. Even though it's not true, at least it'll not be for the want of trying.

* * *

I rush into Ruby's just before twelve, still sweaty and grubby from digging the plot. I should have finished earlier but I was determined to clear another foot. There's a small crowd in the bar, no more than twenty people, standing around drinking cups of coffee. Where are the hundreds who were baying for blood last night?

The coffin is still open. I go over, cross myself and kiss Bear Man lightly on the cheek.

"May the light of heaven shine on your grave," I say quietly.

I step back, finding a place to the right of Ruby. She looks impressive in a black dress edged with deep red. I knew I should have put on a clean shirt.

"Anyone else?" she says, glancing around the room, but no one comes forward until she nods to one of the barmen. He nails the coffin shut, each blow of the hammer rebounding round the silent bar.

"Who wishes to speak?" Ruby says.

Old Joey starts. "Men like Bear Man'll soon be a thing of the past. You could trust a man like him. Reckon we'll not see his kind again."

I don't recognise the next man who steps forward, a heavily bearded miner holding his battered hat between his hands.

"My name's John Maddison," he says in a gruff voice. "William was a good friend to me as a boy, stood up for me when an older boy was picking on me. It was just like him, always standing up for others. But when he was ten he just up and disappeared, him and his ma. I couldn't believe it when I ran into him a couple of days ago. Still recognised him, after all these years. We were supposed to meet last night." He pauses, struggling. "That's why he was in town…"

He turns away, all choked up. As Frances I could go to him, put an arm around him. But not as Frank. I look to Ruby and Clarice, but neither of them step forward.

"None of us should blame ourselves," I hear myself saying aloud. I flush as I feel people's eyes upon me but now I've started I have to carry on. "None of us shot Bear Man. The man that pulled the trigger is the one to blame."

"Frank is right," Ruby says, looking at Clarice. "Sennen is to blame."

"And justice is still squeezing him tight around the neck," Old Joey says. "Bear Man's been avenged."

"What do I care for vengeance?" Clarice says. "It does not bring 'im back. I wish…" She flings herself onto the coffin. "I love you," she sobs. "I love you."

Through tear-blurred eyes I watch Ruby go forward. She puts her hand on Clarice's shoulder, trying to ease her away. But Clarice will not be dislodged, hanging on to the coffin, sobbing and sobbing. I catch Ruby's eye, shaking my head slowly. She seems to understand, stepping back, waiting for the sobs to subside. People shuffle their feet, looking at the ceiling, the array of bottles behind the bar, anywhere but at Clarice.

Minutes pass.

But eventually the intensity lessens and Clarice slumps towards the floor. I step forward with Ruby, helping carry Clarice away from the coffin and over to one of the tables. She lays her head on her arms, spent.

"Perhaps you should lie down," Ruby says.

Clarice looks up, her face red and blotchy. "Non."

"Are you sure?" Ruby says.

"I am staying."

Ruby gives Clarice a final hug, then gets up and goes to stand at the head of the coffin. "Hangtown has no chapel and no priest," she says. "Lord accept that we do what we can for the soul of our friend, William Burns." She takes a small bottle of water out of her bag.

"*De profúndis clamávi ad te, Dómine*," she says as she starts to sprinkle the water onto the coffin.

Silently, I mouth the words of the *De profundis* prayer, keeping in time with Ruby till the end. I echo her as she makes the sign of the cross. So do Clarice and the French miners. The rest of the crowd stand with their heads bowed.

"Please give eternal rest to the soul of our departed friend," Ruby says. "I pray that you absolve him from every bond of sin and lead him into the holy light." She stands for a moment with her eyes closed, then steps back from the coffin.

"Can I have anyone who's wanting to carry the coffin?" Old Joey says. A number of men go forward. I have never been a pallbearer but I want to play my part. I join the group around Old Joey. He takes charge.

"We'll have us two groups. The first'll take him out of the bar and halfway down Main Street. The second, from Main Street to the cart that'll finish the journey out to the graveyard. We're all here out of respect for Bear Man and we don't want nothing going wrong. No coffins slipping and sliding. It's all down to the pairings."

He runs his eye along the lineup, sucking his teeth and tutting occasionally. "You there," he says, pointing to a dark-haired young man. He doesn't look far past sixteen, with scarcely a hair on his soft cheeks. "You're the smallest. Are you sure you're up to it?"

The young man reddens. "Yessir," he says.

"Right, you'll be at the front. And you, Frank. You'll be alongside him."

Old Joey carries on sorting through the volunteers. I nod to the dark-haired lad.

"I'm Frank," I say.

"Zachariah," he replies.

"How did you know Bear Man?"

"He helped me and my pa when our wagon got stuck. How about you?"

"I met him out hunting one day in the woods."

"Are you Pistol Boy?" he says. "He told us about you. Up in the woods. Thought you were going to shoot..." He trails off.

I look down at the coffin. Big and solid-looking. It's bound to be heavy, Bear Man was the biggest man I've ever seen. I hope Joey was right putting me and Zachariah at the front.

Old Joey has sorted out the other pairings and lines the rest of the first group of bearers up behind us. "Right, here's how it's going to be. We're going to slide this coffin off the table and into your arms. I'm putting a couple of extra men at either end. They're going to help you lift it onto your shoulders. Ready?"

I shuffle into position with the others. Zach and I stand opposite each other, waiting. There's a creak as the coffin slides forward. I brace myself.

Oh God, it's heavy. Even with the extra men at either end.

"On three I want you to lift and settle it onto your shoulders."

I'm never going to be able to lift it.

"One, two, three."

The coffin soars upwards. I'm doing barely a thing; someone else is taking the strain. And then the weight is back. I stagger as the hard edge of the coffin bites into my shoulder. A sweat prickles below my skin.

"Can you manage?" Old Joey says.

I force some strength into my legs, I will not disgrace myself. "I'm fine," I say, through gritted teeth.

At Old Joey's command we take our first unsteady step. Ruby walks ahead of us, tolling out a single note with a handbell on each step. Slowly we follow her out of the bar, the coffin banging and bumping against my shoulder on every step.

"Careful here," Old Joey says as we manoeuvre down the few stairs from Ruby's to the street.

We sway along Main Street, past Sam's Stores, following the bell. It's a sound from long ago, the clanging bell in the church in Dunquin, from the days before the famine when there was time to give the dead a decent burial.

Clang.

Clang.

From the corner of my eye I can see miners stopping their business, standing still, hats removed, heads bowed, watching our progress up the street.

Clang.

Clang.

"Pause here," Old Joey says. "It's time for the changeover."

We halt close to the big tree where Sennen still swings. Slowly and carefully each pairing is relieved of their burden by the men from the second group of bearers. I step away from the coffin, rubbing at my sore shoulder, glad to have done it, glad that it's over. I look up at Sennen. His face is livid now and the stains on his trousers unmistakable. Will anyone bother to bury him? I wonder again if he did it.

Clang.

The coffin's moving again. I fall in behind it. There were twenty mourners when we set off from Ruby's, now there are more than a hundred. An empty cart waits at the edge of town. A man sits in the driving seat, holding two brown horses in check. He jumps down and helps the pallbearers slide the coffin onto the back.

Men stop their digging as the funeral procession passes, some of them joining us, swelling the crowd even more. The graveyard's about a mile out of town, a piece of flattish land, dotted with wooden crosses. The trees are turning to reds, coppers and golds. It's a beautiful place, with the mountains beyond. There's a grave already dug, the hole gaping near one of the trees.

Ruby walks forward, taking a second bottle of water from her bag. She sprinkles it into the grave, saying, "Dear Lord, please bless this grave and appoint your holy angels to guard it. Through Christ our Lord. Amen."

The second group of pallbearers positions the coffin over three long straps next to the open grave. Ruby sprinkles the coffin again with holy water.

"Dear Lord, let the soul of William Burns rest in peace. May you have mercy upon him and grant him eternal rest."

She makes the sign of the cross again. And then slowly the bearers take up the straps and lower the coffin into the earth. It makes a gentle *thud* as it hits the bottom of the grave. The men step back. Clarice takes up a handful of earth and scatters it onto the coffin. One after another, the mourners take their turn filling in the grave. At last it is done.

I lean against a tree, watching the miners drift back to their work. This is the closest to a Catholic funeral I've been to in years. I feel hollow. Bear Man had proper prayers, a crowd of mourners. I close my eyes.

"Frank."

It's Ruby's voice.

I'm not ready to open my eyes.

"Frank," she says again. "We are going back to the bar, Clarice and Joey, other friends. Come with us."

I shake my head, eyes still closed.

"You cannot stay here alone." I feel the warmth of her arm as she slips it through mine and force back the sob that rises in my throat. "Please come."

I drag my dirty sleeve across my tear-wet face, then let Ruby guide me away from the shelter of the trees and out of the graveyard. The miners have resumed their frenzied digging but I am quiet as we walk slowly back into Hangtown.

Close to the edge of town I hear a familiar bark and Goldie comes bounding out of the undergrowth. She circles round me, a big dog smile on her face, her whole back end wagging. In spite of myself I am cheered by her and pause to fondle her ears. Clarice too finds comfort, bending down and burying her face in Goldie's neck, holding her close.

Our moment of peace is interrupted by the sound of a horse cantering towards us, a cheering rider on its back. We stand back to let him pass. Behind him he drags a body, bumping and bashing against rocks and stones in the ground.

"Is that…was that Sennen?" I say.

"Guess someone decided it was time to cut him down," Old Joey says.

"Where's he taking him?"

Old Joey shrugs. "Out beyond. Food for the buzzards."

I watch the rider till he passes the bend in the track, then turn around and follow the others back to Ruby's. We enter through the garden, Ruby leading the way upstairs. We pause in the second-floor hallway as Ruby unlocks the door.

"Come in, come in," she says, crossing the darkened room and throwing open the wooden shutters to reveal a large parlour. The view is almost the same as from the room I stayed in, but a floor higher, out onto the garden and the hills beyond. Light glints off varnished floorboards and glass ornaments in a dark wooden sideboard opposite the windows. There is colour everywhere—a day bed, richly upholstered in red, gold and green; two fat, red armchairs; a large couch in dark green; intricately patterned rugs. A huge painting of the sun rising over the mountains adorns one of the walls. Between the two windows stands a bureau and a finely carved chair. At the far end is a closed door.

"Please make yourselves comfortable," she says.

I opt for one of the armchairs, Old Joey for the other. Clarice collapses onto the daybed. John Maddison and a miner who looks vaguely familiar stand on either side of the fireplace.

We have barely settled ourselves when there is a knock at the door. Ai-Li bustles in with a silver platter heaving with tortillas, tacos, bread, cheese and fruit. She is followed by another girl with a large pot of coffee. They set down their burdens on a couple of tables on either side of the large green couch.

"Come, eat," Ruby says.

The men move first, piling up their plates. I stand, uncertain, looking over at Clarice slumped on the daybed. She looks exhausted, like she has nothing left to give.

"Shall I get you anything?" I say, going over to her. She doesn't respond, sitting listless, staring at the floor. "You should eat. It will help."

"Frank is right," Ruby says, sitting down next to Clarice. "You want tortilla?"

"Later." She puts her head on Ruby's shoulder.

I leave them and go to get myself a plate of food. It's been a long morning and I'm hungry. I have developed a taste for Mexican food these weeks in Hangtown and help myself to a couple of chicken tacos, a slice of tortilla, bread and cheese.

"He had a great eye for the right place to dig," I hear the unknown miner say. It's the first time he's spoken, and I suddenly realise who he is—Blue Shirt from the trial last night.

"I wish I did," John Maddison says. "I'm down on Log Cabin Ravine, but it ain't giving me much. It sure is a lot harder than I expected."

"I'm up by Cedar Ravine. A group of men took out fifty pounds of gold there in a week in July. I've a lucky feeling."

This is always the conversation between miners. Everyone knows of someone who's had a big payout, but it's never them. Gerry and I were so lucky. I sit back down on my armchair and bite into a chicken taco. Garlicky tomato sauce spurts out onto my chin. I wipe it away quickly, hoping no one's noticed.

Opposite me Ruby gets up and goes over to the desk. She unlocks the right-hand drawer and takes out a bundle of folded cream-coloured sheets of paper, tied with string and sealed with red wax.

"This is Bear Man's will," she says. "Do you want to sit while I read?"

She remains standing as the men sit themselves down. She picks a slim knife up from the desk and slides the blade along the edge of the paper, breaking the seal. The room is silent except for the rustle of Ruby unfolding the paper, pressing it flat. She clears her throat.

"I, William Theophilus Burns of Hangtown, El Dorado County, California, being of sound mind and body do make and ordain this my last will and testament, whereof I have hereunto set my hand and affixed my seal this third day of October eighteen hundred and forty-nine."

Third of October. That was the day we met him coming into town. I remember my relief when I saw him up ahead, my certainty that we'd be safe with him beside us. Two weeks later and he's dead and buried.

"First. I desire that out of the money I have on hand after my death, all my just debts and funeral expenses shall be paid.

"Second. I give the sum of two hundred dollars and my horse, Flint, to Old Joey from the stables."

Old Joey lowers his head, nodding.

Ruby continues. "Third. I give the sum of one hundred dollars to Ted Galloway, along with my pick and shovel. May they bring him the luck they brought to me."

"Maybe your luck *is* changing," John Maddison says to the miner from the trial.

"Fourth. I leave to Ruby Alvarez my pocket watch." There is the briefest of pauses, like there was more to read but she's decided against it.

"Lastly, my will and desire is that all of the land I own, my vines and the remainder of my gold shall be given to Clarice Cossonnet. May she know at last the love I hold for her in my heart."

Clarice gapes at Ruby, blinking, like she can't believe what she's just heard.

"Gentlemen," Ruby says, "if you wait in the bar downstairs, I will bring the bequests."

I get to my feet with the others but as I'm almost at the door Ruby takes my arm, pulling me aside.

"Please stay with Clarice," she says. "I do not want her to be alone."

I listen to their steps along the wooden corridor and down the first flight of stairs before shutting the door and turning back into the room. Clarice is still sitting on the daybed, staring out the window, jaw slack, almost in a trance. Maybe she'd rather be left in peace, left to think her own thoughts.

"I wish I'd known him longer," I say, at last. "He was a good man."

"'E was the best man I ever met," she says, her eyes shining with tears ready to spill. "And because of me 'e's dead. 'E gave his life up for a filthy—" She starts to sob, shoulders heaving, gulping in air. I can hardly bear to look at her face, the pain written there. I go to put my arm around her but she flinches away.

"Filthy," she sobs.

"Bear Man didn't think so," I say gently. "He loved you."

"I killed 'im."

"No, you didn't. It wasn't your fault."

"Filthy. Dirty," she says, clawing at her hair on each word. I go to grab her hands, to stop her, but she backs away. "Sold by my own brother," she screams. Her voice dies away. "After 'e'd finished with me," she whispers. She collapses into the corner, burying her head under her arms.

I have no clue what to do. I wonder if I dare risk going to fetch Ruby.

The door opens. Ruby crosses the floor in quick, light steps, stopping only to place a steaming cup on one of the tables. I feel like an intruder as Ruby crouches beside Clarice.

"Come, Chickadee," she says, putting her hand on Clarice's arm, encouraging her to get up. But Clarice remains slumped on the floor.

I wonder if I should leave.

"This time is hard, I know," Ruby says.

Clarice's face remains hidden. She doesn't respond.

"You need rest," Ruby says. "I make a drink to help. Will you bring, Frances?"

I pick up the pungent brew from the table.

"Drink this," Ruby says to Clarice.

Clarice accepts the cup in silence. She takes a sip, her face puckering.

"I know is bad taste. Try to drink quickly, Chickadee."

Clarice is biddable now, like a worn-out child. She gulps down the potion, then lets Ruby help her up. They walk slowly across the room, disappearing through the door on the far side.

I sit down on the daybed, not sure what to do with myself. I should be working, but I'm tired, so tired. It's forever since I had a proper rest. I lay my head down on the arm of the daybed, closing my eyes.

"You look worn out."

I sit up with a start, embarrassed that Ruby has caught me drifting. I can feel a speck of drool at the side of my mouth and wipe it away quickly with the back of my sleeve.

"Sorry," I say.

"You work too hard."

"I'm trying to get the plot cleared, ready for building our store."

"Starting a new business is difficult. You do not have to do all alone."

"I haven't been able to find anyone to help, not since Gerry left."

"Why don't you come to me?" She smiles. "What help do you need?"

"Men. Three or four strong men to clear the site, a few skilled men to build the store. But I've been looking. Everyone would rather be digging for gold."

"You look in the wrong place. You should look in Ruby's, at men losing at Monte. Gamblers work if you pay gold."

Is it that easy? "Thank you," I say.

"You're welcome."

"How's Clarice?"

"Sleeping. The valerian has knocked her out."

"I didn't know about her and Bear Man. He never said."

"No, not to anyone, especially not to Clarice. He never wished her to feel—how do you say in English? *Compeler*...? Obliged?"

"She told me about..." I hesitate. "About her brother."

"He is one son of a bitch. He sell her to a pimp in Sutter's Mill. This is where Bear Man find her. She make a new life here. I trust you keep this secret?"

"Of course," I say. "I'm used to keeping secrets."

"Yes. Yes," she says. "I am much interested to know why you become a man."

"I have not *become* a man," I say, prickling. "I just pretend..."

"I do not wish to offend. I am interested in why you pretend."

There is so much I would say. About why I started, about how hard it's been, worrying about being caught, never feeling quite myself, wondering whether I'll ever be Frances again. Instead I smile, rueful. "There are things I miss. But the trousers," I say, standing up and thrusting my hands deep into my pockets, "the trousers make up for a lot."

CHAPTER THIRTY

Dunquin, June 1846

I take one last look along the row, checking whether any weeds have escaped my notice. One last nettle sits sly a few feet away. Stooping, I pull it out, grasping it tight to avoid the sting and placing it in my sack.

I always hate the prospect of weeding but there's a certain satisfaction when you get down to it, rooting out the enemies of our crop, the things that'll damage our yield. I look back at the field—neat, tidy, weed-free rows of strong, dark green plants. Eight inches high already, they'll be blossoming soon, ready to harvest by September.

I walk up to the top field where my da's working. I hear him before I see him, bellowing out "The Wearing of the Green." I grew up with rebel songs but none more than this one. He looks up as I join in.

For the wearing of the green, for the wearing of the green
They're hanging men and women there for the wearing of the green.

He holds the last *green*, a deep note in his gruff voice.
"Shall I give you a hand here?" I say, when he's finished the song.
"You could start on the next row for me," he says.
"How are the other fields?"
"Doing well. It looks like we're in for a big crop."

"They love the rain, potatoes."

"It's the cereals that are suffering. They could do with a bit of sun."

I could do with some myself. I'd like to get from the start of a trip to the end without the heavens opening. I want to lie on my back on the hill above the scalp, the sun on my skin, my sweetheart beside me.

"You're humming that tune again," my da says to me. "It's not one I know. Where did you pick it up?"

I picked it up in bed with Kitty. It's a song she wrote for me, words of love and joy. I wasn't aware I was humming it till he spoke.

"It's one of those ones that sticks in your head," I say, flushing, glad I wasn't singing the words out loud.

"Hum it again, I want to learn it."

I don't want to hum it. It's for us, this tune, for Kitty and me. We're always singing it. It's precious. I don't want to share it, even with my da. But I can think of no reason not to give him the notes so I start to sing.

"*De dum de de de dum dum.*"

"*De dum de de de dum dum,*" he repeats, then nods for me to carry on.

"*De-de de de de-de de de dum.*"

We carry on through to the last line, me leading, him following. And despite my reluctance, I'm enjoying it. My da hasn't the greatest voice but he picks a tune up quickly. And I've always loved making music with him. We carry on along the rows, singing in chorus while the weeds are ripped out and thrown in the sack. In no time we're finished.

"Ah, we've done a fine job there, Frances," my father says, looking at the field. "You're a great help to me, a son as well as a daughter."

"I enjoy helping you. I always have."

"And thank you for teaching me your tune."

"Kitty's the one you should be thanking. She's the one who made it up," I say, smiling, but his face changes.

"I would if I ever saw her. She never visits. It's always you running over there."

I'm not sure how to respond but before I have the chance to form a sentence, he carries on.

"Your mother worries about all this time with Kitty."

I look at the ground but say nothing.

"She wonders what would have you trailing off to Ballyferriter in all weathers to see a friend," he says.

I can hardly take a breath, my heart racing, my face colouring. I try to calm myself as he carries on. "Frances," he says, and his voice is gentle, so gentle I'm fighting to keep the tears in my eyes and not running down my cheeks. "Frances, you know I love you. I've let you make your own decisions. And maybe I was wrong in that. But you always had a will of your own, ever since you were a little girl. And till now that will has taken you in the direction of good sense. But there's no future in this. No future at all with someone who can't marry you."

My mind's jumping in all directions, wondering how to get through this without losing everything that matters to me, trying to pin a hold on what he's saying, what he means, what he knows. I turn his phrases round in my head, trying to understand.

Never visits.

No future.

Can't marry.

Would things be all right if Kitty visited more often? Would that have more of a future? Does he wish I could marry her?

Marry her? Jesus, where's my mind at? He'd never want me marrying a woman. None of them would. What is it he thinks he knows?

"My ma worries too much. I'm enjoying having a friend, that's all. And I'm sure Kitty would love to come visiting."

"This isn't about Kitty. It's about you. Why won't you tell me who you're spending your time with? Who is he, Frances?"

"Who's who?"

"This fella you're spending all your time with. Is he married? Or a drunkard? Is that why you don't want us to meet him?"

Thank God, it's only the same old nonsense my mother was badgering me about last year. "There is no fella, Da," I say, laughing with relief. It's the wrong thing to do.

"This isn't a laughing matter," he says, and he's angry now.

I almost never see him angry. "I'm sorry, Da, I didn't mean to annoy you. But there is no fella. Honestly, you and my ma don't need to worry. I'm not in any trouble."

"So where are you, all these nights away from home? You're not telling me it's all spent at the Gormans. I wanted to give you the chance to tell me the truth yourself. But if I have to speak to Kate Gorman, I will."

Since nearly the start I've known that Kitty's ma had heard my da playing, that my ma knew of Missus Gorman. I've carried on as if they would never meet, as if they lived six hundred miles apart, not six. But put my father and her mother together and that's the end.

I should have admitted to a fella. Is it too late? What will he think if I tell him I've been seeing a married man? How proud will he be of me then? But if I don't make up something, he'll be off to Missus Gorman's.

"What do you want me to tell you?" I say, at last.

"About this man you've been seeing. Is it serious?"

"No, Da. There was someone, but it's already over."

"Who is he?"

"You wouldn't know him, Da. He lived in Dingle for a while. But he left last month."

"Why didn't you want us to meet him?"

"I didn't think you'd like him. And I knew there was no future in it." I mumble my response, eyes down, hoping I look properly ashamed. "He was..." and I hesitate, as if dreading telling him the truth. "He was a...a Protestant."

"A Protestant!" he shouts. "Oh Jesus, Frances."

"I'm sorry, Da. It was a mistake."

"A mistake? Jesus, Frances. A Protestant? That goes far beyond a mistake. My God. How on earth did you ever get yourself mixed up with a Protestant?"

"He was preaching near the market in Dingle. Somehow we fell into conversation."

"Not one of those hypocrites from Colony Gate? Jesus, Frances, you haven't turned, have you? You've not become a Protestant?"

"No, Da, no. Of course not."

"What were you thinking?"

"I'm not sure I was thinking at all," I say, not able to look at him. "But he's gone now. He's away to be a missionary." The lies are coming thick and fast but I'm hoping it's got him off going to see Missus Gorman. "I won't be seeing him again."

"Has he left you in any kind of trouble?"

"No, Da, no. He was very honourable. Very chaste."

"Does anyone know? This is the kind of thing that could destroy your reputation."

"No, Da, no one knows. We were very careful about that."

"And you're sure he's gone. You're not just telling me that so you can carry on seeing him?"

"No, Da, I swear," I say, tears in my eyes, hearing the suspicion in his voice. "It was a mistake, a terrible mistake."

His eyes are shining too. He rubs the back of his hand roughly across them. "I would never have believed this of you, Frances. Your mother's been at me about you for months and I've been telling her to leave you alone. I always thought you were my sensible girl. Always thought I could trust you. And here it turns out you've been lying to me all this time."

"I'm sorry, Da. So sorry," I say, crying now, for how I've lied to him, for how I must go on lying to him. And knowing that even if I do, my life with Kitty will never be the same again.

CHAPTER THIRTY-ONE

Hangtown, October 1849

"I wonder if you're busy on Friday. Perhaps you will mark Day of the Dead with Clarice and I? I think will help her," Ruby says. We are sitting down to a midday meal in her salon. I have seen her most days since the funeral.

"Day of the Dead?" I say.

"Is when we Mexicans remember our dead, a time when their souls visit the living."

"In Ireland, they say the souls of the dead walk the earth on All Hallows Eve. It was one of the best times when I was a child—fortune-telling, big bonfires, jack-o'-lanterns—"

"What are jack-o'-lanterns?"

"They're turnips you carve into scary faces."

"I have eaten turnip. Is horrible taste."

"Oh, I know. I never liked eating them either. But I loved making turnip lanterns—cutting the top off for a lid, then hollowing out the inside. I used to make the mouth all big and jaggedy and always triangle eyes. The excitement when you lit the candle for the first time and the whole face glowed, all scary and mad. I loved it."

"This sounds fun."

"It was. And we'd play lots of games too. There was one I loved where you'd hang an apple on a string from the ceiling and try to eat it without using your hands."

"You have All Hallows Eve since you are in America?"

"No, not here. Not since…" Not since the first year of the famine, when we thought we would all pull through. Before people started to die.

"You look so sad," Ruby says. "What are you thinking?"

I shake my head. "The past."

"You mostly never talk of Ireland."

"No. Those last months…" I close my eyes. "There was so much death…"

"I sense your heartbreak from when first I meet you. I know how is like. I lose people too," Ruby says. "On All Souls Day I welcome them back. That is what Day of the Dead is for. My mother, who die when I was a little girl. But for me, especially I think of a woman I love. Her name is Carlita."

A woman I love? Does she mean…? I stare at her, looking for the answer in her face. "What happened to her?" I ask.

"She is murdered by her husband, four years ago." She gets up and walks over to the window, her back to me.

"This is how I know Day of the Dead will help Clarice," she says, at last.

* * *

"Ruby's Reward," I call to a couple of passing miners. "Only eight dollars a bottle."

"What in hell is Ruby's Reward?" one of them says, pausing by my table.

"It's the finest drink this side of the Rockies. Here, try some," I say, offering him a small glass.

He knocks it back in one. "Son of a bitch," he says, gasping.

"It's powerful stuff," I say. "A bottle will last you ages. And it's half the price of the brandy Sam's Stores is selling."

"Half the price?" his friend says. "Give me a try."

I wipe the glass on my trousers before refilling it. He takes it in his filthy hand, brown from the digging. He is more cautious than his friend, sipping it slowly. He nods. "I'll take a bottle."

"A bottle it is," I say. "And be sure to come back. I'll have plenty of other things to sell soon, once my partner gets back from San Francisco."

I never thought I'd be a hawker but I've been pushing my poitín at every passing miner from a table in front of the tent for the past week. There's seven dollars profit on every bottle and it's going faster than I can make it. I'm telling everyone who buys it about the store. That creep Sam won't know what's hit him once we open.

Ruby was right, it wasn't hard finding losers from her Monte tables willing to work for gold. Well, maybe "willing" is going too far. The first couple of days were difficult, trying to sort out the shirking and the skiving, the arguing and fighting, having to act the tough man to get any work out of them at all. Jesus, I was worn out, nearly ready to go back to building it myself. But then I found Iron Willie. Before California, he was a foreman building the railroad. He soon licked the others into shape. Willie knows all about building and is well on the way to completing a proper two-storey wooden building, far better than the small cabin-store I had planned.

I pack the last couple of bottles of poitín back into the tent and walk round to where the store is taking shape on the plot behind me. Tom, a scowler in a red shirt, is sawing planks in what will be the main part of the store.

"Where's Willie?" I shout over the noise of the banging that's coming from above. He gestures upwards with his head.

The ladder to the second storey is at the back of the shop in what will be the storeroom. I climb the rungs, pausing in the hatch at the top to look around, a feeling of satisfaction at the progress they've made.

"I see you've finished the walls," I say to Willie as he comes over to me.

"What do you think, boss? We've got the windows just where you wanted them."

For all his strength he reminds me of Goldie sometimes, wanting to be stroked. Though he snarls plenty at the men if they're not pulling their weight.

"It looks to be a grand job, Willie."

He beams at me. "They'll hold back any amount of rain, now we've finished chicking them. And I'll have the roof on by the end of Friday. That leaves the rooms up here to finish, the counter downstairs, the staircase and we're done."

I catch myself whistling as I make my way back to the tent. A few weeks ago I thought I'd be sleeping in here until Christmas, snow falling all around me. Now I'll be wrapped up snug and warm above my very own shop. I sit down on the cot, looking around me—the poitín pots, the still, a basin, clothes hooks. Not much to make a home with. I'm going to treat myself to a new bed. And maybe a couple of Indian rugs, like Ruby has in her salon. Perhaps a wardrobe, I think, as I take a clean shirt off one of my hooks.

I run my fingers through my hair before setting off up the street to Ruby's. A flickering light in the window catches my eye as I approach. I stop, staring. It's a jack-o'-lantern. I carry on up the steps and into the bar, grinning. There's a lantern on nearly every table, jagged mouths and eyes gouged out of pumpkins.

"You like?" Ruby says, coming over to me.

"I love them."

"I want to surprise you. Are the lanterns correct? I do not have turnips but I try with pumpkins."

"They're perfect."

"And the apples. Come, look."

She leads me over to the far corner where a dozen apples hang from the ceiling on strings of varying lengths.

"This is right?" she asks.

"It is, though I've never seen quite so many hanging at once," I say, laughing. "Have you had a try at it yet?"

"No. You show me?"

"First, you stand under the apple," I say, guiding her into position, my hands resting on her shoulders.

"I mean *you* to do." She laughs, squirming away.

"You first," I say, pulling her towards the apple again.

"There are plenty of apples," she says, smiling, her eyes bright. "We do together?"

"It's a deal." I take up position at the apple next to hers. "Now put your hands behind your back. It's best to hold one hand with the other," I say, clasping my left hand with my right. "It helps when you're tempted to use them. And then you try to take a bite."

I open my mouth wide, trying to get my teeth into the apple while watching Ruby out of the corner of my eye. She starts laughing as the apple spins away from her.

"This is more difficult than I think," she says.

"I know." I grunt in frustration as my apple slips away again, rolling round my face and past my ear.

"Half an ounce says Ruby takes the first bite," a voice says. I look up. A couple of miners are standing watching us.

"Done," the other one says, offering his hand to shake on it. He laughs. "I can't believe you're backing a woman against a man."

"He's no man," the first one says.

I look around nervously.

"He's only a boy," the miner continues. "Ruby'll take him. Come on, Ruby."

I can't have her beat me now. I rock forward onto my toes to get a better angle on the apple. I'm at an advantage over Ruby anyway who's half a head shorter than me, even with her fancy stacked-heel ankle boots.

I open my mouth so wide it feels like my jaw might break and carefully rest my top teeth on the apple. Steadying myself, I push my lower jaw forward. I've got ahold of it now between upper and lower. I just need to bite down. Careful, careful.

A cheer erupts as I sink my teeth into the crisp fruit.

"He don't look like such a boy now," the betting miner says.

I stand back, munching the juicy flesh, relieved.

"I see you like to win," Ruby says.

"Well, I couldn't be losing at my own game. Especially with a bet like that on," I say, giving her a knowing look.

She smiles. "Perhaps next time I challenge you to a Mexican game. For now I congratulate you with champagne. Come, we sit down?" She nods her head towards the barman as we take our seats at a table near the bar. He rushes over with a bottle of champagne and two glasses. There's a soft hiss as he eases the cork from the bottle and begins to pour.

"To victory," she says, clinking her glass against mine.

"Oh, I do love champagne."

"Me also," she says. "Is—" But I do not get to hear her thoughts. "Marco," she calls to the big, swarthy man making his way across the bar.

I stand up, looking for Gerry.

"Welcome back," Ruby says, beckoning Marco to sit down. "How was the trip?"

"Excellent," Marco says. "I have ev—"

"Where's Gerry?" I ask.

"He's not here," Marco says. "I have—"

"Where is he?" I say, feeling an edge of panic.

"Gerry is in San Francisco. I have—"

"Has something happened to him?"

Marco shakes his head. "I have a letter for you." He reaches into his coat and pulls it out.

I take it from him, my mind whirling. Why hasn't Gerry come back? I don't want to read the letter here. If it's bad news, if he's not coming back…

"I'll see you later," I say to Ruby.

"Frank," she says, her face full of concern, "don't go."

I shake my head. "I'll see you later," I repeat.

I walk down the street, the letter gripped in my hand. Surely Gerry wouldn't off and leave me here? Behind the tent I see the store looming. In less than a week it'll be finished. What am I going to do with a shop and nothing to sell?

Goldie sticks her head through the tent flap. I can tell from her face that she's wagging her tail.

"At least I've still got you," I say as she circles around, pleased to see me.

The letter is still clutched in my hand. I set it down on the bed while I fetch a bottle of poitín. It burns in my throat as I take a swig. I pick the letter up and unfold it.

San Francisco—25 October 1849
Dear Frank,

There is so much I want to be telling you but there is things I cannot be putting in a letter they will have to wait for my return. You should see this place it is nowhere near the size of New York but the hustle and bustle is mad new people arriving every day. Everyone is either trying to sell something or buy it. The docks are full of abandoned ships sitting empty after their crews heard about the gold.

Marco was great introducing me to all sorts of traders. I have made lots of contacts good people for the future selling all sorts from shovels to oysters. There is a wagon on its way with plenty of supplies on it.

I expect to be with you within two or three weeks if all turns out like I am planning. Keep your fingers crossed for me.

Your friend and partner
Gerry

"He's coming back," I say to Goldie, relieved. "Your Uncle Gerry's coming back."

* * *

I don't know what to expect as I walk up Main Street on Friday morning. Day of the Dead, it doesn't sound too encouraging. Ruby mentioned something about skeletons. It made me nervous. But I want to do what I can for Clarice so I've brought Goldie with me. Clarice has always loved my dog.

"Isn't that right?" I say to Goldie as she trots along beside me.

Ai-Li is still serving breakfast in the dining room at the back. I catch her eye and smile before turning right past the reception desk. Goldie's toenails click up the stairs beside me. There's a mirror on the second landing. I check my appearance quickly as I pass it, then knock on Ruby's door.

"Come in."

She looks magnificent today, in a deep red blouse and long black skirt. I have never known anyone with so many glamorous clothes. Not that I envy them. It's hard to imagine myself in a skirt now. I'm not sure how I'd find a way back to looking like a woman again. Anyway, I like the clothes I wear, the soft cotton of my shirt, my patterned waistcoat, the warmth of my woollen trousers. Everything but the binding. I hate crushing my breasts, day after day. There's no comfort in it.

"Make yourself comfortable," Ruby says, indicating the fat red armchair.

But my eye is taken with the dark wooden bureau that stands between the two windows. Usually it's closed up, neat and tidy. But today it's open, covered with all sorts of objects displayed at different levels on boxes, drawers and shelves—figurines, flowers, candles, fruit, bread, little skeletons and skulls. There's a painting of a raven-haired woman, skin a deep golden-brown. I realise I've been staring and look away.

"You're welcome to look. Let me show you. Here at the top is Saint Catherine of Bologna, the patron saint of artists," Ruby says, indicating a sculpture of a haloed woman. "She is here for Carlita. And this is Our Lady of Guadalupe, for my mother." She points to an image of an olive-skinned Virgin surrounded by rays of light and wearing a crown of stars.

"And this is Carlita," she says, picking up the portrait that had caught my eye. She looks at it for a moment before handing the small gold frame to me.

Her skin is darker than Ruby's; hair black, swept off her face; cheekbones high; eyes an almost black-brown. A slight frown plays across her fine features.

"She's beautiful," I say.

"More beautiful in life," Ruby says. "Sometimes I looked at her and scarcely believe she is mine."

There can be no mistaking her meaning this time.

I feel myself flush. "I wondered, you know, if…After what you said before. I've never met…" I stop, not sure what words to use.

"I do not mean to shock you. I think you…" It is her turn to trail off. She looks away from me.

"No," I say, reaching out and taking her hand, "I mean, yes. I mean, no. No, I'm not shocked. And yes, you thought…Yes, me too." I let go of her. I know my face is crimson by now, can feel the burn on my neck and ears. I wish she wouldn't look at me, wish she would say something.

"Have you known other…?" I say at last.

"Sapphists," she says. "That is the word I think you search for, the word for women who love other women. And yes"—she smiles at last—"I have known a few. But Carlita was different. Carlita I love with all my heart. Even after she broke it."

"What happened?" I say.

Her face darkens. "Her brother find out. He make her—" She stops, interrupted by a knock at the door.

I glare at it. *Go away.*

"Come in," Ruby calls.

Clarice slips inside. "Sorry I am late," she says, her voice flat. She looks pale, hair unwashed, unbrushed, like the life's gone out of her.

Ruby goes over and hugs her. "Come, sit down," she says, guiding Clarice to the couch. Goldie pads over and settles on the floor next to Clarice. "I am showing Frances my altar," Ruby continues. "I make for my mother and my friend Carlita. Things that remind me of them."

Clarice nods without looking. Her hand lays still on Goldie's head.

"I think we can make one to remember Bear Man," Ruby says.

Clarice nods again, but there's no interest.

"Do you have breakfast?"

Clarice shakes her head.

"Oh, Clarice, you must eat. You make yourself ill. He will not want you wasting away like this." She rings her serving bell. A few minutes later Ai-Li appears. "Please bring a jug of hot Mexican chocolate," Ruby says.

When Ai-Li has gone Ruby turns to Clarice and I. "Soon we have something to eat. And then we go to the cemetery to build Bear Man's altar together."

"No, not the cemetery," Clarice says.

"Yes, the cemetery. This is the way in Mexico."

"But your altar is 'ere," Clarice says.

"That is different. My mother, Carlita, they are not buried close by."

"Non," Clarice says, her jaw setting. "You cannot make me."

"Is for your own good," Ruby says, "to help you."

But Clarice just says non again.

There's a knock at the door. It's Ai-Li. She carries a steaming copper jug over to the bureau, filling the air with the sweet scent of chocolate and cinnamon. I watch her leave, wishing I could go with her, away from the awkwardness in the room.

"Have some bread and chocolate. *Pan de muerto*, special bread for today," Ruby says. She goes over to the bureau and starts slicing a loaf of iced bread, marked with dough shaped like crossed bones. She brings a couple of slices to Clarice with a silver cup of hot chocolate. "You dip the bread in the chocolate," she says. "Eating will help you think." She watches as slowly Clarice raises a slice to her mouth and takes a bite.

"My answer is still non," Clarice says.

"Do you want some bread, Frances?" Ruby asks, as if Clarice has not spoken.

"Yes, please," I say, pretending all is well. I dip the *pan de muerto* into the chocolate, then take a bite. It melts in my mouth. "This is good."

"We make for the dead. To remember them," she says, looking at Clarice. "To welcome them. So they know they are not forgotten."

"I 'ave not forgotten 'im," Clarice says, anger in her voice. "I will never forget 'im. But I do not 'ave to go to the cemetery. My Bear Man is not there."

We sit in silence, the sounds only of dipping and eating sweet bread, drinking rich hot chocolate.

"You do not have to go to the cemetery," Ruby says eventually. "I only try to help."

Clarice looks up, a shadow of a smile for the first time today. "I know," she says. "I know. And I want to do something to mark this Day of the Dead for 'im. Perhaps we can go to the vineyard?"

* * *

Old Joey is tacking up when we arrive at the stables half an hour later. The carriage is like nothing I've ever seen—small and light, room for the driver and a passenger at the front, another two passengers behind. And red. Whoever heard of a carriage painted red? With red leather seats. It could hardly be less like the hefty wagon I came across the country in.

"Where did you get the carriage?"

"You like?" Ruby says, smiling her big gap-toothed smile.

"I love it."

"I have it made in San Francisco."

Old Joey checks the harness of the two big black horses that have been hooked up to the carriage. "S'all ready," he says to Ruby.

"Thank you, Joey, you take good care of my horses."

He grunts. "You be careful with them."

"I am always careful," she says, laughing. She loads a hamper into the carrying box at the back before climbing up into the driver's seat.

"Get in, Frank," she says, patting the seat next to her.

I put my foot on the shiny silver metal footplate and climb up beside her. There's not much space. I can feel her all down the left side of my body. I adjust my position, holding myself stiff away from her.

"Ah, here is Clarice," Ruby says.

"I 'ave brought a few things," Clarice says, climbing on board and settling the wicker basket she's been carrying at her feet. "Goldie," she calls. My dog, who's been hanging around the stables, scrambles her way up and sits down, head resting on Clarice's lap. We are ready to go.

"*Arre caballos!*" Ruby calls, clicking the reins against the dark backs of the horses. There's a spark of excitement in her face. "*Arre!*" The carriage moves forward at a brisk pace, Ruby paying no heed to the miners milling about Main Street. "*Arre!*"

The horses move quickly from trotting to cantering and I flinch as one miner leaps aside. I'm back in the streets of Cork. They would have driven over the top of you, the rich people in their carriages. Clattering past, their faces turned away, as I dragged myself towards the harbour and the boat to America. I was filthy after two weeks on the road, sleeping in ditches and under hedges, my feet hurt and bleeding, my heart in a thousand pieces.

We're galloping now, trees and miners and picks and shovels whizzing past in a blur. I'm going to be sick.

"Stop," I shout. "Stop."

I need to get off this carriage, away from these people.

"*So caballos!*" Ruby says, dragging back on the reins. We slide to a halt, dust and dirt filling the air, one of the horses snorting in protest.

"What's wrong?" Ruby says.

"I have to go," I say, jumping down from the carriage.

I start to walk back down the track towards town. I try to whistle for Goldie but my throat's too tight.

"Frances! Frances!"

I don't turn back to see if she's following. Instead I start to run.

CHAPTER THIRTY-TWO

Dunquin, July 1846

There was no sign of the islands when I arrived on Clogher Beach ten minutes ago. Now the mist has cleared enough to reveal the smudged outline of the Great Blasket. I wish I could escape there for a few days. I'm worn out, explaining to my ma and da over and over how I met the Protestant, why I liked the Protestant, how I knew it would never work with the Protestant, why I'm glad I have nothing to do with the Protestant, how sorry I am that I lied about the Protestant.

I stoop to gather another handful of seaweed, wondering how I'm going to find a way to see Kitty. It's market day tomorrow. I have loved my market days with Kitty, flogging my wares in the morning, a sup of beer at a tavern before an evening at the scalp. But they're over. I'm not allowed to go. Not allowed to market, not allowed to Ballyferriter, not allowed anywhere but the church, the house and the fields. I've been under supervision ever since I told my da that big lie.

"Frances. Frances."

I look up. It's my mother, marching across the beach.

"Are you not finished yet?" she says, her face tight and grim, as it always is these days.

"I'm nearly done," I say, picking up a long brown frond. I hoist my damp sack onto my back and follow my ma up the beach.

* * *

"Peig, can you do me a favour?" I whisper as we're getting ready for bed. "Can you pass a message to Kitty for me without ma knowing?"

"Oh Jesus, Frances. I don't know."

"Please. I'm not doing anything wrong."

"I know. I'm just not sure I'll be able to manage it. She's watching me too."

"Why's she taking it out on you? It's not your fault."

"Ma thinks I knew about you and the Protestant. She thinks I helped to cover it up."

"How do you know?"

"She was on at me about it yesterday. Why had I let you carry on after such a man? Why had I not said anything to her about it?"

"What did you tell her?"

"The truth. That I knew nothing about it. That I couldn't remember you exchanging so much as a glance with any of that lot from the Colony."

"I'm sorry, Peig. I never meant to get you in trouble."

"It would be easier if I knew the truth. I haven't said anything to Ma and Da, but I still find it hard to believe that you were in love with a Protestant preacher."

"You can't always choose who you love," I say.

"No, you can't. But I don't think this Protestant's who you love. I'm sure it's someone else."

"Someone else?" I say, my heart pounding so loud I'm sure she must be able to hear it.

"You can trust me with the truth. I'm on your side, Frances. I won't tell anyone else."

I glance at her, biting a sliver of skin on the end of my thumb, trying to see her thoughts without her reading mine. Does she really know? Or does she only think she knows?

"So if not the Protestant, who do you think I love?"

"I think you love Kitty Gorman."

I try to laugh as if it's a ridiculous notion but what comes out is more of a squeak. "Kitty? What makes you say that?"

She doesn't answer for a minute and I'm wondering what she's going to say and whether I can bluff it out or whether it would be a relief to go ahead and tell her the truth. But then she says, "I saw you kissing her at Hallowe'en."

* * *

I'm up in the top field, rinsing off yesterday's seaweed, ready for digging it through the manure. But I can't settle to it. I keep looking down the hill to the path from Dingle, looking for my ma and Peig. Even though it's only eleven and they won't be home from market for hours yet.

I'm desperate to know whether Peig has managed to pass a message on to Kitty, whether Kitty has sent a message in return. We were up late last night, whispering in bed till long past dark. The chance at last to talk to someone about how I feel about Kitty. And someone that knows her too and likes her. I wish I'd told Peig sooner.

I look down the hill again. There's no one coming. I turn back to the manure, trying to focus my energy on forking in the seaweed. I'm about halfway through the sack when my da joins me.

"You're getting on well there, Frances," he says. "I'll just get the other shovel and I can give you a hand."

"You can have this one. I was about to go and check on the soup."

"Oh, the soup," he says, disappointed. "I thought we might finish the seaweed together."

"I don't want the soup to burn. Ma'll be looking forward to it after the market," I say.

"You know I only want what's best for you, Frances."

"I know, Da."

I walk back down towards the house, feeling heartless but knowing I can't be talking with him. It was talking got me in all this trouble in the first place. I kick a stone, watching it skitter down the path. There's a speck of a person in the distance on the road from Dingle. I watch for a minute but no one else appears round the corner, no donkey. It's not them.

I carry on down to the house. The soup is bubbling away, its aroma filling the kitchen. I put it on earlier this morning: chopped vegetables, pearl barley, the bones of a chicken, a couple of bay leaves. It's in no danger of burning. I give it a good stir anyway.

There's a rap at the door. "Is anyone home?" The door opens. It's her, it's Kitty. "Peig told me you were in trouble."

She comes over to where I'm standing, wrapping me in her arms. I want nothing more than to lose myself in her embrace, let her enfold me, take me away from these last terrible days. Instead I pull away. "Someone might see," I mutter.

"What might they see? A girl hugging her friend. Girls do it all the time, Frances."

It's never a good sign when she starts calling me Frances. "I'm sorry," I say. "But they're watching me."

"Who's watching you?"

"My parents."

"What are you talking about?"

"My parents. The curfew. The Protestant."

"What?"

"Didn't Peig explain?"

"She said you were in trouble. What's going on?"

"I hardly know where to begin."

"If you've met someone, some man—"

"How can you say that?"

"What am I supposed to think?"

I hear the hurt and confusion underneath her anger. "Please Kitty," I say, taking hold of her hand. "There's no one else—there never will be. You can trust me."

She looks at me for a long moment. "I'm sorry," she says, "I know I can. On the walk over here I came up with a hundred different stories about what kind of trouble you were in. And then when you didn't want me touching you…"

"I do want you touching me. But it's too risky here. I'm in so much trouble already."

"What is this trouble?"

Before I answer, I go to the door and look out down the road from Dingle.

"What are you doing?" Kitty says, following me out.

I carry on to the corner of the house where I can see the path from the fields, then walk back to where she's standing, staring at me like I've gone mad. "I was checking to see that my ma and da aren't coming. Let's go back inside, we mightn't have long."

She follows me into the house. I take a deep breath, getting my thoughts clear. "My parents were suspicious about where I've been going, all these nights I've been spending with you. I had to make up a lie to stop them finding out about us. They think I'm in love with a Protestant preacher. Now they don't trust me and I'm not allowed out anymore."

"What?"

"They think I'm in love with a Protestant."

"I don't understand."

"My da was questioning me about you. I had to say something."

"But why a Protestant preacher?"

"So they couldn't track him down. I was trying to protect you. He was going to come and see your ma."

"My ma?"

"To check whether I'd been going to stay at your house. They'd have found out we were lying. They'd have stopped me seeing you."

"It feels—"

The door opens. I look up to see my da standing there.

"Good day, Mister Moriarty," Kitty says, giving him her best smile.

"And to you," he says, smiling back.

I'm able to breathe again; he hasn't heard anything. But then, as if my ma's whispering in his ear, his face turns serious. "It's a while since we've seen you, Kitty," he says.

"It is. We've had a wet old time of it this last six months."

"Not at the market today then?"

"I was there first thing. But I finished early and thought I'd come for a visit."

"I see. Yes. Well…"

"Kitty and I were about to go for a walk," I say.

"Were you now? Well, I don't know about that."

"We're not meeting anyone else. I swear to you, Da, it's only a walk. We'll be back before Ma's home."

He stands quiet for a minute, looking me in the eye. At last he nods.

"Thanks Da," I say.

I walk with Kitty as far as the gate but as soon as I'm through it I take off down the hill, running at full pelt, the thump of Kitty's feet behind me. We clatter along the road until at last I stop at the track up to Dunmore Head.

I stand panting, waiting for her to catch up.

"Jesus," Kitty says, breathless, "what got into you?"

"Sorry," I say, smiling in spite of everything, taking in the pink of her cheek, her hair wild round her face. "I just needed to run."

"You'll be the death of me," she says, but she's smiling too. "Where are you taking me?"

"Up to Dunmore Head," I say. "There's an old rock up there where I go to think. There's never anyone else about."

We're quiet as we start the climb up the headland. In ten minutes we reach my spot, the big flat stone in front of the old ruined fort wall.

"At last," I say, sitting down, "somewhere we can talk properly."

"You should have seen your face when your da walked in."

"No wonder, now I know we've been caught before."

"What do you mean?"

"Peig saw us kissing at Hallowe'en. She told me last night."

"Jesus. Is she going to tell?"

"No. Though sometimes I think it might be better if my parents knew the truth. They're on at me morning, noon and night—*the Protestant* this and *the Protestant* that. At least you're a Catholic."

She drops her eyes, pulling her shawl over her head, a demure virgin. "Bless me, Father, for I have sinned. My last confession was two weeks ago. These are my sins: I have let my lover besmirch her reputation with a phantom Protestant."

"Three Hail Marys," I say.

"And I've left her to the cruel punishments of her tyrant parents."

"Another six Hail Marys and five Our Fathers."

"And it's more than a week since I had her groaning and gasping and melting in my arms."

"You are one wild woman and no mistake," I say, feeling myself blush.

She smiles, then looks at me, her face intent. "Wild I may be, but wildness won't help fix this problem with your parents. And I need it fixed."

"I don't know if it can be fixed. I've not been out of their sight for more than half an hour since Saturday. My da might ease up, but my ma? She'll never forgive me."

"Your ma will come round."

"I don't think so. When she's not actually complaining out loud about the Protestant, she's tutting and huffing and rolling her eyes at me. They go on about the English but I may as well be living under a curfew. I don't know if I'll ever be allowed out overnight again."

"There has to be a way. I miss you, Frankie. Sometimes I miss you so much I feel I could die of it."

"I miss you too. I miss holding you. I miss talking to you. I miss lying next to you, drifting into sleep, waking up with you in the morning. I'm frightened we may never have those things again."

"Of course we will. Your ma's angry now but she'll soften."

"You don't know her like I do. She's hard to shift once her mind is set. She says I can't be trusted with men, that I've no judgment if I could be taking up with a Protestant. I'm worried she'll bring a matchmaker in."

"Has she said so?"

"Not so far."

"She can't go marrying you off."

"Maybe not. But she's stopping me going out, she's stopping me spending nights with you. I've been trying to find some way round her this last week. But then Peig gave me an idea last night. She's planning to follow Liam to Australia. I think we should do the same."

"Australia? Surely you're not suggesting we go there?" She stares at me, shocked.

"Well, maybe not there, but somewhere. Maybe England, maybe America."

"Are you seriously saying we should leave Ireland? That we should emigrate?"

"I'm saying my mother will never let up while I stay here."

"You're doing it again," she says, getting to her feet. "You're making all the decisions for everyone."

"I wasn't deciding."

"I have a right to a say too, you know."

"I know."

"This isn't just about you, Frances. I have my mother to think of. Have you given her a second thought?"

I haven't given her mother even a first thought but I don't say so. "I've got a family too," I say. "I've got people I'll have to leave behind. But I thought it would be worth it. I want to live with you, to be with you every day. Don't you want that?" My voice has been raised but now as I realise that perhaps she doesn't, it comes out soft. "Don't you want to be with me?"

She looks at me, her face a fury one minute, then softening, then furious again. She goes to speak but all that comes out is an angry puh of breath. She shakes her head and I can feel my world falling apart.

I thought if only I could see her, speak to her, that we'd find a way through together, a way to make it right. I bury my face in my hands, my body hunching over, my knees coming up towards my chest. I wish that I could roll away, squeezed up into a ball, rolling away from the pain and confusion, the trouble in my life, rolling down the headland, towards the edge, dropping free into the sea.

"Shush," Kitty says. I feel her sit beside me, her hand resting lightly on my back. "Shush, darling." The tears come spurting out of my eyes and it's all I can do to stop myself from howling. "It won't be like this forever, Frankie. We'll find a way round your ma. I promise."

CHAPTER THIRTY-THREE

Hangtown, November 1849

Goldie's nails *click-click-click* their way up the stairs. I follow her, enjoying the satisfying *clunk* of my boots against the wood, the firmness of the handrail. She turns at the top, tail wagging, face smiling, excited.

"I know," I say. "It's great, isn't it?"

The builders have finally left and Goldie and I are exploring our new home. The parlour at the back runs the breadth of the house with two windows looking out towards the hills. It hasn't a stick of furniture in it but George, the carpenter who made Bear Man's coffin, has nearly finished a table and chairs for me. And maybe I'll get a couch or a couple of armchairs, like Ruby has. I wonder how much they cost.

I've taken the bedroom at the front, overlooking the street, so I can hear if anyone comes knocking when I'm upstairs. All it's got in it is my cot and Goldie's blanket. But my new bed's coming tomorrow.

"I suppose you'll want feeding," I say to Goldie. We clatter back down the stairs to the stockroom. As I break chunks of bread into a bowl, she sits waiting, drool gathering at her cheeks.

"Nearly ready," I say, adding a generous dash of milk. I carry the bowl out to the back step as she prances around me. Leaving her scoffing, I go back inside. It's cold tonight and I'm glad I won't be in the tent.

I should eat. Maybe a bit of bread and jam. I go through to the store to fetch a jar of blueberry preserve. An array of goods arrived by wagon from Gerry a few days ago. My arms are aching from hefting boxes and stacking shelves, moving some things three or four times before I finally settled on the right place for them. The store is really coming along now. The shelves behind the long side of the counter are stacked with all sorts of jars and tins—pickled vegetables, fruit in syrup, tinned beef, pea soup, oysters, salmon, herrings, walnuts, pickles, relishes, chutneys and preserves. I love the bright colours— tins of yellow and red, green and blue—and the light of the lanterns glinting off the glass jars.

Down the opposite wall are barrels of flour, oats, cornmeal, dried beans and coffee. Kettles, cooking pans, saddlebags and saws hang from hooks in the ceiling. The guns are displayed on the back wall to the right of the door to the storeroom. To the left is the drink— bourbon and brandy along with my Ruby's Reward. I've a couple of blankets on the counter and more out in the back, and a drawer of mending materials—needles, spools of thread and buttons. There's also a drawer of shaving brushes, razors and soap, though from what I've seen of miners, I doubt they'll sell. But the tobacco and matches will, and the candles and lanterns too. Gerry's done us proud.

I've a few more boxes and crates to shift to the storeroom, the big coffee grinder to set up. And Willie's coming back to fit the pot-bellied stoves—one in the store, the other in the parlour. I should be ready to open tomorrow afternoon.

I look around the store, scanning my shelves of food, wondering what to eat. A jar of pickled potatoes catches my eye, sickening me. How many Irish families could I feed with what's in this store?

I don't want anything now. Instead I go back through to the workroom and let Goldie in. She pads behind me into the store. I'm glad of the company as I set about finishing shifting the crates. I don't know what I'd do without this dog. She's a friend to me, especially this last week when I've been avoiding Ruby. I can't face her since the Day of the Dead. I know I was rude but sometimes that woman's far too nosy for her own good.

I'm nearly finished with the crates when there's a loud knocking at the door to the store. I'm not keen to open up; it's late and it's dark and there are robbers everywhere. But Gerry and I vowed to run a friendly store so I walk cautiously towards the door.

"Who is it?" I call.

"Open up," comes the reply.

I peer out through the window to the street. It's that little shite Sam from the other store.

"What do you want?" I say, drawing the bolts and edging the door open.

He pushes hard against it, almost knocking me over.

"So this is it?" he says, stomping down towards the back counter, looking the store up and down.

"What do you want?" I say again.

"From you, nothing," he says and spits a wad of tobacco onto my clean floor. He stares at me, defiant, and I notice again his strange pale eyes. I have never liked the look of him, nor the smell. And a skinful of drink hasn't improved him. Goldie hasn't much taken to him either. She's growling softly beside me.

"That's one mangy critter you got there, boy," he says. "Suits your stinking store." He spits again and this time it lands on Goldie's flank.

She responds with a furious bark, which develops into a deep, fierce growl.

"You keep that varmint away from me, boy," he says, drawing a knife. "Else I won't be responsible."

"Don't you dare threaten my dog," I say, pulling my pistol. "And get out of my store."

He sways before me, eyes fixed on my pistol.

"Ain't nothing here worth staying for," he says at last. "You ain't got the balls for business."

* * *

I wake with the sunrise, not sure at first where I am. Apart from the few nights at Ruby's, I've slept under canvas for months. I wonder how long it will take me to get used to the wooden roof above me. Time to get up and get on with my day. George is going to fit shutters to my bedroom but for now there's nothing to stop everyone knowing my business. I duck into the corridor to wash and dress, then carry on down the stairs, ready to start the day.

The store's ready for business. I stayed up last night after Sam's little visit, too angry for bed. Muttering about what I'd do if I got my hands round his chicken neck as I cleaned gobs of tobacco off my lovely wooden floor. But it gave me the energy to finish the displays and move the last couple of crates. Now all that's left is to set up the scales—a big one for provisions, a small one for gold. I won't be like

Sam, weighing as far out of sight as possible, looking to cheat people. No, everything's going to be up front for the customers to see.

I open the smaller wooden box and gently lift the scales out onto the middle of the counter. They're made of brass, two weighing pans suspended from either end of a horizontal bar. I take the brass weights out of the box and fit each one into the correct wooden dimple. The larger scales are a different type, much heavier, made of cast iron, with arms of different lengths and a counterbalancing weight to give a measure of what's in the pan.

I stand back from the counter, looking around the store, the tins and jars carefully stacked, the pots and pans hanging from the ceiling, and now the weighing machines on the counter, ready for work. That's it. Everything's ready. I go to the door and turn the sign to Open.

Back behind the counter, I wait for my first customer. Up on the wall the clock ticks. I've never lived with a clock. God, it's loud. *Tick. Tick. Tick. Tick.* I go back to the door and look out. Further up the street a couple of men are digging a hole, looking for gold. A cart rumbles by. A man in a black hat rides past.

I go back in, disappointed. When are they coming? I want to be weighing things for my first customer. I scoop some meal out of the barrel and put it in the weighing pan. It clunks down with a satisfying metal note. I start shifting the counterweight along the arm. Four ounces. Nothing. Five ounces. Nothing. Six ounces. The pan lifts a bit. Seven ounces. It rises further and settles in balance.

"That's seven ounces, sir," I say, practising my shop voice.

I jump at a knock at the door.

"Hello," a voice calls.

"Come in," I say, tripping over my own feet as I rush towards the door. I'm almost there when it opens to reveal George, the carpenter.

"How do?" he says. "I've brung your furniture. The cart's out front."

"Bring it round the back," I say. "It'll be easier for unloading."

It takes six trips before we have it all up the stairs. I leave George putting the bed together and go and arrange the table and chairs in the parlour. He's finished by the time I get back.

"You've done a grand job, George," I say, looking at the big solid bed.

He grunts but I think he's pleased. "I'll do the shutters tomorrow."

"That would be great, thanks."

The meal is still hanging in balance when I return to the store. I empty the pan back into the barrel and return it to the scales. I'm barely back behind the counter when there's a sharp knock and the bell clangs as the door opens.

It's Ruby, resplendent in a severe black dress edged in scarlet, her hair tied up with a red ribbon. She's a handsome woman.

"I am not sure if you are open but Willie say to me he has finished."

"Yes, last night. What do you think?"

"Is beautiful. I like the long counter. And so many tins and jars. What choice. You show Sam what a store is supposed to be."

"He was here last night. He said I didn't have the balls for business."

I'm expecting concern, perhaps, or sympathy. Instead, she throws her head back and lets out a full-throated laugh. It's impossible not to join in, and as I laugh I realise how much I've missed her.

"I'm sorry about last week," I say. "I didn't mean to be rude."

"I am sorry too," she says, touching my arm. "I think maybe I should not interfere. I only wish to help."

"You have helped," I say gruffly. "You found me the builders. I'd still be digging the foundations if it wasn't for you. Come on, let me give you a tour. Do you want to start upstairs or down?"

"I'm in your hands," she says, arching an eyebrow. I find myself blushing.

"Well, this is the store," I say, then wonder whether I could sound more stupid.

"You do a good job," she says. "I like how you hang the equipment from the walls and the ceiling. Everything so easy to see. Gerry will be pleased."

"Do you think so?"

"Of course. Other people too. They will want to come to your store."

"I hope so."

"I am sure. But I know what is like when you first open, waiting to see if anyone come."

"I haven't had a single customer yet."

"They will come, soon enough. But you need to make sure everyone in the diggings knows. Perhaps handbills in the bars and wooden signs on the routes to Hangtown?"

"I remember seeing one for Ruby's when we were working down the river. I knew about your place before I'd seen it. And then Bear Man told us all about it on our way into town. That was the first time we met him, up in the woods."

"Yes, he tell me how a crazy boy nearly shoot him."

"It's hard to believe he's dead."

"I know."

"How's Clarice?"

"The vineyard help her, such a beautiful place. I think she move there. Bear Man already start to build a house. Willie will finish for her. But before she moves, I want her to learn to use a gun."

"I could teach her to shoot. She should get a dog too. I don't know what I'd do on my own without Goldie."

"She's a special dog. But you need people too, Frances."

"I know," I say.

"Come to the bar again, soon."

"I will."

"Promise?"

"Promise," I say, looking forward to it already.

It's quiet after she's gone and I'm beginning to worry that I'll never get any customers but then the bell rings and the door opens to a tall man with a huge beard wearing a battered hat.

"How do?" he says.

"Can I help you?" I say.

"You take gold?"

"Yes," I say, smiling, remembering Sam's rudeness when we asked him the same question. "Sixteen dollars an ounce."

He turns his back on me, fumbling with his clothes. Eventually he hands over a leather pouch, still warm and slightly moist. I take it, trying not to think where it's been. Carefully I shake the gold out into the right pan. The nuggets are tiny, nothing bigger than a flea, but he's got a good number of them and the pan dips down. I place the 1920 grain weight on the other side, but it's not heavy enough. I add the 960 grain but still the right-hand pan is down. I take them both off and replace them with the 3840 grain. But it's too heavy.

I can feel little prickles of heat on my face. I thought this would be easy.

"Where've you been digging?" I say to try to cover my lack of skill.

"East of town on the American. Been there a week."

"I started there myself," I say as finally the combination of 1920, 960 and 480 creates a balance. "That's seven ounces you've got there."

"How come you ain't digging now?" he says.

"There's more than one way of making money here."

"I guess," he says, but I can see he's not convinced. He'll learn, I think, as he swaps more than half his gold for a few weeks' food and a bottle of Ruby's Reward. We're undercutting Sam's Stores, but we're still making at least ten times what Gerry paid for things, twenty times on some items.

We plan to divide the profits three ways—a third for me, a third for Gerry, a third for Ireland. But after another thirty minutes on my own I start worrying about whether we'll have enough customers to make a profit. I'm thinking about spending the rest of the day making signs to advertise the store when the bell clangs again, ushering in a stocky miner.

"So you're open at last."

"Since this morning."

"I been watching. 'Bout time for a choice in this town." He walks round the store, peering at my displays, lifting things up, then putting them back down again.

"Can I help?" I say.

"Well, I see you're cheaper than Sam's Stores. Not much cheaper, mind."

"I don't weigh false, so you get all that you pay for. And there's a better choice."

"I see that," he says. "Well for now, all I'm needing's a pick, but I'll be back when I stock up again."

The wait for the next customer is not so long but instead of another bearded miner it's a clean-shaven gentleman. "Doctor Charles," I say, rushing forward to embrace him.

"Good to see you, Frank. How are you?"

"I'm grand. Do you like my store?"

"*Your* store?"

"M & R's—Moriarty and Ryan's. Me and Gerry are partners."

"Congratulations. I take it that you found some gold?"

"That we did. Out by Log Cabin Ravine."

"I am so pleased for you. I've often wondered how you've been getting on."

"How about yourself? Did you strike it lucky?"

He laughs. "I think I must be the unluckiest miner in the whole of California. Or maybe just the most inept."

"Perhaps you'll do better here. There've been some big strikes in Hangtown."

"My gold-digging days are over. I've been doctoring my way round the diggings, trying to decide whether to stay in California or go back East and find that girl my parents keep expecting."

"Go back? Jesus, you can't be thinking of doing that trip again? Stay here in Hangtown. We could do with a doctor."

"The name's a little off-putting."

"It was Dry Diggings till six months ago. Then they hanged some fellas for thieving…" I stop. That's not going to encourage him. "I'm sure it won't be called that forever."

"They have the strangest names, some of these mining camps. Rough and Ready, Grizzly Flat. I even heard of one called Murderer's Bar. So what's Hangtown like?"

"There's a few bars, though I only go to Ruby's. The food's great there, Chinese and Mexican mostly."

"I must say I do like Mexican food. I'd never tasted it till Sacramento but a Mexican woman ran the most wonderful restaurant there."

"Well, you'll love Ruby's. And it's not just the food, there's entertainment too. Lucia Hernandez is coming for a week. I've heard she's all the rage in San Francisco."

"Lucia Hernandez? I saw her in Sacramento. She's quite a performer."

"Shall we go and see her on Saturday night?"

"I'd be delighted."

CHAPTER THIRTY-FOUR

Dunquin, July 1846

I wake with a smile on my lips. I will see Kitty at market tomorrow. Ma told me I could go last night. Da's been working on her, convincing her I've learned my lesson. I have—there'll be no more Protestant preachers. Ma will be there too, of course, I'm not allowed to be roaming the countryside on my own yet. But there's hope for the future.

These last few weeks have been a torture. I don't know how I'd have gotten through them without Kitty. She's come visiting every week, charming my ma and da. I miss our time alone, but at least I've been able to see her.

I sit up, stretching. The sky's already tinged with gold but in the bed opposite, Peig and Lizzie sleep on. They've never been early risers. Quietly I start to dress, ready to get on with my day.

The door creaks as I slip from the bedroom to the kitchen but no one stirs. I sit at the cold hearth, tying on my boots. Dolly and Daisy will be ready for milking. I may as well get on with it.

It's a beautiful morning, the air fresh, sea calm. I stand looking out towards the Blaskets, breathing in the day, then turn and walk up the path to the shed. Daisy lets out a low moo as I open the door. I always milk her first, she wouldn't give me peace if I started with

Dolly. Of all the things I do on the farm, nothing is more satisfying than milking—the rhythm, the warmth of Daisy's flank, the sound of the liquid hitting the pail.

I'm on my way back down to the house with the two pails of milk when I notice a red-haired woman walking up the path from the village.

It can't be. What would she…It is, it's Kitty.

I put my pails down and wave to her. She breaks into a run. I would run to her too, but it would make me want to sweep her into my arms and who knows if someone else is up and would see us out the window. But I wave again, smiling.

She arrives panting and I can see immediately that something's wrong, her eyes red and puffy like she's been crying for hours.

"What is it? What's happened?" I say.

"Oh God…"

"Is it your ma?"

"It's the potatoes. All our potatoes…" Her voice is shrill with panic, eyes wild.

"What's happened?"

"The whole crop. It's all gone. Every plant…"

I stare at her, not wanting to believe her. "Are you sure?"

"Of course I'm sure."

"Oh, Kitty." I go to put my arms around her, not knowing what else to do but she's stiff and shrugs me off.

"I can't," she says.

I step back, not sure what to say, what to do. I stand there feeling dazed. This can't be true. The harvest's not due for another six weeks. How can their potatoes be rotten before they're even harvested? "How do you know?" I say.

"I noticed the first spots on Monday evening. I didn't want to believe it was back. But there were more on Tuesday. Now every plant's shriveled and black."

"Have you checked the potatoes themselves? Maybe it's only above ground."

"It's everything. It's all rotten."

"Oh God," I say.

"It's everywhere in Ballyferriter. Everywhere. And beyond. The whole crop's gone from Ballyferriter to Clogher. Rotten. I had to cover my face from the stench."

"There's no sign of it here," I say, crossing myself in a silent prayer that we'll be safe.

"Lucky you," she says, her tone bitter.

"Thank God our crop's not spoiled," I say, but immediately regret it, touching the wooden pail three times to ward off the bad luck of speaking it out loud. "We need our potatoes, same as everyone else. And it means we'll be able to help you and your mother out."

"Why on earth would your family help me and my ma?"

"They're good people. They help their friends. Of course they'll help you."

"We're hardly going to be top of their list. They'll give to family first, then neighbours."

"But you are family," I say, my voice quiet, not wanting to be overheard. "Family to me."

"Maybe, but not to them." She turns away, looking out to sea.

I wish I knew what to say but I can think of nothing.

"I'm sorry," she says at last. "This isn't your fault."

"I won't let you and your ma starve."

"I know you'll try. But we've no food, no money. And Burnham's agent'll be after the rent in November, as if this year is the same as any other. What can you do that will sort that out?"

"Maybe there'll be public works again."

"Ah Jesus, Frances. Don't you know the English? When have they ever given a damn about us? We could all rot to death and what would they care?"

She's crying now. Not loudly. Just tears pouring down her face. I put my arms around her, holding her as she weeps.

CHAPTER THIRTY-FIVE

Hangtown, November 1849

I wish I hadn't told Doctor Charles I'd go out tonight. I've been run off my feet today, miners queuing up to give me their gold. But a promise is a promise. I fiddle with my red cravat, checking my reflection in the window. The silky material reminds me of my best petticoat, the red-and-blue-striped one I wore to the cake dance the day I met Kitty. I stare at my ghost self, my short hair, flattened chest. What would Kitty make of me dressed like this? I push the thought away.

I clatter down the stairs and out into the street. There are always plenty of miners around in Hangtown on a Saturday evening, looking for a drink, a bet, a fuck or a fight. Tonight's no different. I make my way down the street to Ruby's, nodding here and there at men I recognise.

Even before I open the door to the bar, I can hear the noise of the crowd. I take a deep breath and go in. The heat of two hundred sweaty miners hits me. I scan the bar looking for Doctor Charles but all I can see are beards, beards and more beards. My eyes light on Ruby, sitting close to the stage, whispering into the ear of a woman I've never seen before. They both burst out laughing.

I turn away, worming a path through the throng.

"Frank," a voice says beside me as I reach the middle of the room. It's Doctor Charles. "Sit down," he says, gesturing to the chair beside him. It puts Ruby and her blond strumpet directly in my sightline. Not that it's anything to me. I shuffle the chair to the right and focus my eyes on Doctor Charles.

"I made sure to get us a table," he says, leaning over and talking close to my ear. "Ruby warned me it would be busy. Lucia Hernandez is quite a draw."

"Ruby? You know Ruby?"

"Yes, I've been staying here."

I fight down a spark of jealousy. Ruby's my friend. And I knew Doctor Charles first. I should have been the one to introduce them.

"I've waited to order," he says, "but I know what I want. *Pollo con salsa de mole*," he pronounces with a flourish.

"Consal…?" I say. I haven't really got to grips with Spanish yet and rely on the English translations in the menu.

"*Con salsa de mole*. It's chicken with the most delicious sauce of chili, peanuts and chocolate. I had it on Wednesday night and it was one of the best things I've ever eaten."

"Oh," I say, nodding. I look at the menu but hardly see it, busy as I am watching Ruby out of the corner of my eye. She kisses the blonde on the cheek, then shows her to the exit at the back of the bar that leads through to the hotel lobby. I watch her watching the blonde's retreat. She looks at me as she turns back to the bar but I look away.

"I think I'll have the chow mein. I do love Chinese food," I say, my voice sounding loud and shrill in my ears. I look up again, watching Ruby as she starts to work her way round the bar, pausing at tables, checking the needs of her guests, laughing here and there. I feel myself staring and turn back to Doctor Charles in time to hear "choice." God knows what he said before that.

"You were right about Ruby's," he continues. "I've been in a few mining towns and this is quite the finest establishment I've encountered."

"So you're enjoying Hangtown?"

"Indeed I am. This might be the town for me. I've had plenty of work in the few days I've been here."

"Doctoring?"

"Yes, I took a bullet out of a man's leg yesterday evening. And I've seen a few men with scurvy, a couple with toothache."

"It must be great to be able to help people."

"It is. But I'm sure I can help more people than I can treat myself. I'm even more convinced of my ideas about the spread of cholera. And what better place to study it? I've started to think that it's God's will for me to be here."

"Do you really think you can find a way to stop the cholera?"

"I think it's possible. I have my theories, as you know, and here I can test them."

"Imagine if you really could find a cure."

"Well, I'm going to try at least."

"Do you think you could find cures for other fevers? Like famine fever?" I say, wishing my voice didn't waver.

"There are lots of different kinds of fever—typhus, typhoid, scarlet fever. It would be hard to know from here whether famine fever's a separate disease or whether people are succumbing to the other fevers because they're weak from hunger."

"It's killing thousands in Ireland. Please, can you try?"

"I don't think so," he says, his voice gentle. "I can't study it from America, not knowing clearly the symptoms, the onset, the conditions."

"I know them. I know all about them," I say, carrying on as if tears hadn't started leaking down my face.

"I'm sorry, Frank," he says. "I have more chance with cholera. I've seen it for myself. I think it would be too hard for me to find the cause of famine fever."

"But you think there is a cause? And a cure that can be found?"

"I think scientific study will reveal the cause of all diseases. And in time provide answers to cure most of them."

"The English blame us for the fever, for the famine. Have you heard of Charles Trevelyan? Sir Charles Trevelyan?" The tears are flowing and I am almost shouting now. I can feel people looking but I can't help myself.

"No, I don't think so."

"He's the English official in charge of famine relief. He says the famine is God's judgment, God's way of teaching the Irish a lesson."

Doctor Charles tries to speak but I talk over him. "He blames the Irish, the people who are starving, the people who have nothing. He's not interested in a cause or a cure, not to what ails the potato, not to the diseases ravaging the people. It's providence, he says, dealing with a 'surplus population.'"

"This is the man in charge?" Doctor Charles says.

"Yes," I say, a mocking laugh rising from the bitterness that lives in my guts. "The man in charge. God alone knows how many are dead already, but it's not enough for Trevelyan."

"It must be—"

"They were dying in droves in their cabins and along the side of the roads when I was leaving Ireland. It's got worse since then. The ships we left in—'coffin ships' they're called. Did you hear about Grosse Île, the quarantine station in Canada? Thousands died there, shoveled into mass graves."

Doctor Charles is staring at the table now, looking anywhere but at me. But a man to his left is gawping at me. He nudges the fella next to him. I rub my tears away furiously. "They say that what you can't change you have to learn to accept. But there are things you should never accept. The English have cheated and lied to excuse what they've done in Ireland. There'll be a day of reckoning for Trevelyan and the landlords and the rest of the bastards who left the people to rot and die. It's on their heads. And may they burn in hell for it."

My chair scrapes the floor as I get to my feet. "What are you staring at?" I say to the man behind Doctor Charles. He's taller than me but I don't care anymore.

"Frank, please sit down," Doctor Charles says.

But I can't. The tears have gone now I'm on my feet. I'm ready for a fight and I don't care who with. I feel a twinge of disappointment as the staring man turns away.

"Is there a problem?" It's Ruby. I should've known she'd come over. She's always looking out for any trouble, stepping in to nip it in the bud, to smooth it over.

"No," I say, my tone short. I shrug her hand off my arm.

"I don't know what your problem is, asswipe, but show the lady a bit of respect."

I turn to the big blond man who's addressed me. "Fuck you," I say.

I know he's going to hit me, I want him to hit me, but I want to hit him too. My right fist bores into his gut as his collides with my left eye. My head's going backwards but still I drive my fist into this fucker's gut, hard, hard, as hard as I can, wanting to hurt him. I swing again—but he's out of reach, pulled back, arms flailing, two of Ruby's men dragging him away. I'm grabbed from behind, one arm forced up my back, marched and steered between tables, the crowd opening like magic before us.

I don't struggle. Whoever's got me could snap my arm in a second. And I'm done now anyway, feeling a strange kind of relief as I catch a glimpse of myself in the mirror, my eyebrow cut, blood dripping down my face and onto my crisp white shirt.

My captor pushes me through the door from the bar to the hotel lobby before letting me go. I turn to face Marco.

"Sorry," I say.

He shrugs. "You've gone crazy tonight." He fishes a handkerchief out of his pocket and hands it to me. I put it to my eye where the blood is still flowing. It's beginning to hurt, a lump forming on my brow.

The door swings open to reveal Ruby. She says something to Marco in Spanish but all I catch is "gracias." He nods his head and then he is gone.

Ruby turns back to me, puffing herself up. She's not a tall woman but she looks powerful.

"I'm sorry, Ruby," I say, before she gets the chance to speak. "I shouldn't have been fighting in your bar."

"Why do you do this? He beat you if my boys do not stop him."

I shrug. "I don't know."

"'I don't know.' This is the excuse of a child, not a grown woman."

"Shh," I say. "Keep your voice down."

"Or a grown man," she says, louder than ever. She continues quietly. "I worry about you, Frances. You seem to be looking for a fight. I am right, no?"

I shrug again. "I suppose so."

"But why? You know what is like in towns like this. A man can lose his life like that." She clicks her fingers dramatically in my face. "And I, for one, do not wish to see that."

A drawling Southern voice interrupts before I can reply. "Oh Ruby, do you mind if I disturb you?"

I turn around to look at the speaker. It's the blond woman. I glare at her.

She laughs. "Why, that isn't any way to greet a friend."

"I'm not your friend," I say.

"Not yet. I'm Loula-Mae. Loula-Mae Adams."

She offers her hand, straight out, like a man, though she's wearing a low-cut emerald dress. I'm so surprised that I take it. Her grip is firm, not what I would have expected.

"Frank Moriarty," I say. Then realise what I'm doing and withdraw my hand. I go back to glaring but she laughs again.

"You sure are touchy, honey. That how you got you a busted head?"

My mouth opens to tell her to mind her own business but Ruby cuts across me. "Is there something you want?"

"Well yes, but I can go find one of your staff. You seem to have your hands full with Frank here."

"I'm fine. Sorry, again," I say, looking at Ruby. I turn away towards the exit to the garden.

"Please, Frank, wait," Ruby says. She turns back to the blonde. "What you are looking for?"

"Sarsaparilla. Lucia's decided it's the one thing to settle her nerves tonight. You know how she gets when she's performing."

"Of course. I send a glass through. Is there anything else?"

"No, that's everything. Thanks Ruby. I'll see you after the show. Nice to meet you, Frank." She makes her way back down the corridor, then disappears through the door to the dressing room.

"I don't know what is wrong with you," Ruby says to me, her face a fury. "First you pick a fight with a man twice your size. Then you act like a pig to Loula-Mae. She is an old friend. I hope you will like her."

"You like her enough for both of us."

"What do you mean by that?"

"Nothing."

"This does not sound like nothing."

"I just don't like her."

"You don't even know her."

"I know her type. Flirting and carrying on."

"Are you…You're not jealous, are you?"

"No," I say, but I can feel myself going red. I didn't like seeing some other woman laughing with Ruby, touching her. I wanted it to be me.

"You don't need to be jealous about me," Ruby says. She reaches out to touch my arm but I jump back like I've been branded.

"Leave me alone," I say, pushing past her. "Just leave me alone."

CHAPTER THIRTY-SIX

Dunquin, November 1846

I lie quiet, listening to the sound of my sisters breathing, letting my eyes adjust to the dark. I need to hold on to these last moments. Tomorrow I leave for America.

The chance to live with Kitty at last. I never thought I'd see the day, especially after the Protestant preacher. She turned me down flat then, when I asked her up at Dunmore Head. I never expected her to change her mind. But then, I never expected the potatoes to rot again.

I remember her coming to me that day at the end of July to tell me their potatoes had rotted. I kept thinking, This can't be happening. Not again. This can't be happening.

"I can't think here," I said, wondering if my ma would let me go up to Dunmore Head with Kitty. "I need to be able to think."

"I've been up half the night thinking," she said, "and I keep coming back to the same thing." She took a deep breath. "I have to leave. My ma has a better chance without me."

"Leave Ireland?"

"It's the only way."

I stared at her, hardly able to believe what she was saying.

"You've never wanted to leave," I said. "What about your ma?"

"That's who I'm thinking of. Maybe she can make enough for herself with her singing and the wakes and laying out of bodies. And maybe the agent will let us off the rent till May. And I'll get a job in America and I can send her money for food and for rent."

I stood there wondering what part I played in her plans.

"You said I," I said.

"What?"

"You said, 'I have to leave.' Are you…" I swallowed, trying to keep the tears at bay. "Are you not wanting…Do you not want—"

"Of course I want you to come," she said, putting her arms around me. "Of course." She knelt down on one knee then, looking up at me. "Frances Moriarty, will you come with me to America?"

"I will," I said, my heart brimming. "I will."

Someone's stirring next door, scraping out the ashes ready to lay the fire. I get up, throwing my shawl over my nightgown.

"Morning, Da," I say as he bends over the hearth.

"Ah, you're up. Grand," he says.

"Shall I finish that?"

"No, sit yourself down. I've it nearly done."

I take the chair on the far side of the hearth, watching his big strong hands laying in the sods and tinder. He turns to light a taper from the lantern to get the fire going. He has started to look old these last few months, his hair more grey than black now, the lines more deeply etched into his face.

Our crop failed a few days after Kitty's, most of our potatoes ruined. What survived won't last my family till summer, though at least I'm one less mouth to feed. There's five dead here in Dunquin this last month. And worse to come, I'm sure of it.

"You'll manage without me, won't you Da?"

"Of course we will. Of course. The girls'll help more and there's plenty of cottiers wanting work if I need them."

"It's hard to be leaving at a time like this."

"Don't worry about us, Frances. We've enough oats and barley to last us, the pig to sell for the rent. And you know how your mother's always been, squirreling coins away all over the house. We'll get by."

"I'll send money, as soon as I've got work in New York. I'll send all I can, you know I will, Da."

"Of course I know. You've always been a good girl, the best a father could want."

He looks up and there's no hiding the tears in his eyes.

"Oh, Da," I say, starting to cry myself.

He comes and puts his arms around me. I bury my wet face in his neck. He smells of smoke, the fields and the tallow soap my mother makes. I've never thought much about his smell but today I breathe it in greedily, hoping I'll never forget it.

"I wish it wasn't so far," I say, lifting my face at last. "I might never come back."

"I know. But you're right to go to America. I would in your place. You'll get a decent chance there, not like in England. Kitty too. She's a grand girl. I'm glad the two of you will be together." He holds my eye for the longest moment and I wonder, does he know? Is he telling me he knows?

But then there's the creak of my mother's step on the stairs down from the half loft and the moment is gone.

* * *

"Why don't you go and meet them?" my da says.

"What?" I say, turning back from the window.

"Kate and Kitty. Why don't you go and meet them? You're like a hen on a griddle, waiting."

"I am not," I say, though he's right. I've been back and forth to the window this last thirty minutes. They should have been here by now to help us prepare for the wake. An American wake it's called. It's for me, leaving. Kitty was having one in Ballyferriter last night. They're happening all over Ireland, especially in the west where the hunger is the worst. Still, it feels strange to be preparing a wake for myself, as if I'm already dead.

God alone knows where everyone will fit; the whole village will turn out. We've a lot of the work done, bottles of poitín brought down from the old cabin, a great pot of vegetable broth prepared.

"I'll come with you," Peig says.

Soon we're hurrying along the path from the house down into the village, a vicious wind biting at our faces.

"God, it's bitter today," Peig says.

"Maybe you should go back."

"No, I'm coming."

"Do you think something's happened to Kitty?"

"No, I'm sure she's fine. They'll have been held up somewhere along the road."

"What if she's changed her mind?" It's out before I can help it, a fear I didn't even know was there.

"Of course she hasn't. She loves you. I see it all the time, the way she is with you, the way she looks at you. Sometimes I wonder how no one else can see it. If you were a man and a woman, everyone would be talking about marriage."

"I wish I could marry her."

"At least you'll have a life with her. You can be together whenever you want."

I hear the catch in her voice. "Sorry, Peig. Here's me caught up in my own worry when you've no word of Liam."

"I understand. I'd be the same. If I had the chance to be with him at last, I'd be terrified it would all fall apart at the last minute. But it won't."

"Do you really think so?"

"Of course, stop worrying. I bet we'll meet them before we've walked five minutes."

But twenty minutes later there's still no sign. Where are they?

"I think you should go back," I say to Peig. "Look at the sky—it's going to pour soon. There's no point us both getting soaked."

"I'm not leaving you on your own, not on your last day. We'll find somewhere to shelter if we need to."

We've barely gone another hundred yards when I feel the first fat drops. The weather comes in fast here. I quicken my step, pulling my shawl up, Peig at my heels. I'm sure there's a cabin somewhere near here, half-hidden from the road by an overgrown hedge. Maybe round the next bend. I'm almost running now, wanting to get inside before it really breaks.

And then I see them, Kitty and her mother, crouched at the side of the road.

"Kitty," I shout, gathering up my skirt and breaking into a run. As I get closer I can see something lying on the ground between them. Not something, someone. I slow my step, the pounding of my feet unseemly. "Oh God." It's an old woman, old and very, very thin, thinner than anyone I've ever seen before, just skin, bone and filthy rags. Grey hair straggles round her skull face. Her eyes are shut.

"Is she…?" I say.

"No," Kitty says quietly, standing up, but she shakes her head slightly, shutting her eyes. It won't be long.

"Should I fetch the priest?" Peig says.

"I think so," Kitty answers.

I watch Peig turn and run back down the path to Dunquin. I'm relieved she's gone, away from this diseased and dying woman. Half of me wants to run after her. Instead I turn to Kitty. "She'll be an hour, if the priest's in at all. I hope it's long enough."

Kitty shrugs. There's not much either of us can do about it.

"We should get her inside," I say as the rain starts to come on heavy. "There's a cabin near here, off that lane up ahead."

"Do you think we can move her?" Kitty asks her mother.

"We can try. Can you lift her from the other side?"

Kitty bends down, putting her arm round the woman's waist. Together, Kitty and her mother get to their feet, the old woman moaning and swaying between them. She seems to have lost all power in her legs. I stand looking on as they struggle to keep her upright.

"Where's this cabin?" Missus Gorman calls.

"Sorry," I say, coming to my senses. "Here, follow me." I pick up Kitty's bag and hurry past them, guiding them along the path to the cabin. I knock on the door but don't pause for an answer. The place is empty, not so much as a blanket or a stool. It's cold and damp and I can hear dripping where the rain's coming in. But it's better than nothing.

Kitty and her mother ease the woman carefully onto the earthen floor.

"There, there," Missus Gorman says. She starts crooning a lullaby, like the old woman's a baby at the start of life, rather than facing her last hours.

Hear the rain fall, hear the wind blow
You are safe here, sweet child, sweet love

Kitty squats against the wall of the cabin, listening and watching. I go over and sit next to her.

"Do you know who she is?" she asks.

I stare at the woman, trying to place her. We're only a couple of miles from Dunquin; surely I must know her. I lean closer but the smell coming from her is fearsome. Not just the piss and shit but a putrid smell that turns my stomach. I feel a terrible wave of pity. Pity and revulsion.

I don't know how Missus Gorman can bear to be so close. She has an old piece of rag and is wiping the woman's forehead as she sings, tending her with gentle care though the woman looks like she's past noticing.

"How long have you been with her?" I say quietly.

"Perhaps an hour before you came. We found her lying at the side of the road. We couldn't leave her there."

No, though some would have.

"Looks like famine fever," I say.

"I think so. Though the hunger's nearly done for her anyway. There's grass stains round her mouth," she says, her voice cracking. "Grass, she's been eating grass. How desperate would you have to be to be eating grass?"

Kitty and I lapse into silence, watching as Missus Gorman carries on mopping the woman's head. She's stopped singing now. Leaning closer to the woman, she starts to speak.

"O my God, I am heartily sorry for having offended Thee,
And I detest all my sins because of Thy just punishments."

Kitty and I join in the prayer.

"But most of all because they offend Thee, my God,
Who art all-good and deserving of all my love.
I firmly resolve, with the help of Thy grace,
To sin no more and to avoid the near occasions of sin."

With barely a pause, Missus Gorman carries on into the Apostle's Creed. I'm not even sure the woman's still breathing but I pray with all my might, wishing her peace, wishing her away from the pain of this life.

Missus Gorman crosses herself. "May the Lord Jesus protect you and lead you to eternal life. Amen." She sits, looking at the woman for a long time.

"Dark days," she says at last, standing up and turning towards us. "We're in dark days. I'm glad the pair of you will be out of it."

"Come with us, Ma. Please."

Her mother takes Kitty into her arms. "My place is here. I know it in my heart."

"I can't be abandoning you—"

"You're not abandoning me. You think I don't know you, Kitty Gorman? You think I don't know you've been thinking of me with this move to America? This poor woman's death doesn't change the fact that we both have a far better chance if you go."

She strokes Kitty's hair, holding her while she sobs.

"You too, Frances," she says, looking at me. "Make us proud in America. Take the chances you'll get there." She holds her free arm out to me and I go to her, letting her sweep me into a hug with Kitty.

We stand together, holding one another, not saying anything. I breathe deeply, trying to calm my heart. I will miss her so much, this sweet, generous woman who made my lover the woman she is. I will miss all of this—my family, my home, my people, my fields, the land, the sea, the music, the stories.

At last we break apart, laughing a little, wiping our eyes and our wet noses with our sleeves. Missus Gorman bends down, fiddling with Kitty's pack.

"I wanted you to have this," she says, handing the wooden flute to me. "I remember that first day you came to visit my Kitty. The big clumsy fingers of you, dropping it on the floor. But then you played it and I could see the heart of you. Think of the happy times when you play it. Think of the happy times, not this accursed famine."

CHAPTER THIRTY-SEVEN

Dunquin, November 1846

It seems like I'm awake before I've even been to sleep. Maybe it was being back in bed with Peig and Lizzie, maybe having Kitty in the same room, maybe Missus Gorman's snoring. I don't know, but I have barely closed my eyes all night. Instead I've lain here worrying.

The wake was a grim business with none of the usual storytelling. The talk was of what lies ahead, for us and for those we leave behind. A few people knew the old woman who died—Eileen Mitchell she was called. Another name to be added to the list of those lost—the Garveys, little Mickey Kavanagh, the two Connors, Bridie Moore, Matt Fitzgerald. They've been parading through my head half the night. How many more before this famine's finished?

And Manus O'Brien brought news of food riots in Dingle, a group armed with pitchforks, shot at by Burnham's henchmen when they tried to get at the grain store.

But it's my own future that's really preying on my mind. Mine and Kitty's. People had plenty of advice for us at the wake—watch out for the fever; avoid the soup kitchens; sleep somewhere sheltered; follow the main roads; steer clear of the towns; find a seaworthy ship; keep your belongings about you; look out for cutthroats.

Neither of us has ever set foot beyond Dingle. But in a few hours we'll be starting a walk of more than a hundred miles, off the peninsula, out of Kerry into Cork and onto a ship to take us to the other side of the world.

How are we supposed to avoid the towns if we follow the main roads? Don't the main roads go through the towns?

What do I know about choosing a seaworthy ship? And if by chance I find one, how will we get on our feet when we get to New York? We don't know a single person there—only the name of a distant cousin of a neighbour of Kitty's. Aidan Murphy. And a possible address—Orange Street in New York—though no one's heard from him for two years.

I've been turning it all over in my mind for hours and I'm exhausted. I should try to get some sleep. Instead I get up, not able to stand another minute of tossing and turning. My clothes are laid out ready on the chair. Quietly I slip out of my nightgown and into my petticoat, not wanting to disturb Peig and Lizzie, asleep in one bed, Kitty and her mother in the other.

Out of the dark, Kitty whispers, "Frankie, is that you?"

"Yes," I whisper back. "Go to sleep, it's still early."

"You're not going to sleep."

"No, but that's because I can't."

"Maybe I can't either."

Through the dark I see her sit up and slide her legs out of the bed. She gropes on the floor for the clothes she discarded last night.

"Come on," I say, once she's dressed, "let's go through to the kitchen."

The embers are barely glowing and I kneel down, blowing gently, wanting to get the fire going again. But Kitty puts her hand on my shoulder. "There'll be time for the fire later," she says. "Come on, let's go for a walk."

"It's still dark," I say, but I get up and follow her outside, wrapping my shawl around my shoulders against the cold. Dawn's a way off, but the light from the moon glistens on the sea. We walk slowly down the path from the house towards the village.

"How do you feel?" Kitty says.

"I don't know. Nervous. It's such a long way."

"I know. There'll be no coming back. I think this is the hardest part, saying goodbye. It'll be easier when we're on our way."

"Do you think so?"

"I do. Goodbyes are always hard. Hard for us, hard for them. But we know we can support our families better from America than here. And we won't be a burden."

"I've been worrying about what we'll do, how we'll get by. What if we can't find work?"

"Of course we'll find work. Everyone says it's the land of opportunity."

"But we don't know anyone there."

"We know each other. That's enough. We can be together, really together."

"I've wanted to live with you for so long, I can hardly believe it's finally going to happen."

"Believe it," she says, turning and pulling me close, kissing me in the dark while Dunquin sleeps.

It takes my breath away and my fears. I don't need to know all the answers; we can work them out together.

"Mmm, I love kissing you, Kitty Gorman," I say as we break apart.

"I love kissing you too, Frances Moriarty."

I touch her face gently. "I could never have imagined loving anyone like this."

"We'll be grand, you know. You'll look after me and I'll look after you."

It's still quiet when we go back inside and I set about the fire with energy, adding kindling as I get a flame. Kitty's right, it'll be easier once we're away, for us and for everyone else. Once the fire's going we'll get some stirabout on. We'll have breakfast and then we'll be off. There'll be plenty of time for crying on the journey; there's no sense in dragging it out here.

I add sticks to the fire, wait for them to catch, then a few sods of turf from the basket. As the fire takes hold I smile up at Kitty. She winks back at me. Everything will be fine. We'll be together, our whole lives together.

"I'm away to milk the cows. Do you want to give me a hand?" I say.

"I've never milked a cow in my life and I've no intention of starting now. But I'll keep an eye on the fire."

I make my way for the last time up to the old cabin. The cows greet me as usual, nothing different in the day for them. Will they notice it's not me tomorrow? Will they grunt and snort and moo for Peig instead?

I love these cows, their sturdy legs, their solid bodies, the noises they make like they're talking away to me. I pull out the stool, nestling in beside first Daisy, then Dolly. The milk comes fast and easy. "You be good for Peig and Lizzie," I say, the tears welling up.

I stand up, pausing to scratch both cows behind the ears before making my way back down to the house. It's getting light now, the sun coming up behind Mount Eagle. I've not been gone long but the kitchen is a different place when I return. My da and Missus Gorman are up and dressed and sitting by the kitchen table while Kitty sits at the fire, keeping her eye on a pot of stirabout.

"—a great player," Missus Gorman's saying as I go in.

"She's had a talent for the music since she was no age," my da says.

"I suppose she takes after you."

"I can't imagine life without music," Da says.

"No, nor me. I think I'd go mad if I couldn't sing."

"You'd my heart torn last night with 'Dark Rosaleen.'"

"She's a sad song, there's no doubt," Missus Gorman says. "A sad song for a sad country." She starts to sing it again, quiet but clear.

Woe and pain, pain and woe
Are my lot, night and noon,
To see your bright face, clouded so,
Like to the mournful moon.

We sit, listening to the end.

You'll pray for me, my flower of flowers,
My Dark Rosaleen!

"'Tis a disgrace for the English to be banning that song," my da says.

Missus Gorman shakes her head. "They'll be banning breathing next. They've near enough banned eating. Did you have that terrible corn they sent? It would have cut your guts open."

"We never had it ourselves. We're lucky with the oats and barley. You must take some home with you," my da says.

"Thank you," Missus Gorman says, her voice barely a whisper. My da stands for a moment with his hand on her shoulder, a terrible sadness on his face.

"Shall I get the bowls out for breakfast?" I say. "The stirabout must be about ready."

"Near enough," Kitty says.

"Go and get your sisters up," Da says to me. "Excuse me," he says to Missus Gorman, retreating up the ladder to the room he shares with my ma.

"Peig, Lizzie, it's time to get up," I say, shaking them gently. I leave them dressing, returning to the kitchen. Kitty's mother sits silent at the table, tears glistening on her cheeks.

We are joined after a minute by Ma and Da. My ma looks terrible, her skin grey, eyes red. My mother never cries. I look away, not able to manage the rawness of her. Then glimpse back again. She smiles a little smile, a tear leaking from the corner of her eye.

Oh Ma. I go to her, putting my arms around her, like I haven't for years. It's my da I've been close to; all my life it's been him. My ma's the one I've battled with. I squeeze her tight, wanting her to feel the fierceness of my love for her. She lets me hold her, patting my back awkwardly, till at last we step apart.

"Thanks for your help with the breakfast," she says to Kitty.

"You're welcome, Missus Moriarty."

"Peig, Lizzie," my ma calls sharply. "Get yourselves to this table."

They emerge dressed, taking their places as my ma starts ladling the stirabout into the bowls. We sit, squashed round the table, blowing on the hot porridge for something to do that doesn't need talking. I know I should say something, some special words for my last meal with my family. But nothing feels adequate, so I say nothing.

I have lived twenty-one years. That's a lot of days. Nearly all of them have been spent at home, with my family. I will never see them again. I must talk. "Looks like it'll be a dry day," I say.

"It does right enough," my da says.

"It'll be a change from all this terrible rain," Missus Gorman says.

"Oh, I know. I've never known weather like it," my ma says.

No, no, I've got them off on the weather. That's not how I want it to end. I try again.

"There was a lot of worry last night, times as they are. I wanted to say that me and Kitty will do our best for everyone here. Our very best. I wanted to say that…"

"Sure don't we know it," my da says. "Never a doubt. And I want you to know that we will manage. We've oats and barley and money put past. And we'll help Missus Gorman here too. We're all family."

I can barely swallow my stirabout with the lump filling my throat. They're good people, my family and hers.

"You'll write to us, won't you?" Lizzie says.

"Of course," I say, reaching over and squeezing her hand.

I finish my last few spoons of stirabout and get up from the table. Kitty follows me into the bedroom. I check my bag one last time— other dress, other petticoat, nightgown, saucepan, bowl, tinderbox, blanket, headscarf, oatcakes, boiled eggs, flute, ribbon.

"Are you ready?" I say.

She looks at me and nods.

They're all still sitting round the table when we return to the kitchen. "Well, I think we'll get off," I say into the silence, my voice breaking at the end.

Peig gets up and throws her arms around me. "Be careful," she says. "Good luck."

"You too," I say.

She moves from me to Kitty as Lizzie appears before me, her eyes swimming with tears. My littlest sister. I wrap her up in my arms, feeling her body shaking.

"Oh Lizzie," I say.

My da comes and puts one arm around her, the other round me. I rest my head against his shoulder. My ma joins on the other side and somewhere there's Peig and the five of us hold together, not speaking, just standing clinging onto one another, till my da pulls away a little and beckons Kitty and her ma into our farewell.

"O Lord, be between all of us and harm," my da says.

At last I disentangle myself, groping for my bag, eyes blurred. I open the cabin door to the cold, crisp morning and take my first step away from everything I have ever known. Kitty walks beside me. I wish I could hold her hand. I feel awkward, my lumpy bag bumping against my back, my nose full of snot, aware of their eyes on us.

I want to look round, fix them in my head one last time. But if I do I'll break down. So I keep walking, head down, one foot in front of the other, left foot, right foot, left foot, right foot…

It is Kitty who stops. I don't see it so much as feel it. I stop too, half turning, waving my hand at the little group crowded together in front of the cabin door, watching us go.

"Come on, Kitty," I say as I feel her wavering beside me.

She stands, looking back up to the house, her face a picture of pain.

I want to take her in my arms, promise to make it better. But I can't. "Come on," I say again. "You said it yourself, it's better to get it over with. For them and for us."

She turns at last and we carry on down the path onto the road, heading away from Dunquin.

* * *

"We should stop for something to eat soon," I say, not long after we pass through Lispole.

"If you want," Kitty says.

"Would you rather wait a while?"

She shrugs.

I've been walking alongside her for hours but I may as well have been on my own for all she's talked. I've never known her so quiet. She's gone away inside and I don't know how to find her.

"What about there?" I say, pointing to a large flattish rock in a field to our right. It looks like it was made for sitting looking out across Dingle Bay. There's a stream burbling down one side. I fish my bowl out of my bag and go and fill it.

"Here, have some water," I say to Kitty, handing her the bowl. I reach into my bag and bring out a couple of boiled eggs and a few oatcakes. "Do you want an egg?"

"You have them," she says.

"What about an oatcake?"

"I'm not hungry."

"You've got to eat. We've been walking for hours."

She takes an oatcake and nibbles at the edge of it.

"We're making good progress, past Lispole already."

But she doesn't answer.

We eat in silence, or rather I eat, she sits staring out to sea. In ten minutes we're back on the road, left, right, left, right, keep walking, hope it gets better.

We've made maybe half a mile when a cart comes clattering by.

"Afternoon, ladies," the fella driving it says, pulling up beside us.

"Good day," I say.

"Can I be offering you a lift?"

I look at him, sizing him up. Not much older than us, maybe mid-twenties, friendly freckled face, a scratch of red stubble on his chin. He doesn't look like a cutthroat robber.

"Where are you going?" I say.

"Heading back to Castlemaine."

Castlemaine. I've been repeating the route over and over for days, wanting to get it clear in my head. Dingle, Castlemaine, Killarney, Macroom, Cork, Cobh. I look at Kitty, wanting her agreement, but she's gazing out to sea.

"That would suit us. Thank you," I say.

"Throw your bags in the back there and climb on up," he says.

I sit next to him so that Kitty doesn't have to.

"Jimmy Dowd's my name," he says.

"I'm Frances Moriarty," I say, offering my hand. "And this is my friend, Kitty Gorman."

"So is it Castlemaine you're headed to yourselves?" Jimmy says.

"No, Cobh," I say.

"Are you emigrating?"

"To America."

"America? Have you family there?"

"No."

"That's a long way for two girls to be going with no family. Jesus, I wouldn't be wanting my sisters going off that length of a distance without either me or a husband to be looking out for them."

"We can look out for ourselves," I say.

"Jesus, I hope so. There's all sorts of vagrants on the road, you know. With all breeds of diseases and fevers. Desperate people that might do anything. You want to be careful. Two girls on your own. You're sitting ducks."

I feel like hitting him hard about the head, lecturing us as if we know nothing. But the lift'll get us much farther than I could have hoped on our first day, so I change the subject, asking him about his family.

"Well, no doubt you'll have heard of the Wild Colonial Boy," he says. "He was my second cousin." He starts to sing.

There was a wild Colonial boy, Jack Duggan was his name
Of poor but honest parents he was born in Castlemaine

We pass the next while running through folk songs as the horses trot us along the road to Castlemaine. I'm hoping Kitty will join in, but my girl sits silent.

At Annascaul we follow the road downhill and on towards a long spit of sand jutting miles out into the Atlantic. I look at the sun glinting on the sea, the mountains beyond, listening to the hiss and suck of the waves.

"Isn't it beautiful?" I say to Kitty.

She gives a half smile.

I look back at the beach as we drive past, onwards to Castlemaine.

* * *

"We should look for somewhere to sleep," I say. "It'll be dark soon."

"I suppose," Kitty says.

"Maybe a cowshed. Or an abandoned cabin. What do you think?" I say, trying to keep the conversation going. We've been walking for about an hour, since Jimmy dropped us off at Castlemaine, and she's barely said a word.

"I suppose so."

"But we're making good progress. I didn't think we'd get this far today, did you?"

She doesn't answer, back in her own world. We trudge on in silence, heading southeast, the sun dropping behind us. The cabins have thinned out since we passed through Milltown, half an hour ago. I hope we find somewhere soon. There's a small cabin ahead, but a curl of smoke shows it's occupied. It'll be dark in half an hour, maybe three quarters if we're lucky. It's getting cold. There'll be a frost tonight.

And suddenly, there it is, a whitewashed cottage, set back from the road, an animal shed at right angles to it. It's the biggest place we've seen for miles, far larger than my house.

My house. I've tried not to think about it all day. I wonder what my family is doing, imagine them settled in the kitchen, getting on with their jobs without me. I pull myself back. I can't think about them now.

"Let's try here," I say, walking up to the gate. As I open it, a sheepdog comes running out, barking like mad.

"Good dog," I say, but it pays me no heed, careening round us, barking its lungs out.

"What a fuss," Kitty says, but in a voice like the dog is the most delightful creature on this earth.

"Stop your barking," a woman calls from inside. The dog pays her no mind, continuing to weave in and out between us, barking and wagging its tail.

"Hush now," Kitty says, bending down to stroke the beast's ears. It looks up at her like it's found its own personal saint. Kitty for her part seems scarcely less enthralled, smiling for the first time since we set off. And she's managed to stop the barking.

It's replaced by the sound of a baby crying. The top half of the cottage door opens to reveal a woman with the baby in her arms.

"Dratted dog," she says, snuggling the baby in against her shoulder and stroking its back. "There, there."

"We didn't mean to set it off," I say.

She looks at me then, like she's sizing me up. Her face is lined, mouth downturned. "What brings you hereabouts?"

"We're on our way to Cobh, looking for shelter for the night."

"Cobh," she says. "Emigrating, I suppose?"

"Aye, to America."

"You're not the first and I'd say you'll not be the last before we're done."

There's silence between us then, her making a show of soothing the baby, me wondering did she hear me asking for shelter. Surely she must have heard.

Kitty joins us, the dog at her heels. "Sorry to disturb you," she says. "My friend and I were wondering have you somewhere we could sleep."

I see the woman hesitating, holding the baby closer to her.

"Not in the house," I say. "In the shed."

"The shed?" she says.

"Yes, if you would let us sleep in the shed, we'd be very grateful," I say.

"The shed," she says. "Oh yes, of course, that would be fine. I'd do more if I could, but with the baby…"

"No, we understand, everyone's worried about the fever. Though we don't have it," I say.

"There's plenty of straw. Make yourselves comfortable. And there's logs in the shed if you want to make a fire outside."

"You're very kind," I say.

We make our way round the back of the house to the animal shed. It's a decent size, which is just as well as there are already three cows, a donkey, two pigs and maybe eight or nine hens in it. But the smell's not so bad; it's been mucked out recently. I shoo some of the hens out of the way and start to gather the fresher straw into a big pile to make us a bed.

"I'll go and get the fire started," Kitty says.

"Oh, I'll do that in a minute. I've nearly got the bed ready, you can lie down and rest for a bit. I'll make us some nettle tea when I can boil some water."

"I'll make the tea. You don't have to do everything. We're in this together, Frankie."

She comes over, slipping her arms around me. I feel my heart opening and the fears I've been holding all day slip out. "We can go back. If you've changed your mind. We can set off in the morning."

"Of course I haven't changed my mind. Why did you say that?"

"I don't know. You've been so quiet. I thought maybe you were thinking I wasn't…" I stop, not wanting to say it out loud.

"Wasn't what? Tell me."

"Wasn't enough," I say, my voice barely a whisper, my eyes brimming with tears.

"Oh, Frankie," she says, putting her hands on my arms, looking into my eyes. "You've got to let me be upset without thinking it's about you. It was hard today, leaving my ma, worse than I expected. It doesn't mean I don't want to be with you."

"I'm sorry."

"You don't have to be sorry. But don't be worrying about me loving you. You never need to doubt that."

We sit round the fire, drinking nettle tea and eating oatcake, as the darkness settles in. The moon stands out sharp against the night sky.

"We mustn't stay out too long," I say. "I'm all hot down my front but freezing down my back."

"Why don't you turn around for a bit?"

"Because I want to look at you."

"You can look at me anytime. Go on, get yourself turned."

"I'll finish my oatcake first," I say, dipping it into the tea and sucking it. "I wish we'd some butter. I love a thick spread of butter on an oatcake."

"Jam. Juicy blackberry jam, that's what I want."

"I like a bit of jam myself, at least the jam we had at home. Ma told me they eat a bitter kind of jam at Lord Burnham's, made of oranges. Do you think they'll have oranges in America?"

"I bet they will. They'll have all sorts we've never had. Probably things we've never even heard of."

"Evening," a voice calls from over by the corner of the house. "My ma sent me out with soup for you. I'm setting it here on the window ledge."

"May God bless your ma for her kindness," I say.

"And yourself for bringing it out," Kitty adds.

The lad scuttles away back to his ma and I go and fetch the two bowls of steaming soup he's left for us. I settle back down by the fire, cradling the bowl in my hands, waiting for it to cool.

"Smells good," I say.

"She may think we're lepers, but she has a good heart."

I blow on the soup, then put it to my lips and take a sip. It's still hot, almost too hot, but it's tasty, with barley and split peas and a few greens.

"It'll get us nicely warmed through before bed."

"Am I not enough to warm you through?" she says, with a cheeky smile.

"I'd forgotten how much you like to tease," I say, smiling back, glad to hear her more like her old self.

"I wish I'd the energy for the kind of teasing I like the most."

"We've got plenty of time."

"Let's get to bed anyway. I'm tired out and I can feel a headache coming on."

I leave Kitty dousing the fire while I take the bowls back, knocking on the front door and calling thank you so the woman knows they're there.

Kitty's already in the shed when I return. It's dark inside and my eyes take a long moment to adjust.

"I'm over here," she calls.

I step carefully over to her, not wanting to fall or to tread on her.

"Come and warm me up," she says. "I'm cold."

We're both still in dresses and boots but it's good to feel her in my arms, holding her close, her head tucked in against my shoulder.

"I wish it wasn't so cold," I say. "I want to feel you skin to skin." I pull her in closer, wanting her to feel the pounding of my heart, my love for her. "I can hardly believe that you're here in my arms, that we're setting off to build a new life together."

"I'm glad to have got today over, it's worn me out. But it feels right to be here with you."

She leans forward and kisses me.

"Good night, Frankie. Sleep well."

"Sweet dreams."

* * *

I wake in the dark, needing to piss. I groan, not wanting to go out into the cold, but I have to get up or I'll not sleep again. Feeling my way outside, I crouch behind the shed. It's good to let it out, steam rising from the frosty ground. But it's even better to get back inside. I reach for Kitty, snuggling in against her back, slipping my arm round her waist.

Her clothes are wet with sweat. She's hot, too hot. I put my hand to her head. She's boiling. Her back, her arms, her belly, hot and sweaty. I lie next to her, trying to listen to her breathing. But all I can hear is the blood pounding in my ears.

Stop panicking, Frances. You'll be no use if you don't calm yourself.

Maybe I'm just imagining it, coming back in from the cold. Maybe she's just warm. Gently I touch her forehead with the back of my hand. Her sweat is slick against my skin; she's burning up.

She murmurs as I touch her but doesn't waken.

Should I wake her? I don't know.

I've got to cool her down. That's what Ma did when the children had a fever. I need cold water and a cloth.

There's a stream a few hundred yards back. I hear it gurgling down the hillside as I rush along the road, almost falling over my feet. The saucepan clangs against the stones as I stoop to fill it. It's loud in the silence of the night but I don't care who it wakens.

I feel calmer as I hurry back to Kitty. I remember Lizzie as a child, burning with fever in the night, right as rain the next afternoon. So it will be with my Kitty. This is a passing thing.

I kneel down next to her, dipping my handkerchief in the water and placing it against her forehead. She wakes with a start.

"It's only me," I say.

"My head hurts."

"I got you some water. Here, drink."

"I'm too hot," she says, throwing off the blanket and starting to pull at her dress. "Aren't you hot?"

"You need to rest."

"Everything aches."

"I know, but you'll be better if you rest."

"I feel terrible."

"You'll be better in the morning."

She sits up suddenly. "Oh God," she says, fear in her voice. "You don't think…It's not famine—"

"You'll be better in a day."

"I don't want to die like that old woman."

"You won't," I say, sounding as calm and firm as I can. *Please God, let it not be famine fever.*

"I'm burning, my head's pounding, I'm aching into my bones. They're signs."

"They're signs of lots of things. It's been a hard day, Kitty. All you need is a good rest."

"If it's famine fever, you have to leave me. Promise me, promise me you'll leave me."

"It's not famine fever."

"But if it is. Promise, Frankie. I don't want you to get it too."

Nothing will make me leave her. Nothing. "Lie down, sweetheart," I say. "You need to sleep."

She lets me push her gently back down. But suddenly she's up again. "Oh God, we've got to get away from here. The baby."

"Please Kitty, you're not well. You've got to rest."

She starts to sob. "Don't you understand? Everyone here could die because of me."

"It's not famine fever," I say. "Please rest, at least for tonight. We'll work out what to do in the morning."

I put my arms round her, trying to comfort her but she pushes me off. "Too hot," she says.

I dip the handkerchief back into the water, wiping her face, her throat, the back of her neck. I soak it again, then wring it out at the top of her chest, letting it drip down her front. Slowly, her sobs subside. She lets me ease her gently back down onto the straw.

"Rest now, darling," I say, kissing her temple.

She drifts into a fitful sleep but I lie awake next to her, listening as she mutters and thrashes, bathing her head and neck, trying to cool her. I have never felt anyone so hot, the clothes sticking to her, hair damp, limbs clammy.

She is right, these are the signs.

CHAPTER THIRTY-EIGHT

Near Knockreagh, November 1846

I'm still awake as the new day dawns. The hens have started to flap and cluck and one of the cows keeps mooing. It won't be long before someone comes out to see to the animals. Beside me, my girl lies in the grip of fever.

I get up carefully, not wanting to wake Kitty, and slip out of the shed. The mad dog comes bounding up to me but at least it's not barking. The ground is still frosty white, my breath steaming in front of my face as I walk round to the front of the house. I knock loudly on the door before stepping back to reduce the risk of contagion.

The baby starts crying and I can hear the woman muttering and grumbling inside the cottage. I stand outside, waiting. Eventually the half door is thrown open.

The woman glares at me but doesn't speak.

"Sorry to disturb you," I say. I pause, trying to gather myself. "It's my friend. She's...she's come on ill."

"Ill? What kind of ill?"

"I think it's the fever."

The woman crosses herself. "Oh Jesus, Mary and Joseph. Oh for the love of Christ."

"We need your help."

"Help? You lied to me. How could you do that?"

"We never lied. She's only just got sick."

"I've a baby here. And three children. You've no right to bring the fever to my door. How could you do such a thing?"

I take a deep breath, not wanting to start shouting back. "My friend is going to get better," I say slowly, pronouncing each word. "She doesn't want to risk harming you. All I need is somewhere else for us to stay."

"What you need is to get away from here."

"And we will but she'll die for sure if she's out in this cold wandering around looking for shelter. We need somewhere else to stay."

"What's that to do with me?"

"If you won't help, we'll have no choice but to stay in your shed."

She gives me a look of pure hatred but I don't care. All that matters is getting Kitty well again. If it was up to me, I'd stay in her shed. But I know Kitty. She'd waste her strength fighting me if she thought we were putting other people at risk. She's too good for the likes of this woman.

But I'm not. And I'll use everything I can to make her help us. I step closer to the door.

"Stay back," she says, panic in her voice.

"I won't come any closer if you agree to help."

"You don't give me much choice," she says.

"I'm doing what I have to, same as you."

"What do you want?"

"Do you know of an empty cabin nearby where I could take my friend till she recovers?"

She sighs. "Maybe. But I'm only telling you if you promise me on the life of your friend that you'll leave and won't come back here again."

"I promise that I want away from here and to cause you as little trouble as I can. But I need to borrow your donkey."

"My donkey? Jesus, have you no shame? And after the help I've given you."

"She's too ill to walk. I'll bring the donkey straight back."

"Do you think I was born yesterday? You'll be away with my donkey and I'll never see you again." Her eyes narrow. "I bet your friend isn't even sick, is she?"

"Why don't you come and see for yourself?" My voice is loud but I can't help it. "Why don't you come and see the sweat pouring from her, feel her burning up?" I can feel the tears welling in my eyes. "Please, have a pity on us. Please. I don't want her to die."

A lad appears next to her, his head just visible above the bottom half of the door. I don't know if it's the same one who brought the soup last night. He looks out over the door at me, his hair standing up in ten directions.

I take a step back, away from the door. "Please," I say again.

"Go back to bed," she says to the boy. She waits till he pads away, then turns back to me. "There's people called Riordan lived about a mile down the road. They left in September for Liverpool. The cabin's still empty. It's on the right down a track immediately after a field with a standing stone in it. Take some straw for bedding and burn what you slept on last night. And take an egg if the hens have laid. Apply the white to the soles of her feet. I want my donkey back by noon."

I start to cry with relief. "Thank you, thank you."

She nods curtly, then shuts the cabin door.

Kitty's still asleep when I return to the shed, lips moving, face contorting. I leave her sleeping while I gather our things together, returning the saucepan to my bag.

I need something to carry the fresh straw in. I look around the shed for an old sack but nothing presents itself. In the end I knot our shawls together to make a container. I can feel the donkey watching me as I start to fill it. They are such nosy creatures.

"Good morning," I say, looking over at it. It is a soft grey colour with the cross lines marked out clearly in dark chocolate across its shoulders and running down the middle of its back. It stares back at me with the saddest eyes you ever saw on a living creature. I dig in my bag for an oatcake and break a bit off for the donkey. I reach my palm out flat towards it. The donkey sniffs the oatcake, then picks it up from my hand, its lips brushing against my skin.

"Good donkey," I say, stroking its ears. "I need you to help my girl. You have to be nice and gentle with her." The donkey looks at me again with its big soft eyes, like it understands every word I'm saying, like it knows the sorrows of the world and wishes it could ease them.

My preparations are complete but still Kitty sleeps her fretful sleep. I kneel beside her. "Kitty," I say, gently shaking her. "Kitty, wake up."

She looks confused when first she opens her eyes but then she gives me a faint smile.

"The woman's told me about a cabin down the road. She's lending us her donkey to get you there."

Kitty sits up slowly. I take her hand and help her to her feet, then slip my arm round her and lead her carefully over to the donkey. I can feel how thin she's got these last months.

"Do you think you can get on her?"

"I'll try."

The donkey stands patient as Kitty gathers her energy.

"I'm ready," she says. She puts her foot in my cupped hands and with some difficulty I help her up. She leans forward against the donkey's neck, breathless from the effort, eyes closed, face gleaming with sweat.

I stand close, ready to catch her if she falls. She lays there for a minute or two, not speaking, but then her eyes open and she gives a little nod. We take our first steps into the sunshine, the dog trotting along beside us as we make our way through the yard and onto the road. I'm looking out for the cabin from the first turn in the road, only yards away from the woman's cottage. I don't know how long Kitty will have the strength to hang on to the donkey. Her eyes are closed and every so often she moans in pain.

"Not much further," I keep saying. "You're doing well, not much further," as the donkey clip-clops along. The dog is still with us, sometimes drifting to the side of the road for a sniff along the hedgerow but mostly trotting along by my heels. Every field I'm looking for a standing stone. Maybe the next one. Maybe the next one. It has to be soon. What if the woman was lying? Maybe there is no empty cabin, no track off on the right, no standing stone. She'd have said anything to be rid of me. But surely she wouldn't want to have given up her donkey?

"Not much further," I say again, and this time I'm right. I feel a surge of relief as I see the stone, about five feet high, not quite in the middle of the next field.

* * *

Snow has fallen overnight. I loved waking up to snow when I was a girl, the way it changed the look of everything, how you could shape it in your hands, the fun you could have slipping and sliding in it. Today I hate it. We're not even halfway through November, it has no business falling this early. I'm never going to find wood dry enough to burn. And I have to keep the fire going, sweat the fever out.

I bend down, checking the lower branches of the hedgerow, sheltered from the worst of the snow. I hack at them with Kitty's brother's knife, grunting with the effort. When I've gathered enough I lash the sticks together, heft them onto my shoulder and head back to the cabin. There's snow covering the thatch and on the peaks of the mountains beyond. It's a small cabin but sturdy, made of stone, and does a good job of keeping out the weather. The chimney has a good draw, pulling the smoke outside and not into the room.

Kitty sits in my nightgown, propped against the back wall, much as I left her. She looks up as I enter, a faint smile on her lips. I go to her, relieved. There have been times in recent days when she's not known me, shuffling away as if I might harm her, or sitting lost and bewildered, her face blank.

"How are you feeling?" I say, bending down to kiss her cheek. "Did you manage to sleep while I was out?"

She shakes her head. She has barely slept in days, huddled over as the pain sweeps through her or leaning against the wall, staring into space.

"Maybe later," I say.

I set my bundle of sticks beside the hearth to dry out and load the fire up with the remainder of the wood I cut yesterday. Soon the flames have taken hold, throwing light around the room. I steal a glance at my girl. Her eyes are shadowed with great dark circles, her lips dry and cracked, her cheeks sunken.

"How about an oatcake?" I say, but again she shakes her head. I wish she would eat; it's days since I got something solid down her. All she'll take is the odd bowl of soup that I make with whatever I can forage.

Instead of eating she's drinking all the time. She must have drunk near enough a lake of water this past week, though she can't have passed more than a puddle. I've never known anyone with such a thirst. Thank God there's a well nearby.

"Have you water still?"

"I have," she says, indicating the half-full bowl sitting on the floor beside her. Her mouth has become dry and brown since she's been ill and her voice is faint and scratchy.

I settle myself next to her on the earthen floor. We've not a single stick of furniture but I've covered the floor with the straw we brought from the animal shed. We sit together in silence while my mind looks for something that might interest her.

"I saw a wren when I was out chopping the wood," I say. "I wonder will there be a Wren Day this year after all the trouble last time."

"Maybe."

"Jesus, it's been a hard year. That fella getting killed, Liam, the Garveys…" I trail off. Talk like this won't help her recover. "At least you're on the mend."

She turns her head to look at me. "Frankie…" She shakes her head, tears gathering. "I'm not mending."

"Of course you are. The headaches have eased, the fever's no worse. It'll break in the end, I know it will."

She opens the blanket and pulls the nightgown up. Her belly is covered with a dark red rash, pinpricks in places but bigger blotches too. "I'm dying," she whispers.

Tears leak down her cheeks and I feel them rise in me in response. I push them back down.

"No," I say, my voice harsh, "no, you're not dying, you're giving in. Lots of people recover from the fever. You need to start believing you're going to be one of them."

She stares at me, her eyes full of hurt, shaking her head, and I feel a moment of shame. Softer I say, "You can't die. I won't let you. You're going to get better. We're going to have a wonderful life together."

I go to put my arms around her but she pulls away.

"I'm sorry," I say. "I know you're worried. I'm worried too. But I don't believe God brought us together to tear us apart now."

She closes her eyes, leaning her head back against the wall, shutting me out in the only way she can.

"Please Kitty, please. I'm sorry," I say. But she doesn't answer.

* * *

I kneel on the floor, my hands clasped together. Kitty lies next to me, her legs and arms twitching and thrashing. She has been lost in the delirium these last two days.

"'Hail Mary, full of grace, the Lord is with thee,'" I say. "'Blessed art thou among women, and blessed is the fruit of thy womb, Jesus. Holy Mary, Mother of God, pray for us sinners, now and at the hour of our death. Amen.'"

I take Kitty's hand.

"Blessed Mother of God, in thy mercy hear and answer me. I humbly ask thee to restore thy daughter, Kitty Gorman, to good health. In the name of the Father, and of the Son and of the Holy Spirit," I say, crossing myself. "Amen."

The day is grey and we are set for rain. I go out to the well to haul up more water while there is still light. As I turn the handle I look across to the sombre mountains. I wish we had never come to this place. Kitty was safe at home. And if the sickness had come on there, my ma would have been able to help. Or Missus Gorman, she always knew plenty of cures.

What do I know? Nothing that's helped. Kitty hasn't eaten since half a bowl of soup yesterday morning and she brought that back up ten minutes later. Her arms and legs have become swollen and afflicted by the same rash that started on her belly. This last day a bad smell has come upon her that no end of washing could shift, like she's rotting away from the inside. Yet I remain as healthy as ever while she wastes away.

I return to the cabin with my bucket of water and settle myself by the fire. I sit watching her, thinking of how little time we have had together, the days wasted at home when I could have been with her at the scalp, all those weeks lost to the Protestant preacher.

As darkness begins to settle outside, a change comes upon her. Her breathing eases and she goes over into a gentler sleep. I touch her forehead with the back of my hand but she still feels hot, her breathing shallow. As I mop her face again she wakes, eyes opening. She smiles up at me.

"Thank you," she says, her voice quiet but clear.

"How are you feeling? Do you want something to eat?"

She shakes her head. "Come lie with me."

I lie down facing her, slipping my arm around her. "It's good to be holding you," I say.

She nuzzles in closer, her breath against my neck. "I love you," she says.

"You too."

* * *

I wake to thin morning light, filtering through the windows. It's cold in the cabin where the fire has gone out overnight. I should get it going again.

Kitty lies sleeping next to me. I lean over to kiss her. Her cheek feels cold against my lips.

"Kitty," I say, sitting up and shaking her gently. Her body is stiff and unyielding. She doesn't wake. I put my ear to her heart but can't find the beat.

"Kitty," I say, more urgently, putting my hands on her shoulders and shaking more vigorously.

"Kitty," I shout.

Still she doesn't wake.

"Kitty!" I scream. "Kitty!"

CHAPTER THIRTY-NINE

Hangtown, November 1849

The street is busy as I run from Ruby's, dodging between groups of miners, pushing them aside. I have to get away.

Goldie gives a warning bark as she hears me fiddling with the lock on the door at the back of the store.

"Quiet," I say, sharp.

She yelps as I stumble in the door, tripping over her.

"Out of the way."

My feet are loud as I climb the wooden stairs, slipping once, banging my knee, staggering on, not caring. Near the bedroom window sits my pack. I root down into the bottom of it, my fingers closing on the soft velvet of Kitty's ribbon.

I take it out, rubbing it between my fingers, pressing it to my lips as the tears spill.

"I haven't forgotten you. I haven't stopped loving you."

I'm blubbering now, great wet sobs, spit falling from my mouth onto the ribbon. I fold it up, my hands shaking, and put it into my pocket, wanting to protect it. It's all I have of her.

I try to conjure up the day I gave it to her. What comes instead is the image I've been running from for three years, her dead body in the grave that I dug for her, her face beginning to disappear under the dirt I'm shoveling in.

I slump against the bedroom wall, sobbing, trying to drive the image away. But her dead face remains. I slap myself hard with one hand then the other, again and again. *Don't make me remember. Don't make me.*

The wind is cold, greedy, reaching far below my skin, deep into my flesh, sucking my bones. The kind of cold that stays inside, that won't let go, that hours by a warm fire won't undo.

But I'm not by a warm fire. I'm in your grave, digging. I've been here for hours, wanting to be sure it's deep enough. Not another living creature is in sight. Alone, I dig, in a fury, hating God. He has taken you from me. And he won't let me follow. For days I've been praying— three days, four days, I don't know, I've lost track. Praying for death. Lying next to your cold body, praying for death.

"Please God, in thy mercy, take me too. Please God, don't make me live without her. Please God."

It didn't please God. So now I dig. My hands are raw and the last hour of light is almost upon me before I'm satisfied that it's deep enough. Dragging myself out of the hole, I go back to the cabin. I pause outside, cleaning the mud off my dress and boots, washing my hands.

You are lying where I left you, on the straw bed, the blanket tucked in under your chin. I didn't want you to be cold. I washed you this morning, combing out your hair, making you ready.

Your dress is laid out by the fire. I check that it's dry. I bring it over to you, sitting you forward, pulling it over your head, easing it down your body.

"It's time," I say, but I don't move. I sit beside you, holding you, stroking your hair.

"It's time," I say again.

I hold you under the arms, getting you to your feet. I expect it to be easy to carry you, wasted away as you are. But it is hard, every inch of ground to be fought for. We arrive at your grave with me sweating, the toes of your boots caked with mud.

I look into the hole, wondering how to get you into it. There is no one to help me. I consider it from every angle, getting in and out of the grave, trying to work out a plan. In the end, all I can do is lay you facedown on the edge of the hole. I roll you over and in, trying not to hear the sickening *thud* as you land on your back in the bottom of the grave.

"I'm sorry."

I lower myself in beside you, doing my best to straighten your crumpled body, cleaning the mud from your face. The sampler I made you is folded in my pocket. I take it out, tucking it under your hands, almost crying for the first time today.

Hauling myself back out of the grave, I stand silent. I have no words to pray a sermon. At last I fetch the flute from my pack. For a moment I can't play, my breath too fast and shallow. But then I put the flute to my lips. The tune that comes to me is the first one you ever asked me to play, "She Moved through the Fair."

As the final note lingers in the air, I put down the flute and pick up the shovel.

I let myself slide down the bedroom wall, until I'm sitting on the floor, my face in my hands.

"Oh, Kitty."

Goldie's toenails click across the floor. She settles beside me, head in my lap. We sit together in the dark.

"Good girl," I say, stroking her silky ear, tears sliding down my face. An hour ago I was raging and brawling. Now I'm quiet. "You're a good girl," I say again.

I reach into my pocket and take out Kitty's ribbon. As I tie it round my wrist, I sing, my voice barely a whisper.

Last night she came to me, my dead love came in
So softly she came her feet made no din
And she laid her hand on me and this she did say
It will not be long now till our wedding day

* * *

I wake on the floor, curled around Goldie, a half-empty poitín bottle nearby. The sun is up and somewhere nearby a pickaxe bangs on rock. Even on a Sunday, there's many a miner digging for gold. I wish they'd do it somewhere else.

Sitting up, I rub my face, trying to clear my head. I wince as my hand knocks against my eyebrow. Tenderly I explore the lump with my fingertips. I'd forgotten about the fight. Was that only last night? It feels like a lifetime ago.

Kitty's ribbon is still wrapped around my wrist. It's such a beautiful colour, sea-green like her eyes. I wish I had more to remember her by.

Goldie gets up, stretching, front legs, then back. Her jaws open in a huge yawn. Finally she shakes her head, ready for a new day. If only it was so easy for me.

"Shall I get you something to eat?"

I leave the back door open so she can relieve herself while I prepare her breakfast. As I put her bowl down, I realise how hungry I am. I didn't eat last night. A hunk of bread will do me for now, washed down with the preboiled water I still drink. I should go and apologise to Doctor Charles. I didn't even tell him I was leaving. Maybe later. I don't want people, I want time to think about Kitty.

* * *

The parlour is ready, candles from the store all around the room, freshly baked scone and a bottle of poitín on the table, a dish of snuff on the windowsill. This is how I remember the wakes at home.

Except a wake should be packed with mourners, every one with a story to tell of a life lived, the room full to overflowing, people spilling out down the stairs and into the streets. But those who knew and loved Kitty are on the other side of the world, if they're alive at all. All but me.

Gathering my resolve, I kneel down. "The blessing of God upon the souls of the dead," I say, crossing myself.

I take a pinch of snuff between my thumb and forefinger, place it on the back of my hand and inhale, savouring its intensity, resisting the urge to sneeze. It is years since I had snuff. I give my head a brief shake before downing a tot of poitín.

Missus Gorman would have spoken first. Closing my eyes, I try to imagine what she might have said.

"There'll never be another like my Kitty. I knew it from the day and hour she was born. Right from the first minute she came out, she was staring round the cabin, eyes bright, looking at everything she could see. The most curious baby I've ever known."

I remember Missus Gorman saying these very words to me, one Sunday afternoon a few weeks after I first met Kitty. I was eager for every detail of her life. And Missus Gorman was happy to oblige, always one for a story. A story and a song. She loved her music. Kitty did too.

My hands are trembling as I take Missus Gorman's flute out of my pack. The last time I played it was the day I buried Kitty.

"Think of the happy times when you play it." That's what Missus Gorman said when she gave it to me. "Think of the happy times and not this accursed famine."

I don't know if I can.

I'm interrupted by the clanging of the bell to the store. *Go away.* It clangs again. Can't they read the Closed sign?

I wait, but it doesn't clang a third time. I turn my attention back to the wake. The music should come later, after the stories. Missus—

Bang, bang, bang. Pounding on my back door. *Bang, bang, bang.* Goldie gallops down the stairs, barking loudly. I get to my feet and stomp my way down to the back door, cursing whoever's disturbing me.

"Who is it?" I shout.

"It's me. Gerry."

It stops me in my tracks. Gerry. I've been wanting him back, but did it have to be now? Slowly, I open the door, trying to quell my irritation.

He stands there, grinning. Then his look changes. "Jaysus, what happened to you?"

I tidied my face up as best I could this morning but there's no hiding the scabby lump on my left eyebrow or the black eye. "Nothing," I say.

"It doesn't look like nothing."

"I'll live."

"If you say so," he says, the familiar mocking tone to his voice.

Suddenly I'm glad to see him. "Come in," I say, finding a smile at last.

He follows me up the stairs, Goldie fast behind.

"Would you look at this?" he says, standing in the middle of the parlour, gazing around. "A step up from the tent and no mistake. But what's with all the candles?"

"I was…I was holding a wake," I say, feeling awkward.

He crosses himself. "Who died?"

"Kitty. You remember, the woman I told you about."

"Oh Frank, I'm sorry. What terrible news."

I shake my head. "This isn't news," I say, my eyes glistening.

He looks at me warily. "What do you mean?"

"It's been…She's been dead for three years."

He doesn't say anything for a minute. "I thought so, in the past. I thought that's why you wouldn't talk about her. But then, when you said a wake…"

"I didn't have one when she died. We were on our own, on our way to Cobh. She got famine fever…"

"It's a terrible disease. My sister, Mary, on the ship…"

We are both silent.

At last he looks up. "If this is a wake, where's my drink?" he says, trying to smile.

I pass him the bottle of poitín. He takes a slug, then passes it back.

"There's snuff, too," I say, pointing to the windowsill.

He kneels down as if he were in front of the body. "The blessing of God upon the souls of the dead," he says. He takes a pinch of snuff and inhales it. "That's good stuff, so it is. Is it the one I sent?"

I nod.

"I'll be ordering from him again." He sits down at the table, having a swig of the poitín. "So, are you going to tell me about Kitty?"

"I hardly know where to begin," I say, taking a seat opposite him.

"Why don't you tell me about how you met her?"

"It was at a dance, a cake dance. I suppose you had them in Skibbereen?"

"We did, surely. But I was never one for them. Walking I can manage, but dancing?"

"I've never seen anyone who could dance like Kitty. Better even than the dance master. I couldn't take my eyes off her."

"So did you go and introduce yourself?"

"Me? I was useless. It was my sister, Peig, that did the introductions. All I could do was stand there gawping like a fish."

"Were you worried that she was a woman?"

"You know, you'd think I would have been. But I wasn't, not at the beginning anyway. It was like my entire mind was taken up with how delightful she was and there was no space left for anything else."

"So it was love at first sight?"

I nod. "It was. Right from the start I was smitten." I smile, remembering.

"Love at first sight," he says again. "Can you keep a secret?" He leans towards me. "I'm courting," he says, his voice barely above a whisper.

"What? Who?"

"Someone in San Francisco." He leans closer still, though there's no one to overhear but Goldie. "His name is Shen."

"His?" I say. I knew it.

Gerry nods. "Are you shocked?"

"Of course not. I'm glad," I say, reaching over and squeezing his hand. "What's he like?"

"He's Chinese, from a place called Canton City. His hair is the purest black, in a long ponytail down his back. And his face…" He closes his eyes. "He's beautiful." He laughs. "Jaysus, would you listen to me. Like a swooning girl."

"How did you meet him?"

"At a sale."

"A sale?"

"Honest to God, you never saw a place like San Francisco for sales. Anywhere and everywhere, a big mess of noise, people barging and jostling, craning their necks for a better view, shouting out their bids."

I can tell from his voice that he loved being there, in the thick of it. "So, you met at a sale?" I say, wanting him to get back to the story.

"Sorry, anyway, yes, I was at a sale when a big fight broke out. Well, you know how good I am in a fight. I dived for the table behind the auctioneer for a bit of protection and Shen did the same. And that's how we met."

"We should drink a toast to your happiness."

He shakes his head. "I'm sorry, Frank. You were supposed to be telling me about Kitty and here's me waxing on about Shen."

"I spent half the night crying. Half the day too. I'm glad to hear your news. Kitty would be too. She was so full of love."

"You are too. I can see how much you loved her."

I can feel the tears gathering again. "When I was with her, nothing else mattered. When I was with her I felt more alive than I have ever felt."

As I say the words I realise how much the life has gone out of me these last three years. And I know it's not what Kitty would have wanted.

CHAPTER FORTY

Hangtown, November 1849

I pick up the flute. "I used to play for her and she'd sing and dance. They were good times."

"So it's your flute?" Gerry says.

"It is."

"I thought it must have been hers. You said you couldn't play it."

"I haven't been able to play, not since she died."

It's hard to believe how long it's been. I used to play the flute nearly every day. My own flute, at home, before Missus Gorman gave me this one. I raise it to my lips, not sure I can make my mouth form the right shape.

Gerry puts his hand on my arm. "Take your time."

I let my breath out, breathe in again, out and in again. The song that comes is the one that Kitty wrote for me. I start to play, hearing her singing to me.

From the moment that I saw you
And you whispered to my soul
You have filled me with your loving
With you, at last, I am whole

I close my eyes, seeing Kitty as she was when first I knew her—her turquoise eyes, the thick red hair, her smile. A tear leaks out. I feel it rolling down my face. The way she died has sat between me and my memories of all the good times we had together. I am glad to have them back.

"What a beautiful tune," Gerry says.

"Kitty wrote it."

"She was talented, your girl."

"That she was. Kind, too, and generous. But it was the wildness that drew me to her. I couldn't resist her. Or more, I didn't want to."

"I wish I'd met her."

I nod.

He tops up my glass with poitín. "To Kitty," he says.

"To Kitty," I say, chinking my glass against his. I drink it down, feeling the burn at the back of my throat.

He goes to fill it up again but I wave the bottle away.

"We should have some food or I'll be on my back," I say. "I never could drink on an empty stomach, especially during the day."

"A bit of this scone'll do me rightly. Sure what goes better with poitín than scone?" He breaks off a hunk and shoves it in his mouth.

"Do you fancy a bit of jam with that? There's a jar already open downstairs. Or there's all sorts in the store."

"Jaysus, the store. I've not even put my head round the door of it yet."

"I should have given you the grand tour before," I say.

"Now's time enough."

Goldie follows us down the stairs. I pause at the back door to let her out. She stands in the doorway wagging her tail. "Are you staying in or going out?" I say to her. "In or out?" She doesn't move. I shuffle her outside.

Gerry has gone ahead of me into the store.

"What do you think?" I say as I catch him up.

He doesn't answer at first, walking around, looking. "I can't believe you've done all this on your own," he says, at last, but his voice is subdued.

"Don't you like it?" I say.

"It's far better than I could have imagined."

"There's something wrong. What is it?"

"Nothing. It's only I thought, maybe you'd have more need of help."

I shake my head and let out a sigh of exasperation. "What, because I'm a woman?"

"It's not that," he says, but I'm sure it is. He's always been like that, thinking I can't do things.

"Jesus, Gerry, do you have any idea how hard I've worked?" My voice comes out louder than I expect.

"I can see that. I'm sorry, you've done a great job. Really. The store is fantastic. It's only…" He sighs.

"Only what?" I say, pulling the anger back.

"I thought maybe there'd be enough work getting the store up and running for you, me and Shen. But I can see now there's no room for a third partner."

A third partner? Jesus, he's only just met this fella and he's after giving a great chunk of our business to him. "Would he come if he was a partner?" I say, trying to keep my voice casual.

"Not if he wasn't needed. Shen's proud. He wouldn't be wanting to be here on my coattails, as a favour." He runs his fingers through his hair. "Fuck, he's never going to come."

"Have you talked about the future?"

"Not really."

"Is it serious? You and him."

"I think so. We saw each other every day in San Francisco."

"What does he do?"

"He's setting up a business, importing from China."

"Could he do it here?"

"I don't think so. He needs to deal with the ships." He sighs. "It's hopeless."

"Maybe you could move to San Francisco," I say slowly, thinking as I speak.

"I was worried about leaving you in the lurch."

"You wouldn't be leaving me in the lurch. I've been managing the store on my own so far. I'm sure I could carry on."

"But it's supposed to be our business."

"It still will be. I'll run the store, you find the supplies."

"The supplies are easy, now I've the contacts made."

"There'd be no store without them," I say.

"I wouldn't want to be taking the money if you were doing all the work. I amn't some English landlord."

I pause, wondering why it's me who's trying to persuade him. "Don't you want the chance to be with him?"

He doesn't answer for a moment. When he does, his voice is full of doubt. "What if he doesn't want the chance to be with me?"

"Oh, Gerry, then he's a fool."

"Two men," he whispers, "it's supposed to be unnatural. The Church is against it. You can go to jail for it."

"How does it feel when you're together?" I say.

He shakes his head, smiling. "Amazing."

"You only live the once, Gerry. Go to San Francisco. Maybe he'll want you, maybe he won't. But I know you'll regret it if you don't give him a chance."

"What about you?"

"Keep sending me the supplies. And if you're that worried, open another store in San Francisco. We can share the profits from both." As I say it out loud, I'm struck by what a good idea it is.

He gawps at me, then his face breaks out in a huge smile. "Frank, you're a genius. We should celebrate. Let's go to Ruby's, my treat."

"Not tonight," I say, not wanting company. "I'd rather be home tonight."

* * *

"Are you ready yet?" Gerry says, knocking on my bedroom door.

"You can come in," I say.

He sits on the bed as I finish pinning my cravat in place. It's green silk, a present from San Francisco.

"What do you think?" I say, turning towards him.

"It suits you," he says. "I knew it would."

I take a final look at my reflection in the little shaving mirror. The lump's gone but the black eye's still visible.

"You'll do," Gerry says. "Come on, or we won't get a decent seat."

It's almost dark as we walk up Main Street to Ruby's.

"I'm looking forward to a night out," he says.

"Me too," I say, though it's not entirely true. He's been trying to winkle me out of the store since Sunday. I ran out of excuses today.

Ruby's bar is not yet heaving but it's busy enough for early evening, with many tables already taken. I suppose Lucia Martinez is still drawing the crowds, even on a Thursday night. There is no sign of Ruby. Gerry had breakfast with her a couple of days ago but I haven't seen her for nearly a week, not since the night of the fight.

"Can I help you?" a waiter says.

"We'd like a table near the stage," Gerry says.

"Of course."

As soon as we're seated, Gerry orders a bottle of champagne.

"I suppose you'll be having Chinese," I say as the waiter departs, leaving us to the menus.

"I have plenty of that in San Francisco," he says, smirking.

"So Shen's a good cook?"

"Shush," he says, looking around. "You need to be careful."

"Sorry. Maybe you—"

Before I can finish, Gerry raises his hand, beckoning to someone across the room. I look up to see Ruby making her way towards our table. She's wearing the dark red velvet dress that I like so much. My face flushes.

"Good evening," she says, smiling. It is a relief, after how I behaved on Saturday, after how I've been avoiding her all week.

"Why don't you join us?" Gerry says.

"Perhaps later," she says. "You have ordered?"

"Champagne," Gerry says.

"Excellent choice," she replies. "I hope you enjoy."

And with that she's off across the room, greeting miners here and there as she weaves her way between the tables. I watch her for a while, then turn back to Gerry, who's watching me.

"So, what's the story with you and Ruby?"

"What do you mean?"

"I know you like her. And she likes you."

"She's a friend."

"But sure the two of you are perfect for each other. Everyone would be thinking…I take it she knows of your…situation?"

"She does. But I don't think she feels that way about me."

"Are you joking? Haven't you noticed how she looks at you?"

"She's sweet on someone else."

"Who?"

I lower my voice, not wanting to be overheard. "Loula-Mae she's called. Travels with Lucia Hernandez. She's her manager I think."

He laughs. "I wouldn't worry about that." He beckons me forward. "Lucia and Loula-Mae are together," he says quietly.

"Are you sure?"

"Of course. Everyone knows it. Well, everyone in San Francisco, or certain parts of it at least. I'm telling you, it's you she likes."

The waiter returns with our bottle of champagne. I think he must be new to the job. He fumbles with the cork like he's never seen one before, his face scrunched up with concentration. At last he has it out with a loud *pop* and a great frothy burst of bubbles. He panics, slopping it into the nearest glass saucer, which immediately overflows onto the tablecloth. He curses under his breath in some language I don't know, then repeats the pouring process with the second glass. Without a further word he sticks the bottle onto the table and departs.

Gerry picks up the nearest half-full glass. "*Sláinte*," he says, clinking his glass against mine.

"*Sláinte*."

* * *

Within a couple of hours, Ruby's is packed, hundreds of miners out for a good time. Every seat at our table is taken—Old Joey, the French boys and Doctor Charles, back for a repeat performance. It's hard to follow the conversation, noise all around me from drinking, talking, laughing and guffawing.

I let the sound wash around me, thinking about what the future might hold. Gerry draws me back with a nudge. He points to the stage where Ruby has emerged from the sidelines.

I watch as she looks out across the crowd, waiting for them to quiet. I know my heart would be pounding, thinking they would never notice me. But she looks calm, not doubting they will pay her mind. There's always been something impressive about Ruby, right from the first time I met her. Confident, capable, brooking no trouble from any quarter. I'm a little in awe of this outside that she wears so well.

As silence spreads around the bar, I study her face—the thick eyebrows, dark eyes, high cheekbones, pink-brown lips. "I like to thank you all for coming here tonight. Even those of you who have no time for a wash this year." Laughter ripples round the room. "My name is Ruby Alvarez and this is my bar. I like to think is the best bar in the diggings. And tonight is graced by the best act in all of California. So please give a gold-strike welcome to the one and only Lucia Hernandez."

Heads turn, hoping for the first glimpse of our star, as Ruby raises her arm towards the left side of the stage. All heads but mine. I look instead at Ruby. I've stayed loyal to Kitty these last three years. Though she told me not to, told me to find someone else if she didn't pull through. I didn't want anyone else. Till now.

"*Don't waste a minute.*" That's what Kitty said, on the way home from the old man's wake. "*Don't waste a minute of your life*"

As a great cheer erupts I continue to stare at Ruby. She sees me watching her as she turns to depart the stage and gives me one of her smiles and a slight inclination of the head. I can feel my heart beating faster. Maybe she does like me.

There's laughter all around me, but I've missed the joke. I don't care. All I want is to go and find Ruby and tell her...

Tell her what? I wouldn't know the first thing to say to her.

* * *

"More. More."

"Bravo!"

Everyone around me is on their feet, clapping and shouting their approval.

Wild cheering greets Lucia's return to the stage.

"Thank you, thank you. You're too kind." Her voice sounds American through and through, betraying no hint of her Mexican upbringing. "And to repay your kindness, I'd like to give you a word of advice. Never get into a fight with an ugly man—he's got nothing to lose."

She waits till the laughter dies away. "Would anyone like one last song?"

"Yes," comes the answer.

"I didn't hear you," she says. "Does anyone want one last song?"

"*Yes*," the crowd roars. I shout with them, happy to join in, now I know it's nearly over.

"Well, I'll make you a deal. I'll sing the verses if you sing the chorus. Is that a deal?"

"Yes."

"Are you sure?"

"*Yes*."

"Here's how the chorus goes:

For we won't go home till morning,
We won't go home till morning,
We won't go home till morning,
Till daylight does appear."

She stands at the front of the stage, conducting us in a couple of rehearsals till she's satisfied with our performance. It's hard to believe this sparrow of a woman has the biggest and burliest of rough tough miners doing her every bidding. With a nod to the pianist, she's off into the first verse, her voice rich and strong, filling the room.

We're all met here together,
We're all met here together,
We're all met here together,
To eat and drink good cheer.

"Now it's your turn," she says as the piano plays on.
"For we won't go home till morning."
Voices join in around the room but Lucia's not satisfied. "Louder,"
she calls out.
"*We won't go home till morning.*"
"All of you."
"*We won't go home till morning,*"
"That's better."
"*Till daylight does appear.*"
"Now it's my turn," she says and she's off again, with lines about
singing, dancing and "kissing lasses dear." She doesn't need to urge
us this time as the chorus bellows out around the room. I find myself
smiling as I listen to the final verse, *The girls we love them dearly, And
they love us, 'tis clear.* How bold for her to sing these words if what
Gerry says about her is true.

"One last time," she calls. She sings the chorus along with us,
holding the final note long after everyone else has faded away. The
crowd breaks out into rowdy applause, feet stamping, loud whistling,
banging on tables. She bows to the front, to the left of the room, to the
right, then back to the front. A chant of "Lucia, Lucia," goes up around
the bar as she disappears at last from the stage.

"I told you she was good," Gerry says, leaning over so I can catch
his words.

Cries of "More, More," continue to ring out around the room. But
after several minutes it's clear that there will be no more. As the calls
and foot stamping die away, there's a sudden rush for the bar.

I scan the crowd for Ruby, but all I can see are hefty miners. "I'll
go and get us more drinks," I say, hoping the bar will give me a better
vantage point.

"I'll go," Gerry says, standing up. "What do ye all want?"

To go to the bar myself, I think. "I'll have a beer," I say.

"Beer then wine, you'll feel fine. Wine then beer, you'll feel queer,"
Gerry chants, then guffaws to himself like it's the funniest thing
anyone's ever said.

"What?" I say.

"I'll tell you later," he says, still smiling as he finishes taking the orders and departs for the bar.

"She's quite a talent, Miss Hernandez, don't you think?" Doctor Charles says to me.

"That she is."

"You'd never expect such a big voice to come out of such a tiny woman."

"I suppose not." I look around the room, half an ear on what Doctor Charles is saying.

"—breakfast with her manager."

It suddenly occurs to me that I haven't seen Loula-Mae this evening. Maybe that's where Ruby is.

"—wonderful to have a musical talent. Mama played the piano but my fingers never could quite get the hang of it. Did you—"

There she is. Through a gap in the crowd I glimpse Ruby taking a seat at a table on the other side of the room. The gap closes and she's gone again.

"Sorry," I say, cutting Doctor Charles off in mid-sentence. I squeeze between a couple of groups of miners, heading in the right direction, my heart pounding.

At last I get a clear view of Ruby's table. I should have known. Loula-Mae sits there like a puffed-up cat. Gerry knows nothing. Lucia's lover, my arse. She can't even be bothered to be backstage after her performance.

I go to turn away but at that moment Ruby looks up and sees me. She beckons me over.

"Come, sit down," she says.

There's only one seat free and of course it's next to Loula-Mae. I'd rather sit down next to a rattlesnake but can think of no excuse not to take the chair offered. At least Clarice is on the other side, in conversation with a couple I don't know. I will talk to them.

"Nice shiner," Loula-Mae says.

I scowl by way of an answer, which sets her off laughing, just like she did on Saturday evening. She truly is one of the most aggravating creatures that God ever put on this earth.

"Oh sugar, you surely do need a little fun in your life. Have some champagne." She puts her own lipstick-marked glass in front of me and fills it till the froth is threatening to spill over the edge. She gets to her feet. "Well, I guess I better go and see if Lucia's ready yet for company. Bye for now."

I stare at the bubbles rising in the glass and try to think what I should say. The bar is full of chatter, everyone talking but Ruby and me. Next to me, Clarice continues her explanation of grape growing and wine making.

I risk a glance at Ruby. She's looking at me. I look away, embarrassed. I shouldn't have been so rude. I don't even know for sure what Ruby's feelings are for Loula-Mae. Let alone her feelings for me. That's what I'm supposed to be finding out. I wish I could slink away and start again another day, a day when Loula-Mae is far away and Ruby's forgotten all about her. Instead I say, "I—" just as Ruby says, "You—"

We both give way, waiting for the other to speak. Ruby inclines her head towards me, indicating that I should go ahead.

"I was wondering if…if I could…if you had, perhaps, if maybe I could see you later." I stare again at the champagne, sure she can see straight through to my thoughts.

Her hand on my arm gives me the courage to look up again. She smiles. "I finish in an hour. Come to my rooms."

* * *

There's no need to panic. I've been in Ruby's rooms before. In her parlour, at least. Never in the bedroom. I'm not ready for that, not yet.

I've got to stop jumping ahead. It's not as though I'll be seeing her bedroom tonight. I may never see it. She's forever with this Loula-Mae. But when she touched me this evening, I'm sure there was a feeling between us.

"You're quiet," Gerry says.

"I'm tired."

"Shall we go home then?"

"Oh, well, not quite yet. Not for me anyway. You go. I need to see Ruby," I say. "On business," I add as an afterthought.

"Business, is it? Maybe I should come."

"Ah, there's no need. I can handle it."

"I'm sure you can," he says, smirking.

"I'll see you later," I say, though it's ten minutes yet till Ruby's expecting me. I want away from any of Gerry's speculating. I'm nervous enough as it is.

"Good luck," he calls as I make my way from the table, "with your *business*."

To my relief, the hotel lobby's empty. It gives me the chance to get a proper look at myself in the mirror. I adjust my cravat a fraction to the right, then twitch it a little to the left. There's a dark smudge on my cheek. I lick my finger and rub it off, but there's nothing I can do about the black eye. I lean forward, drawing back my lips to expose my teeth, checking for fragments of food. I put my hand up to my mouth and breathe out while trying to sniff in at the same time. Not too bad—a bit beery, but not unpleasant. Unless you don't like beer. Finally I run my hand through my hair, smoothing it down at the back. I stand back for one last check.

"You look beautiful."

I turn around, embarrassed at being caught preening.

"Shall we go up?" Ruby says.

I nod, speech having deserted me for now. Ruby leads the way, skirt swishing, black leather ankle boots clipping up the two flights of stairs to her rooms. She slips the key out of her pocket and opens the door. The only light is from the fire blazing in the hearth.

"Have a seat," she says. "Do you like a drink?"

"No, thank you," I say. I've been drinking soda water this last hour, wanting to feel in control of my senses. I settle myself on the couch, watching as Ruby moves round the room, lighting lanterns, then pouring herself a glass of port. She's so self-contained, going about these domestic duties with the same quiet efficiency that she showed onstage.

"Were you not nervous tonight, introducing Lucia?"

She turns and smiles at me, and I notice again the gap in her teeth I like so much. "Not really. But Lucia, she is sick before every performance."

"She seems so confident."

"Once she starts she loves to perform. But beforehand?" She shakes her head.

"I'd never have guessed."

"Do you enjoy the show?" she says, coming and sitting on the armchair nearest to the couch. I am disappointed that she hasn't sat down beside me, disappointed and relieved.

"She's a great performer," I say as if I'd been hanging on Lucia's every word.

"At least you like one half of LuLu."

"LuLu?"

"Lucia and Loula-Mae. That's what I call them."

"Gerry told me they're courting."

"They are. I want you to meet them; they're old friends. But you do not seem to like Loula-Mae, so…" She shrugs.

"I'm sorry I was rude."

"Why don't you like her?"

I can't say "Because I thought she was making eyes at you." It's my turn to shrug. "I think we got off to a bad start."

"You should give her a chance. She look after me, when Carlita…" Her voice is low and I can hear the sadness there.

I wait for her to go on.

"When Carlita leave me, I don't know how to bear it. I live in Santa Cruz then. Carlita lives on a ranch a few miles from town, with her new husband. She want us to be friends, but I feel too proud, too angry. Six months later, she is dead. He beat her from the first night after the wedding. She have no one to turn to. I still wonder, sometimes, if I have been her friend…"

"It might still have turned out the same."

"I know."

"It's hard losing someone you love. When Kitty died…"

She leans forward and takes my hand. "Kitty?"

I grip it tightly, my eyes shut. "My lover, Kitty Gorman. She died of famine fever, when we were emigrating."

"I'm sorry, Frances."

"I loved her so much. So much," I whisper. "I didn't know how to save her."

"I know what is like to have someone you love taken from you," Ruby says. "And to blame yourself, to torture yourself with what you should do differently."

"I nearly went crazy when Kitty died. God alone knows how I got from Knockreagh to Cobh. I have no real memory of it."

"The days after I hear about Carlita…" She shrugs again. "I remember almost nothing."

We're both quiet. The clock ticks, time passing a beat at a time.

"Maybe it's always that way when it's someone who really matters to you," I say, at last. "I think I've been frozen these last three years, in my heart."

"It won't be like that forever."

"It's changing already. I've been…" Oh God, am I really going to tell her? "I've been having feelings for someone new," I say, wishing I wouldn't blush at all the wrong times.

"Anyone I know?" she says, her voice soft, eyes down, not looking at me.

"You," I say.

She starts to cry.

I sit, not sure what to do. What I want is to slide from the couch, to kneel in front of her, to put my arms around her, to hold her close till she's cried out all the sadness. But I'm not yet sure of my ground. I fish a handkerchief out of my pocket and hand it to her.

"Sorry," I say, "I didn't mean to upset you."

"No," she says, wiping her eyes. "Is only...Is a long time, for me also."

I can feel my heart thumping as she looks up again, as she looks at me, as she smiles.

And in a moment I am on the floor in front of her, kneeling up so that my head is close to hers, my arms reaching for her as she does for me. I pull her to me, feeling the smallness of her frame, the softness of her dress against my fingers, her breath on my cheek. It is so good to hold her, to have her in my arms.

We hold each other close, not saying anything until at last she turns her face towards me. She looks at me for a moment. And then we kiss.

Bella Books, Inc.

Women. Books. Even Better Together.

P.O. Box 10543
Tallahassee, FL 32302

Phone: 800-729-4992
www.bellabooks.com